A HAVEN OF SMOKE AND RUIN

Cover design by Maria Spada

Editing by Nice Girl Naughty Edits

ISBN: 979-8-9872533-0-4

CONTENT NOTES

<u>This book is set in the world of A River of Ash and Bone, and although it's not necessary to read it first, it would help provide some context for the characters and the setting as well as the past events that are referenced throughout.</u>

Please be aware that the content in this book may not be suitable for all readers.

This book contains graphic violence and sexually explicit content. It's a post-apocalyptic new adult novel, so expect discussions of a global pandemic/virus, as well as blood, death, gore, zombies, and profanity.

The warnings are as follows:
- Recurring thoughts of anxiety
- Parental neglect/abuse
- Loss of a family member
- Mentions of parental abandonment
- Mentions and brief descriptions of military-controlled testing facilities

This is a why choose romance (MFMM), meaning there are multiple men to one woman.
Due to the list above, reader discretion is advised.

To anyone who battles their own anxieties like Sera, I see you, and you're not alone.

CAMP

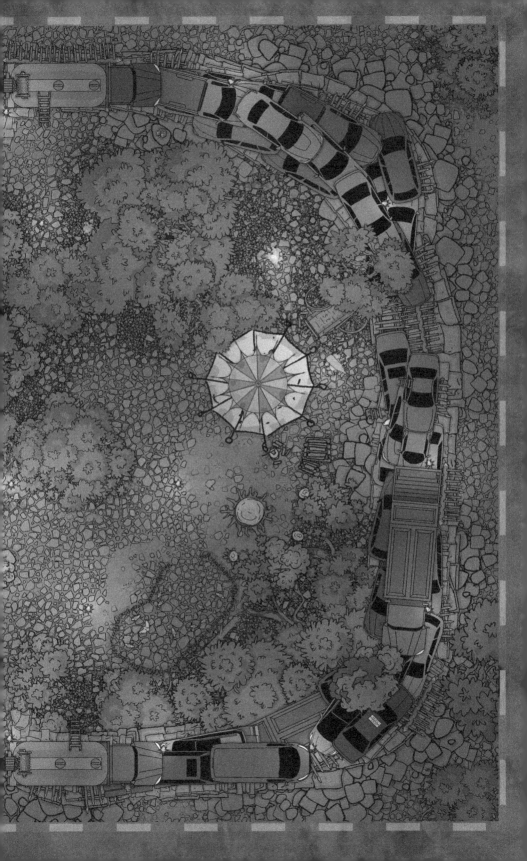

CHAPTER 1

Drawing in a deep breath of the smoke-laced breeze, I closed the gate to the coop behind me, taking care to make sure the lock slid neatly into place. After issues in the past with the lock failing and the chickens escaping, there was now a little hand-painted sign nailed to the front that encouraged all visitors to be extra cautious.

The chickens were noisy, clucking absentmindedly as their sharp beaks pecked eagerly at the grains scattered on the ground. The scents of straw and dirt were comforting, and I was already counting down to my next visit.

A husky voice echoed from behind me, and I gave myself an internal pat on the back for only startling a little.

"I wouldn't have guessed you were a fan of chickens," Jake drawled, leaning up against the chipping paint of the building across from me with his arms crossed. His brown hair shone a dull honey in the sunlight and he must have trimmed his beard recently because it looked neater than usual. "Y'know, the mess and all."

I rolled my eyes, containing my excitement at seeing him to just the barest twitch of my lips. I loved when his drawl grew deeper and more pronounced. Usually on the rare occasions when he was angry, but also in casual conversation when he was relaxed. "Yeah, well, that's the thing about assumptions, right?" Really, I thought the chickens were adorable. Loud, sure, but each one had such a unique personality, and they had so much energy. It had been a long while since I'd spent any time around animals, and I missed their playful antics. I'd been pleasantly surprised to discover they kept livestock when I first arrived, as I certainly hadn't any.

A gravelly chuckle filled the air. One of my favorite things about him was how easily his smiles came, and how obvious it was when he was genuinely amused, not faking it to seem interested. I soaked up every golden drop of his attention, the sun shining a bit brighter whenever he flashed those brilliantly white teeth. Heidi adored him, and even Nadira and Jamie had warmed up to him quickly, which was no easy feat.

Brushing my hands off onto my dirtied pants, I cast a quick glance around for Ryder, both concerned and yet not when I didn't see him. It wasn't often that he got pulled away from my side to take care of something around camp, but it wasn't unheard of. Like me, he hadn't yet found his niche, and so we tended to stick together. At least I thought that was why. We'd never discussed it, but I didn't mind the company. The familiarity was comforting.

Jake pushed off the wall with a grunt. My gaze caught on the flex of his biceps as he uncrossed his arms, then flicked back to those deep brown eyes. "If you're looking for pretty boy, he's helping Caelan with something over by the front gate."

Figured the one time I actually checked to see if he was there, someone would see and call me out on it. "No, just looking for Nadira. She was supposed to meet me," I lied easily.

A wave of sympathy washed over Jake's expression. "I saw her with Heidi earlier, going over nausea remedies. I think Halli mentioned wanting to plant chamomile and peppermint so she could try out some recipes that are supposed to help. It's been a good few years since our last pregnancy, and after we lost most of our crops, those specific plants weren't something we put the focus on cultivating."

A loud thud sounded from somewhere behind him, and that he didn't even flinch was impressive. More cabins and buildings were being constructed, which River told us was mostly her influence. She'd arrived not too long before us, and had managed to talk her men—who ran the camp now that their father died—into being more lax with whom they allowed entrance, which meant they needed more lodgings to accommodate any new arrivals and even some old.

Years prior, an incident with a cluster of raiders passing through had left its mark on the camp, making them reluctant to welcome newcomers. Then the conflict between them and the group I'd been living with had come to a head last month. When Ryder's father, the man who'd run our group, had taken River to use as a bargaining chip knowing that her men would trade anything for her, she'd used that time to convince us to accompany her back here when she escaped. Meaning that we didn't burn up with the rest of his men in the fire she'd inadvertently started.

The triplets knew all about what it was like to have an asshole parent who only looked out for themselves, which was most likely why they let Ryder join us here despite his position as his father's reluctant right-hand man. That he'd taken advantage of the chaos during the fire and turned on Gunner—stabbing him through the heart—had worked in his favor. I was grateful each and every day that he'd accepted their invitation because I hadn't been sure I'd be able to leave him behind. We had a complicated relationship, borne mostly of wordless conversations, thoughtful gestures, and shared proximity, but I wouldn't trade it for anything. That quiet acceptance was everything to me.

The discordant clucking at my back brought my wandering mind back to the present. My cheeks flushed with embarrassment, that only worsened when Jake shot me a reassuring wink.

"That's awfully kind of Halli," I finally responded, touched that she'd taken the time to care for my friend. "We're all hoping it won't be as bad in her third trimester."

That devastating grin of his was distracting. "At the very least, maybe the farm has something we can use in the meantime."

We stood in silence as I processed his words and sorted through my confusion until it dawned on me what he was referencing. "That's right, you're due to make a trip up there in a few... months?"

"We're fixin' to leave in a couple of weeks, depending on a few things."

"Oh?"

"Gotta make sure they've got enough fresh meat stocked for when we're gone, since Jeremiah and I've been doing the bulk of the hunting when we're not helping with construction."

Time had flown by, or maybe the timeline had moved up; either way, I hadn't realized he'd be leaving so soon. In fact, I'd pushed it from my mind so successfully that its now looming presence was unsettling. The thought led to a strange tickle in my stomach, and I quickly shoved it aside before it bloomed into something more anxiety-inducing.

"Oh," I repeated, weakly this time. I didn't dare say anything else with my mouth suddenly so dry.

His lopsided smirk said that maybe my concern wasn't as subtle as I'd hoped. His name sounded in the distance, accompanied by a loud clanging.

"I'll see ya around, Sera," he murmured as he gave me a look I couldn't place and sauntered off.

My stomach churned with unease as I watched him leave. In just weeks, he would set out on a journey beyond the walls, the possibilities for disaster endless. I'd grown used to running into him all over camp, eating meals together because of our shared social circles and letting him introduce me to new people.

What if something happens while he's gone? Or he gets ambushed in the middle of nowhere?

My lips twisted. I had a man to see about a job, and if I wanted to understand a lick of the instructions I'd surely receive, I'd have to pause my worrying for the time-being. I scoffed under my breath, toeing at the dirt under my heel with the tip of my mud-splattered boot.

Unlikely.

"This is all of it," Nix said, throwing open the doors to the rickety shed and revealing shelves stacked haphazardly with medical supplies. "Throw out anything like bandages or gauze that's been damaged by time or age, and anything with broken packaging that's been exposed to dirt and can't be disinfected. Then sort the supplies by category and mark down our inventory on the sheet I gave you. That sound good?"

I nodded, giddy with the prospect of having my own job. It was nothing glamorous, but maybe this was exactly what I needed to get rid of any lingering stagnancy: a real way to contribute.

His smile radiated kindness. "Once this has been sorted, maybe we can start some lessons. It never hurts to have another person trained in first aid."

My chest warmed. "Yes!" I coughed. "I mean, yes, I would love that. Thank you. I was taught some things growing up, but there's a lot more I could learn." A dull ache, the memory of loss, brushed along the edges of my senses before fading away.

"Good. I've got to help River with something, so I'll check back in later, yeah?"

"Sure, give her my best." I rolled up my sleeves, looking over the tiny, stuffy room, and decided that wading in would be the best approach.

I worked for hours, losing myself in the monotony of sorting, cleaning, and inspecting. Exhaustion hounded me, but it was pleasant rather than crushing, and my bones ached with a smug satisfaction.

Hours of work later, my shirt was damp with sweat, and my knees were covered in grime from kneeling on the unforgiving floor.

The sound of rustling fabrics filled the small space as I dug through an overturned bin full of gauze packs when the heat grew unbearable. Or perhaps it had been unbearable for some time, and I'd been too busy to notice. I had a bad habit of working through my discomfort instead of taking a break to make it better.

My joints protested loudly as I stood and cracked the door open wider, propping the wedge of wood under it to make it stay, and groaning at my first gulp of fresh air. I knew I had to stop incentivizing my work with normal, everyday things, like a sip of water, or oh, I don't know, dust-free air?

The windows in the shed were so high up and coated with dust that there was no way I could've caught a glimpse of the outside, especially while focused on my work, which was why I was so surprised to find the sun hanging low in the sky. Somehow, almost the entire day had passed me by. I took another deep breath in, pleased at how the evening breeze caressed my hot, sweaty face.

Using the back of my arm—the only part of me that wasn't covered in complete filth—I brushed the strands of hair that had escaped my ponytail back from my face and cracked my neck with a soft grunt. My muscles throbbed from sitting in odd positions for hours upon end, but the deep sense of fulfillment outweighed the stiffness. I'd gotten so much done, although there was still a lot more to finish. Maybe if I weren't so concerned with doing the job perfectly, it would have gone quicker, but I was. The supplies had to be organized just so, and I couldn't sort them into dirty, dusty bins so I'd ended up wiping those down as well, and of course I had to think of how we could repurpose whatever was too damaged to be used for their original purpose rather than throwing them out.

"Sera," a deep voice shouted. I propped my hip up against the door frame, content to wait. Seconds later, Nix came into view, jogging the rest of the distance to stand in front of me. "I'm sorry I'm late," he huffed. He was panting heavily, dark waves plastered to his forehead and cheeks tinted pink. I remembered that he'd told me he was meeting River and must've made a face because he rushed to clarify, looking adorably awkward. "No no no," he assured me. "We were moving furniture in for Heidi, for the baby. Took longer than we expected."

I laughed, and with a soft clap, shook the dust from my hands. "You finished getting the nursery ready, then?"

He nodded. "Looks great. She's really excited. The walls are covered in art the kids made, and Shiori even made a mobile to hang over the crib that Jake and Caelan built."

Just picturing it made me want to tear up. Sweet, optimistic Heidi had been my light in the darkness during my time at Gunner's camp. Always smiling, always telling stories, making sure everyone was comfortable. She deserved the world.

"Well, I like to think I got a good amount done," I said, sweeping my arm towards the shed. "Although maybe not as much as you'd expected."

He peeked inside, jaw dropping as he took in the space. "This is amazing, Sera. It looks so much cleaner, which was half the problem in the first place. You didn't need to stay so late either. Next time, feel free to leave whenever you're too tired or you get hungry. I honestly hadn't expected to find you here this late in the afternoon."

"If you don't mind, I think I'll go grab some food now." My stomach growled loudly, and I gave him a sheepish smile. The scents from dinner were making their way over, and they were making my mouth water. We must've been having meat and potatoes, because I could smell the signature spices that Will liked to season them with.

"Go ahead, and you can come back anytime tomorrow. Just find me when you're finished, and we'll get started on those lessons."

I gave him a grateful nod and set out for the tent. If I had to guess, it was right after the first dinner rush. Most people had come and gone by now, so I was surprised to spot Nadira, Thomas, and Jake standing near the entrance. My walk slowed, and I kept my small smile to myself. I could sense his presence even in the dark, as if all that silent, brooding energy channeled into physical touch. Scanning my surroundings, I found Ryder sitting off to the side on the grass, long limbs sprawled out and eyes already locked onto me. His dark hair had grown long over the past few months, curling ever so slightly where it hit his neck and covering his ears, and those eyes that were laser-focused on me appeared so dark that they seemed black. Nothing like the deep, rich brown that I knew them to be.

He pushed to stand when I grinned at him, falling in step with me as I walked over to join the others. Neither of us spoke a word, even in greeting, instead defaulting to our usual comfortable silence. With anyone else, the quiet made me fidget and squirm, but there was something about him and the way he simply *existed*. Solid and strong and immovable. I craved it.

"There's my girl," Nadira said, pulling me in for a quick hug. Her springy curls were pulled back into a loose bun, using a scrunchie I knew Thomas had made for her last week. Her dark skin was practically glowing, and I didn't think it was all due to the dying rays of sunlight. I was glad my friend had found happiness here.

I nodded at Thomas in greeting and smiled at Jake while Ryder hovered silently at my shoulder, happy to ignore the pleasantries.

"What are you all doing here? I thought you liked to eat earlier?"

"I got caught up helping Naia and Thomas waited for me," she explained. "But now you're here." She beamed, taking my arm in hers and guiding me past the parted canvas that made up the tent.

"How'd it go?" Jake asked, tugging lightly on a dark curl that had escaped my ponytail and shooting Ryder a sour look when he grunted.

Honestly, I had no earthly idea why they disliked each other so much. Ryder spent half the time ignoring him or staring at him in distaste, and Jake took any chance he could to irritate him and try to provoke a reaction. I knew he was likely harboring resentment over Ryder's relation to his father, but wasn't the fact that he'd killed him enough? It was for the others.

"Good. I got a lot done."

Everyone grew quiet as Ryder spoke, his voice raspy from disuse. "Got what done?"

Inwardly, I cheered at the confirmation that he was listening despite his prior silence, although I tried to keep my expression under control. "I started cleaning out one of the supply sheds today, and when I finish, Nix is going to train me."

His frown was small before it smoothed out. "I see."

My enthusiasm dimmed somewhat, soon forgotten after Nadira grabbed my attention once more, telling me all about her day as we got in the short line while the others were content to listen to us talk.

CHAPTER 2

I flew awake, breathing fast, and realized almost instantly that I was soaked through with sweat.

A groan escaped my lips as I threw the heavy covers off and sat up. There was something so intangible about my nightmares. They were infrequent, and disappeared like smoke when I woke up, leaving a vague, sickening pit in my stomach. I could never recall exactly what I'd dreamed about, just that whatever it was made me toss and turn all throughout the night. Although I supposed that was normal nowadays. All of us had things we'd rather forget.

I felt worse for those who were old enough to remember the outbreak. I couldn't imagine going from a regular life to a worldwide pandemic, especially one with a mortality rate of 94%. Considering I'd only been two during the initial outbreak, and three when the Paleo virus–named for the era it was dated to after being discovered by a group of archeologists when a swath of glaciers melted–mutated.

All travel had been suspended, never to be reopened after things went to shit, but that didn't stop the virus from spreading over every inch of the globe and decimating the population.

When the virus mutated in the following year, everyone thought they'd finally caught a break. That maybe they'd have a chance to re-cover, to develop methods to combat the spread, now that the virus could only be transferred through blood and fluids. Those hopes were dashed when they realized what this new, twisted version of the virus was capable of.

The living dead filled the streets and any chances we had of recover-ing the state of the world before the outbreak had vanished. It was then that I lost my parents to the ensuing pandemonium. The end of life as we knew it. Rates of infection decreased, but humanity was irrevocably changed.

No matter how hard I tried, I couldn't recall if those hazy im-ages of panic and screams were manufactured through other people's retellings or my actual memories.

Still, there had been plenty of close calls after Ben had taken me in. He'd always liked to refer to himself as a prepper, and he sure had been prepared. A friend of the family, he'd only ventured into town once every few months to gather supplies and see a friendly face. Otherwise, he was holed up in his mini-fortress.

Pushing my memories away before they grew too dark, I scooted to the edge of my bed and lowered my bare feet to the cool, textured wooden planks so I could get a better vantage point of the world outside my window.

The sun had just risen over the horizon, casting a soft golden glow across the trees and turning their spring growth a hazy yellow. I sat still, deciding that I wouldn't be able to fall back asleep. Unlike the others back at Gunner's, I liked to rise with the sun. That moment when the fog slowly lifted and revealed the weather for the day was my favorite.

Every now and then, I even managed to sucker one of the other girls into watching it with me, usually through bribes.

The morning sunlight filtered through the glass, bathing the modest room in a cozy amber radiance. The odd belongings scattered about and covered in highlights brought a smile to my face. A group of people including Anna, River, Halli, Shiori, and the twins had come over almost daily in rotations our first week to help us adjust: bringing dried food that we could store in the cupboards in case we missed a meal, glassware, utensils, and knit blankets, as well as cute homemade decorations like the paintings the children Nerese and Naia watched had done from berry paints, and the macrame tapestry Shiori had woven out of old clothes. A technique she declared she'd never be repeating after her hands cramped for three days straight once she finished.

When we first arrived several months ago, we'd slept in tents for the first week. Then some of the people here had traded accommodations so that we could experience running water and privacy. It still amazed me that they'd developed a system to run water to the cabins. I'd never experienced anything like it before. Well, I was sure I had at some point, but I had no recollection of it now. Like any glimpses of my parents, it was locked behind a wall with all the other things I'd been too young to commit to memory.

There was one larger log cabin near the second fire pit that Heidi had been given that had been standing before the camp was ever formed–for when she gave birth and needed a separate room for the nursery and for guests who could stay and help–and she'd insisted on sharing it with someone. According to Jamie, she and Heidi hadn't quite felt like being separated yet and they'd moved in together, just like old times when we'd all shared a room wherever we stopped for the night. If Nadira hadn't already moved in with Thomas, she'd probably have joined.

Unlike them, I moved into a small cabin on the perimeter of the largest clearing. There was no separate bedroom, just a king-sized bed across from the wide fireplace and a luxurious bathroom. I was sure I'd be lonely at first, but it turned out that the silence was bliss. No yelling, fighting, or dashing outside to piss in the grass and hoping no-one jeered at you. I woke up alone each morning and took a moment to greet the day, showered in peace, and fixed myself a cup of fresh tea. The gratitude from having my own space, but still being so close to others was immense, and it felt like I was rediscovering myself more and more each day. There was still something missing, something I hadn't been able to put into words yet, but it was through no fault of my accommodations.

Whenever that vague sense of restlessness cropped up, it was quickly dismissed. Sometimes it chafed that I'd only ended up here out of pure circumstance, the results of the actions of people much braver and more confident than I, but I tried not to focus on that. To have everything I could ever want, yet still be unable to pinpoint the cause of the unfulfillment that plagued me, was a special kind of torture.

I'd never felt more accepted or safe than I did here, and I'd do anything to keep it, but the best part was that I didn't have to.

No strings, no requirements, no restrictions.

Freedom.

Ryder would never admit it, but I could tell he felt similarly.

My shower was long, and even though Grey had reassured me that there was no limit to the amount of water we could use, I still felt mildly guilty after twenty minutes. The sensation of the water running off my skin, warm and slick from the custom body soap Halli and Priya had created in their spare time, was like nothing else, and I relished the feel of a clean scalp.

All throughout the day, I would catch whiffs of lavender and thyme as my hair moved. Its length was easier to manage too now that Jamie had cut it to my shoulders, and without the oppressive summer humidity making my curls frizz, they fell neatly in loose spirals. Jamie complained the entire time she'd worked on it how unfair it was that it didn't tangle like her curly red mane did.

Freshly showered, damp hair pulled back into a high ponytail, I snagged a few carrots from the basket River had dropped off the other day—sitting atop the latest book she'd leant me—and left my little cabin, heading out to start work.

I was only halfway to the shed when I heard the commotion. Rounding the corner of the large barn-like structure they liked to use for camp meetings and mind racing with new possible emergencies, I found the center of camp, abuzz with activity. Hushed whispers were punctuated by exclamations and laughter, and the longer I watched, the more confused I was. What were they all gathered for? I searched the crowd for a familiar face and was relieved to find River and Grey up towards the front of the camp, hovering close to the guard shack and speaking in low tones. Driven by curiosity, I headed in their direction.

"Oh good," River breathed when she saw me. Her hair swung as she grabbed Grey's arm and tugged him along with her as she approached. They were largely recovered from the night she'd escaped, and it was good to see them looking so healthy.

"What's going on?" I whispered, still lost as to why everyone was congregating here.

"We have a visitor," Grey stated plainly, gaze darting towards the unfamiliar man standing off and to the side.

My eyes snagged on his tall frame, and I wondered how I hadn't noticed him before, towing over everyone like he was. Not just tall but large, and made more imposing by the way he stood; almost like a soldier. Jet-black hair fell to his shoulders, contrasted by gray eyes so light they appeared translucent as the sun hit him. They were only made lighter by the presence of his heavy black brows. He watched us talk, face devoid of all emotion.

"You don't know him?" I asked faintly, still somehow unable to look away. He didn't quite qualify as handsome, not like Ryder did with his sharp allure or Jake and his boyish charm, but there was something captivating about his sheer presence. Nose crooked as if it had been broken so many times it would no longer heal straight, frown lines formed from years of stress framing his firm lips, and a strong jaw covered in black stubble that seemed purposefully maintained. I sucked in a breath when his heavy stare landed on mine, frozen by his stare.

"Earth to Sera," River hissed, waving a hand in front of my face and breaking my concentration. I blinked, glancing back at him, but he had looked away. Her lips twisted upwards in a smirk, but she quickly moved on. "Apparently, he's just passing through. He saw the smoke, and since this area has been pretty picked clean of food, thought he'd take a chance. We're going to set him up in one of the almost finished cabins for a quarantine period just to be safe. Would you mind bringing him dinner later?"

I blinked again, surprised by the question. Of all the people here, she was asking me? She trusted me? I was a nobody, brand new. Even so... I gave her a resolute nod, pleased that she'd asked. After all she'd done to bring us here, settling us in and helping us adjust, I'd do anything to give back. I was eternally grateful we'd met, even if it was under awful circumstances. A brief memory of when she was locked up in that small concrete room flashed through my mind.

Her exhale was full of relief. "Good. Okay. I'm going to escort him there and then our day is full, so I'm glad I can count on you."

River's words warmed some part of me I hadn't even known was cold. For so long I'd felt useless and weak; a product of my environment, and that wasn't to say I'd suddenly stopped, but it was convenient to ignore as the days went on.

"I'm happy to help," I rasped.

River beckoned him over, and my heart beat faster as he took long, loping steps in our direction. Now that he was closer, I could tell he was maybe less than a decade older than me. Dark circles smudged the delicate skin beneath his eyes, and his forehead bore deep grooves earned from years of harsh survival, but that gaze... So clear and focused.

We stared at one another in silence until Grey gave us a quizzical look and spoke up, explaining to him their next steps. I tore myself away from their little group, heading off to meet Nix and hoping that the manual labor would clear the cobwebs from my brain. I was overdue for some clarity.

P leased by my progress, I chose to break for dinner. The quiet had been nice, but I was ready to be surrounded by the constant murmur of conversation.

I had spent so much of my life in silence: the emptiness of my house after my parents died, the days Ben spent holed up in his study reading and writing, the time I'd spent on the run after... after.

There was something incredibly soothing about sitting in the large tent the camp had designated for meals. Breathing in the smoke from the fires they used to cook around back, the swirl of dust motes illuminated by the suns rays where it snuck in through pinholes scattered across the canvas, the low hum of activity as people grabbed their meals—not to mention the delicious smells of freshly cooked food.

I tugged self-consciously at the ragged pants I was wearing, grateful that their dark color hid most of the dirt I'd collected from working and that none of the fraying holes were wide enough to expose anything important, when the distant sound of coughing drew my attention, followed by a muffled groan. Worrying my lower lip, I made the executive decision to check it out. Lunch could wait.

The sound grew louder as I diverted from the path around to the side, where shadowed by trees and surrounded by shrubs, Heidi stood. She was wearing a dark green dress, her face soft and glowing, freed from the tension I hadn't even noticed she'd been carrying as she'd worn it since the day I met her. One of the girls must've done her hair—I know it bothered her to no end that she didn't know how to—because a long, brown braid wrapped its way across her head to lay across her shoulders. My eyes drifted down to the bump she was clutching. It grew a little more each time I saw her, and was large enough now to show beneath her clothing.

Close enough to see her unusually pale color, my pulse skyrocketed. "Are you okay? Hurt?" I asked succinctly, hands hovering over her arms in a desperate attempt to do *what* exactly, I wasn't sure.

She laughed softly and brushed the heavy braid over her shoulder to fall against her back. "I'm okay. I was just heading to grab some dinner when something set me off. Must be the scent of the chicken stock they're using because it didn't sit well with me last week."

My muscles relaxed when I realized there was no immediate emergency, and I nodded, gaze shifting once more to her rounded belly. It struck me that before Heidi, I'd never seen a pregnant woman. I'd read enough to know the entire process: the trimesters and development, conception and birth–a large chunk of the books in Ben's extensive library had been medical in nature, leftover from his late wife–but I'd never actually seen one.

She looked so settled, even underneath the thin sheen of sweat glistening off her pale skin. Still, I wondered. Was she happy here? Did she feel safe? Doubts swirled in my mind as I absently scratched at a spot on my arm, watching fascinatedly as it turned blotchy, the irritated pink color mingling with my freckles.

"What's wrong?" she asked gently.

The words bubbled up before I even had a chance to think over them. "Are you... settled in here? Enjoying it?"

Heidi cocked her head, confusion bleeding into understanding. "You're not?"

I glanced away. "Of course I'm happy, I just... Don't you worry about what would happen if the walls fell tomorrow or zombies got in? Just a couple months ago, someone sabotaged the fence. Doesn't it worry you that it's so easy for something to go wrong?"

"Have you been feeling like this since we arrived?"

When I opened my mouth to speak, I realized my throat was choked with emotion, so I settled for a nod. The very real fear of if something were to happen plagued me often. Who was to say I wouldn't end up with another group just like Gunner's out of necessity? The fact that I'd managed to keep myself alive at all after being forced from Ben's home was due to sheer luck.

Things were even more tense knowing that the camp was only just replenishing some of the food stores that were depleted when the camp's old leader was paying off Gunner, believing that it would keep him from attacking the camp. The food they'd discovered in the bunker last month had alleviated everyone's minds somewhat, but we still needed the surplus that the farm would provide in trade. It was all everyone could talk about.

"Oh, Sera," she whispered, and cool hands grasped my shoulders with a light touch. "What you must think of me. I had no idea you were worrying so much while we were all adjusting."

I'd put up a good façade when I was back at Gunner's–projecting confidence for my own safety–but underneath I was a roiling mess of emotions, and they were finally making their way to the surface now that we were somewhere safer. I was about to brush it off, horrified at the thought of upsetting her, but she firmed both her grip and her voice. "Listen closely. I know you only ended up with us because you had nowhere else to go. You were lost, starving, and dehydrated. It was a wonder you could stay on your feet at all. You may have been desperate enough to take a chance on strangers, but it was a decision all the same. It required courage. Not only that, but you survived months on your own before finding us, and you fit right in once you did."

"It was luck," I pointed out. "If not for Ryder..."

"I was so grateful to Ryder for keeping such a close eye on you." She smiled wistfully. "He stepped in immediately. Took one look at you and that was it."

The memory of it, stumbling onto their base after following the scent of freshly cooked meat, made me cringe. I couldn't believe I'd been so reckless. But she was right; I'd seen him in the distance and walked into the open without thinking twice. Immediately, I'd been supplied with fresh food and filtered water and ushered over to Heidi and Jamie for a change of clothes.

"You're wrong," I mumbled, clearing my throat. "He was just... Maybe I remind him of someone."

Heidi's smile was indulgent, and as though she'd realized the worst of my emotions had passed, she withdrew her hands from my shoulders. "That man is smitten with you, Sera. I don't know how you can miss it."

But I had to. I had to miss it, and she had to be wrong. To get my hopes up would crush me. He was so closed-off, capable of both a heated and icy fury, but not affection. Blunt as he was, he'd have said something otherwise.

I shook my head. "So you like it here?"

"Like nowhere I've ever stayed before. All I've ever wanted was to be a mother, from the moment I helped my mom deliver my siblings to taking care of them when she passed, and I can do that safely here. Well, as safely as I can. Survival is the art of adapting."

With a deep inhale, my senses suddenly attuned to my surroundings, like we'd been conversing in a bubble. The sound of the birds cawing overhead, the sudden chill that swept in along with the cluster of clouds hiding the sun.

Heidi sighed, opening her arms for a hug, and I was quick to throw my arms around her middle. "Now if you'll excuse me," she said as she pulled away, "I've got to go find some of those rosemary crackers that Anna likes to hoard."

I laughed softly, watching her braid swing as she left. Remembering my promise to River, I headed to the tent and ate my meal in record time before preparing a tray for the stranger. Even if he'd eaten lunch, he was most likely starving. It had taken me at least a week to adjust after I arrived so that I wasn't constantly hungry despite having eaten.

Balancing his tray, I took care as I climbed the steps up to his cabin. The door juddered from my knock, and I cringed, looking around to see if anyone was watching. I'd had to use my elbow, and had clearly overestimated the amount of force I would need to be heard.

A low voice called out from within, telling me to enter, so I used my hip to prop the tray up and twisted the knob, rushing to get inside before I dropped anything.

He was fortunate. Tonight we were having split pea soup, which was a rarity.

Once inside, I was taken aback at how dim it looked. None of the candles were lit, nor were the torches. Only the fire roaring in the hearth and the fastidiously cleaned and recovered windows provided enough light to see from. I strode over to the wooden table just outside the small kitchen, admiring the workmanship of the structure. The cabin was still in development, dusty and with supplies lying here and there, but the walls were solid, showcasing a rustic woodgrain, and the interior was nearly finished. It felt safe, like everything a home should be.

Once the tray was firmly on the table, I stood, my attention pulled in his direction as if magnetized and was startled to find him watching me right back. Sprawled in a comfy-looking chair beside the fire, flames casting harsh shadows across his face, he sat there like he owned the place. He wasn't classically handsome–his features hewn from granite, not marble, and his jaw a bit too square–but all the same, his strong characteristics made up a picture that was hard to look away from.

"Thank you," he rumbled. His voice was just as I'd imagined, deep and rough.

"Why are you here?" I blurted without thinking and immediately regretted it, lips pressing together tightly in case I embarrassed myself any further.

"Was just passing through when I saw the smoke and was hungry enough to take a chance."

He didn't elaborate, and I vibrated with curiosity, but resolved to stay quiet so it didn't seem like I was pumping him for information.

Finally, after a period of tense and assessing eye contact, the corner of his mouth crooked upward, and he looked towards the fire before continuing. "Military activity had increased in the area, and supplies were all but gone."

"So you'd never consider staying if you could?"

He shrugged in response, hesitating like he wasn't sure how much to reveal. "I have a friend to check up on. A mutual survivor. We make it a priority to meet up every year, give or take. He didn't show, so... I'm going to find him. I know the general area where he was staying last."

I brushed my fingers together where they rested at my side, the repetitive movement soothing. "That's going to be tough."

He dipped his head.

"I'm Sera, by the way."

"Kasimir."

Kasimir. Even his name was powerful. It wasn't one I'd ever heard before, even in my books, and I found myself liking it.

An idea hit me, and I prided myself on weighing the words in my mouth before speaking them aloud. I hoped I wasn't overstepping. "We're sending a group up north to trade with one of the surviving farms. If you wanted to join them, I'm sure they could always use another person."

"Safety in numbers, hm?" he asked, settling deeper into the chair. I became acutely aware of the fact that I'd been hovering in the center of the room this entire time. "I'll consider it."

The way he looked at me, it felt like he was considering something else. The air in the cabin charged, and the heat from the fire became unbearable. All at once, my skin was buzzing, and my stomach filled with an oddly warm sensation. It scared and fascinated me in equal measure, and I decided I'd had enough.

"Well," I said brightly. "Enjoy your soup, and by the looks of it, your quarantine will be over tomorrow, so maybe I'll see you then."

Bright gray eyes observed me as he nodded. I had the brief notion that he could see inside my body, could sense my odd reaction to him and read the thoughts straight from my brain, and left in a hurry before I felt any more exposed.

CHAPTER 3

The following week passed in the blink of an eye. I finished cleaning out the shed, and Nix followed through with his promise to try to teach me everything he knew. Occasionally someone would stop by to say hello or bring us something to eat, but otherwise we spent most of the day walking all over camp for demonstrations. Taking me to the kitchens to show me the lavender oil they had on hand for burns, to the sections of the forest within the fencing to teach me how to identify pine trees, and how their needles could be used for treating colds, coughs, or even infections. He had me gather some just so we could go through the process of washing, trimming, and drying them for use. My brain was bursting with all the new information, and that was only after a couple of days. The real challenge would be retaining it all, and I still had a long way to go.

Nix had just finished showing me some of our herbs and how we could repurpose them when I'd spotted Kasimir's powerful stride as he made his way through the camp. He was alone, and people stepped out of his way to let him pass. Halli, noticing my focus had shifted, followed my stare. I looked away immediately, but not before her eyes filled with mirth at having caught me.

I shoved him from my mind, ignoring Halli's inquiring glance, and jumped back into the conversation with Nix on the lemon balm they'd just planted. Though it was silly of me to think she'd forget. She pulled me aside after Nix wandered off to speak to Merikh, who'd stopped by to check on the garden.

"So," she said, eyes sparkling.

"So nothing. I don't even know him. There's just... something about him."

"There's something alright. He looks like he eats nails for breakfast."

A snort escaped me. "I grew up... sheltered. Seeing all these different people, it's just a shock to my system." The unspoken words were that seeing someone who looked like *that* made it hard to think.

"I get it. River was much the same, honestly."

I thought of River, seeing her around camp so in love with her guys, something I hadn't even known was a possibility before I'd met them. Merikh, Nix, Caelan, and Grey doted on her relentlessly at every opportunity. That she could've ever felt like me at first was reassuring.

"How's it going with your mending skills? You were trying to learn a few weeks ago, right?"

Her laugh said that my topic change wasn't quite as smooth as I'd hoped. Even so, her face brightened. "It's going well. Shiori's trying her best to teach me, but I can hardly even thread the needle after a full day of work, so progress is slow. Besides, Naia lives to distract her and then we all end up forgetting what we were doing in the first place."

"That sounds like Naia. I don't know where she gets her energy." I stretched my arms over my head to get rid of the tightness in my muscles when I remembered Heidi's predicament. "And you're looking into growing mint? Jake mentioned it the other day."

She lifted her long braid off her neck and wrapped it into a tight bun using the tie on her wrist. The thin bracelets stacked beneath it jangled with the movement, a sound I associated solely with her now. "The seeds won't take. We got fortunate with the others that River found, but these are some of the few that are just too stubborn to grow."

"Is that something the farm might have? Actual mint we can bring back, so there's no standing around and waiting for disappointment?" I asked. Knowing next to nothing about cultivating a garden, I was sure there was some reason it wouldn't work.

"You genius! Yes, it's definitely worth a shot. In fact, we could probably trade for a variety of cuttings that would be much less temperamental than seeds."

Her praise was unexpected, and nice to hear. I fiddled with a loose thread hanging from my shirt, hiding a pleased smile.

Nix's voice rose, cutting into our conversation and drawing our attention. "You know damn well you can't. Things are too busy here, and you were just gone. Kasimir's already requested to go. You don't think he'll be enough of a replacement?"

Halli looked just as confused as I was.

"It's not about whether he's 'enough,'" Merikh growled, crossing his arms. "He's not even planning on staying with them the entire way. Do you really want Jake or Casey out there with one less person for even the smallest stretch of time?"

Nix's response was drowned out by the blood rushing to my head so fast that I swayed where I stood. Did he mean... Was Jeremiah okay? Why wasn't he going on the trip anymore? I felt like I was hovering outside my body, watching myself in sheer horror as I marched in their direction and interrupted their heated argument.

"What the hell is going on?" I demanded.

"Jeremiah broke his leg working on one of the new cabins," Merikh said absently, sparing me a glance. "And Nix here doesn't think I should accompany them in his stead."

"I'm not saying Jake has to go with just Casey," Nix insisted, clearly exasperated. "I'm just saying we need you here, and that they'll have to wait. With the added patrol on the fence and the construction, we can't afford to spare anyone else."

"We've waited long enough! The camp needs this—"

"I'll go."

Both heads snapped to me while I stood there frozen on the spot, wondering what had just possessed me to speak. My fingers were numb with adrenaline, heart thudding rapidly in my chest with the knowledge that I'd just made what felt like a life-changing statement.

Merikh raised his eyebrow and gave me an assessing look. "What makes you think you could handle it?"

I tipped my chin up, anxiously aware that he had a point, but reluctant to admit it. Yes, I was inexperienced, but I'd lived on my own for months, and just from the last few days I probably had more fresh knowledge of healing salves and treatments than Jake or Casey did. Surely I could be an asset? The more I thought about it, the more right it felt. I could pay River back for bringing us here by keeping her men safe within the camp and taking Merikh's place.

"I can help," I said firmly. Maybe if I sounded confident enough, they'd buy it. Judging by Halli's horrified stare, I might've missed the mark. "I can bring along supplies, barter for anything you need, and help keep an eye out for threats." The words sounded stilted coming from my dry mouth. With Casey, Jake, and most likely Kasimir going, they would have the muscle covered. But what if they needed someone smaller for certain tasks? Someone to stay up and keep watch while the important people slept?

Merikh stared at me, and I was sure the next words to leave his mouth would be no, but he surprised me.

"Fine."

Nix made a noise, casting an incredulous glance his way. "What do you mean, *fine*? She just got here. She shouldn't have to be shipped right back out again."

"I *want* to help." They didn't need me here like they did the others. I'd been a victim of circumstance for too long, going wherever life took me instead of taking charge. This was my opportunity, a chance to help the camp, to help the others who'd saved me just because they could. I was no River—I'd heard endless stories of her bravery and courage from the people here—but I still wanted to help contribute instead of languishing here while I could be doing something *bigger*. Taking hold of the fears that plagued me and confronting them head-on instead of allowing them to control me, with the added benefit of making sure Jake stayed safe.

"You'll stay by their sides at all times," Merikh cautioned, both a warning and an advisement. I nodded, ready to agree to anything. "If you want to change your mind, you just need to speak up."

Nix seemed hesitant, but reluctantly agreed after some coaxing from Merikh. "We'll cram in a few more lessons," he informed me. "Broken bones, swelling, scrapes. Hopefully, you won't need to use any of it, but just in case. And I'll pack you a kit to bring."

A terrified excitement consumed me, and my stomach twisted itself into knots at the magnitude of what I'd just committed to.

What the hell have I done?

The amount of time between when I'd volunteered myself to go and when we were actually scheduled to leave passed by like nothing. I resolved not to tell my friends, because I knew they'd try to talk me out of it, and it wasn't like they visited often enough to see the mess borne from my thorough packing. Based on our conversations prior, it was clear they didn't feel the same restlessness as I did. They wouldn't understand and it would just lead to an argument.

Muttering under my breath, I rifled through my bag one last time, making sure I had everything I needed. Extra sets of clothes, disinfectant, hair ties, a can opener, hygiene products, and an aluminum water bottle were just a few of the items I spotted as I did my final check. Someone else would be bringing rations for us to split.

Keeping myself busy so that I didn't focus on my nerves, I slung the bag over my shoulder and forced myself from the familiar surroundings of my cabin, exchanging the cozy comfort of the small wooden structure for the unknown.

This is it, I gently reminded myself. Nerves formed a fist around my lungs and made it difficult to breathe. You can do this. I slammed the door on the pessimistic thoughts that tried to creep through, wondering why a nobody like me was taking a valuable space in their group.

There was no going back. I had to be strong.

The glimpse of Ryder standing near the gates as I approached–dark hair and darker clothes swallowing the sunlight overhead–calmed my racing thoughts until they came roaring back at the sight of Kasimir standing beside him.

I felt a bit like prey, being stared at as I was, one set of piercing gray eyes and another so deep they appeared black. I slowed to a walk, grateful when Grey came bounding up the path and stopped at my side. He followed my gaze to Ryder, then glanced back at me.

"He's a persistent one, huh? Soon as he heard you were going, he demanded to go as well."

Emotions overwhelmed me, threatening to send me spiraling, but were too chaotic for me to pin down. Relief, fear, affection, confusion, hope–all of them eclipsed by the single thought that he's leaving for me. I hadn't seen him in days, and just the sight of him was welcoming, remote expression and all.

"Yeah," I replied weakly. "Persistent."

Grey's mouth opened, but I pretended not to see and quickly pulled ahead to stave off any unwanted questions.

The two men were silent as I joined them, and I wouldn't have put it past either of them to not have spoken a single word to one another, even to introduce themselves.

"Ryder, have you met Kasimir?" I asked, gesturing towards the hulking man beside him. They were around the same height, but where Ryder was lean and a tad shorter, his toned muscles hidden away behind his fitted clothes to make him appear deceptively slender, Kasimir's frame was broad and imposing, with powerful shoulders that stretched the fabric of his clothing, and one glance at his build would tell you he could put you through the floor.

Fuck.

My cheeks heated. *Not like that.*

Both men gave each other stoic nods, looking stiff and uncomfortable.

Relief flooded through me at the first glimpse of River as she turned the bend, accompanied by Merikh, Caelan, and Nix. Jake loped alongside them, and Casey brought up the rear. I hadn't officially met Casey, though I'd seen him around camp. The older man was loud, outgoing, and always helping someone with something or other. It made sense he'd be accompanying us. He seemed capable and strong. Maybe I could learn from him.

Jake took in Ryder and Kasimir with a quick assessing glance, confusion briefly dancing across his rugged features, as he gave them a small tip of his head in greeting. His eyes flicked to me when I emerged from where I'd been standing almost behind the two men and his familiar, nascent grin transformed into a scowl the minute his gaze landed on the bag in my arms.

"No," he growled. He whirled around to face Merikh, the suddenness causing River to take a quick step back before she planted her feet in the dirt and crossed her arms. "Why didn't you tell me?"

"Clearly, because we knew you'd pull some shit like this," Merikh said flatly, a faint hint of exasperation weaving its way through his words.

Beside him, Nix held his hands up like he had nothing to do with it. "She volunteered. Don't take that away from her just because you're scared."

Jake scoffed, and I felt a sudden rush of embarrassment at being discussed, like I wasn't standing right there. He spun on his heel to glare at me, throat moving on a thick swallow. "Stay here," he ordered.

I blinked rapidly, drawing my head back. "You must be joking."

He crossed his arms, leveling a look my way that told me he wasn't up to negotiations.

"Surely, you don't think you can just hand out commands and I'll follow along? You have no say," I hissed, mortified that he would single me out like that. I was nervous enough as it was, and if any of them had a glimpse of just how much, there would be more voices than just his telling me to stay behind.

I straightened my spine and lifted my chin. "Fuck off," I declared, walking back to Ryder's side and catching a hint of the smirk he'd aimed at the small crowd behind my back. How could Jake speak to me like that in front of everyone?

Nix's voice was soft as he quietly explained that Ryder would be accompanying us as well. Sure enough, Jake took this news with nothing but a small frown. Was I really so weak, so incapable that he didn't trust me to defend myself? Defend them? Or to at least not be a burden?

River shot me a concerned look, and my nails bit into my palms as my thoughts raced and threatened to escalate. Was everyone thinking it?

Do I look so obviously out of my element?

"Enough," River told a now sullen-looking Jake, to which she received a grunt in response. His jaw remained uncharacteristically tight, but at least he was no longer talking. Would he be like this the entire time? Grumpy and distrusting? It was a side of him I'd never seen before. She took a deep breath, then continued, addressing the entire group. "As you know, Jeremiah is injured, and Sera is going to be taking his place. Ryder will accompany you as well, and Kasimir will be present for most of the journey. You have a list of things we need and can trade at this time, as well as the route, so all that's left is to be safe and quick. We can't afford to put this off any longer." She sent a cutting glance toward Jake. "So you will say thank you for the additional support and let it go."

At her increasingly irritated tone, Nix slipped a hand into River's while Caelan flanked her other side, dropping an arm around her back. Kasimir watched them interact curiously.

I set my bag down and crossed my arms, taking the role of speaker since the others had elected to stay quiet. "Sounds good," I said, more confidently than I felt. I appreciated that River didn't pull me aside to check in with me, that she didn't single me out or second guess my conviction. She took what Merikh had told her at face value, treating me as an important member of the team.

My stomach dropped when someone out of view shouted, and Nadira, Jamie, and Heidi appeared, making their way over to where we stood.

"Wait!" Heidi panted, spreading her stance to breathe heavily. "I was sick," she gasped. "Thought we were too late."

"You weren't supposed to know," I mumbled, plucking nervously at the band on my wrist. "I didn't want you to worry. River was going to tell you after I left."

That earned me a nasty look from all but Heidi. "We wish you wouldn't go," she said. "But we understand that we can't order you not to do something that you clearly feel you need to." That was accompanied by a glare at Jamie, who seemed to be holding back some choice words. "We need you to come back safe and sound. We love you very much–" Heidi choked up and Jamie rolled her eyes good-naturedly, pulling our friend into her side.

"What she said," Jamie grumbled. "If you don't come back, I'll go kick your ass myself."

Nadira nodded. "I'll help."

I gave a watery laugh as I pulled all three into a tight hug, blinking rapidly so that none of the pooling moisture escaped.

"Good luck on your adventure," Nadira whispered, eyes sparkling. "I hope it achieves everything that you're expecting it to."

Not trusting myself to speak, I nodded, giving them one last squeeze before I walked back over to the others. Casey gave me a wide grin as he approached, holding out his hand to give me a firm shake. His near-silver hair was cropped short, and his bag was the largest of them all.

"Nice to officially meet you."

Some of my nerves dissipated at his genuine greeting. "You too. Have you done this before?"

Crinkles gathered at the corners of his eyes as his smile deepened. "Yep, for half a decade or so. A walk in the park. Just stick with me, kid."

A walk in the park. Sure.

CHAPTER 4.

A dog's bark echoed from behind a nearby house, and I cringed at how the loud noise shattered the tense silence. It didn't seem real to be outside the camp, far enough away that the wide arc of layered fencing was almost entirely obscured by the rounded wall formed years ago from the shells of abandoned cars. From here I could just barely hear the dull hum of conversation, of movement; all the sounds that had become so familiar and comforting to me after such a short amount of time. Each step away from my newfound sanctuary was like lead in my heart, bringing me back to the day we arrived not even a couple of months ago.

We came to a halt after what felt like ten minutes but could've only been five when Jake turned around from his spot in the front to face us, giving me a severe look. Those golden-brown eyes lacking any of his previous teasing.

"Now's your chance," he told me. "You can turn back right now. Or even hole up in one of these empty houses for a few days if you're so desperate to prove yourself. You won't lose any face and there won't be much danger. It's the best option, the *safest* option."

Oh, Jake.

"I'm not going to do that," I said firmly. A brisk gust of wind sent a leaf flying onto my shoulder and I brushed it off. "I didn't ask to go because I wanted to make myself look good, or gain points with anyone. I'm going because I believe I can be an asset. Because..."

How ridiculous would that sound if I told them it had felt like a compulsion? To burn away my fears by running straight toward them instead of away? He'd turn me right back around, protests be damned. As would the others. "Just because," I finished weakly.

He scoffed, pinching his lips together and running his hands through his hair. The bright sun overhead illuminated harsh shadows over his furrowed brows, and for a brief moment, I didn't even recognize the person looking back at me.

"Whatever," he muttered, shaking his head.

We walked for hours just like that, Jake in the front, sullen and wordless, with the others trading positions every so often. Behind me, Ryder had fallen back to walk beside Kasimir but Casey matched my pace.

Our surroundings grew more urban; the ghostly remains of a civilization that no longer existed. The infrequent quips and whispered observations stopped until we were walking in complete silence.

I couldn't help but morbidly glance at the insides of the twisted and wrecked cars we passed, compulsively checking each for skeletons. Each time I saw something that might be the hint of one, my heart dropped a little further and raced a little faster.

The next car, some kind of monstrosity of a truck lying on its side, revealed a bundle of bleached bones tangled in rags hanging over the steering wheel. I sucked in a quick breath, tempted to look closer. It was startling to be confronted with death up close.

A firm hand on my shoulder had me glancing up to find Ryder staring at me with a small, sympathetic grimace. He shook his head once, steering me into the center of the group so that there were bodies on all sides blocking my view of the cars, then let me go. Kasimir's arm brushed mine from where he walked to my right, and I wondered if it was an accident or not.

Jake made a slashing motion with his hand from the front, and we fell still. Casey slowly lifted the weapon at his side, his almost constant affable expression replaced with something much more serious.

I kept a wary eye on the surrounding landscape, carefully examining each pile of rubble, each hollowed out car and dark shadow. I hadn't heard anything, but I trusted Jake's instincts. Matching my inhales and exhales to Kasimir's deep, level breaths, my head began to rid itself of that awful throbbing tension from the adrenaline. My grip on my knife ached, I was clutching it so tightly.

Something crashed behind us, and I whirled around to face the sound. My heart pounded. Was this it? My first up close and personal encounter with a zombie? I'd never felt quite so vulnerable in my entire life.

Ryder crept forward a couple of steps, carving knife clenched firmly in his hand and his face a mask of concentration.

His jaw tightened at the rustling noise coming from the car closest to us, shoulders sagging just the barest inch in relief when a black cat darted out from its undercarriage and streaked up to our group, stopping to sniff Ryder's pants.

We all breathed a collective sigh of relief, shaking out our stiff muscles and watching as the cat examined Ryder. It sat on its haunches at his feet, mouth still slightly open from all the sniffing, and stared up at him. It didn't dare make a sound, almost as if it knew that we were in a more populated part of the city–outskirts or not.

Casey huffed a silent laugh, crouching down and clicking his tongue once to get its attention. It eyed him warily, taking a few hesitant steps in his direction. Casey rubbed his fingers together to make a dry shushing sound and outstretched his hand so the cat would come closer. It did, albeit warily, getting close enough to sniff his fingers before rubbing its entire side along his hand. Casey's grin was dazzling, and he beckoned me to come crouch by him to greet it as well. I took slow steps, careful not to scare it, but it didn't even seem to notice or care about my approach. I dropped to my knees beside Casey, following his lead when he inclined his head toward my hand and extending it so that the cat could sniff.

It turned big, green eyes onto me, neglecting Casey's hand to come look at mine. This close, I could see that a sizable chunk of its right ear was missing, as was the tip of its tail. Its whiskers twitched as it leaned its head forward to sniff me, a low purring sound leaving its body as it tucked its head into my hand, repeatedly rubbing its fur along my nails to be scratched. I'd never seen a cat up close before, let alone touched one. There was a stray that used to hang around when I was younger, but it never let me get close. A surprised breath left me when its body vibrated with a rusty purr.

Its fur was covered in dust and dirt, but it was still incredibly soft to the touch. Casey nudged my side, looking down at me with a small, proud grin. I grinned back, elated by the entire experience and fell into a lull petting the small, friendly creature, trusting the others to keep us safe. It rolled onto its side before shifting to its back and letting me rub its stomach, giving happy little wriggles with its paws up in the air.

"A girl," Casey whispered.

I beamed when she rolled back onto her feet and nudged my hand once more. "Mila," I whispered back. My mother's middle name.

A quick glance up had my smile faltering as I stared into the intent gazes of the other three men accompanying us. Jake watched my hand while Ryder's eyes had dropped to my mouth. Kasimir just looked puzzled. I sighed, shifting my balance, and Mila took it as a sign, rushing off to go plant herself near Ryder's feet once more. Casey stood, knees creaking, and reached out a hand to help me up as well. I reoriented myself, that time spent with the cat doing more for my nerves than any number of affirmations or deep breathing. A sense of calmness returned that I thought had left behind for good the second we walked out of camp.

Jake continued in the same direction as before and in unspoken agreement, we all fell in behind him, Mila included. We walked for what felt like miles just like that, sticking to the lone road just on the edge of the city.

Mila ran off at some point, much to my disappointment, but a mile later the small black cat was once more trailing behind Ryder as he walked.

"She likes you," I murmured, when it finally felt like a safe enough area to speak.

He shrugged, watching as she skillfully navigated her way through the rubble. "She just smells the jerky in my pocket."

At the sound of his deep voice, she surged forwards to wind her way through his ankles with a purred trill, almost tripping him.

I pursed my lips, trying not to laugh. His expression was so disgruntled, I almost couldn't resist.

"If you say so."

Mila once more pranced happily after him as we walked until the faint remnants of pink threading through the inky sky had almost completely disappeared over the horizon. The trees that surrounded us filled the air with scents of earth and decomposing leaves. We were all slowing down, and I knew it wouldn't be long until we stopped.

Sure enough, not ten minutes later, Jake pulled to a stop to examine a nicely sized clearing lined by trees and the occasional bush.

"Here?" I asked, watching as Jake slung his bag down and Casey followed suit.

"Here."

I flung my bag off, a low appreciative groan leaving my throat at the lack of weight on my back. All the pressure in my shoulders faded as I rolled them out, my sweat cooling where it soaked the back of my shirt. I twisted around to try to relieve the tension in my spine, just in time to catch Jake's eyes before he turned his head. Things had been stiff between us the entire day.

It made sense for us to camp out in the forest. The likelihood of running into a zombie wasn't zero, but it was much less likely than if we were still on the outskirts of the city. Even with my limited experience on the outside, I knew they were more commonly found in civilization, or the echoes of it. It would've been better if we'd come across some kind of structure to sleep in for the night, but we hadn't seen anything for miles after we decided to enter the forest.

Mila meowed, rubbing against Ryder's ankles while he looked at her like he wasn't sure what to do with her. The little cat had followed us that entire distance, sometimes lagging behind, sometimes running ahead, but ultimately ending up by Ryder's side.

I made my way towards them where he was rolling out his sleeping bag and bent down to scratch her cheek, her body vibrating when she purred loudly. When Ryder finished setting up his things he switched his gaze to me, and it sent a strange thrill through me to have his complete attention.

"Like this," I murmured, distantly hearing the others move about as they gathered the supplies for a fire. I held out my hand to Mila, letting her sniff, then used the backs of my fingers to stroke her cheek. Ryder looked at me dubiously, pushing his dark brown hair back from his face and grimacing when a piece fell free to hit his cheek. It had grown almost to his ears over the past several months and would need a trim soon. He never did know how to deal with it when it grew long enough to fall in his eyes. I couldn't help but laugh as I smoothed it away.

"Come on," I encouraged, reaching out to take the hand balancing on his knee and pulling it towards the cat. His exhale was shaky, and his skin warm and dry, fingers covered in tiny cuts and scrapes from working around the camp with callouses on his palm. I took a shallow breath as I held it in front of Mila, grinning when she gave a little trill and mashed her face into his hand. A quick peek at his face revealed a quiet happiness as he let the little cat maneuver his hand as she liked.

I continued to hold his hand in place before deciding that he had it under control. Though my skin brushed over the back of his when I went to pull away, and the accidental graze brought with it a wave of awareness. Solemn brown eyes stared into mine, a hint of surprise in their depths.

A rush of dizziness washed over me, making me stumble as I went to stand. Certain I was about to go flying backwards and humiliate myself, I could only blink when a large hand shot out to grab my knee and keep me balanced. I didn't dare look at Ryder again, instead offering him a mumbled thank you.

A quick scan revealed everyone to be doing their own thing. Casey poked at the robust fire with a long stick, while Jake sorted through the food, and Kasimir was nowhere to be found. My face grew hot when I realized how completely in my own world I'd been just seconds ago. The heat seeping through my jeans at my knee kept me from completely brushing it aside.

"How can I help?" I asked, voice slightly strangled. I cleared my throat and took a few steps closer to the fire.

Casey's voice rang out from behind me. "You can get me some more wood for the fire." A quick sweep of the ground inside the clearing revealed it to be clear of branches and other debris. The grass was sparse in some areas, circles of flat dirt peeking through, and anything loose must've been gathered by Casey when we first arrived.

Guess I need to go into the forest... The gaping maw of darkness beyond the scattered trees was far more intimidating than it should've been.

I took a deep breath and pushed the long sleeves of my shirt up my forearms as I picked my way through the overgrown bushes at the edge of the space, trading the comforting light from the flames for the heavy gloom cast by the trees. Now that night had fallen, the branches cast long shadows against the ground, the fading light from the fire giving them sinister silhouettes.

Hopping over the trunk of a fallen tree, I listened as the low murmur of Casey and Jake's distant voices faded out of earshot. Thankfully, the moon was out tonight, and cut through the areas of the trees that hadn't yet filled out after the long winter. I picked up sticks here and there, skipping the ones that were too thin and wouldn't provide much fuel.

A branch cracked behind me, and I turned to give Jake shit for not even trusting me to do this alone when I realized... *who the fuck is that?*

Immediately, I berated myself for not paying closer attention. How the hell had someone managed to sneak up on me without me noticing?

The figure was shocked into stillness before tripping over itself to reassure me.

"So sorry, I wasn't expect–I didn't mean to scare you." The man's hands shot up as he squinted at me. "This looks really bad. I'm sorry it's not daylight out because I think that would make this less sketchy. I just saw the smoke from the fire and... is there a sanctuary around here or something? You just look so... *clean.*"

I blinked as I searched for a response to his rambling, still half-frozen from shock.

"Promise I'll be on my best behavior," he added, lowering his hands slowly and keeping his palms open by his sides. "I'm late to meet someone and I need to rest for a bit somewhere safe if I want to keep going at the same pace. Thought whoever started the fire might know of something."

At least he wasn't lying about that. Dark circles sat heavy beneath bright blue eyes, and his hollowed cheeks were just beginning to show signs of gauntness. His thick blond hair was growing out from what had to have been a shorter cut, judging by the awkward length, and he looked to be about my age. Maybe a little older.

There was no way I could go back and ask the guys what they thought. They'd either tell me I'd imagined him from exhaustion or would lecture me for not getting them immediately. Jake couldn't micromanage *everything*, right? I had things under control just fine all on my own.

My teeth left indents in my bottom lip. The others would say no, but I knew what it was like to need refuge, if just for a night, so who was I to act like the gatekeeper to the place I called home now? I knew River would give him a chance. So I would too.

"Yeah," I replied, checking to make sure nobody was coming. "Actually, I do." I proceeded to give him the best instructions I could. We weren't far anyway, and it had been a pretty straight path to where we were now. Hopefully, he'd find it just fine.

"Thank you," he said. "I'll remember this."

"Just tell them Sera sent you," I tacked on.

He nodded, and just like that, he was gone. I hadn't even gotten his name. At least I didn't have to worry about Jake seeing him; who knew how he'd react if he found out what happened.

It felt strange to go back to my original task after meeting a whole *stranger* all by myself, but needs must. Up ahead, there looked to be a large graveyard of fallen branches. A closer inspection revealed they were not too large for me to carry and in perfect condition. I silently cheered, crouching down to add them to my pile, so focused on gathering them I didn't notice the shadow looming above me until it spoke.

"Good find."

I swallowed my scream, only relaxing when I saw Kasimir standing above me. *Holy shit, I thought that stranger came back to finish me off.* Had he heard me talking to that man? Did he know?

"That for me?" he asked, sounding amused.

Guess not.

I noticed the branch pulled back defensively in my hand and snorted, tossing it down with the rest.

"I'll have you know I could do a lot of damage with that branch," I joked.

He bent down to collect branches without even being asked, black hair hiding his face from view. "I don't doubt it."

My cheeks flushed with heat, and I gathered the kindling at a quicker rate. A tug on the branch I was currently lifting had my eyes flying up to land on Kasimir, who was holding the other end. He gave me a rare smile, and revealing a dimple on the right side of his cheek. It somehow tempered his other intimidating aspects: his tall, large stature, the pale scar running from his temple through the corner of his right eyebrow, and those penetrating eyes tinted silver by the moonlight.

I gave a shaky laugh, relinquishing my end so that he could add it to its own stash. His smile was gone just as quick as it came, but I'd already committed it to memory.

CHAPTER 5

"I don't understand how you don't even need to look at a map," I grumbled under my breath, brushing the sweat from my forehead with the neckline of my shirt. The air was cooler today, but I was still soaked through with sweat from the exertion, and each step sent shooting pains through my tired feet.

Jake huffed a bitter laugh. "I've taken this trip almost every year since we first began trading with them. Speaking of, we're going to have to stay further to the west for the next few days if we want to steer clear of the local testing facility."

It was amazing to me that he'd memorized exactly how to avoid it., but I was grateful he had. The facilities were military controlled, and had cropped up after society had fallen, testing everyone who passed through their doors, and according to rumors, whoever they could pluck unnoticed from the streets. They didn't discover the gene that indicated immunity until several years after the virus was released, and had yet to discover how to synthesize it, but that didn't stop them from trying.

Even the recent claims that they'd grown more ethical in their practices didn't stop people from giving them a wide berth. The only person I'd ever known who had been to one was River.

We approached the edge of the city limits, about to enter a larger stretch of empty land. The quiet was welcome, if not a little daunting. Our group had already encountered a moderate number of the undead, largely handled by Kasimir and Casey, who wore their efforts on their clothes. Only when the ambling, skeletal bodies were far enough away and didn't pose as big a threat did we try to sneak past.

The first sighting had made my limbs tremble, and I'd stood frozen on the spot, watching as it staggered ever closer. I'd seen them before, of course. It would've been almost impossible not to have. But never up close.

I'd spent so much time in the shadows growing up, shielded from everything that could possibly cause me harm. Some of my worst anxieties revolved around decaying figures of flesh and bone, but actually facing them down had distilled my nightmares into something tangible. I had let them rule my life for far too long. With every new experience, I realized how much I'd never really *lived* due to my constant fear.

Others faced the undead frequently, like it was no big deal. River had survived out in the open for years, for fuck's sake. But Ben had kept us so sequestered that we rarely encountered them, and when we did, he took care of them. When I'd fled and ended up with Gunner, others had taken the confrontations onto themselves. I never liked to recall the time I'd spent on my own between those two periods. Waking at the slightest of noises, staying deep within the forests to avoid other people, and sleeping in trees so that I was less of a target, even if I'd been perpetually worried about falling out. At even the slightest hint of a zombie, I'd fled swiftly and silently, not stopping until I'd put at least a mile between us.

The killing of a zombie was so visceral, as they would get back up missing pieces if their heads weren't crushed or damaged enough to incapacitate them for good. I knew it was me or them, but sometimes I doubted I had what it took to make that final blow. The consequences if I couldn't would be devastating. A single fresh bite could take up to five minutes to turn someone, and during that time, they could still be killed by normal methods. With the advanced strength a newly turned had, there was no choice but to take them out while they were still *them*. I could think of nothing more painful—for me or those I was with—and each step further away from camp tugged incessantly at the survival instincts that told me to hide and stay still.

A furry presence twining around my ankles nearly sent me flying when I lifted my foot. I muttered a low curse, catching my balance at the last moment and giving Mila a quiet scolding that devolved into ear scratching.

"I could walk to the same place twenty times and I'd still probably need a map," I said.

Casey snorted from where he walked beside me. "Some people just aren't good at navigating," he said. "It's all about street names and landmarks."

All heads faced Kasimir as he spoke. "Everyone has their strengths and weaknesses. If you're smart, you'll befriend someone whose skills compliment yours."

Mila darted back to trot alongside Ryder as he nodded in agreement. The gray sky made his eyes appear darker than they were, but I liked them both ways, chestnut from the sun or sable from the clouds.

As the conversation lulled, self-consciousness hit me once I realized how loud my breathing had become. And had I always been lagging so far back?

Of course, Jake noticed. He could shove the concerned look he gave me.

"Do you need us to stop for a bit?" he asked.

I sputtered before finally finding the words. "No! Fuck off."

"What the hell, Sera? It's okay to need a moment."

"Oh yeah? Because you haven't taken one, and you haven't asked anyone else either."

His brows creased. "That's not... I wasn't..."

"That's what I thought. Just leave me alone."

Casey chuckled, patting him on the back as he passed him. "Tell us some more about the route."

Jake grunted. "It's going to be open terrain like this for the next day or so. There's a decent-sized forest northwest of us, and that's where we're heading, although we'll have to pass through some more urban areas first. We're looking at a week of travel left, at least. Less if we make good time. The farm isn't too deep into Pennsylvania."

"We've got... what, like five hours of daylight left?" I asked, directing the question to anyone but Jake.

Casey nodded, pulling a bottle of water from his bag and taking a sip. His gray hair was matted down with sweat, making me feel a little better about my slowing pace. Going from helping around camp and even before that, traveling with Gunner, had not prepared me at all for how much energy this trip was going to take. Each day we'd walked from sunup to sundown, and it was because of me that we had to take frequent breaks.

As much as I wanted to keep going, sometimes I needed to get my breathing under control. To sit and give myself a pep talk to keep moving. I'd noticed the others creating more and more reasons why they needed to stop, but I was fairly certain they were really for me. Though, of course, Jake had to be blunt about it. It was humiliating to be singled out. And even worse, I'd gotten a full night of sleep, unlike the others who had traded off on watch. Even my nightmares couldn't penetrate the bone-deep tiredness whenever we settled for the evening, but I'd tried. They'd refused to let me take a turn yet, no matter how much I insisted.

I didn't want any handouts or special treatment. I wanted to get back to camp and be able to say that I pulled my own weight and participated just like the rest of them. That's why I tried to take on as many as the more manageable tasks as I could, like making sure everyone was supplied with small bites to eat throughout the day and keeping an ear out for any suspicious sounds.

Watching Casey take another sip of his water made me realize how thirsty I was. I pulled my bottle out and frowned at how light it felt. Guess I hadn't noticed just how much I drank earlier. Tilting it back to take a gulp, I squeezed my eyes shut when my next was just a few leftover drops. My throat convulsed painfully at the lack of the cool liquid it had been anticipating.

Shit.

With a discreet movement, I tucked it back into my pack. No use in making us waste time just for me to refill it. My throat could deal.

A nudge at my elbow preceded a bottle being thrust into my space. I looked up at the scarred hand holding it, following the length of his arm until my head tilted back and my gaze landed on Kasimir's face.

"Here," he said gruffly.

I was hesitant at first, reaching out slowly to wrap my hand just below his on the metal cylinder. His pinky brushed my thumb as he let go, sending a flutter through my stomach. I pulled the bottle closer, my movements jerky, and brought it up to my lips. Able to feel that there wasn't much left in his bottle either, I wiped my sleeve across my mouth after just a gulp and screwed the cap back on.

"Thank you," I murmured, thrusting the bottle back into his hands awkwardly. All I did was take a sip of someone's water, so why the hell was it so embarrassing?

I lost the battle to keep looking ahead like nothing was wrong and let my gaze fall to the dirt. *If everyone could just pretend like I'm not acting strange for no reason, that would be amazing.*

"I can't believe she's still here," Casey said with a glance towards Mila, taking the attention off me.

Ryder's gaze followed Casey's, and he shrugged in response.

"She feels safe with you," Kasimir told him.

The corner of Ryder's lips quirked up in a miniscule smile, and he shook his head. "I feed her," he replied softly. Like she realized we were speaking about her, Mila gave a little meow and rubbed up against his ankle.

"It's *you* she likes."

Ryder looked past Casey to me and his barely there smile disappeared. "We'll see if she stays."

I ducked my head and pulled my bag up over my shoulders, then hastily tucked in all the stray pieces of hair that had fallen out of my ponytail over the past few hours. Backpacks were easier to walk with during the day and could hold a large number of items, but they were a safety hazard. To wear something attached to me that could be grabbed at any moment was a nightmare. But I had no choice. If we wanted to bring the maximum amount to trade with, there was no other option.

We walked in silence for hours, keeping a wary eye on the sky overhead. The clouds had gathered tightly as the day went on instead of dissipating, and the air gained a crisp, fresh scent. The longer in the day it got, the more the temperature dropped. It was much too cold for an average April day, and my teeth chattered as we walked.

The first few flurries had my jaw dropping. Twisting my arm, I watched as a translucent snowflake melted onto one of my scattered freckles where I'd first felt the icy numbness. I twisted my head to squint up at the sky, startled to find it a lightened gray color, even though the sun had clearly set for the day and we were well into the evening.

Little bumps raised on my arms as a cool breeze swept by, more flurries landing on my exposed skin. We'd had some more frigid nights this past week, even a few frosty mornings, but this was totally unexpected.

Shivers wracked my body as I rubbed my arms, only serving to spread the melted ice further across my skin to be ambushed by the cool air. We couldn't sleep outside like this. A fire wouldn't be enough to stave off the cold, nor would our thin sleeping bags.

Jake must have realized this too, because up ahead, he and Kasimir were already on the lookout for any structures that we could potentially spend the night in.

A snowflake landed on my nose and I quickly scrubbed it off, then tried to brush the chill from my palm off onto my pants. It was disorienting to have gone from a sunny day just yesterday to being thrown back into winter weather. We certainly hadn't packed for it.

With no warning, a warm weight covered my shoulders. Ryder took the ends of the blanket he used on cooler nights and tucked them in where my arms were pulled tight to my chest, making sure the blanket covered as much as it could.

"You're going to need it later," I said quietly. "You should put it back into your bag where it can't get wet from the snow."

He tilted his head, completely ignoring me, and pulled the blanket tighter around my shoulders. "I don't care if it gets wet," he finally said, his voice gruff. "You need it more now than I will later."

I clutched it closer to me with shaking fingers, noticing Mila's head poking out of his light jacket where he'd nestled her in from the cold. I paused to take them in: the furry little bundle tucked against his chest, his reddened cheeks and long, damp eyelashes framing eyes made light from the sky.

Once I realized he was watching me with just as much scrutiny, I faced the front, taking a few quick steps forward so that I could hear Kasimir, Jake, and Casey's murmurs, only catching the tail end of whatever they were discussing.

Bringing the soft fabric up to my face to shield my freezing nose, I discreetly inhaled the familiar scent of him infused with the fabric. A comforting blend of jasmine and something deeper.

"-nearby," Jake muttered.

Casey grimaced. "Better than nothing. And I bet it has some heavy doors."

Jake was about to reply, but froze when he noticed me. His lips twisted downwards before he turned back around. Was it me? Did I do something? It felt so strange to be as angry with him as I was and yet still be worried about him. We'd barely spoken since our fight, and I missed the easy camaraderie we used to have. But not enough to forgive him yet.

Before I could dwell too much on it, Kasimir spoke.

"That?" he asked, pointing at the large structure in the distance. It looked like... I squinted. A church?

"That's it. We've passed by it before, but never had a reason to go in. It's the only building for the next several miles. There were some houses further out, but I don't think we should try for them."

I would've thought Kasimir immune to the cold with all that muscle mass had I missed the slight shiver that racked his body. *Huh, guess he's human after all.*

We all trudged towards the church in a single file line as the winds grew stronger. I fought hard to keep my shuddering under control, because if any of them stopped to check on me during the short walk, I'd never live it down.

A muffled meow sounded behind me, followed by some almost silent whispers, but when I glanced back, Ryder's face was blank, and he was looking straight ahead.

The closer we got to the church, the more signs of civilization I noticed. When we finally reached the singular gravel road that led to it, I took one look and opted to stay on the grass because of the number of cracks, potholes, and vegetation that had consumed it over years of disuse. The parking lot was in a similar state, almost entirely covered in green and swallowed up by nature, like the church itself. What must've once been a dull white color, the building was now a dirtied gray, with bushes and vines creeping up against the sides. A tree had fallen on the roof at some point, though not hard enough to break it as far as I could tell from where I stood. Somehow, amazingly, the stained-glass window at the front remained intact. Dirty and scratched, but uncompromised.

I sighed when, after several minutes of holding my breath in suspense, Jake called from around back. One look at the large, heavy wooden doors that were sealed shut at the front of the building and Jake had circled the building to find a different entrance.

The snow was coming down harder now, melting in my hair where it wasn't covered by the plush blanket and chilling my hands where they clutched at the edges.

"Come on," Ryder murmured, placing a hand on my back to urge me along. We trudged down the path along the side of the church, Jake waiting at an open door that faced the forest to our left. I followed Kasimir and Casey inside, grimacing at the stale air, so different from the crisp, snow-chilled atmosphere outside.

I joined the others in taking my gear off, pleased at the slight increase in temperature once Jake shut the exterior door, then examined the space. The ceilings were higher than they'd appeared outside, soaring overhead in an arched shape and decorated with small windows that let in some of the light from the bright, snow-filled sky above.

Casey, who'd left to explore one of the side rooms, called out, his voice echoing from the rafters. "Best not to start a fire." He made his way back to us with a grunt. "No ventilation, and I don't want to suffocate in my sleep. We're better off hunkering down in one of the smaller rooms than letting the cold in just to light something. There's a daycare room with blankets that we can use, though I doubt we'd fit on the cots."

Kasimir nodded. "Agreed. Won't do us any good to let the cold in just to start a fire that we'll need to stay up all night to keep an eye on." His black hair was damp from melted snowflakes, clinging to his flushed cheeks and neck and making him look more approachable somehow. Younger. Less intimidating. Though his deep voice remained as commanding as ever, echoing around the hollow chamber and making it sound as if there were three of him speaking at once.

It didn't feel like the world had ended here. With no signs of life nearby, no scents of decay or remnants of violence staining the room, it was like the virus had never happened in this little corner of the woods.

The weight on my shoulders lifted as Ryder pulled the blanket off.

"I'll hang this up to dry. I don't want it to soak through to your clothes."

"Thank you," I said, my voice tripping slightly over the words.

He reached into his jacket with one arm while the other was occupied by holding the blanket, and passed me a little ball of fur.

Mila made a snuffling noise as she stretched out in my hands, then curled right back up again, probably desperate for the warmth she'd just lost.

"Sweet girl," I whispered, cooing little sentiments at her while using the backs of my fingers to scratch the top of her head. "Such a cutie."

I pulled her close to my chest, lifting my head to see Ryder staring at me, frozen in place. He spun around as soon as he realized he was still standing there and took the blanket to the back of the room, draping it as best he could.

I accidentally locked eyes with Casey, who glanced between me and Ryder with a smirk he quickly wiped away, shaking his head and looking to the ceiling.

"What can I do?" I asked, convinced that any sheepish blush would be lost in the redness of my cheeks.

"Just stand there for now," he replied.

I frowned, looking around at everyone as they all found something to do and feeling inexplicably useless and small. Why wasn't I automatically aware of how I could help? All I was doing was proving Jake right. The stress of the journey so far had run my brain ragged, and we had a long way to go yet. Fatigue from an entire day of walking had me swaying on my feet, so I tensed every muscle I could to remain still and not stand out.

Maybe it was the cold, or that I was missing my friends and the comforts back at camp, but to my horror I felt a prickling behind my eyelids. Squeezing my eyes shut to stave off any tears, I clutched Mila just a little closer and pretended that if I couldn't see them, they couldn't see me.

The illusion shattered as a hand grasped my elbow. I cracked my eyes open and breathed a sigh of relief when there was no film of tears blocking my vision.

Jake stood in front of me, hiding me from the rest of the room and wearing a mild expression. His golden-brown hair was dark from the snow, his scruff already well on its way to a beard from several days of growth and still looking somehow soft.

"Can you check if there's a kitchenette? At the very least, they might have seasonings left we can use," he said quietly.

It could've been exhaustion, or emotion, or that he knew just the right thing to say exactly when I needed to hear it that led me to forget about my irritation with him as I lifted my free hand to brush the backs of my fingers against the side of his jaw, exhaling slowly.

This close to him, I could smell the fresh, wintery scent of snow on his clothes, blending in with his usual aroma of juniper. He should smell awful, like me. Like sweat and drowsiness and dirt.

My hand moved again, another gentle stroke against all that unruly stubble.

Rough and warm.

Just like I'd thought.

Only I dropped my hand like it was on fire as the silence stretched on and I took in his stiff posture. He stood frozen, muscles firm and tense, chest barely moving. I'd think he wasn't breathing if not for the slight puff of mist between us from our breaths mingling with the cold air. The only thing not still like the rest of him were his eyes. Deep, turbulent pools of brown locked onto my face with a startling intensity, their usual golden hue gone.

"Ha," I laughed weakly, backing up. Just when I thought it couldn't get worse, I had to embarrass myself and make things awkward. "I'll go... Uh, do that," I muttered, pointing towards the recesses of the church that hid more doors before scurrying away, keeping my ears peeled for any sign of his reaction behind me.

I didn't know if I was relieved or embarrassed when I heard nothing.

Relieved. Definitely relieved.

A nudge at my leg had me stirring awake.

"Come on sleeping beauty," someone said. "Time to get up."

I groaned, rolling over from my stomach to my back, and shielded my eyes from the bright cloudy light filtering through the dirty windows overhead. A quick glance down to check out whatever the warm weight was against my side revealed Mila curled up into a ball and sleeping away.

Kasimir stood above me, arms crossed. "The snow didn't stick last night, so we're all set to spend the day traveling."

He picked his way back over to the door to do who knew what while I knuckled my bleary eyes.

"Oh." He paused, scarred hand grasping the door frame. His clothes today were new in rotation, a stretchy and form-fitting long-sleeve black shirt, and a pair of worn cargo pants. "Here." He tossed something at me. "Thought you might like it, since you love flavoring your water with ginger." It landed in my lap, no larger than some of the coins I used to scrounge around the house when I was little, and Ben would give me random tasks to keep me occupied.

Kasimir left before I could even thank him, so I switched my attention to the bright item on my blanket. I picked it up, crinkling the plastic it was covered in as I untwisted the sides to pull it off. It looked like… candy? Bright red streaks mixed with dull white, and a distinct peppermint scent floated off the sticky surface.

I dropped it on my tongue, pleased at the sudden burst of flavor. The stale taste was overridden by a surge of sugary mint. It reminded me of Ben, of the tea he used to make me whenever I was sick, and had just solidified itself as my favorite treat.

Tucking the quick-dissolving candy in my cheek, I was loath to throw my blankets off. Somehow the moth-bitten fabric had retained a comforting smell beneath the scents of must and age.

Thinking back to last night, how the guys were miraculously satisfied with just their sleeping bags so that I ended up with all the blankets we'd scrounged up sent warmth through my chest. Though it still chafed that they treated me differently. If they could stick it out for a night in the cold church without extra comfort, I could too.

I spent a few minutes petting Mila while the candy grew so thin that it only took a few crunches of my back teeth to finish it completely.

"I'll be back," I whispered to her, giving her an extra little scratch under the chin and tucking her deeper into the pile of blankets once I stood up.

The adjoining bathroom was empty, so I used the tube of homemade toothpaste someone had left out to scrub my teeth and the bottle of water left on the sink to rinse. Then I poured a tiny amount into my hands to scrub at my face, feeling more human with each passing second. A glance at my face in the grimy mirror revealed my gray eyes to be lighter than I expected, untouched by any of the stress I'd expected to cloud them. My face was shaded pink from windburn, obscuring the light brown freckles that were sprinkled across the bridge of my nose and onto the apples of my cheeks. Despite my chapped lips and unruly, brown curls tangled above my shoulders, I felt *good*. Today was a fresh start, and after a solid night's sleep, I was ready to tackle it.

"Breakfast," Casey called.

I dried my face then followed the sound of voices, rounding the corner of the kitchenette to find Jake seated at the table and Casey standing at the counter. Casey nodded towards one of the empty chairs, and it struck me how similar he looked to Ben from some of my earliest memories of him.

"Kasimir and I made a small fire outside to boil water for the oats we brought," he said. "Best part is that the kitchen had bowls already."

That was good news. We'd brought a few dishes along with a pot and pan that we could use if we were unable to scavenge one from wherever we were staying that night, but unless there was a water source nearby so we didn't have to waste our potable supply, it was a hassle to store them until we could clean them.

Jake tried to catch my eye as I sat, but I brushed him off, still too hurt to hear whatever he had to say. His callous words had wormed their way deep, and substantiated every stray thought I had about myself whenever things got tough.

I tucked into the oatmeal, using the tarnished silver spoon laid out beside the bowl, and made a low noise of surprise at the hint of cinnamon and brown sugar underneath the sweetness of the powdered milk. I was sure that the oats that we'd brought were unflavored. "This is really good. I didn't know you could add season oatmeal like this."

Casey chuckled, gesturing at the little array of containers spread out across the counter. Cinnamon, salt, pepper, cumin, brown sugar, paprika, and what might've been rosemary were just the few closest to me. "I made yours just how my daughter used to like hers."

Jake ducked his head to take another bite, but not before I caught the sympathy on his face. Clearly, Casey's daughter hadn't just grown out of oatmeal with brown sugar and cinnamon.

I had no idea what to do or say. An uncomfortable silence blanketed the kitchen, only broken by the sounds of our utensils clinking against our bowls. "Tell me about her?" I blurted out between bites.

Casey's smile grew. How he didn't once lose it was a miracle to me; like talking about his family brought him comfort instead of sadness. "She would be about your age now, actually. She was the spitting image of her mother, golden brown skin and chestnut-colored hair. Even got her brown eyes. Unfortunately for her, she inherited my personality and then some. Just my luck that she got my stubbornness and not my wife's everlasting patience."

I hadn't known that he'd had a whole life at some point and it had been taken from him somehow. I knew he was at the camp alone, though I didn't know what circumstances had led to it.

"I doubt she thought it was unfortunate at all," I said quietly.

His snort was soft. "Yeah, well... I suppose not."

It was easy to forget about loss when you were consumed with surviving, with living and providing. It was harder shaking it off in the silence, in the quiet parts of life. I felt my own memories rising to the forefront and clamped down on them before they threw me back into a place I didn't want to be.

We finished quickly after that, the conversation dying down as we focused on finishing our food and packing up for the remaining days of travel. The somber mood faded as we went about our morning, working in a familiar routine. It didn't take long until we were shutting the door of the church behind us, propping up a piece of wood against the outside to secure it.

Reality hit when the trees thinned out after several hours of walking, exposing ragged buildings in the distance. I already missed our zombie-free interlude, and the worst part was that I knew we had a lot more to face before we arrived at the farm.

Everywhere I looked, there were signs of snow from the previous night. Slushy puddles gathered in dips in the road, and a fine layer of crystals coated the sparse grass. The air still had a crisp bite to it, but it was nothing like the freezing temperatures from before. Maybe when the sun hit its zenith, the lingering chill would disappear altogether.

We resumed our brisk pace, but Kasimir hovered far enough back that Jake stopped.

"Come on, old man," he taunted. He was angled so that only I could see his mischievous grin.

"I'm only thirty," Kasimir grumbled as he caught up. "And you don't look much younger anyway, so who the hell are you calling old man?"

Jake gave him an assessing look. "Huh, I never would've guessed." He pointed at Ryder. "Then I'll pass the baton off to him. He looks young enough to get away with it."

"I'm twenty-four," Ryder muttered, looking as if he'd bitten into something sour. "Not that big of a goddamn difference."

"If he qualifies, then I certainly do," I declared.

Kas gave me an odd look. "Just how old are you?"

"Twenty-five," I said, frowning. "Do I not look it?"

Everyone stopped to evaluate me, and I blushed under the attention. "Don't answer that," I muttered. I knew stress had added some years, but I hadn't thought it was *that* bad.

Casey grunted. "I've got you all beat. Why don't you hit your fifties and then you can start judging who's old and who isn't."

I smothered a laugh at Kasimir's disgruntled expression.

To my relief, we steered well clear of the distant buildings as we walked, sticking close to the road beside the trees. Several hours later the nearby burbling of a creek reached our ears, so we decided to stop and replenish our supply, drinking what we had stored first so that the new filtered water would last longer.

Ryder tilted his head back to get every last drop, the muscles in his throat working with every swallow, a soft, satisfied sigh parting his lips when he finished. He used the back of his arm to wipe his mouth, and my eyes were riveted on how his shirt clung to his skin as he moved. Beside him, Jake pulled the bottom of his shirt up to wipe the water he'd just liberally splashed himself with, exposing a lean, muscled abdomen...

Casey coughed from somewhere behind me, and I just knew my cheeks were scarlet. It was easy to pretend I wasn't aware of them back at camp, since I could choose when and where I saw them. But out here, spending every second in their company... a girl could only take so much. I didn't want to scare Ryder away. He'd declined multiple offers in my presence over the time I'd known him, and I knew that if he had any idea of how attractive I found him, our relationship wouldn't be the same.

Not to mention my appreciation for Jake. Our fight the other day didn't erase weeks of him gaining my trust, making sure I'd settled in okay, involving me in things around camp and just looking generally edible.

It was for the best that nothing could come of it. Connections were a liability; good in the moment and devastating when something went wrong, no matter how much I occasionally wished things could be different.

Case in point, the piece of jerky that Ryder slipped to Mila as she wound around his ankles, accompanied by a soft pat to her head and a whisper. He was so *good*, and it pained me that he didn't see it. That he felt like he was still living in his father's shadow.

I crouched down when Mila came trotting my way, using my nails to scratch her cheek. "Who's a good girl," I cooed, letting her twist her head this way and that to move my hand wherever she wanted it.

"She's so friendly," Kasimir said as he crouched down beside me, watching the little cat.

"I think she's just a lonely people person. Though Ryder is clearly her favorite. I mean, doesn't the man notice that we all feed her and she still clings to him?"

He grinned at that. Everyone was amused by the way Mila stuck to his side, using him as a touchstone whenever she broke away during the day to do whatever cats do.

"I used to have a cat," he said suddenly, and one glance at his profile revealed him to be just as surprised as I was at the sudden confession. Unless it was a trick of the light, the tips of his ears were turning pink.

"You did?" I prompted, hoping he'd keep talking. The deep, sure sound of his voice was soothing, especially when paired with the running water to our right.

"His name was pebbles. He had white and gray fur, and he always liked my mom the best."

If I was surprised before, that was nothing compared to now. I'd not once heard him speak of his family or his life, barring his friend.

I looked at him again, and... yep, his ear was *definitely* pink where it poked out from beneath his long, black hair. It was endearing, watching the huge, intimidating man get flustered.

"I've never had a pet," I confessed. "My... Ben, he had a few goats, but that was it. He'd raised them from babies after he found them wandering around his property in the days following the outbreak."

Kasimir nodded. "Pebbles passed well before the virus, which was probably for the best. Sometimes just seeing the number of strays looking for food..."

Mila chose that moment to open her mouth wide and chomp down on my hand. I squeaked, using my other hand to pry her off gently. She hadn't broken the skin or anything; in fact, her teeth had hardly made a dent. It was the suddenness that had startled me. Clearly, I'd ignored her cues that she was getting overstimulated.

Kasimir made a low noise and reached over to grab my hand, pulling it up so that he could peer at it. Maybe the feel of his skin on mine did nothing to him but for me? It was intoxicating. Watching his heavy black brows furrow while he used his thumbs to massage my hand, light gray eyes scrutinizing the indents left by her teeth... it brought a level of awareness that our interaction had previously been lacking.

The scent of vanilla wafting off his skin–from the soap Priya had gifted him–was hypnotizing. It was similar to the rose one she'd given me when I'd first arrived, proud to show off the latest batch of soap Halli had taught her to make.

"It's fine," I told him, needing space if I didn't want to humiliate myself completely.

He made a displeased sound and let my hand slide from his, but not before helping me back to my feet.

"Thank you for the candy, by the way. I loved it."

A frown marred Jake's face as he approached. "What candy?"

"A peppermint," Kasimir grumbled.

"I didn't know you liked peppermints, Sera."

I shrugged. "Neither did I."

He opened his mouth, but Casey spoke over him. "Looks like we've got less than a week to go," Casey informed us, turning to Kasimir. "You'll reach your friend about a day earlier than that."

It hit me that I'd managed to forget he was leaving. A dull ache radiated in my stomach at the thought of him going off alone, of never seeing him again. It made me wish I only admired his looks, and not the way he snuck Mila treats whenever he thought no one was paying attention, or how every time I fell behind he slowed down so casually that nobody but me noticed.

I knew better than to get attached to someone new. Everyone left eventually, whether by choice or circumstance.

CHAPTER 6

The tension riding our group was almost as thick as when we'd first set out. A heavy blanket of weighted silence was cast over us so that all we could hear were our measured breaths. It seemed I wasn't the only one out of sorts from reentering a more populated area.

Rolling my shoulders out, I stepped around a pile of unidentifiable rags. My muscles were stiff from a mixture of both dread and anticipation. We'd already encountered several zombies that morning, and it looked like things were only going to get worse. Even the cool breeze chilling the sweat from my flushed face and exposed arms didn't quite erase the sense of foreboding that crept up on me a mile back.

The memory of what could have been still occupied the forefront of my mind. Only the sharp inhale from someone in front of me had signaled that something was wrong. Once Kasimir's hulking form had moved to the side, I saw Jake shake the bony hand off his ankle before aiming a well-placed kick at its skull. It looked like a zombie had managed to wedge itself halfway under a car and get stuck, surviving out of spite and who knew what, getting so lucky as to intercept Jake as he walked by.

I never would've seen it, and if I had, would I have reacted as quickly as he did? Would I be bent over my bitten ankle right about now, as the virus pumped its way through my veins? What about Mila? What if she'd disappeared down the maw of the very creatures that occupied my nightmares each night? It was becoming too real, and the realization that I had only myself to blame for this, that there was no turning back, only through, had me biting my tongue until the metallic taste of blood filled my mouth. It took more courage than I thought I had to keep putting one foot in front of the other until the last remnants of my fight or flight died down into a more manageable wariness. I had to keep reminding myself of the reasons I'd set out on this trip in the first place. My optimistic attitude from that morning felt miles away.

We were all deadly silent, which was how we heard the clang in the distance. Everyone froze in place, holding their breath to listen closer. It was instinctive, the way we didn't move a muscle, and the hairs that rose on the back of my neck told me that this wasn't another Mila, or something stuck where it shouldn't be.

Casey made a series of hand movements that I had no chance in hell of deciphering. I gave him a desperate, questioning look while everyone else moved forwards to flank him. Grasping the handle of the blade at my side, my slippery palms made it difficult to get a comfortable grip. The world stood unnaturally silent, and a gust of wind ruffled the hair clinging to my neck.

The first screech came seconds later.

It was a ghastly, grating sound, coming from whatever had just stumbled out from behind the closest building, much nearer than I'd assumed.

The body in front of us looked fresh, and there weren't many of those these days. I could only tell because it was less... decayed than the ones

I usually spotted from afar. Not only that, but it had the vocal cords to shriek upon seeing its prey, and it evaded the obstacles scattered about with an unerring accuracy. A pair of torn pants hung from its frame, accompanied by a ragged shirt. All its clothes were the same dull color, as dark as the brownish-gray pallor of its skin.

I stood frozen at its speed, combined with the haunting wail coming from its throat. Not only at the discordance of such a sound, but the fear it inspired. We'd been so careful to keep quiet and here this zombie was, making enough noise to raise the dead.

"Stay back," Kasimir barked at me, louder than I'd ever heard him speak, before he swung the ax that was usually strapped across his broad back over his shoulder and *launched* it at the approaching zombie.

I couldn't stop the helpless noise that escaped my mouth as I watched it move with an agility that it had no right to have in death, throwing itself sideways so that the weapon clipped its arm instead of its skull.

A curse left Kasimir's lips as he stood weaponless before it. My eyes widened as I noticed the second zombie emerge from a shop front, attracted by the noise; watching as it grew closer to Jake, who didn't seem to notice it, too preoccupied with the threat in front of us.

"Look out!" I shouted, making the terrifying, split-second decision to run forward. I put on a burst of speed and hefted the machete over my shoulder–courtesy of Grey–bringing it down onto its shoulder.

The jarring, grating noise of steel against bone sent a shudder down my spine, but I had no time to pause.

It was already lunging forward, even with my blade still lodged in its body.

Without a single word, Jake spun around and took it to the ground with one swoop of the nail-covered bat he carried. "Don't do that again!" he ordered, already spinning away from me to face the other zombie that had just turned the corner.

I huffed, shaking my hair out of my face and bending over to grasp the handle, gagging slightly at the sucking noise as I wiggled it free.

When I stood straight, the others were still facing the initial zombie and the new one that had come from that same direction.

Even I knew it was unusual behavior for them to just stand there and calculate. They weren't supposed to be capable of logic, of reason, yet there it stood, looking as if it were plotting the best path to eat us all.

The guys didn't dare rush forward. It was clear that this creature was more capable than those they'd run into in the past, and there was no telling what it would do if they approached.

What I wouldn't have given for a long-range weapon right about then. The gun River gave us was still tucked away in Grey's pack for emergencies, but even with all the noise we were making, it would still do more harm than good.

The sight of another grotesque body had my stomach dropping. Blood rushed to my head so fast it made me light-headed, leaving what was left in my limbs to run through my veins almost sluggishly. I was keenly aware of every breath I took, the pounding of my heart threatening to drown out the sounds around me. This one was clearly older than the others, missing parts and pieces all over, and wearing only threadbare rags. I could see bone through the torn, pale gray skin on its cheek.

They exhibited an almost pack-like mentality, deferring to the one that seemed to be... stalking us? Pacing in a semi-circle and snapping its jaws like it was standing behind some kind of imaginary line drawn in the asphalt.

"Fuck," Casey spat.

Kasimir nodded. "Apt."

I snuck up close behind Ryder, trying not to divert his focus, but he glanced at me anyway. "You should stay back," he muttered, voice low.

I didn't bother to dignify him with a response. What if they needed me? What good would I be if I hid myself away from the fight? Yes, I was scared. I was more scared than I could ever remember being. But I was strong too, and I just had to keep reminding myself of that.

It happened so fast I didn't even have time to blink. The one in charge darted forwards, shrieking at the top of whatever lungs it still possessed, while the others took this as a signal and started at their own paces, unable to choose who exactly to go for first.

The lead feinted right before hitting Casey so hard that he went barreling backwards. There was no way he could've gotten his weapon up in time to skewer it before it reached him.

My mouth flew open in horror. I looked at the others, only to find that they were circling the remaining two.

They seemed to have the situation handled in front of me, so I turned my attention to where Casey was grappling with the zombie behind us.

I took a deep breath in as I watched it roll him onto his back, and exhaled as he tried to throw it off, thinking of the best way to approach so that I didn't make things worse. I was afraid to do nothing, but afraid to do anything, and each option would have consequences I had no control over.

Right before the fear could take root and numb me, an opportunity presented itself. Casey managed to push away the wriggling zombie just enough that he was able to deliver a strong kick to its midsection, leaving a sizable chunk of space between them.

Letting adrenaline and impulse take over my movements, I bolted in their direction and used my machete like a bat to bludgeon its skull as I passed over them both.

The blade connected, the impact jolting us both and jerking the zombie sideways...

But it kept moving.

A cry of frustration left my lips as I tried to pull the blade back and found it to be stuck in bone.

I watched in horror as it repeatedly snapped its jaws at Casey, moving closer and closer to where he lay pinned. It was relentless, despite the blade in its head, despite Casey's best efforts to shove it away with his working hand, and I knew I had to act.

"Hold on, Casey," I muttered, getting a firm grip on the leather. I jerked the handle to the side as hard as I could, hoping the blade wouldn't slip free with the movement. I must have taken it by surprise because there was hardly any resistance, and we flew back fairly easily. The momentum sent us straight to the ground, the weight of the undead body landing on top of me and the hard surface at my back knocking the breath from me so that I was gasping for air.

Casey's eyes locked with mine. I took in the flat, grim line of his lips, the way he clutched his arm close to his chest, the angry red flush that took over his face.

"Sera!" Jake thundered, his deep voice consumed with fear and pain. Time moved in slow motion as my lungs seized, trying desperately to pull in a breath. The zombie on top of me twisted to try to face me, and I cursed my helplessness, trapped in my own body and inches away from a predator.

I squeezed my eyes shut, knowing that Jake wouldn't be able to reach me in the time it would take for me to get bitten. Nor would Kasimir, or Ryder, who were even further back.

The absence of the weight on my chest hit me first. I drew in my first full breath as I looked over at Casey, where he grappled with the zombie he'd just yanked off of me. I was only a foot away from them, watching in horrified silence as Casey gripped its head and twisted, wincing when the zombie, with one final burst of movement, sunk its teeth into his throat.

Everything fell silent, save for the ringing in my ears. I met Casey's gaze as he dumped the unmoving body to his other side, his eyes glazing over with each passing moment. The injury too severe, and he was dying faster than the virus could take hold—a small mercy, but not to me. Not right now, as I watched every excruciating emotion pass through him.

"Sorry," he mouthed, his face a rictus of pain. The blood that had flowed so freely from his throat was beginning to slow, and none of the frantic attempts the others made to stifle it had helped. My only consolation was in remembering how excited he was to see his wife and daughter again, stating it as the reason he could even leave the camp at all with any sense of peace when I'd asked him more about them last night. I hardly even noticed the flurry of movement around him, Kasimir crushing the zombie's skull just out of view with his boot in case.

Casey's eyes grew dull, and I turned my head back to face the sky, uncaring about the painful scrape of the pavement against my scalp.

How had this happened? How? Just this morning he was laughing, reminiscing, teasing. And now... I fought the urge to empty my stomach, focusing on drawing air into my lungs instead. I couldn't even process it, that he wasn't here anymore.

"Look," Jake said grimly.

I sat up, ignoring the burn in my chest, to find him holding Casey's arm up. An angry bite graced the skin of his wrist. Streaks of inflammation wound their way up his arm and stopped just below his shoulder, an ugly jaundiced red. He'd already been bitten, and I hadn't noticed, maybe even before I'd first stepped in.

Kasimir crouched down beside me; eyebrows furrowed as he examined my face. "Are you okay?"

I had no words.

When I tried to speak, nothing came out. I felt adrift, and lost. Vulnerable. Suddenly the worst possibilities were no longer just around the corner or reserved for someone else–someone far away from us–they were right here, and closer than ever.

My face stung, my arm throbbed, and I could tell from the blood on my shirt that I must've gotten some cuts when I landed on the ground, but the pain was distant. Just out of reach.

Shoving aside Kasimir's concerned look, I rolled over onto my hands and knees and pushed myself to a standing position. From there, I stumbled over to Casey, staring down at his lax face. I noted absently that someone must have closed his eyelids, because they were shut now. The others spoke in hushed whispers, but I couldn't wrap my brain around what they were saying.

Someone clasped my arm and tugged me gently away from the body. Jake leaned down to peer into my eyes and quietly informed me that Kasimir would be staying behind for a few minutes to wrap things up and that we were going to settle for the night, preferably back in the direction we'd just come. We needed to wash the blood off, and there was a guaranteed creek we could use.

I nodded, already averting my gaze to focus somewhere in the distance. I had so many thoughts I was struggling to process that it was hard to walk straight. It was like my brain was trapped, running over the same images again and again and again. It wouldn't move forward, just circling around the same anxious thought pattern, never reaching a resolution. A small part of my mind worried that I was being a burden by not being more aware of my surroundings, but my endless stream of consciousness quickly overrode it.

At some point during the walk, Jake let go of my arm. We continued in silence, only to be joined by Kasimir what could've been minutes or hours later. Even the scents of the forest when we reached it did nothing for me. Surrounded on all sides by the endless green, I thought I'd feel somewhat better, but I'd never been more dazed.

Eventually, we reached the clearing that we had stopped at earlier in the day. I could see glimpses of the water through the trees but had no motivation to get clean.

Everyone placed their things around the glade, and I followed suit, dropping my bag where I stood. Jake turned to me, but I shook my head. His fists clenched, and a muscle in his jaw popped, but he relented. "I'm going to go gather wood for the fire," he said, heading off in a random direction. I watched until I could see him no longer, then put my attention back on everyone else. Kasimir left to help him, leaving just Ryder and me.

I waited for him to leave too, unsure of what I would do next but struggling to force myself to move when he started in my direction. He placed his hand on my shoulder, and I tilted my head back to meet rich brown eyes watching me to see if I would protest. When I didn't shake him off, he slid his hand down the tan skin of arm to clasp my hand, fingers warm and comforting in mine. Even the shock of his touch didn't jolt me out of whatever stupor had consumed me.

Ryder picked up the bag I'd dropped with his free hand, then led me through the maze of trees in the direction of the creek. I could smell it before it came fully into view, the scents of earth and sediment going a long way to soothe all the numb parts of me.

His hand slipped free from mine, and I mourned its loss. He set my bag down and approached the bank, beckoning me to follow.

So I did.

I grabbed the bar of soap from my bag and greedily inhaled its lavender and thyme scent, once again sending thanks to Halli for working with Priya to create it, and waded into the river, clothes and all. Ryder stayed on the bed of rocks, facing away from me. I looked my fill as I let the soap pass between my hands, mesmerized by the slimy texture. His hair was longer than I'd ever seen it, hugging his ears with a slight curl. His frame was leaner than Kasimir or Jake's, but broad and defined nonetheless. He was so familiar to me, yet brand new at the same time.

The water was chilly, but not so much that I couldn't bear it. I lifted my arm to lather my hair and yelped at the sharp pain in my shoulder. Ryder spun around, instantly scanning the space for threats but calming once he realized what the issue was.

Tears of frustration flooded my eyes and obscured Ryder from view as I realized I couldn't even wash myself properly. The icy numbness from the past several hours receded–courtesy of the soft, rhythmic lapping of the water at my chest–but in its place were all the aches and pains that I had been oblivious to.

Ryder's mouth tipped down, and he hesitated before stepping into the creek to meet me. We stared at one another, standing maybe about a foot apart until he closed the distance between us and set his large hands on my shoulders to turn me around. They were so warm that it felt like they were imprinting themselves on my skin. Like I'd wake up the next day to find marks in the shape of his hands on my skin for all eternity, his fingerprints a part of me like the freckles on my face.

I went easily, trusting him to do whatever it was he wanted to do.

He reached around me to take the slippery bar of soap from my grasp and lathered up his hands, placing them onto my scalp. I missed the silky texture of the shampoo and conditioner we used back at camp, but this was all I could bring in the way of hair care to make as much use of the space in my bag as possible.

He used his hands to massage my scalp methodically, brushing his thumbs along my temples and behind my ears in soothing circular motions, and using his nails to lightly score my skin. I tilted my head back further into his grasp, unable to help the low, content groan that escaped my throat. His hands froze, and a sharp breath left his lips, almost hidden by the sloshing of water. A few seconds later he resumed the treatment.

The cuts on my face stung and my arm throbbed where it hung aimlessly by my side, but I was easily distracted by the pleasure of having my hair washed. No one had ever done anything like this for me before, and it was exquisite, comforting and thrill-inducing all at once. Once my hair was sufficiently lathered, he wound it around his fist several times, then gently tugged. I tipped my head back easily, allowing him to submerge my curls in the water and rinse all the product off. At the angle my head was at, I could easily look up at his face to watch him as he ran his fingers through my hair. An intense look of concentration dominated his features, and it was endearing how focused he looked on making sure I was taken care of properly.

He let my hair slide through his fingers and took a step back. I spun around to face him, the frigid water lapping at my collarbones, and held out my hand for the soap bar. I was desperate to scrub the blood, dirt, and sweat off.

Only when I lifted my arm, he noticed my slight wince. Ryder's expression became mulish, and he shook his head. I was confused up until he took a step forward and telegraphed his intentions by fingering the fabric near my shoulder.

He meant to undress me.

Would he wash me as well? The rest of my remaining apathy burned away from the adrenaline and heat coursing through my veins. I'd done nothing but entertain a few possibilities, and already I was sure my face was scorching. Maybe he was just going to help me wash over the fabric, but somehow, I knew that wasn't the case. We stood in relative silence, with him resolved and me wide-eyed as we stared at one another, our bodies rocking fluidly from left to right with the force of the current.

I nodded.

He stepped closer, his large hand landing on my waist and grasping the hem of my shirt. My flush deepened at the gasp that left my mouth. He ignored it–thankfully–waiting once again for permission. I inclined my head, and he slipped my shirt off in a way that I was able to keep my injured arm at my side rather than lifting it. I'd take any opportunity I could to erase the earlier images from my brain, and this was working well. His movements were perfunctory and clinical, and I felt slightly ashamed for noticing every nuance of his touch, the way his fingers skimmed my ribs and his other hand tightened on my bare shoulder to keep me balanced.

Ryder turned me around and hovered his fingers over the clasp of my bra under the water. I hung my head to give him more room without my hair in the way and stood to my full height, so that he could see what he was doing. Before I knew it, his fingers were brushing the skin of my back as he fiddled with the little metal hooks, the bra releasing into my hands. My full breasts were exposed to the frigid water when I sank back down, nipples straining and sensitive from the cold.

And there we were, him standing behind me with my shirt in his hand and me completely bare from the waist up in front of him. My breaths were embarrassingly rapid. I knew he was going to leave any second, I could feel it.

"Will you wash my back?" I blurted without thinking. Anything to keep him there with me, so that I didn't have to be alone with my thoughts.

His exhale was audible, and when he waded out of the creek without another word, my heart sank. Only he set my clothes down with care... then made his way back to me.

"Yes," he responded quietly.

My shoulders tensed, whether in anticipation or nerves, and I focused on relaxing all my muscles so that I didn't jump out of my skin when he touched me.

His first touch against my back was tentative. Only when I stood completely still—no reaction at all—did his movements gain more confidence. He lathered up his free hand, placing it flat against my shoulder blade. Both of us froze at the contact before he widened his surface area. He flattened his palm and paid special attention to working my shoulder muscles. I groaned happily, hanging my head once more.

His soapy hand moved further down to the small of my back, and I swore I could feel every callous and line in his palm. My breathing sped up as he traced the line of the scar I knew crossed my lower back, from when I'd tried climbing our fence when I was younger and had gotten caught on the barbed wire at the top.

I'd never been touched like this before—never been touched at all—and my body was sending conflicting signals to the melancholy I had been carrying around all afternoon.

His movements were stilted and reverent at the same time, and he seemed almost relieved when he was finished.

"Thank you," I said as I turned, holding my free arm out for the soap so I could get my front, face, and everywhere else I could reach.

Ryder stared at me with eyes wide and lips parted, damp hair clinging to his neck and an appetizing water droplet rolling down his collarbone. His irises had all but disappeared, lost to the growing darkness of his pupils.

Just as soon as I asked what the problem was, did I realize I had turned around—at my full height—sans top. I was standing before him with my fucking tits out, completely exposed and unaware of it. Yeah, maybe we'd had some sort of chemistry a second ago, but what if it was just me? The poor man didn't consent to getting flashed when he offered to help me out.

"S-Sorry," I stuttered as I tried to get the word out, pulling my uninjured arm back to clasp it across my chest.

His jaw worked several times, but no words left his mouth, and he swallowed thickly before giving up. I shifted my gaze to his forehead so that I'd stop scrutinizing him. Oh, I was so humiliated. "Well, thanks," I squeaked, a clear dismissal.

He nodded, still looking slightly dazed, and stepped close to hand me the soap bar so that I didn't have to stretch my arm out, since the other was still occupied with covering my nipples. I swiped it from his hand, our fingers brushing.

"Call if you need me," he rasped. "I'm just going to... wash up. Over here." He gestured to a spot in the shallows, closer to the bank.

This close, I could see his shirt-plastered chest rise and fall rapidly with each breath he took, and I quickly looked away. "Yup, sounds good. Definitely."

He sloshed over to where he said he would and faced away from me as he stripped his shirt off. I was met with acres of pale, smooth skin, broken up by the occasional scar. It felt a little intrusive to be staring at him like I was, but... were those cigarette burns along his shoulders and back?

I'd known his dad was a piece of shit, but to actually see his effect on Ryder... it was heartbreaking. I turned away as he washed himself, using the soap he'd collected from my bar before he handed it back to me and finished up cleaning myself off, paying special attention to the open wounds on my face. They felt small, but I wasn't taking any chances with infection.

We finished around the same time, and I hovered awkwardly in the water as he dug the towel out from my bag and held it up outstretched to cover his face. I grimaced at the dirt and rocks under my toes when I waded out of the creek, missing when I could put on a pair of fresh, thickly knit socks after my baths. Shivers racked my body, the cool air chilling my already cold skin from the water temperature.

He had set my shirt down on top of his, I noticed, and it was thoughtful how he hadn't let it touch the ground. I briefly considered putting it back on, but I wanted to wear something clean. I stopped in front of Ryder, allowing him to bundle me up in the towel, and clutched it close, wishing it was a little larger so that my legs wouldn't be as cold and exposed. He used his own towel to squeeze the water from my hair.

"You'll be alright," he murmured, breaking the silence. "You can handle anything."

I nodded woodenly, reality rushing back in at his words. My eyes flew wide when he pressed a gentle kiss to the top of my head. I could smell my soap on his skin, lavender and thyme mixed with the lingering jasmine scent of the lotion Anna had given him when he first arrived and had nothing to his name. I was ashamed to say I'd noticed immediately when he'd begun wearing it, the flowery scent intoxicating on his warm skin.

It only hit me after we left that he'd stood there–most likely freezing, if how I felt was any indication–while he'd focused only on making sure I was comfortable.

I headed back to the clearing, brushing aside the irritated look Jake gave Ryder when he noticed both of us had wet hair. I didn't have the energy for whatever the fuck was bothering him now besides Ryder's general existence.

The fire was already roaring when I sat beside it, the heat soothing. Ryder shook out my sleeping bag behind me and laid my blanket on top, and I scooched back so that I could wrap myself up. I spent long minutes staring into the flames, waiting for my hair to dry and trying to keep my mind occupied. The sky darkened, but I still didn't feel like I could rest yet. Occasionally, I felt the weight of Jake's gaze, but never checked to confirm.

At one point, Kasimir crouched beside me. He pulled a small flask out of his bag and silently passed it to me. I took a large gulp, flinching at the sour taste. All my fear, my grief and shock, was dulled at the edges by the liquor. I trusted them to protect me, to keep me safe just for the night. And when I went to lay down, limbs heavy and drowsy from the drink, I listened to the soft voices around me and the dull crackle of the campfire and allowed my eyes to drift closed.

CHAPTER 7

I rubbed my tired eyes, wishing I felt more rested. I'd woken to the bright light of day piercing through my eyelids, but only when I sat up did I realize that it hadn't been this bright in the morning since I was back at camp.

"Did I sleep in?" I asked Jake with a frown.

He eyed at me from where he was crouching nearby, jabbing a stick at the dying fire and sending smoke spiraling into the air. His answer was short. "Yes"

Great. That was so very helpful.

"We decided to take a day," he added with a shrug. "Thought you could use the sleep."

That stung. Was I holding everyone up? Had they chosen to wait a day because they thought I would be a burden if we ran into something? My thoughts inevitably led to the previous day as I looked around camp and realized what was missing. Who was never coming back.

"Don't keep us here on my account," I muttered, throwing back my blanket. I stood on shaky legs, gathering my things to head down to the creek, when Kasimir, who had been silent up until that point, interjected.

"We need a day to regroup. Everyone feels Casey's loss, not to mention you need to take it easy on that arm."

Jake nodded in agreement. Ryder faced away from us, the tips of his ears pink. Not sure what that was about, but it was clear they were all on the same page. Despite my suspicions that they were only trying to mollify me, I would take them at their word.

"Fine." I left them behind, heading down to the water to splash my face and brush my teeth. Its temperature was slightly warmer than the previous day, but still cold enough to shake off some of my exhaustion. My mind wandered to last night as I went through the motions of getting ready, pleased to have a little more time to myself than usual.

I'd tossed and turned for what felt like hours, drifting in and out of sleep, and though it was clear, the others had been awake as well, they hadn't said a word to me about keeping them up. I'd managed to stay asleep at one point...

Heat infused my face as I recalled what had happened once I'd finally drifted off. Not even what must've been a few hours later, I'd woken up gasping for air, breaths sawing in and out of my lungs so hard that it was painful. The last vestiges of my dream clung to me but all I could remember was blood and screams. A noise in the dark had me snapping my head up to assess the threat, but I relaxed when I saw it was only Jake. I could just barely see his silhouette in the dim light of the moon, bending over to fiddle with his bedding. I laid back down, mopping the cool sweat from my face..

I hated the helplessness I felt. Lonely, and vulnerable, things I thought I'd finally shaken off after I left Gunner. I rolled my head to look at whoever was lying closest to me, finding Ryder a few feet away. He looked so peaceful; long limbs tucked into his blanket and a lock of dark hair resting on his cheek. The tension that he always carried with him was missing in sleep, and his features were more relaxed than I'd ever seen them. I worried my bottom lip, debating my next move, but in the end, it was too dark and I was too exhausted to deny myself what I really, truly wanted.

Gathering my blanket close to my chest, I stood as quietly as possible. Without thinking too hard about what I was doing, I tiptoed over to the bare patch of grass about a foot from Ryder and laid my sleeping bag down. I snuggled up tight in the blanket, twisting on my side so that I was facing him and mirrored his deep breaths, in and out. Before I knew it, my eyes had grown heavy, but I kept my gaze on him even as they fluttered shut, this time drifting off into a dreamless sleep.

Oh, shit. Was that why he'd looked so strange this morning? Because he knew exactly where my bedding was when the night had started since he'd helped me lay everything out, but when he woke, he noticed I'd moved into his space?

I headed back to the little glade, clearing my throat as I approached.

Ryder and Kasimir appeared to be deep in conversation, absently patting Mila's head as she rubbed against their legs, so I sauntered over to Jake instead where he was half-hidden by the trees.

"The plan is to just sit here all day?"

"So what if it is?"

"We need to get moving. I'm fine to keep going."

"We're not staying here for you, Sera."

"Like hell," I grumbled.

His eyes flashed. "Would it be so awful if we were? Why are you so angry about it? What's wrong with a little extra help?"

"What do you mean, what's wrong? First you tell *everyone* that I have no place even being here, then you ask in front of everyone if we need to take a break for me to catch my breath, and now we're spending a whole day doing nothing just because of my damn arm! It's like you live to prove your point."

Jake's voice when he spoke was frigid. I'd never seen those golden brown eyes so cold. "Enough. It has nothing to *do* with you being weak or a liability. I don't have some secret plan to make you feel useless, or to make myself seem justified in saying what I did. I *know* you can handle it, okay?"

"Then why even say it?"

"*Because you were supposed to be safe!*" he shouted, running his fingers through his hair and leaving it disheveled. "You were supposed to be safe," he repeated lower this time, "back at camp where you were protected and taken care of. Hell, half the reason I could even leave was because I knew that you'd be comfortable in your cabin and would reap the benefits of whatever we brought back. But to have you risk your safety... and for what? To prove yourself? Because you got bored? I can't handle–I just can't."

I hadn't thought my frustration capable of being so easily swept away.

"You don't understand," I whispered. "I didn't do this to make you upset or because I thought it would be a fun adventure and I was bored. I came because I thought I needed it. Because I didn't want to be afraid anymore. I woke up every day letting my fears rule my life, and it was time I put them to rest."

My hands trembled, and I tucked them under my arms to hide it. He frowned but didn't comment, instead looking at me with something akin to pity but it wasn't. That much was clear. It was a certain kind of understanding mixed with affection.

His hand covered my knee, a warm, reassuring weight.

"I see." He cast his head down to look at the ground as he said, "I didn't mean to get so upset with you or embarrass you. I was just worried. It's not safe out here and, somehow, I didn't mind going if I knew that everyone I cared about was still tucked away back at camp." He huffed a laugh, but it lacked the humor that it usually held. "I couldn't care less about my own safety, but yours? Yours I care about a great deal for. The day you arrived... everything changed."

Of all the things that could make me soften towards him, that was the biggest. I felt my walls drop, and cupped his hand on my knee, using it to lean forward. "That feeling you have about me, I feel that exact same way about you. It should matter to you just as much to keep yourself safe for the ones that love you."

He looked up, and I blinked rapidly as what I said finally filtered through to my brain. "Or something like that," I muttered, pulling my hand back and standing.

"Sit down so I can look at your arm," he demanded, quickly tucking away the smirk that had crept over his lips.

I huffed, making sure to sit with as much reluctance as I could.

"Relax," he said softly. "I just want to make sure you're alright."

I leaned towards him and pushed up the sleeve of my sweater so that he could look at my injured arm. It hadn't bothered me too much that morning, but I also hadn't taken a good look at it.

Jake touched my arm with a gentleness I'd forgotten he was capable of, tentatively palpating the area where it ached the most. Even still, I couldn't suppress my wince at the contact. He'd just pulled his hand back, when without even thinking, I reached out with my other hand and clamped his to my arm.

"S'fine," I murmured. I certainly wouldn't be explaining that I'd flinched more from the touch of his skin against mine than from pain.

The corner of his lips quirked. "If you say so. My uncle was the same, jumpier than a jackrabbit in a thunderstorm."

I snorted. "Okay, cowboy."

He finished carefully prodding at the area I'd landed on yesterday, but it never started to hurt like I thought it would. The stiffness in my muscles had released overnight, so I had almost a full range of motion again.

He nodded to himself, switching his attention to my face.

"These'll heal up fast," he rasped, brushing his thumb along the edge of one of the scrapes on my cheek. "They're not too deep. Just make sure to keep them clean."

The dull throb of my abrasions was drowned out by his sheer proximity. Maybe it hadn't dawned on him how close we were, but I was overcome but the realization. I could see the individual strands of bronze and honey mixed into his brown hair as he bent his head to finish his examination, the delicate splay of his lashes against his tanned cheeks when his eyes lowered, the surprised, minty exhale of his breath as he found me staring.

Moving was impossible, captured by his gaze as I was, with that large hand still cupping my cheek. The tension that had first appeared when we were still at camp came roaring back with a vengeance, and suddenly I was aware of every shaky inhale and exhale that left my lips, the subtle twitch of his fingers against my skin and the tightening of his mouth.

I wanted him. I missed him, even though he'd been right beside me all this time.

It was freeing to even think. What had begun as playful in the past–a way to help me settle in when I'd first arrived, to make me less of a stranger and more approachable in a time when I was soft-spoken and closed off–had shifted until it became something I no longer recognized. I'd made an invaluable friend, but somewhere along the way, it had turned into something more without my permission. One day I'd woken up and the flirtatious jokes and sidelong glances had had a ring of truth to them.

Jake's eyes dropped to my lips, and a strange thrill ran through me. His hand slid from my cheek to my jaw, thumb moving in a sweeping motion against my uninjured skin.

I was close to begging him to move. His thumb moved to the side, brushing against my lower lip, when a branch cracked somewhere nearby.

Jake shot to his feet with a low growl, and I was quick to follow. I'd known the real world would catch up to us; it had been foolish of me to pretend it wouldn't, even tucked away as we were. The forests were no safer than the cities were no more safer than the countryside. It was just an illusion.

Ryder and Kasimir quiet beside the smothered fire, scanning beyond the trees, and Jake jumped into action. "Pack," he ordered us, already reaching over to grab his bat. "I'm going to check it out."

I opened my mouth to protest, but one glimpse at his quelling glare and I closed it. While Kasimir was securing the communal items near the fire, I rolled up my sleeping bag and gathered my scattered belongings. Ryder took care of both his and Jake's items and within minutes we were waiting with bated breath for Jake to emerge from the trees.

Sure enough, just minutes later, Jake came barreling back through the clearing. My heart dropped at the smudge of dirt on his cheek and the dark stains on his bat. His grim face confirmed my suspicions. "It's not safe here anymore," he said. "Where there's one, there's a chance for more and I'd rather not risk it."

Kasimir looked my way.

"I'm fine. Let's just move on from here."

"There?" I repeated, pointing at the vast lodge in the distance in disbelief. I tried not to look too skeptical, but it was hard.

"I'd recognize it anywhere. I went every year with my parents and brother to celebrate my mom's birthday." Emotion flitted across Kasimir's face before he continued. "There were hearths in all the rooms with a lot of light from candles and torches. They might even have some non-perishables stowed away, and there was a wood-fire oven in the kitchen. The best part is that they were closed for the winter, so in those months when the virus was first spreading... they probably never had a chance to reopen."

It really did sound like a good idea; it was just such an imposing building, a little too large to barricade properly and a hotbed for nomads.

Fortunately, it was in the middle of nowhere, and the odds of some-one being there this very second were low. I hoped.

With an actual destination in mind, we moved quicker than usual, and it took us just an hour or two to reach the building that Kasimir had pointed out.

It looked to be about two or three stories tall, and while the win-dows on the first floor were mostly discolored and cracked–some even shattered–those on the top floor looked to be in decent condi-tion, if not permanently stained with dirt. The lodge had a cottage feel, enhanced by the overgrown ivy that had all but swallowed up the light sandblasted stone exterior. It possessed a kind of elegance, visible in the long circular drive that was now full of cracks and potholes. The hedges that were no longer neatly trimmed dominated the edges of the drive in such a fashion that it was almost as if they were forming a maze, and stunning stone and timber columns joined to form an overhang over the front doors–which were boarded over.

"I would've liked to see this in its prime," I said wistfully, trying to imagine all the dilapidated and unkempt areas as sparkling clean; families and friends hovering outside for one last word before head-ing to their cars, or the couples bundled up against the cold and desperate to get inside to warm themselves by the fire. The luxury reminded me of when Ben had tried to give me a spa day once when I was younger. Apparently, it was something his sisters had done when they were children, forcing him to prepare the ingredients for their face masks and making him fetch them damp towels and cucumber slices for their eyes. He thought it would give me a dose of normal, and so we headed out to the garden to pick a few cucumbers, a couple slices for our eyes and the rest for snacks, along with the other supplies we'd need. It had been fun, and though I never knew what we were missing, he sure did. The memory was a lot like this place, occupied by the ghosts of people who'd once stayed and had experiences that I would never fully understand but desperately wanted to.

"I don't want to pry these off yet if we don't have to," Jake said as he pointed at the barricaded doors. "I want to keep that illusion of disuse while we're inside. Maybe there's a back entrance that's more discreet."

We all nodded, following behind him as he rounded the corner of the building, picking our way through the hedges and overgrown shrubs. I cursed as I stumbled over a rock, grabbing onto Kasimir's arm to keep from falling flat on my face. He clamped his hand over mine to steady me, murmuring something softly as he kept me upright, but I couldn't catch what it was.

"Thanks," I said, letting go as soon as I was stable and rushing forward to catch up to the others. It only occurred to me later that he hadn't let go until I'd pulled away.

At the back of the inn was a wide, lush field that backed right up to the forest. We were elevated, and over the tops of the trees in the distance was a long, winding row of mountains. A patio that had since been consumed by nature stretched along a wide wall punctuated by several large top-to-bottom windows. The lower half–about my height–was boarded up, although I was surprised that the exposed glass at the top hadn't shattered over the years.

"This will do," Kasimir said, drawing my attention. He prodded at a metal door that looked like maybe it led to the kitchen. It was one of the easier, unobstructed forms of entry, but how would we get inside if it was locked? It wasn't like we could kick down metal, and I didn't want someone to get tetanus or something equally awful.

Jake walked up to where we were standing holding a large piece of wood, and without a single word, hefted it backwards and brought it down swiftly against the rusted doorknob. We all watched as the handle fell to the ground with a clunk. Jake tossed aside the log and gave the door a gentle push, grinning proudly as it swung open. "Tada," he exclaimed, making a weird little movement with his hands. I snorted, brushing past him to head inside, when a hand on my shoulder stopped me.

"Let me check if it's safe first," Kasimir said gruffly.

I rolled my eyes but waved him on. When Jake went to go with him, I grabbed his arm. "Absolutely not. If I'm a damsel, so are you."

"Speak for yourself," Ryder commented, pushing past us both with Mila on his heels. He shot me a playful wink before he rounded the corner.

Jake used my distraction as an opportunity to slip out of my grip. "Ah, come on, not gonna let a little thing like a wink take you out?"

I snorted, joining him in the doorway. "Fuck you, St. James"

He barked out a laugh as he ushered me in, shutting the door behind us, then waited with me in the moderately sized, dusty kitchen until both Kasimir and Ryder had called out that they'd checked over the entire building.

"Finally," I huffed.

"If you wanted to rush off and possibly get eaten, that's all you had to say," Jake said with a smirk.

Pushing off from the counter, the row of spices on the far counter caught my eye, and the smile dropped from my face. It was hard to keep my thoughts from wandering to Casey during the day, but I often saw things that reminded me of his absence. I wish I'd gotten to know him back when we were still at camp. Everyone was going to be devastated when we told them.

"Come on," Jake murmured, almost like he'd known where my brain had gone. I followed him out of the kitchen and into the bright main room. The sun shone in from the uncovered sections of the windows, illuminating the dust motes swirling in the air. It was very open, almost the entire interior being visible from where we stood. A glance up revealed a mezzanine lining the entire perimeter of the upstairs, the rooms tucked away behind it. Directly above us was a larger platform up against a silver beam that ran along the wall of glass, with a set of steps leading to the mezzanine. I walked towards the center of the room and craned my head back to see what it held, only to find a small dining area. There looked to be around ten tables, arranged so that its occupants could leave their rooms to eat on the same floor and gaze at the view outside.

Against the far wall was a huge stone hearth that spanned the entire room. I ran my finger across one of the dusty white sheets covering the furniture and Jake helped me pull it off to reveal a large, luxurious, round gray couch facing the fireplace. Smaller sheets covered what must've been individual recliners placed along the width of the glass wall every few feet. I could easily picture how stunning it must've been in its prime. Dark woods mixed with stone to create a welcoming environment, and the ornate chandelier overhead gave it an understated elegance. The air smelled of must and age, but it was nothing like the scent of some of the buildings that had not been closed off over the years.

I followed Jake across the room, noting as the floor changed from a soft carpet to hardwood. He stopped at the bottom of the wooden staircase to call up to Kasimir and Ryder as I walked over to the reception desk. It was harder to see in this area, the light from the window across the room not filtering as far. The main entrance probably had windows at some point, if the doors weren't glass to begin with, but since almost the entire wall in the entryway was boarded up, it was impossible to tell.

"A rustic experience," I whispered, reading from the dusty brochure I'd plucked from the front desk. I had severe doubts about what they deemed to be rustic, although, if I'd read that right... excitement filled me as I rushed over to the guys and jabbed my finger at the text in bold. "They have a well! They use well water! I saw nothing when we were out back, but I also wasn't looking for one."

Jake looked at Kasimir, who had just descended the staircase, and my heart sank. "What, you think it's dried up?"

"Not necessarily," Jake replied. "But it all depends on if they have a hand crank or not, and even if they do, there might be too much rust to use it."

I nodded. I knew that was a possibility, but the prospects had made me too excited to really sit down and think of the limitations.

"Good find," Kasimir added with a soft smile.

Jake did a double take when he noticed. It was times like these, when Kasimir was less on the defense for things trying to kill us, that I remembered his mouth wasn't frozen in the shape of an assessing frown.

"I wanna fire up that wood oven tonight," Jake said as he walked over to the desk I was standing by and ran his fingers through the dust. "Might try to catch some fish so we can have somethin' fresh." Good thing Grey had reminded him to pack the collapsible fishing rod.

Ryder spoke from somewhere above us. "I'll check out the chimney. I want to be able to light a fire if the temperatures drop and I wouldn't want us to suffocate."

That didn't even occur to me. Not for the first time, I wondered how I would get by if I were alone. I let out a slow breath. That was the whole point of this, to absorb as much knowledge from them as possible.

"I'll look for anything we can eat," I offered. "There were no awful smells in the kitchen so they probably had the forethought to dispose of all the perishables before they closed up for the season, but still, maybe there's something we can use."

The approving nods I received had me spinning to face the other direction so that they wouldn't see the look on my face.

Ryder volunteered to go with Jake as I walked back the way I first came, who easily agreed that it was safer to go out in pairs, although I could hear the tension coating their words. I still didn't know what the hell was the issue between the two of them. Most of the time, things were fine. Some judging looks and maybe a little attitude, but they functioned alright together. There was some underlying frostiness in the interactions between the two that I hadn't been able to pick apart yet. Maybe while we were staying here, it would be a good time.

Hands on my hips, I surveyed the kitchen from where I stood at the entrance. It was dusty, and darker than the rest of the building since its only light came from what filtered in through the floor to ceiling windows in the main room. Starting with the row of cabinets closest to me, I quickly got to work in the hopes that I could finish before the sunset, and soon stripped off my heavy outer shirt once I was in real danger of soaking it through with sweat.

Ryder found me, what felt like hours later, sitting on the floor with various jars lying around my legs. I'd methodically looked through every single cabinet and the large, walk-in pantry, but had only acquired a handful of things we'd be able to eat.

I laughed when I saw his face. He'd tried his best to get all the soot, but there was a streak near his jaw that he'd missed.

"Come here," I urged him, pointing to the one bare spot in front of me.

Even with no idea what I wanted, he came. Once he'd settled into a crouch, I used my thumb to wipe at the stubborn black stain, smiling triumphantly when it was gone after several tries.

"I'm not the only one," he mumbled, pulling his sleeve over his thumb to wipe at what must've been leftover dust or dirt on my face. I'd encountered a fair amount of spiderwebs and mouse droppings, but the dust had been the worst offender.

"So you found something?" he asked.

I swept my arm out towards the various jars at my side. "Some jams and preserves. No telling if they're still good, but as long as they don't make us sick..."

He nodded. There was a fine line when eating scavenged food despite knowing it had soured over the years, but taking a chance on something when there were other options available? The extra food wasn't worth the risk if we opened the containers and found mold or rot.

"Good find. We can try them out later. Jake got back a little bit ago, but he didn't want to disturb you, so he's dressing his catches in the other room."

I must've been too focused to notice when he came in. I wrinkled my nose at the thought of covering the fancy tables with fish guts.

Like always, Ryder knew exactly where my mind had traveled. "He laid out some sheets first, Seraphim."

His casual use of my full name had my hand twitching where it rested on my ankle. I hadn't heard it in so long, maybe a few weeks before his dad's death, and was beginning to think I never would again. He was the only one who used it anyway, other than Ben.

He laughed quietly. "You always were so particular about where things were prepared."

The sound of the kitchen door opening was loud as Kasimir strode in, his shirt and sections of his pants damp and clinging to his skin. His wet hair stuck to his neck, and the many veins in his arms were practically bulging. I hadn't known muscles could be that large.

"Was worried it had dried up at first and it took a while for the rust to filter out, but it works. Should still boil it but," he shrugged, "water is water."

It was a battle to focus on his words and not that droplet clinging to the edge of his scar and drawing my gaze to those light gray eyes, but the hand Ryder extended to help me up snapped me out of it. "Perfect," I said, leaving them both behind.

Ryder would tell him what I found. Was I going through a late puberty or something? Surely others else didn't have this much attraction to everyone in sight. It would be easier if it was just their looks, but I was drawn to *them* too. To Ryder's introspective nature, and how Jake could be all brash energy in one second and deadly serious and commanding in the next. Even Kasimir's steady presence, tempered by his dry humor and those flashes of vulnerability, was impossible to resist. I couldn't keep running like this.

I groaned, burying my face in my hands. *What the hell am I going to do?*

The fire crackled and popped loudly, the wood we'd gathered easily catching alight. The reflection of the flames against the interior of the hearth created a warm, welcoming glow that illuminated the large room. A faint scent of smoke filled the space, but nothing like when we had fires outside and it was right in our faces depending on the breeze. I was surprisingly cozy, belly full from the meal that Jake had prepared, and the sips of whiskey from the bottle I'd found intact in the cabinet where they kept their liquor.

"We have to have this more often," I said as I ate my last bite.

Jake laughed. "What, fish?"

He looked edible sprawled out in the large leather chair, jeans hugging the broad width of his thighs snuggly and his hair shone gold by the flames.

"Mmm, yes. It's been ages since I had fish and it's just as good as I remembered."

"Had fish a lot then, did you?"

"Wouldn't you like to know, cowboy?"

I supposed it was a fair question. They knew next to nothing about me, and I was just sated enough to tell them. Ryder knew a little more, but not much. I moved my feet and Mila meowed at me where she was curled up beside them, looking adorably disgruntled as she tried to get comfortable again.

"As a matter of fact, I did. Ben liked to fish. He only brought me along once, but it was enough for me to realize I liked the taste but not the acquiring." I noticed Jake and Ryder exchanging glances from the corner of my eye, but was too preoccupied with the rhythmic swirling of the liquid in my glass to confront them on whatever their deal was.

"I used to fish with my father," Kasimir said.

Everyone grew silent, waiting to see if the elusive Kasimir had anything more to say.

"Oh, fuck you," he grumbled when he noticed how raptly he held our attention. He'd decided not to drink, assigning himself the job of keeping watch through the night, but the others were. It was reflected in Ryder's hesitant smile, more a smirk, and Jake's easy laughter–even louder than usual.

My head was light, and I had no right to feel as secure as I did, holed up in this space and surrounded by them, like nothing in this world could touch me.

The blanket draped over my torso fell down the length of my arm as I shifted, exposing the bare skin across my upper chest to be warmed by the fire instead of the stifling heat of the blanket. I sighed happily, curling my body tighter and glancing up to find Kasimir watching–no, *staring*–at me. Resting my heavy head against the back of the chair, I looked back at him until he raised an eyebrow, then I giggled, leaning back to face the high ceiling.

It was tempting to doze off right where I lay, the blanket soft and heavy draped over my limbs and the spirits weighing my body down. The deep, quiet voices were lulling me to sleep, and as much as I wanted to stay awake a little longer with them, it was impossible to keep my eyes open...

I woke up gasping for air. I must've slept for hours, as the room was mostly dark aside from the pale glow coming from the hearth, the fire just embers–though I was coated in sweat like it was still roaring–and I could see the moon shining through the glass overhead. The room was silent, only punctuated by soft snores somewhere off to my right. I slowed my breathing, the images of whatever my nightmare had been about fading more with every second that passed.

"Seraphim," someone whispered, and I jerked my head up at the sound. "Just me," Kasimir murmured.

One by one, my muscles relaxed, and I let out a relieved sigh. "Forgot you were staying up," I croaked. A few moments of silence, and then it hit me. "Where did you hear that, anyway?"

He hesitated. "Overheard Ryder earlier." I could hardly see his face from this angle–just the odd ray of moonlight gracing his cheek and catching on the taut line of his scar as the clouds shifted–making it impossible to guess what he was thinking just from his shadowed features.

A quick glance around revealed Jake and Ryder to be sleeping, Mila curled up on the lap of the latter.

"Why don't you use it?" he finally asked.

"Dunno," I whispered sleepily, tucking my head to rest it more comfortably on the pillow someone must have tucked behind me while I slept as I watched him. "Just stopped at some point. Was too long for people to say."

"I like it."

I liked the way he sounded when he said it.

"So use it," I murmured, shyness making my face heat.

He made a soft humming noise under his breath. "Maybe I will."

"...Kas?"

"Kas, huh?"

"Just came to me. Short, like mine."

His laugh was soft. "You can call me Kas all you'd like, Seraphim."

My smile couldn't be contained, blooming in response to his deep voice saying my name.

CHAPTER 8

I sat at the table with Jake and Kasimir, as I swallowed my last bite of oatmeal, the hint of cinnamon still clinging to my throat. That Jake had remembered my preferences and added it without me even having to ask made my chest warm. Casey's absence was palpable. He should've been sitting there with us, cracking jokes and telling stories.

Jake leaned back in his chair to watch the sky from the uncovered glass near the ceiling. "Might try to catch some more fish for lunch today."

"My arm hardly hurts anymore," I said, albeit reluctantly. It still throbbed if I focused my attention on it, but it was no longer the sharp, biting pain it had been the previous day. "Suppose that means we should move on soon."

Maybe my unwillingness to leave was obvious, because Kas's face softened at my words. It was incredible watching his face transform. Even those half-lidded glacial eyes had thawed somewhat.

"Hold on," Jake said, pausing to dig for something in his pocket and presenting it to me almost shyly. I plucked it from his hand, instantly recognizing the red and white stripes.

"How did you know?"

"I asked Kasimir what that candy was that you liked so much," he grumbled. "I grabbed a handful a couple days ago from that restaurant next to the store where you found that protein bar under the shelf."

Kas smiled to himself as he continued eating, and my brows crept higher. "You mean the restaurant that was practically falling apart? You never should've risked it!"

He shrugged, looking completely unrepentant, and leaned back in the metal chair to adjust his lazy sprawl. "Say thank you, Seraphim. Consider it a part of my apology."

Guess that means there'll be more to come. I shook my head. "Thank you, cowboy."

Ryder entered the room on a yawn, with vestiges of sleep clinging to his tired eyes and tousled hair. "How do you feel about heading down to the creek to bathe?" he asked us.

Everyone was in agreement that we should get clean while we still could, and in the end, we'd all ended up in the frigid water except for Jake, who'd woken up early that morning to bathe alone, which he received a short scolding for. Instead, he stood several feet away, keeping an eye out for anything that didn't belong.

In truth, he was in more danger over there than we were, even oblivious to the noises around us. Zombies seemed to have an odd dislike of the water, and they refused to enter when faced with a lake or a creek, even to pursue their prey.

"Jake!" I called from the water. "Can you toss me my soap?" I'd wanted a chance to rinse myself off first thoroughly without worrying about losing it, so he'd agreed to hand it to me whenever I asked.

"Yes ma'am," he answered. His smirk when I spun around was wicked.

I laughed softly, catching it when he tossed it and turning around to wash myself. It was getting easier to compartmentalize, to stay out of my head and savor the moment, admiring how the sunlight danced off the ripples of the freezing water, casting a sparkling, golden glow.

Washing away the grime and weariness I'd accumulated since my last bath, I felt almost like a new person. I hadn't bothered to strip this time, instead scrubbing off both me and my clothes at the same time for efficiency. In front of me, Ryder was already wading to the grassy bank. I was about to do the same when Kasimir called out behind me.

"Seraphim?"

My head grew light, like every other time he'd said my full name today. "Yeah?"

"Can you take this with you?"

The deep timbre of his voice resonated through the air and made bumps rise on my chilled arms. It took me a second to register his request, and I spun around, ready to fulfill it, only to stop short at the shirt in his hand.

As my gaze landed on him, time seemed to freeze. Droplets of water glistened against his pale skin and his muscles rippled beneath the water's surface, distorted by the current. Black hair, damp and unkempt, framed his face, and his strong jawline, now partially obscured by several days of stubble, added to the rugged nature of his features. But it was his piercing gray eyes that transfixed me the most, dancing with a glimmer of amusement. They bore into mine with a depth that urged me to look away, and although it was almost impossible, I did, shifting my gaze to his chin. Slowly, his lips curved into a knowing smile.

He waded closer, his steps deliberate and unhurried. As he handed me his shirt, our fingers brushed in a fleeting connection and the touch sent a jolt coursing through me.

The water hugged his bare hips, lapping against the treasure trail on his abdomen, leading down... I snapped my eyes up, but they lingered on his broad chest. Covered in various scars—some deep and some shallow–and punctuated by dips and curves, he was beautiful. Trepidation held my tongue captive.

Someone coughed behind me, and I jumped into action. "Yeah." I cleared my throat. "I'll take it with me."

"Thank you," he rasped. "It was in the way."

The high-pitched, nervous giggle that left my lips filled me with mortification and I quickly made my way back to Ryder and Jake, where they waited. "Well, happy to help. Of course. So very happy. To help, that is," I said, stumbling over my words and struggling to regain my composure, my face warm with a mix of embarrassment and intrigue.

When I reached the rocky bank, I smacked the wet shirt into Jake's chest, interrupting his dedicated stare at the tops of the trees with his arms folded, lips pursed tightly to keep from laughing.

"Pains in my ass," I muttered as I squeezed the water from my shirt. The scents of sediment, mud, and moss were thick in the air, but it was better than sweat. I bent over to wring my dark hair, the limp waves sad and flat from the creek water.

It didn't take Kas long to join us. I was careful to keep my eyes fixed on a nearby tree, and not on his damp, exposed body or the many droplets that were currently winding their way down his bumpy abdomen.

I was the first to leave, the others trailing behind me, as we made our way back to the building in the distance. Thoughts of the cozy interior had me moving faster, excited to strip off my wet clothes and get into something dry so I could curl up by the fire for a snack, but a noise had me jerking to a stop. I held up my hand so the others would fall quiet and listened intently.

There it was. Up ahead, something was crouching in the bushes. A zombie? A deer? It was impossible to tell, and I wouldn't have noticed if not for the flash of white as it hunkered down. I crept forward, at a loss to how it hadn't noticed us. I guessed it wasn't impossible. We tended to move soundlessly when out in the open, and the trees offered some protection.

Once I moved past a particularly large tree, I was able to get a clearer view. It was a... boy? No, a man. He was kneeling, cradling his foot and gritting his teeth.

He was clearly injured. What if he needed help?

I rushed forward, only to be jerked to a stop by a brick wall. Oh no, silly me, it was just Kasimir's huge fucking arm yanking me back into his solid body.

"Let me go," I hissed, squirming in his grip.

Jake forged ahead to investigate further while I was stuck back with Kas. What if he scared him? Or insulted him?

Kasimir grunted as I stomped down on his foot. "Stop that, damn it."

"Let me go help them!"

The man was now looking up at Jake, who stood before him, Ryder at his side. Kas spun me in his arms so that we were face to face and I could no longer watch the confrontation at my back. I wriggled again, cursing him under my breath. Did he think me too weak? Too useless to approach a threat first?

Kasimir used one hand to tip my chin up, the other still banded tightly around my waist–and shit, how strong did he have to be to have such an iron grip on me with just one arm?

"I don't want you to be hurt," he grumbled, gray eyes searching mine. I was close enough to see the flecks of navy near his pupils.

"What do you care?" I argued. When would I stop being treated like I was made of glass? Why did I even come if I was just another thing for them to protect, another weight on their shoulders?

His sigh was long and gave me a moment of pause to realize just how close we were. Low, calm voices filtered through the trees behind me and I relaxed some, satisfied that things were going peacefully and there was no imminent danger.

"Is it so wrong of me–of us–to want to keep you safe?"

I frowned. "I'm not your little sister, or a child. I can protect myself, and I don't appreciate being manhandled out of situations."

"No, definitely not either of those," he replied, his words a low rumble.

My eyes widened, and I knew it was for the best when his arm loosened. I slid down the front of his body, grateful to have my feet back on the ground. Although I felt every excruciating inch of friction as the fabric of our wet shirts rubbed together, of the pressure of his solid chest against my softer one. My stomach twisted in anticipation, and I was thankful for the lightly padded bra I'd made sure to put on that day, hiding the worst of my inopportune interest in him and his proximity.

The worst part was how out of my control I felt, my desire sending a fizzing energy to my head, and I would've given anything to be able to easily dismiss it. All the novels I'd read, and I never knew real life could feel like this.

His sharp breath sent me stumbling back, letting the fabric of his shirt slip through my fingers when I hadn't even consciously grabbed onto it.

"Good talk," I mumbled, my movements coltish as I approached the trio, hoping that I didn't look as out of control as I felt. Jake and Ryder wore suspicion clear on their faces, arms crossed defensively as they watched him.

"You must be Sera," the man said in greeting. Standing at his full height, he was a little shorter than Ryder, which put him at about Jake's height. I hadn't yet seen anyone surpass Kasimir, who stood several inches above them all.

The man's hazel eyes seemed tired. Greasy, brown hair hung to his shoulders and tangled in clumps, and his beard looked like it had grown a couple inches and then just stopped. His clothing was torn, and his ankle was bleeding freely. It was difficult to tell under the blood, but there seemed to be bruises covering his exposed leg where the fabric had been ripped away, probably during his injury. He looked like he could collapse at any moment.

I rolled my eyes. "Well then. Not a zombie? Or a murderer?"

He blinked, shifting awkwardly.

"Come on," I huffed, saving a quick glare for the others. The poor man was unsteady on his feet, probably starving and dehydrated, and they were making him stand through an interrogation?

He followed me across the overgrown lawn, and I grabbed onto his arm when he stumbled the third time to keep him from falling. He shot me a grateful smile. "Thanks."

"What's your name?"

"Liam."

"Alright, Liam. We can get you cleaned up and something to eat, then you can talk about why you were creeping in the bushes and staring at the place we've been staying for the past day. Deal?"

When he didn't answer, I glanced over at my left. Liam stared at me wide-eyed, his expression impossible to place. "Deal," he confirmed weakly.

I spent the next several hours fussing over Liam. Feeding him leftover grilled fish and watching, fascinated, as he scarfed it down. I wagered he hadn't even tasted it. Grabbing a towel from the linen closet near the bedrooms on the second floor, I raised my brow at the guys until they reluctantly offered up pieces of clothing. Pants from Jake, a shirt from Ryder, and socks from Kas. Luckily his shoes were in good shape, and although clothes were scarce, I knew the others had several other sets they could live on until we reached the farm.

Then I accompanied him down to the creek we'd just left and sat him down in the grass before me, making him sit still as I cut his hair with the rusty scissors I'd found in a drawer in the kitchen, then shaved his beard with the straight edge Jake had lent me. I'd never thought Ben letting me make him over for fun, shaving him and cutting his hair whenever we had our pampering days, would come in handy, but I'd already used those skills on Ryder, and now Liam too, it would seem.

After, I sent him off to the water to bathe, giving him my soap to use.

The man who emerged from the water clutching the spare sheet was not the same man who'd been crouched in the bushes. His hair was a soft brown color once rid of the oil and filth, the top longer than the sides–which I'd trimmed short. Free of blood and dirt, he was actually quite handsome. Liam's lanky form further cemented my theory that he'd been hungry for a very long time, and he shivered as he pulled the sheet tighter. It slipped somewhat, revealing the edge of a deep scar, but he tugged it back up before I could see what it was.

"I'll be right there," I informed him, pointing at the crop of trees to our right and facing away so he could get dressed, hoping my presence felt soothing and not stifling. It was a little surprising that the guys hadn't put up a fight about me accompanying him alone, whether because of the risk of zombies or just being around a stranger alone, but it was a nice burst of reassurance to be trusted to handle my own.

He announced when he was done, and I turned to find him fully dressed, the clothes hanging off his frame. The sun hung low in the sky, and the growing shadows only served to emphasize his weariness. The man was practically falling asleep at my feet.

"Great. I'm sure you just worked up an appetite so now we can grab some more food."

He stopped me with a gentle clasp of my arm. "Hold on, how can you afford to feed me? I don't want to use up all your supplies."

I smiled, patting his hand. "You're not. We have enough to spare."

True, we had a limited amount of jerky, granola, cans, and various other foods, but with Jake's fishing, we hadn't had to dip into our rations at all over the past day. I knew hunger, and I didn't want him to feel like an imposition.

He didn't protest any further, just gave me a hesitant smile back.

CHAPTER 9

"I came because I saw the smoke. It's just me here," Liam said as he leaned back in his chair.

Jake cursed. "Of all the things, I hadn't thought of the smoke."

"Nor had I," Kas said with a frown.

"So... what, you were going to steal our food and... slit our throats?" I asked.

He looked horrified. "Absolutely not. I–" His offense melted into shame and his voice grew quiet. "I thought... maybe you might have extra food. That I could take some and rest nearby for a bit before heading back. I wasn't going to kill anybody!"

"Why are you alone? Where are you based?" I gently prodded.

Liam hesitated, and Kasimir shifted closer to the edge of his chair to scrutinize him further. "My family's alive. They live a couple of hours away back at our homestead." He paused, but no one interjected. It was clear he was nervous to tell us everything, but the desperate hope radiating off him kept him talking. "I was scavenging for us. They..." he grimaced. "It's hard for them to go out. My sister is sheltered. She doesn't understand what it's like out here, so it's my responsibility to do it. But everywhere I look is picked clean, so every day I travel a little further only to return with scraps."

I frowned. Why did it sound like he'd spent the last twenty-something years hiding under a rock? "What do you mean they don't know what it's like? How is that possible?" *Everyone* I knew had suffered from the effects of the virus, whether from losing loved ones to the infection in the early days or through learning the hard way how to survive amongst the zombies.

Liam's eyes darted to the window. "We were in a facility, okay?"

The negative reactions around me were unexpected. Jake was the loudest, his scoff echoing off the walls.

"Why is that such a bad thing?" I asked the room.

"Because we all know the military ain't gonna find shit," Jake spat. "'Specially not a cure. It's just an excuse to get a free ride, and in exchange for what, some blood samples? A few shots?"

Whatever their personal thoughts on the matter, we all knew it wasn't like that. Even from the little I'd heard about what happened inside the facilities, I knew they involved more strenuous procedures. That there was more involved than mere shots and samples.

"He's right." Liam's voice was bitter. "They keep you like their own personal pets, telling you what to eat, when to sleep, to exercise, to fuck. But even despite the controlled environment, having access to food and shelter..."

I shifted uncomfortably in my seat. The situation sounded eerily similar.

Ryder placed a hand on my shoulder, murmuring just for me to hear. "It's not the same. And it's not fair to them, but those in the facilities are resented because they have an easy time of it just because of their DNA. A whisper here and a joke there about preferential treatment, regular meals, and indoor plumbing, and it's enough to make the nicest person bitter."

Covering his hand with mine, I gave it a squeeze.

"Why aren't you still there? Last I heard, they hadn't discovered a cure for the Paleo virus."

"I–They just didn't need us anymore. We couldn't stay forever, and there's only so much you can get from the same person's body before it's not worth the extra mouths to feed." He grimaced, twisting his mouth into an ugly sneer that darkened his features. "Gave us a plot of land, some food, some defenses, and fucked off. Closed the facility and moved to a more populated area up north."

My intuition insisted that he was telling the truth, but it still seemed like there was something he wasn't saying. Though I didn't think it was anything dangerous. Or maybe it was just that I was struggling to see deceit in him. He looked too tired, too worn thin. It didn't escape my notice that he hadn't told us how they'd ended up at the center in the first place and which of them was immune.

Kasimir took over, his expression once more impassive. "So they threw you out into the real world and left you to fend for yourselves."

Liam nodded, his eyes shuttering. Poor guy was exhausted.

I stood, tucking a stray curl behind my ear, and made to grab for the aluminum water bottle I'd found under the reception desk and washed earlier. "Here, I refilled it with fresh water. Why don't you head up to one of the bedrooms and get some sleep, and we'll talk in the morning."

If it were anyone else, their suspicion would have been too strong to accept the offer, but he just stared at me, warily accepting the bottle and taking a big gulp. "If you insist," he rasped, still looking at me oddly before making his way up the stairs.

"Absolutely not," Jake whispered after one of the doors shut upstairs, and Kas folded his arms across his massive chest.

Ryder huffed. "Hate to agree with the cowboy, but he's right, we can't waste any more time."

The look Jake leveled on him was filled with scorn.

Fuck. I thought of the dark circles under Liam's eyes, the desperate hunger as he ate, and the pained manner in which he regarded the world. "Please," I begged, my voice cracking midway. "I want–*need*–to help him. Haven't you ever been stuck? And wished so deeply that someone would come to your aid?"

Like I'd flipped a switch, the faces before me morphed from uncompromising to resigned.

"There's no set date for us to get to the farm," Jake said gruffly. "Hopefully, everyone back at camp will think we chose to stay an extra week or two to recover from the journey rather than..." He didn't finish. We all knew what he meant.

"And your friend?" I asked Kasimir. "Can he wait?"

Kasimir's steely gaze softened, and he gave me a hint of a smile. "Yes, Seraphim. Ethan can wait."

Ryder sighed, and a heavy hand landed on the top of my head to ruffle my hair. "Our Seraphim, such a soft heart."

I wondered if anyone else noticed that he'd said "*our*."

"Y ou're sure you want to come?" Liam asked.

Kasimir grunted. "You're struggling, yes? We can help. Teach you to fish and scavenge properly so you all don't starve." The morning sun made the gray of his eyes translucent, and he raised his hand to shield them.

"Maybe kick your family into gear while we're at it," Jake muttered from somewhere to our left.

I frowned. It hadn't sounded like his family was incapable of helping, more like for some reason they'd just decided not to and had piled it all on him. The ideal scenario was that they were open to learning.

"It's great that you were given the property and resources, but they're only useful if you know how to utilize them. Anyone can claim a home, but it takes work to establish a system to provide for yourself," I explained.

I felt for him. Even with Ben teaching me everything I needed to know to survive after he was gone, we'd always assumed I'd still be living in the home I'd grown up in. Maybe if I'd been less cowardly, I wouldn't have thrown my lot in with Gunner. Then again, I wouldn't have met Ryder, or ended up in the haven that was their camp. But Liam had something I didn't. If anyone could make it, it would be him; he just needed a little guidance.

Ryder shot me an odd look, and I shook my head. He knew a little about Ben, but not everything. Not how hard it had been when he grew sick and I took on the bulk of the work. Flashes of the night I'd been cast out filled my vision. The threats from the men who'd thrown me from the house echoing long after I'd fled, the ragged sound of my gasping breaths, because I'd been too afraid to even cry, fearing that I would draw something from my nightmares out of the shadows.

A flash of warmth drew me from my thoughts, and I quickly realized that Jake's hand had brushed against mine, a brief reassuring touch. I'd have thought it accidental if he didn't accompany it with a tilt of his head. I just smiled, twining my pinky with his.

"We can work with your family to find their strengths and that way it's not just you shouldering their continued survival, but there are alternatives if not. It doesn't make you less worthy if you don't want to keep on like you were," Jake said.

Liam's face fell. "Continued survival," he said. "Last year, our biggest fear was the chicken shortage or the facility being breached."

I cringed when Ryder snorted. Sometimes it was easy to forget how hard he'd had it. Dealing with a father that provoked him daily–whether personally or through his treatment of others–and had created an antagonistic environment that Ryder felt compelled to combat behind his back. Missing his mother. Losing everyone important to him.

If Ryder was any less sure of himself or had a lesser sense of justice, I wouldn't be standing where I was. His father would still be terrorizing other survivors, taking resources from wherever he wanted, and enabling his men. A rush of affection ran through me, and I sidled up next to him, wrapping my hand around his arm while he walked to anchor myself. I held the words back even though I was bursting at the seams to tell him how proud I was of him.

Instead, I just squeezed his arm where I held it, offering him a beaming smile. His aloofness faded into a distracted confusion as he looked down at me, and he stumbled slightly before righting himself.

"I'll have what he's having," Jake muttered from behind us.

I ignored him, reaching out to twirl a strand of soft, dark brown hair at Ryder's temple around my finger. "Let's get you a haircut soon, yeah?"

He shivered, probably from the cool air against his exposed skin, and nodded. I'd always cut his hair for him back when we were still with his father. The first time I'd offered, I couldn't believe he'd agreed. To let me near him–a stranger–with sharp scissors was unthinkable. His hair had fallen below his shoulders before I'd realized he wasn't going to cut it on his own and could no longer resist asking. Since then, I gave him regular cuts, just enough to keep it out of his eyes and off his neck.

"Good," I chirped, patting his neck and stepping away to reach in my pack and pull out a piece of jerky for Mila.

Kas chuckled, as if I hadn't seen him sneaking her pieces of his fish last night. Every day I was convinced we'd wake and find her gone, but so far she'd decided to stick by us.

"You know how to get back there, right?" I asked Jake. We'd boarded over the exit when we left that morning, making it look uninhabited once more, but good, secure shelters were hard to come by, and I'd hate to lose that one. We wouldn't have even found it if not for the zombie that threw us off course, and I was sure it would factor into future trips now that we knew of its existence.

"I remember," he replied, baritone voice reassuring.

I nodded, noticing Liam's limp out of the corner of my eye. If we weren't on such a deadline, I'd have insisted we stay behind so that he could have more time to recover.

As we walked, I kept an eye out for a branch that could function as a kind of walking stick. The less pressure he put on his ankle, the quicker it would heal. Anything that could make the trip back a little easier for him would be invaluable. He'd already taken some expired pain medication–after a short discussion where I'd had to reassure him that was what it was for when he'd refused at first, saying that he didn't want to waste it on himself–and had used some of our supplies to bandage his ankle before we left.

It took me at least ten minutes to spot one both long and sturdy enough to support his weight. Everyone wore odd looks as I darted past them to grab it, grinning when I handed it to him and realized it came to his chest.

Liam looked from me to the stick, stunned into silence. "Thank you," he said quietly, taking it from my grasp.

Jake huffed, reaching over to snap some of the lower twigs off so that they wouldn't catch on his clothes. When he straightened, he looked Liam dead in the eye and said, "You'd better not be leading us into a trap. You won't like the outcome."

"I'm not."

Kas brushed past us all, along with Ryder, who clicked his tongue at Mila to get her to follow along.

Only a short few hours later, we stood before a robust fence that enclosed a large plot of land. The grass was overgrown and riddled with weeds, and in the distance, I could see a large house that looked to be built from... "Is that steel?"

The roof was topped by a large sheet of metal that resembled a rainbow. It was shaped in a half-circle and covering the sides of the home. The building looked to be about one story, and the front-facing exterior seemed to be made of some kind of metal that was darker than whatever was used on the roof, but it was at least five times the size

Ben's home had been. A closer look at their land revealed a large fire pit at the back of the house, along with some other shapes resting against the sides.

"We think it was built before the outbreak, and that they just cleaned it up and cleared the area when they passed it off to us. Should be noncombustible, and in the winter the snow slides right off."

"Damn," Kas murmured. I nodded in agreement, taking advantage of our stillness to gulp from my bottle and use a splash of water to rinse my face. At least I was no longer panting. It had only taken us a couple of hours to reach Liam's home, and most of it was spent on rural paths and heavily wooded areas, not a soul in sight.

A voice from across the field rang out, and we all cringed at the shrill volume, watching as the figure in the distance waved their arms.

I noticed the guys giving each other looks behind me and gestured at the gate. "After you."

After fiddling with the extensive locks, Liam led us inside. The sweet scent of wildflowers filled the air, and as we approached, I released the meadow behind their home was filled with them. The one thing I didn't see was food.

"No garden?"

"No."

"So just flowers," Kas said flatly, unimpressed.

Liam grimaced. "My sister... The one time I brought her with me, she found them in some bulk bag in the back of a shop. Brought them back and just threw them all over the ground, said it'd be a miracle if they grew and that's how we'd know we belonged here."

"Course there were only flower seeds left," Jake muttered, "who in their right mind is looking for pretty things when they're starving?"

"She considered that her contribution, and I didn't dare bring her back with me—not that she would come. Too loud and no sense of danger. Besides, it's... it's my job," he uttered under his breath.

I braided my damp hair back to keep it off my face while he talked, using one of the many hair ties River had gifted me when I'd first arrived after witnessing my struggle to secure my hair back when I was at Gunner's camp. It was my favorite, second only to the one Nadira had gifted me once she had access to fabric scraps again, a light purple color with a velvety texture.

The closer we got to the house, the clearer the figure standing outside became. Petite with slim curves and freshly washed red hair that fell to the middle of her back. My gaze went back and forth between the siblings, unable to process what I was seeing. She was well-fed, rested, uninjured, and apparently ecstatic to see her brother.

"What did you find?" she exclaimed, rushing over to her brother and peeking in the bag at his side, frowning when she saw it was almost empty.

Liam cleared his throat. "Morgan, this is Sera, Kasimir, Jake, and Ryder. They're going to be helping us for a while."

It was only then that she snapped her attention up to the tall men behind me and grinned. "Well, hello there."

I bristled being ignored, surprised that she hadn't commented on her brother's limp or the excess padding around his ankle.

Morgan tucked her hair behind her ears and leaned closer. "Welcome to our home." She smelt of something floral and sweet, nothing like the sweat and dirt that clung to my skin. A wave of shame hit me when I realized how I must look in comparison.

A raspy meow rang out, and I glanced down to find Mila rubbing against my calf, startling when Morgan squealed. "Oh, you have a kitty! How cute," she gushed, bending over to pet Mila and laughing nervously when she hissed in response. "Anyway, come in. You can meet my dad."

It was impossible to resist looking at Liam to gauge his response to her, and his frown, paired with a sigh, told me exactly what I'd suspected.

Everyone filed past me to follow her into the strange-looking dwelling, and I found myself missing Casey more than ever.

"Dad!" she shouted as she threw open the door.

A startled breath escaped me at the sight of the cluttered great room. Napkins, unwashed utensils, various supplies, and fabric liberally coated the inside. It smelt of dust and disuse, and the sun coming through the long window against the front exterior wall above the door illuminated the stale air. Under the disarray, their furnishings were in good condition, only showing minimal damage.

"For fuck's sake," Liam muttered. "I just cleaned it before I left." I tried to see it from his perspective. It must've been frustrating to come home from scavenging to find even more work to do, because it was clear he was the only one who minded the mess.

Morgan gave an unflattering snort. "It's just trash, Liam. You're so picky."

His teeth ground audibly.

Ignoring the bickering siblings, Jake marched over to their father and introduced himself. They were stark contrasts beside one another. Their father was pale, lacking Jake's golden tan, and his eyes were rimmed with dark circles. Even his dark hair, so different from his children's shades of red and light brown, was patchy and missing in places.

He looked up at Jake in bewilderment. "Anthony."

Peering towards the rooms at the back of the house, I waited to see if anyone else would come out and introduce themselves. Liam must have caught me because he stopped arguing with his sister to inform me that his mother had passed years ago, and that it was just them in the home.

"Oh..." I said, realizing all eyes were on me. "I'm very sorry."

Morgan waved a hand. "Ridiculous, right? All those medical professionals and not a damn one of them could save her."

Jake shot me a look of panic, like he'd be expected to go over and rub her back or something while making soothing noises, and the laugh I suppressed came out as a choked cough.

"Well," I said brightly. "This is nice. Always nice to make new acquaintances."

There was a smothered sound behind me, and we all stood in awkward silence for several prolonged beats.

"Is there somewhere we could talk privately?" Ryder asked bluntly. I loved him for it.

"Sure," Anthony said, finally rousing himself to speak. He pointed toward the hallway to our right, past the kitchen and dining area, that must've contained a set of rooms. "Last two doors on the left are our guest rooms; you can talk there."

Ryder led the way, shutting the door behind us after we'd all entered. It wasn't the biggest room, but it wasn't so small that we were packed in like sardines either. It was nicely decorated, fairly clean, and there was a single barred window high up on the wall. The word spartan came to mind.

Only once I'd finished examining the room did I realize how close we all were. I cleared my throat, backing up until I bumped into the bed behind me. Even still, I had to look up to talk to them. "So," I said.

Kas laughed softly.

"Okay," Jake said. "We can walk out of here right now, give them directions to the camp, and send them on their merry way. We don't have to stay here and get involved in their family dynamics."

That idea sounded better and better by the minute, but I kept returning to Liam's dejected posture when he'd sat across from us earlier. He was reaching his breaking point, and it didn't seem right to abandon him when he needed help. "They have such a nice home; what if they don't want to pack up and leave just to share a space with others? Shouldn't we help them regardless and let them choose after?"

"If that's what you want. I don't know if I like sending anyone we barely know back home anyway."

"Why are we vetting people? Can't the people back home do that?"

"Maybe since pretty boy's dad almost killed us all," Jake replied drily.

I sucked in a shocked breath. Surely, he wasn't trying to imply... I'd heard all about what happened before the girls and I had arrived. They'd been wary *well before* Gunner had started sniffing around and making a mess.

Ryder was silent, but his eyes told a completely different story. Pain flashed for a split second before his gaze fell flat, like he'd squashed any semblance of hurt the second it flared. I'd seen him do it countless times around his father, and I wasn't sure it was even a conscious choice anymore.

"That's not fair," I snapped, careful to keep my volume low. Kasimir wouldn't know the context, but I did, and I wasn't going to let Jake make Ryder think it had anything to do with him. "The triplet's dad, the *actual fucking leader* of the camp, was the one trading with Gunner secretly before he died. Ryder had fuck all to do with it." Jake damn well knew that and had only said what he did to provoke him.

Jake's shadowed brown eyes widened a fraction. "You're right," he said. "I'm sorry. I just don't want to send anyone toxic back to them. For all we know this is just a big elaborate trap and they have plans to murder and eat us."

"That's a bit much," I replied faintly, sick at the very idea.

A discreet glance at Ryder revealed him to be wearing a familiar blank mask. It broke my heart. Every time he started to seem a little more comfortable, a little more free to express himself, he shut down again and retreated back behind his defenses. I wanted to reach out so badly, but didn't want to put him on the spot or make him think it was pity that made my hand itch to hold his.

"It's a moot point anyway," Kas interjected. "I don't think he can make the journey with that ankle, especially not as their sole provider and protector."

"So we stay and help. Teach them how to survive, judge their character, and offer them the option before we leave, if all goes well."

"We start immediately," Kas said. "Find out where they're sourcing their water, how they're treating it, what food they have and what their individual skills are. Liam just needs some guidance, but the others are still unknown."

His authoritative tone sent shivers down my spine and filled my mind with thoughts of him giving me orders in a very different context.

"Seraphim?" he asked, seeking confirmation. I nodded rapidly, willing my cheeks not to darken, though his gravelly tone didn't help.

That was enough of that. I cracked the door open, exiting the room to find Morgan speaking animatedly to Liam, who was massaging the space between his eyebrows while their father looked on.

Kas came up beside me, took one look at the scene, and grunted.

"Yup," I said, popping the p at the end.

Finally, our presence was noticed. Morgan turned our way with a wide, calculating smile. "There you are. Will you be staying?"

The way she'd worded it was off-putting, as we were discussing a leisurely vacation and not something vital to keep her family from starving.

Jake crossed his arms. "I'm not sure what Liam told you, but he injured himself while out scavenging and met us while looking for shelter."

Morgan scanned Liam from head to toe, raising an eyebrow when she spotted no gaping, devastating wound.

Liam sighed. "My ankle."

"It's our understanding that you're relatively new to surviving on your own. We're prepared to go over your provisions, show you how to scavenge properly, and teach you the basics," Jake continued.

"What, like there's a cafeteria around the corner we somehow missed?" she teased, wilting in the face of Jake's lack of amusement.

"Berries, edible plants, fish, rabbits, anything you can identify or catch and prepare on your own. One person can't do it all," he said pointedly. Their father had the good sense to look away in embarrassment, though Morgan scoffed.

"You're right." Anthony said. "It's not fair of me to let my son do it all, and I'm prepared to learn."

Judging from Liam's incredulous stare, this must've been the first time his father had expressed such a sentiment. I wasn't sure if he was just saying what we wanted to hear or he actually meant it. Only time would tell.

"We can't stay for too long," Kas added. "Just long enough for Liam to recover so you're not completely fucked."

"We only have two spare rooms," Morgan informed us, flipping her hair over her shoulder. "You could always share with us? I'm sure two of you would love the chance to have a bed to yourselves, and the other two... well." She shrugged. "You can trade."

I wasn't sure what little set up she was envisioning in her mind–probably some endless rotation of the guys in her bed while I was pawned off on her brother or on my own–but it was a relief when Ryder jerked his head sharply. "We can make the two rooms work, thank you."

My head grew light as I imagined the different possibilities.

How the hell am I going to survive the next few nights?

CHAPTER 10

"I'm sorry, you have *how* much food?" I exclaimed.

I stood beside Liam as we watched Kas inspect the hand pump for their well, thinking once more how similar their compound was to Ben's. It was just missing his weird infatuation with cow-printed decor and the remnants of his half-finished projects lying about.

Liam shifted the weight off his injured ankle and looked down with a small shrug. "Around a half dozen cans, along with some spam. Some bags of rice and a few potatoes I found growing nearby. It's probably less now since I was gone."

I cast a helpless look at Ryder, who lurked silently behind us, looking grim. "That's... it's incredible that you've kept yourselves fed for an entire year."

Kas pushed himself to a stand, raising his arms up over his head to stretch and groaning when he heard his back crack. He wore a dark short-sleeved shirt today, and it clung deliciously to every dip and curve in his torso. His dark hair gleamed under the midday sun and brushed the back of his neck, slicked back like he'd brushed his hand through it too many times. The entire picture it formed was irresistible.

Liam's bony elbow hitting my side made a strangled noise leave my mouth, but the smirk he quickly hid had me giggling helplessly. Kas looked to us both for an explanation, but his seriousness just made me laugh harder, so Liam cleared his throat and spoke for me. "Just tired, I think."

It felt so damn good to just let go, and when my giggles tapered off, I focused back on the scene before me, only to realize Kas and Ryder were watching me intently.

"Well–" I began.

Ryder's grin was mostly teeth as he shook his head and started the walk back to the house. Kas followed, shooting me a suspicious look that threatened to make me lose it all over again.

Liam waited until they were a little further ahead to start walking. "So."

"So?"

"What's going on there?" he asked, inclining his head towards the two men cresting the hill in front of us.

"I don't know what you mean." Was it that obvious? That he'd picked up on anything was a little mortifying.

His slow grin told me that I wasn't fooling anyone. "Don't you?"

"There's nothing."

"Sounds like that's half the problem."

I gave a startled laugh and elbowed him gently, remembering too late that his balance wasn't so great at the moment.

Thankfully, he caught himself. "I'm right, aren't I? I've never seen a group of people so tense and determined not to stare at each other too long."

"Fuck off," I coughed.

We walked through the front door to find Morgan crowded up beside Jake, hand on his arm and chatting excitedly about something. Anthony, Kas, and Ryder stood nearby having a discussion about the supplies they were standing over.

"Oh good, you're back!" Morgan exclaimed. "I was just telling Jake here about how we wash up. We have a solar shower bag on the side of the house that we use with rainwater we collect. You're welcome to try it in the coming days."

"You'd love that, wouldn't you," Liam muttered in his sister's general direction.

Just under several hours of being here and it was already clear that there was no love lost between the two. The siblings carried a weird tension, half envy and half disdain, though Morgan hid hers well behind a happy mask.

My brows flew up when Jake spoke. "Morgan and I are going out to get a rough idea of the land and what we might be able to utilize. I'm banking on finding something we can use to supplement dinner tonight."

"Do you need us to come?" I asked. The odds were low that anything would happen when we were so deep into the forest, but that didn't mean they were zero, and I worried about him. Maybe taking just Morgan wasn't the best idea.

He shook his head, chestnut-colored hair brushing his shoulders with the movement. Lines bracketed the corners of his mouth under his growing scruff, and dark circles deepened by the day under those soulful eyes, yet he still remained one of the most handsome men I'd ever laid eyes on. "Ryder's coming. Kasimir is hanging back with you and Anthony to get things in order around the house."

"I'm injured, not dead," Liam interjected somewhat bitterly, and I understood. He'd been taking care of his family for so long on his own that it most likely stung to be pushed aside and made to feel like his previous efforts weren't good enough, even if that wasn't what was happening.

Kas stood straight and said, "I know. You're a vital part of making things work after we leave. While you recover, you'll be learning as much as you can about dressing and catching meat, setting traps, water filtration, and gardening techniques." He raised a hand to stave off any protests when Liam opened his mouth. "I know it's not exciting, but it's necessary. All things that we've learned from years trying to survive and passed on by the people we've met on our journeys that you didn't get a chance to learn firsthand."

Liam's mouth was tight, but the previous frustration had dimmed. "Fine."

The others left after our discussion ended, and I settled in with Anthony and Liam to listen to Kas and chime in when necessary. We sat in plastic folding chairs around the large wooden table in the dining room, directly across from the kitchen. I could see the front door from where I sat, but it was mostly tucked away behind the wall that separated the kitchen from the foyer.

Hours passed as we took turns speaking, pausing at times for Anthony to jot down notes in the aged leather notebook he held. There was an odd sense of solidarity in sitting there beside Kasimir, glancing at one another in affirmation when we expanded on something that the other knew a little less about.

At one point after I loosened my ponytail, irritated that it was pulling too tight, one of my shorter curls slipped free to rest on my shoulder. I was glad Jamie had cut it because it was much easier to have less to wash and care for, but I hadn't considered the fact that it would be harder to tie back. Without breaking his sentence and before I could move it myself, warm fingers brushed against the exposed skin next to my tank top strap as Kas wrapped it around his hand and tucked it safely behind my ear in one smooth movement. When I dared to peek to my right, those light gray eyes watched me intently, drifting down to the curve of my neck. All my energy went towards holding back a violent shiver. It had been a casual touch, but all I could feel were his roughened fingers dragging against my skin, leaving a trail of heat wherever they moved.

Liam's gaze shot to mine, the curve of his mouth sly. I glared daggers in his direction, grateful that Anthony had recaptured Kas's focus with another question.

Fuck you, I mouthed.

"Do we need to take a break?" Kas asked, finally catching on. Thankfully, his voice sounded amused and not annoyed. When he shifted to rest his arm on the table, I caught a whiff of the vanilla fragrance that always seemed to cling to his skin, mixed with an underlying scent of sweat. Fuck, maybe I really was broken if even his sweat was attractive.

"Nah," Liam said. "All good here."

Kas frowned, eyes darting between us, but I gestured for him to continue. He turned his attention back to Anthony, but I was hyper-aware of his elbow resting on the table and just ever so slightly touching mine, and sending a tingling sensation throughout that spot. Did he know? Was it purposeful? Hell, at this point the what ifs would make me spontaneously combust before the sun ever set.

We eventually switched from survival tips to stories, and I'd discovered more about Kasimir than all I knew up until that moment combined.

I learned that he vividly remembered what it was like to see the bodies piled in the streets in the early days of the virus, when there was no system in place to collect them. That he couldn't make eye contact when speaking of his family, and that there was nothing he loved to eat more than the tea his mother used to make using the orange peels from the tree that grew in their backyard.

All the little facts and interests Liam and I pulled from him painted a new picture of someone carrying around so much more pain than I'd realized. He was all alone in the world aside from his friend, and had been traveling for so long. *When was the last time he had a home?*

The door slamming behind us interrupted the easy conversation we'd had going and yanked me back to reality.

I straightened in my seat, watching as Morgan clung to Jake's arm while she whispered something that I couldn't quite hear. The small, bitter part of my brain that I tried to ignore wondered why he hadn't shaken her off yet.

"Find anything good?" Anthony asked as he shut his notebook.

"Oh! We found some morel mushrooms, which look sooo odd, but I guess they're a good find, and some ramps and some greens, plus the nearest creek is around thirty minutes to the west which isn't so bad," she gushed, looking up at Jake. "Isn't it amazing? We never would have known without Jake and Ryder."

Liam blinked, and I covered a smile with my hand. "I'm well aware of where the nearest creek is," he said.

"That's excellent, darling," Anthony said absently. "And thank you for agreeing to help us," he told us.

I let the others answer him. It felt wrong to take his praise when I hadn't really done anything. It was the guys who'd foraged with Morgan, and Kasimir who'd coached him.

Ryder caught my eye, but I looked away before he could notice that anything was wrong.

"So, dinner tonight?" I asked, running my finger along a divot on the table's surface.

"Rice with sauteed morels, ramps, and chickweed," Jake informed me.

My stomach growled on cue, and I pressed my hand over it to try to muffle the sound.

Just like that, everyone burst into a flurry of action. Jake and Ryder brought their finds to the kitchen, while Morgan carried in the bucket of water I hadn't noticed she'd brought. Kasimir headed outside to get a fire going in the large fire pit on the back of their property, and Anthony followed behind him with a cast-iron skillet as he talked about the dwindling supply of firewood Liam had cut for them several weeks ago. I moved between groups to help as needed, sighing happily at the faint scent of smoke once the fire was going.

After dinner, we all stood around the dying fire, soaking up the heat as the last of the sun's rays went down and trading stories.

Mostly Jake and I, as Liam and his family didn't seem very inclined to talk about their time in the facility, Ryder didn't much want to recall his time with his father, and Kas was private by nature.

My stomach buzzed with nerves as I thought about what would come next. Jake had told them we'd be alright sharing the two rooms, but would we? Surely, he wasn't expecting all three of them to pile into one bed, so who would be rooming with me? I stared at the dancing flames as I considered all the possibilities, watching as the wood crackled and embers rained down onto the grass. I hardly noticed when Anthony, and then Morgan, excused themselves, Liam following not long after.

The rest of us decided to stay out a little longer, enjoying the sweet scent of the wildflowers mixed with the smoke. It wouldn't be so easy to relax without the robust fence in the distance.

"Hot as hell," Jake muttered, the last word stretched lazily by his drawl. Considering he was standing right over the fire as he stoked it, I wasn't surprised.

"Your accent," I began haltingly.

Jake gave me a solemn, knowing smile. The spectrum of colors from the flames played off the golden highlights in his hair and made his eyes shine.

"I know you've been at the camp for years but..."

"I was born in Texas," he said. "I was five years old when my uncle and I took a trip to Delaware to visit family. My parents and brothers stayed behind because they had work and prior commitments, but I threw a fit until I got to go with him."

I almost regretted asking when I noticed the way the corner of his lips twisted bitterly. I should've known the question would bring up memories that he'd rather forget.

"You don't have to–"

"No, it's fine, honest. I told you when you first showed up at camp that you could ask me anything, didn't I?"

Beside me, Ryder took a deep swig of water, giving us the illusion of privacy.

"We drove up here. It took days, but there was nothing my uncle loved more than the open road. Once we arrived, we stayed for several weeks until reports of the virus started pouring in. Before we could even start to drive back home, Delaware implemented a travel ban. So we stayed." There was a wealth of emotion in his last words. It was starting to sound like he never got to see his family again. How much of them did he remember? Enough to miss them like I missed Ben? Or was it more the hazy grief for a person that was gone from your life before you could really know them, but you lived with the knowledge that they would've been someone important to you? Like I felt for my parents.

"We were miraculously fine for that first year. We almost never left my grandparents' house and were extremely careful. One day a neighbor had stopped over for something–I can't even recall what now–while my uncle was out grabbing supplies for the next few weeks. She must've been carrying the virus because the very next day my grandparents passed, side by side. We buried them out back. Well, he did. I watched from inside."

My heart ached for him. So much loss.

"What about your uncle?" Kas asked, proving he'd been listening diligently the entire time.

"Somehow, he never got sick. We lived in their home until the mutated strain of the virus started making the news, then we left to find a more isolated area."

"You never went back?" Ryder asked. "To Texas?"

Jake shook his head, coming over to sit next to me on the grass. He rested his arms on his bent knees, watching as the wood in the pit shifted and sent sparks flying. "We couldn't. It was pandemonium for so long, we had no choice but to wait it out. We lived here for about eleven years before he passed, courtesy of a nasty cut that got infected. I struck out on my own and happened to stumble on the camp nearby. So you see," he said, taking a deep breath in, "my uncle practically raised me, and that southern drawl stuck with me like glue. It had to've, considering it was all I heard day in and day out."

A pained look crossed his face. "Sure, I could go back to Texas if I was determined enough, but I'd have no idea where to start, and the odds... well. Best to just stay here. There's nothing left for me there."

I leaned over to brush his shoulder with mine, a small show of solidarity, and his answering smile was softer than usual, affectionate. I knew what it was like to feel unmoored, but it must have been worse for him, not knowing how his family was and then losing his only connection to them.

I took a slow inhale of the brisk night air, letting it fill my lungs. "I know the feeling."

Instantly, I felt the collective weight of their eyes. Sure, so I didn't share that much, but having so much of their attention on me? It was daunting.

"I don't suppose you'd tell us how?" Ryder asked, fingers twisting in the grass where he'd decided to rest on my other side. His eyes were fixed on mine, a brown so deep and clear that I could've gotten lost in them.

"Sure." The word left my mouth in a rush of air. "A family friend raised me. He'd come to check on us in the weeks following the outbreak and found me alone in the house. My parents were upstairs... gone." I cleared my throat, looking up from my hands, only to be snared by Kasimir's gaze. He was so solid, so dependable, and suddenly I had the strength to continue. "I was too young to understand what to do. My mom... well, she must've known. My father had died days previously, and so she prepared me as best she could while as sick as she was before heading upstairs to join him and locking the door behind her."

It stung that I had to rely on Ben's approximate idea of how it had gone down, put together from clues he'd gotten around the house instead of remembering it myself.

I'd made my peace with it all, truly, but I still felt a lingering sense of grief for that little girl, alone in the house with her dead parents upstairs for days on end.

"So he found you and took you in?" Kas asked, crossing his arms across his chest. I paused to watch the moonlight play out across his stern features.

"Yeah. He was a prepper, you see. He brought me back to his compound with him and that was that. I guess he'd originally planned to have us all stay with him where he had the means to keep us safe."

Ryder's mouth turned down, and I knew he wanted so badly to ask what had gone wrong, but his lips firmed, and he stayed quiet. I, for one, had done my requisite sharing for the day and was more than satisfied with myself.

I cleared my throat, brushing a few stray pieces of ash off my pants. Kas and Ryder gave me a break and started to debate on if the fire was low enough to leave.

My earlier anxiety returned, and I once again ran through our possible sleeping arrangements.

I hesitated at the first door as the guys crowded around, watching me with identical frowns. The hallway was dimly lit from the moonlight streaming in from the windows around the corner and the plain white candle Ryder was holding, but it was just bright enough to see their faces.

"Everything okay?" Ryder asked.

I pushed my hair back behind my ears and stood a little taller. "Who's sleeping where?"

Glances were exchanged over my head, a silent conversation I hadn't been invited to.

Jake smirked and brushed the hair that had sprung back into my face over my ear once more. "You're fine, darlin'. We've got it all figured out."

My fingers, that had been rubbing together nervously, paused at that.

He lifted a shoulder. "Everyone else gets to use your full name; I want something that's just mine. Tell me I'm the first one to use it. Tell me you like it better than something obvious like angel."

"Y-you're the first," I confirmed. "And nobody has ever called me angel?"

"I've changed my mind. You've been missing out. I plan to use them both, liberally."

A rush of warmth crept down my neck. Kas laughed under his breath at whatever look I was wearing. "Enough! Who the hell is sleeping where?"

Ryder spoke then, his voice hushed, and all traces of his previous laughter gone. "You're with me tonight."

I gulped audibly and pushed open the door on the left to cover it up. The interior of the room looked similar to the one beside it. A large bed sat in the center against a small rectangular window–the tall wooden headboard coming right up to the windowsill–and two nightstands sat on either side. A large, surprisingly uncracked mirror was secured to the wall on our left.

It was amazing how many furnished bedrooms I'd encountered lately. There was a time where I thought I'd never have a good night's sleep again. But my little cabin back at camp, as well as this bedroom here, were the very definition of luxury. I exhaled a happy little sigh as I set my things down by the door and plopped down onto the edge of the bed, appreciating the bounce. Mila darted inside and leapt onto the bed, immediately heading to one of the two pillows and curling up in the center.

"Nice, huh?" Ryder murmured as he shut the door behind him, then set his things down next to mine and joined me on the bed. He groaned as his body settled into the plush surface.

It was so familiar to me, the sound of his paced breaths, the comforting weight of his presence, and the smokey scent that clung to his skin from the fire we'd just had. I half expected his father to be in the other room, keeping everyone awake with his yelling.

"Just like old times," he said.

It was gratifying to know our brains had gone to the same place.

I let my upper body fall back onto the bed so that we were side by side, inching up so my legs weren't hanging off when he spoke. "You're different now."

Next door, I could hear Kas and Jake moving around as they got ready for bed.

"So are you."

He made an affirming noise. "I'd imagine so."

I rolled my head to face him, admiring the elegant splay of his lashes with each blink, and the sharp curve of his cheekbones. "Not in a bad way," I assured him softly. "I like it."

"You do?"

"Of course I do. You talk more, for one. You're not afraid to give your opinion, and you're not as angry anymore from holding back all the things you couldn't say to your father."

He grunted. "I was never angry."

"That's because you're thinking of anger as something hot and volatile. What you felt for him was far more insidious. Years of hate and loathing had carved you into something sharp and cold."

Ryder met my gaze. "But not now, right?"

"No. Not now." To ward off any doubt he might have harbored, I continued. "You took care of me, and when there were any threats, you took care of those too."

"You shouldn't praise me for that," he said gruffly. "A better man would've killed his father years before I did."

I frowned, turning on my side to face him fully. "You were just a child when your mother died." His face darkened at that, but I continued. "He was all you had. And he had all those men loyal to him, so when exactly were you supposed to have done something?" He opened his mouth, but I cut him off. "You acted precisely when you had the means to, and not a moment before. You timed it perfectly, and then instead of going your own way you came with us back to their camp, even though everyone wouldn't stop giving you death glares."

His lips twitched. "But not Caelan. Or River."

"A fact that drove the guys mad, I'm sure," I teased. It was no secret that they'd been distrustful of Ryder when he'd first arrived with us. River and Caelan had worked magic to get the others to let him stay, and over time, views towards him mellowed until it was only Jake who gave him shit now and then.

"You're an amazing man, Ryder Cross. I'm proud to know you. I was glad when you were with me and the others back then, and I'm glad you're with me now."

Ryder inhaled sharply, face unreadable as he stared at me. "Thank you," he rasped, a rare vulnerability stark across his features.

I smiled and reached out to finger a dark lock of hair clinging to his cheek, withdrawing my hand when my pinky grazed the skin of his neck and he sucked in a breath. His hand shot up to anchor mine, holding it in place.

My lips parted as I moved my gaze from our joined hands to his eyes, surprised at what I found there. Both his icy aloofness and fleeting vulnerability had vanished, and in their place was pure, unfiltered desire.

"Ryder," I gasped as he clutched at my hand tighter against his neck.

He growled quietly before surging forwards to seal his mouth over mine. Shock rendered me immobile until I returned it with just as much urgency, awareness rocketing through me of the rapid beat of his heart thrumming in the vein under my hand. His lips tasted of the honey he'd drizzled in his tea earlier.

A mewling sound unlike anything I'd ever made before escaped me and I spread my hand so that my thumb and index finger were resting against his jaw, holding him right where I needed him. His mouth worked tirelessly against mine, slick noises filling the room as we moved. My hips rocked forwards to seek out his touch.

A rough noise left his throat and all too sudden thoughts of if the others could hear us next door threw a blanket over my frenzied need, sending me backwards to gulp in deep breaths of air. He leaned back as well, panting heavily as he watched me with lowered eyelids; lips swollen and reddened from *me*.

His eyes tracked my every move with a predatory edge, like a hunter assessing its prey. Ryder reached a hand out, chest still heaving for breath, and swiped his thumb over my puffy bottom lip, gaze darkening as he dragged it down.

"We can't," I whispered raggedly.

If he was confused at all, it was erased when my eyes darted to the shared wall of our rooms. Instead of the anger I thought I'd find, there was a resigned understanding, and then there was nothing at all.

When he rose from the bed, brushing his hands through his dark hair and getting ready to sleep, I did the same, careful not to look his way. And when we both got under the covers, so close and yet miles away, I anticipated a night full of awkward tossing and turning and avoidant eye contact. Hence why I nearly jumped out of my skin when his large hand landed on my waist where I lay facing away from him.

"Easy," he murmured, and I let my muscles relax.

Did this mean that he understood? The nuances of why I couldn't take things further? There was nothing between Kasimir, Jake, and I, yet it still would be like a betrayal, the deep attraction I felt for the others a deceit in and of itself without a discussion first.

Spurred on by the heat of his hand through my shirt, I took a hesitant leap and wriggled backwards until our bodies were just barely touching. His presence was so large behind me: heavy breaths stirring my hair and warmth radiating through the thin covers.

He tightened his hand across my waist, using it to tug me back even further until my body was cradled by his, and the synchronized sighs we released let me know that everything wasn't as broken as I'd have liked to believe. He buried his face in my hair, letting out another slow, content sigh, and I let my eyes fall closed to the soothing, rhythmic beat of his heart at my back.

CHAPTER 11

"Morgan, could you go down to pump some water for everyone?" Ryder asked, hands occupied as he prepared oatmeal bars on the counter.

Liam was resting on the couch, and their father was either still in his bedroom or outside looking at the state of the soil with Jake, so it was much quieter than usual if you didn't count the rustling noises Ryder made as he cooked.

Morgan's mouth twitched into a slight frown at the question. Distaste crossed her elfin face as she looked over at where I was sitting at the table beside Kas as we cataloged our supplies. When she realized I was watching, she sent me a discreet sneer before turning to face Ryder.

"Oh, I'm not sure. You really think we need some already?" she questioned, idly twirling a long strand of red hair between her fingers.

Ryder didn't bother to look up. "Yes, I'm sure. You should probably refill the solar shower while you're out there."

Her stare was mutinous, and her honeyed tone did nothing to make him change his mind. "Okay, sure."

Ryder went back to his task, either unbothered by or unaware of her contempt for the job. He was no more talkative than usual, but there was a strange quality to his silence this morning. There'd been no acknowledgement of the kiss last night, and when we'd woken up wound around one another, legs tangled and my head on his broad chest, he'd just traced light circles onto my back until I was ready to get up.

It would be easier to pretend the kiss hadn't happened, but that would be a disservice to us both.

Kas noticed her thinly veiled attitude, though. And as Morgan was preparing to leave, he started to speak. I could tell from the unhappy set of his mouth that it wasn't going to be anything good, so I cut him off with a sharp elbow to the gut.

"Good lord," he wheezed, elbows down on the table and head hanging between them as he tried to catch his breath. "What the hell?"

"You can't make an enemy out of her," I whispered. "She'll refuse to help, put the load back on Liam, and worst case, she'll pitch a fit until we're forced to go. I just want to help them, then get the hell out of here."

He sighed, leaning back in the stiff folding chair and rubbing his temples. "Fine."

I popped a peppermint into my mouth, lamenting that my stash now had one less than before. Jake had caved and given me the rest he'd collected instead of doling them out one by one, so at least I had control over when I ate them. Being able to see exactly how many I had made it easier to actually consume them instead of hoarding them until the end of time. Running my tongue over the grooves in the candy as it dissolved, the cool sensation in the back of my throat went a long way towards soothing my nerves.

After Morgan left, the morning flew by quickly. We'd finished break-fast and were discussing the next steps with Liam, and then Morgan when she returned, when Jake came back in and informed everyone that he, Ryder, and Kas would be heading down to the creek to try to catch some fish and set some traps.

"All three of you?" Morgan asked, resting her chin in her hand. "You don't need a fourth?"

I choked, sending the water that I'd been sipping down into my lungs. Liam grimaced, smacking my back until I gasped and told him to cut it out.

"No, we're good," Jake responded, avoiding my gaze. He was acting strangely this morning; finding reasons not to be around, making plans to leave for the day, and not even asking if I wanted to go. I knew it was smart for him to bring Ryder and Kas, but was he excluding me on purpose?

"I guess I could shower," I said slowly. "I'll refill it once I'm done so you can bathe too when you get back. The sun is out, so it won't take very long for the water to warm up."

"Could just bathe down by the creek," Kas added in his deep, rumbling voice, running a hand over his recently trimmed stubble. He was quiet on a good day, but now it was as if he were made of stone. In fact, that was the first time he'd spoken all morning, aside from the incident with Morgan earlier.

My chest tightened as I wondered if they knew what happened with Ryder. Probably not, but would they even care? Maybe it was all in my head, and I'd assigned them emotions they didn't really feel. That had to be it. I was imagining things, fantasizing that I meant more than I really did.

"We'll figure it out once we're there," Jake decided.

I felt a distinct pang of loneliness even though I was surrounded by people. The only person who'd really acknowledged my presence was Liam, and since he was sitting right beside me, it would've been hard not to.

The guys were quick to leave, gathering their supplies and weapons and heading out within the hour, leaving Morgan, Liam, and me in an uncomfortable, awkward silence. I hadn't seen Anthony yet and hadn't bothered to ask where he was.

Cracks had formed in their family, and soon the house would become a burden rather than a boon if they couldn't keep themselves nourished inside it. Liam was already looking less like death warmed over after several consistent meals and some good rest. The sickly pallor to his skin had practically disappeared, and I'd hate to see it return.

"I'm going foraging." I decided, thinking it a good use of my time. The shower could wait until after. Anything to improve our stores and give their family some much needed food security. I'd already made up my mind to convince the guys to give the family the details of the camp and let them decide on their own whether to head there, but in the meantime, it would be prudent to gather as much as possible for them before we moved on. I could make decisions on my own; there was no law that I couldn't arrange my own task for the day.

"I'm going with," Liam insisted.

I glanced at Morgan to see if she had any objection.

"Don't look at me," she said, examining her nails. "I'm not going out there beyond the fence in the blazing sun with my injured brother and *you* to pick fungus just because you're restless."

Shoving down a flippant response took a moment. It wasn't like I wanted her to go with us, she'd be more of a risk than anything else should something happen, but it would've been nice if she showed a little more concern towards her brother and making sure her family didn't starve. Or maybe it was just that I lacked a deep as hell voice and a six-pack in the convincing department.

Knowing it would be futile, I still tried to convince Liam to stay behind. "Don't you want to rest and recover some more? You could worsen your injury. I won't stray too far from the fence, and I'll have my machete."

He shook his head, mouth set firmly.

"Fine," I sighed.

In no time at all, I stood outside, supplies in the bag around my waist and my machete on my hip, with Liam behind me carrying his walking stick and bat. I stopped once we reached the towering gate, re-thinking my plan to leave, but a deep breath and some optimistic affirmations had me undoing all the locks.

I'm capable. I'm capable as fuck. If the guys can go off and fish or whatever, I can forage, and I'm not even going on my own. I'm an adult who has the power to make on their own. Sufficiently encouraged, I kept going, locking everything up behind us.

We walked for a long while in silence, admiring the warbling sounds of different birds and the fresh scents of the newly sprouting leaves on the trees surrounding us. Small creatures darted through the undergrowth, occasionally crossing our path.

So often I found myself frightened and scared, worried about the future, the present, and the people I cared about. But now, even though we were outside the safety of their fencing, my worries lessened some. The still ambiance of the woods, punctuated by intermittent rustles and chirps, evidence of the vibrant wildlife hidden amidst the foliage, was oddly reassuring. That didn't mean I wasn't still on guard. Several times a close noise had me pausing, hand on my machete as I listened over the frantic rush of blood to my head for whatever had made it, but it was always revealed to be something benign.

"Sera," Liam called from somewhere behind me. I stopped to find him standing beside a tree, leaning heavily on the trunk. We'd been walking for about a couple hours, which was probably far enough for now, so either he was ready to head back, or he'd found something.

"Yeah?"

Once I got close enough, I realized why he'd stopped. Beside him sat a bush adorned with clusters of strawberries, still in the early stages of ripening. Pride and excitement at his find lit up his face.

I approached the strawberry bush, captivated by the delicate, light green berries nestled amongst the leaves. I hoped they would burst on my tongue just like a ripened berry would. It had been far too long since they were in season last.

Letting my fingers drift over the few closest to me, I plucked a smaller one and took a bite, grimacing at the bitter flavor.

Liam laughed, tasting his own. "Edible though."

We plucked the strawberries one by one with care, placing them gently into the canvas bag we'd brought. The soft whispers of the leaves while we worked were soothing, and I was careful not to let them lull me into complacency. By the time we'd grabbed most of the berries, the sun was lower in the sky, still doing its best to combat the cool breeze. The bag was a satisfying weight in my hand.

"You don't think we should've waited for them to ripen?" he asked.

I didn't feel like I should tell him about his pending invitation back to camp without speaking to the others first, so there was no way to let him know that he might not be here long enough for them to ripen at all. Instead, I just landed on, "With the extra mouths to feed this week, I don't think we can afford to wait. If there's one bush, then there must be more nearby that you can pick from once we're gone and they have time to mature."

I fastened the top of the sack and hooked it to the belt around my waist so that both my hands would be free for the walk home. Just because we hadn't encountered anything on the way here didn't mean we would be so lucky on our way back.

"I'm glad you came," I told Liam as we retraced our steps.

"I am too. It didn't feel right to let you go by yourself and I couldn't stay in that house for one more minute, especially with just Morgan to keep me company."

Enough hair had slipped from my bun that I stopped to gather the errant strands and tie them back once more, grateful for the brisk air on my face now that my hair was out of the way. I didn't envy when it came time to brush it. It had been tied back for so long that I knew for sure that it had matted underneath.

After about thirty minutes, I checked on Liam to make sure he was doing alright, and was pleased to see that he was fine. Lucky for us, the foliage overhead was thick enough in most places to prevent us from getting sunburned, and a glance at my wrist revealed my olive skin to be only slightly pinkened, a perk I liked to attribute to my mother's Grecian heritage.

"I'm surprised that was your first time getting so injured," I told him honestly, sucking in a sharp breath as I hopped on top of a particularly large fallen tree trunk and almost lost my balance.

"Oh, it's not."

"What do you mean?"

"I've been hurt before. Had some close calls. I was always too far to make it back that same day, so I just holed up somewhere with whatever I'd scavenged and waited until I healed enough to make the trip home."

There were no words. How long had he been going through this cycle of injuries, close calls, and empty-handed trips, and how hadn't he lost hope yet? I couldn't let him continue on like that. "I'm sorry."

His mouth tightened. "It's my job. My responsibility."

"I don't understand. Why you?"

He shrugged, hand absently brushing against where I'd first seen a hint of a deep scar before pointing towards the uniquely shaped tree in the distance. "We passed that tree a while back, right?"

"Yeah, not too long now. You should spend the rest of the day resting your ankle if you want it to get better."

When he huffed, not dignifying me with a response, I wasn't surprised. It had to get old fast to have people telling you to take it easy every minute.

The acidic taste of the berry lingered on my tongue, and I wondered what we could make with them. I was sure Kas would know. He seemed to have an encyclopedic knowledge of plants.

The rest of our walk went quickly, although we stopped several more times, once to pick some vibrant yellow dandelions, and the others to pick some ramps. Hopefully, we could make some dandelion tea. I'd had it several times with Ben and had always admired its earthy taste along with the tang of the lemon we'd added. If I knew Jake, we'd be having sauteed dandelion greens and ramps tonight, similar to last night's meal, but with enough variety to keep us from getting bored.

"Finally," Liam gasped upon seeing the fence in the distance, and I had a flash of guilt that he might have worsened his injury. I lost my balance on a half-buried tree root, snickering as I caught myself on Liam's outstretched arm.

The loud, sharp sound of my name cut through the breeze, and I jerked my head up to find Kas storming towards us with purpose, eyes locked onto where I was grasping Liam. As I watched him from afar–fury emanating from his colossal form in waves–my heart sank. Black hair cascaded down to broad shoulders, framing a face that wore his displeasure like a mask, and heavy brows knitted together in a dark expression.

CHAPTER 12

At first glance, his eyes appeared to be their usual shade of light gray, like polished steel. But the closer he drew, the more their color darkened to a stormy, almost gunmetal hue; glimmering with hostility. He was mad that I'd left, but why?

My breath hitched, body tensing involuntarily as I braced myself for a confrontation. A lump formed in my throat, holding my words captive. Liam waited diligently beside me, more out of support than necessity.

Maybe because he didn't see what I did. That Kas would never ever hurt me, no matter how upset he seemed.

Tension crackled between us when Kasimir finally reached me.

His deep voice cut through the silence. "Where the hell have you been?"

I raised a haughty brow. "I *know* Morgan must've told you where we went whenever you got back."

"That's not what I meant, and you know it," he seethed. "How could you do something so reckless? What if something had happened?"

It wasn't like I was completely ignorant to his point. I was just too frustrated to acknowledge it right then. "We're here, aren't we?"

"You know better than to go off on your own! You left without any consideration for the risks you were taking. We would've had no idea if something happened to you."

"I wasn't on my own, I had Liam," I refuted, gesturing at the man standing a little further back.

Kas scoffed. "Like he could do anything to protect you. He's been sheltered his entire life."

Liam flinched, taking a small step back.

"You're an asshole," I hissed, punctuating my words with a finger to his chest. "I don't care if you're fucking upset if it means you treat the people around you like shit. I don't have to listen to this."

A look of what could've been chagrin crossed his face. "Seraphim..."

I shook my head in disgust, leaving both Kasimir and Liam behind as I stomped through the brush, past the open gate, and across the large field to the house. When I walked through the front door, Ryder just looked at me silently where he was seated at the kitchen table with what they'd caught earlier. I ignored Jake when he opened his mouth to most likely add to whatever nonsense Kasimir had been on about.

Did everyone share the same opinion? Overprotective, suffocating bastards. All of them.

Whatever Morgan said with that insufferable tone where she sat on the couch, followed by a shrill laugh, I missed it. Too preoccupied with getting to the bedroom before I did something I couldn't take back, like burst into angry tears.

Sitting on the edge of the bed I had shared last night with Ryder and feeling like a disciplined child, I stared at the closed door before me. Half of my mind was working furiously, telling me that I'd made a scene, and who would want to travel with me after I'd locked myself in my room and refused to talk?

The other half was incensed by the injustice of it all. Why was it that they could leave no problem and when I did, it was an issue? I hadn't even been alone. I knew where Kas was coming from. It was dangerous out there, and sticking together was important. But his disappointment hit upon the sensitive part of me that I liked to pretend wasn't as close to the surface as it was. The one that told me I was masquerading as someone who knew what they were doing and would end up getting someone killed for it.

I sat there long enough for my temper to fade some as I realized just how filthy I was. My last bath had been a couple of days ago, and my skin was crying out for soap. I decided to tackle my hair first, because there was no way I would try to brush it once it was wet, and I knew detangling it would take a while.

Just taking it out of the hair tie was painful. Days without brushing, washing it with lake water and bar soap, and using an old sweatshirt as a pillow, had led to matted sections all around the back of my neck and my crown. It wasn't new to me, but each and every time it tested my patience like nothing else.

I started at the ends, using short, quick motions to drag the brush through my hair. The metallic red finish was so worn that the brush was a faded silver color, winking in the afternoon light that shone through the window. It felt like hours that I worked in methodical movements, biting my lip whenever I hit a snag and manually pulling the knots apart in the worse sections.

My arms ached, and I'd only finished the left and right sides. The rest was the worst, sitting in one large chunk. After working on just one knot for ages, I reached my limit and yanked the brush through the knots, tears flooding my eyes at the pain.

"This fucking sucks," I muttered, yanking harder. The door creaked open behind me, but I ignored it.

"Hey," Kas said, laying a firm hand over mine and stopping my progress.

"What?" I snapped, in no mood for whatever the hell this was. If my hair would just cooperate...

"Be kinder to yourself," he murmured. A weight dropped onto the bed behind me as, without a word, he took the brush from my hand, fingers tangling with mine. When a surge of energy passed between us, I jerked my hand back.

A muttered curse rang out behind me as he started working. He had an actual technique, separating small sections to hold in his fist and starting at the very bottom before working his way up. Similar to mine, but less stress on my arms since I wasn't contorting to reach each spot. It was still painful, but my arms were no longer screaming at me, and I was no longer about to snap.

I remained still, unsure of how to respond to this... whatever it was. His touch was unexpectedly gentle, fingers skillfully working through the knots with a tenderness that surprised me.

"My mother," Kas said without prompting. "Her hair was always getting tangled, and on worse days, the entire thing was one big knot. She struggled a lot with her hair, but my father loved it and so she'd refused to cut it short."

The tension slowly leeched from my muscles as I relaxed into his touch, the honesty easing my nerves.

"That was kind of you."

From the rustle of his clothing, I assumed he'd shrugged.

"You miss her?"

His answer was immediate. "Of course. I miss my family every day."

I glanced up, meeting his gaze in the reflection of the mirror to our left. Eyes that had been hard and closed-off now held a glimmer of remorse, a silent apology that tugged at my wounded pride.

My eyes slid closed, squeezing tighter at every painful tug. Frustration mingled with vulnerability as the strokes of the brush became a rhythm, and I allowed myself to surrender to his ministrations, the anger and hurt beginning to dissipate.

It occurred to me just how much progress he'd made when the brush glided through my hair rather than snagging. A soft sigh escaped my lips as the brush coasted through the strands, the rest of my apprehension unraveling with each stroke.

The air around us grew thick as Kas leaned closer. "All finished."

The thud of the brush hitting the bedspread was loud, and my shudder was telling.

With a soft touch, he brushed his fingers underneath the waterfall of hair, fingers trailing along my neck. It was made even more electrifying by the fact that I couldn't see his face. I hoped he couldn't hear my heart beating rapidly in response, but when his other hand drifted to my shoulder to push my hair back and trace over the quick beat in my throat, I knew it was obvious.

"So delicate, Seraphim," he murmured.

My voice was just a whisper. "Kas."

"Wait. Just let me... I didn't mean to upset you earlier," he said, the spell broken.

Bracing for another argument, my earlier irritation returned with none of my doubt. I crossed my arms, rising from the bed and spinning around to face him, my now untangled hair swinging with the movement. "I just don't understand why I should be the one held back? You go off on your own all the time, facing danger without a second thought. Why should I be treated any differently?"

His jaw clenched, teeth grinding audibly. "It's not about treating you differently," he retorted, voice tinged with a hint of exasperation. "I worry because I care about you. I don't want to see you hurt."

A surge of defiance rose within me, my voice sharp as I responded, "I can handle myself. I've faced danger before, and I've come out stronger. Why should I suddenly be restricted just because you can't handle the thought of me taking risks?"

It felt wrong to argue *against* being taken care of. To reject someone just wanting to keep me safe. But that was the whole point of this journey, wasn't it? To prove to myself that I had what it took. That I would be okay when the next instance of my shitty, godforsaken luck hit, and I was alone again.

"It's not about restricting you! It's about looking out for each other. I don't want to lose you. I can't bear the thought of something happening to you because I wasn't there to protect you. It only takes a second to lose someone, and I can't bear that weight again." His eyes flashed, and I realized that underneath that bluster was a fear so deep it rivaled my own.

"I need to feel like I have some control over my own choices. I need to prove to myself that I can handle the challenges that come my way, and I can't do that if you treat me like I'm not capable."

His hand reached out to cup my face gently, his touch both firm and tender. "I can't help worrying about you, Seraphim, any more than I can help missing my family. But I'll try to work with you instead of against you."

I wanted to fight, wanted to huff and shout and push him to the edge, and why was I feeling like this? He was so authoritative when he argued, all that rugged but refined appeal turning into something heated from his conviction, his eyes giving me every ounce of his attention and scrambling my brain so that it was hard to focus. He was saying all the right things, but why wasn't I satisfied?

"Stop being so nice to me, damn it!"

"You want me to be mean?" he growled, the hand on my face slipping down to grip my chin and hold me steady.

"Yes," I replied breathlessly.

His heated gaze dropped to my lips, and in the span of a single breath, our mouths met in an explosion of pure frenzied need. It wasn't gentle, and our teeth clashed as we fought to get closer, all desire and no skill.

In an instant, I knew I hadn't imagined the sparks between us. My frustration over our earlier fight vanished, and now I just wanted to explore him, to...

I reared back, pulling out of his grip easily as I'd known he would let me. I couldn't stop replaying what I'd done in this very same room the previous night. How could I put words to my fears? I didn't even know how to explain them to myself.

Kas shook his head. "This is a bad idea."

A mixture of confused relief intertwined with disappointment. "Sure," I muttered, ducking down to grab my clean clothes and avoiding eye contact. My frizzy curls clung to my shoulders, and I admired their loose softness compared to the tangled mess of earlier, even if it came with the memory of his touch.

A short, unhappy laugh left him. "I don't mean—it's not—"

I cut him off, flinging the door open. "Bye, Kasimir."

Two things vied for my attention and tore me away from my relaxation. The fact that my hair was still damp and sticking to my skin even though I'd used the solar shower hours prior, and the endless bickering in front of me.

Jake and Ryder were in fine form tonight, standing before the fire and arguing like they hadn't just spent days traveling side by side. The animosity from this morning had carried over to the evening with a vengeance, and they weren't content to trade muttered insults any longer.

The overpowering scent of smoke mixed with the aroma of honeysuckle to create a dizzyingly sweet mixture. It was hard to appreciate over the harsh sounds of their disagreement, as was the dreamy reddish-pink hue of the sunset.

"That's not how you fucking do it," Jake snarled, grabbing the stick from Ryder and pointing animatedly at the pot suspended over the fire.

I wasn't even sure what the problem was. Had he hung it too low or something? Built the fire too high?

Ryder snatched the stick back and gritted his teeth. His equally wet hair clung to the nape of his neck and dripped beads of water down the front of his light shirt. At least his was justified, because he'd showered last.

"It looks fine. You're just being a bastard for no reason."

Jake shot him a dirty look. "I've been doin' this shit since I was knee high to a grasshopper, pretty boy. I think I know how it's supposed to look."

"Fine. Do whatever you want. Just don't think it'll get you anywhere with Sera."

"I don't work on a fucking merit system," I interjected sharply.

Ryder's mouth thinned, and he turned just before I could make out whatever the hell he was mouthing to Jake.

"For fuck's sake," I hissed. "Enough. Enjoy your time spreading your feathers or whatever the hell that book said peacocks do to show off."

Kas sighed, muttering something under his breath from where he sat beside me. I was glad the others were still inside because this was an awful example of a cohesive group.

"You'd know about bastards, wouldn't you? With a father like that. I'm surprised Sera even lets you around her with all the shit you put her through."

My back snapped straight. Just what the hell was Jake trying to say? It wasn't like him to be intentionally malicious.

"Shit I put her through? At least I killed the asshole. *You're* the one who made her feel worthless when we left."

Jake huffed. "Yeah, only after letting her suffer there for months while your dad terrorized people."

His expression was twisted into something hateful. The darkening sky didn't help, further emphasizing the starkness of his features and the shadows under his clenched jaw.

Ryder flung the stick to the ground and rounded on him. It was rare that he ever lost the measured control he wore like a shroud. I'd only seen it several times before.

"What the hell was I supposed to do, Jake? Tell him to fuck off and end up dead and unable to protect her? Being his blood didn't offer me the immunity you seem to think it did. It was torture, and I wouldn't wish it on anyone. Constantly walking the line between keeping her safe, opposing him where I could, and appeasing that bastard, and *fuck you* for acting like if only I'd cared for her more, I would have acted differently. It was *because* I l–cared for her that I didn't dare rock the boat. What could I have offered her out on our own? Sleeping in shifts? Starving to death while we tried to stay alive? And as though she would leave her friends." He shook his head, jaw working but saying nothing else as emotion held his voice hostage. Raw hurt overtook his normally impassive expression before he hid it away, like always.

The others didn't understand. He held himself apart from everyone else, and it made them think he lacked the desire to be involved, as if he were too cold to scrounge up interest. But I knew.

I knew that sometimes he was so choked by his anger, his resentment and pain, that he left us alone so that he didn't drown us with them like he did himself. He was suffocating, trying to keep them all inside, so easily bruised by other's perceptions of himself that he didn't even try to dissuade them. In fact, he agreed. He viewed their disdain as his punishment, a deserved sentence.

Jake was shocked into silence by Ryder's outburst, whereas Kas's icy visage hadn't cracked. Based on what he'd let slip before, he probably struggled with the same demons. I didn't know exactly what had happened in his past yet, but I knew it was bad.

"I'm sorry," Jake finally said. "I shouldn't've presumed to know why you did what you did, or how difficult it must've been for you."

Ryder bobbed his head, but he was already locking his emotions away one by one, his expression growing increasingly blank.

I couldn't have that.

"Don't do that," I whispered, wandering over to clasp his hand in mine. "You have to stop with this guilt. You are not your father, and I was never waiting for you to ride in on your white horse and carry me off to your castle."

He flinched at that, and my eyes flooded with tears against my permission.

"Hell, you were everything to me when I needed someone to show me how to be strong. I didn't need a knight, Ryder, I needed a villain to keep me safe until I could do it myself, who had no qualms doing whatever it took and could look past all my less than stellar qualities. I never once confused you for your father just because of your proximity to him, or blamed you for all the reckless plans he made or the hurt he caused. If that was the case, we'd all be at fault. Everyone knew he was up to shady shit."

Jake grumbled something about poor qualities, and Ryder's lips quirked briefly upwards.

I chanced a look up to meet his dark gaze, getting lost in it. "You were exactly what I needed, exactly when I needed it, and I'm eternally grateful to have met you. That's never going to change."

Ryder was slow to nod, and I crossed my fingers that the new lightness in his expression would stay, and meant that he'd really, truly heard me this time. He leaned down to press a soft kiss to my forehead, uncaring of who watched. Kas's face held thoughtfulness, but no confusion or anger, while Jake's groan was loud and obnoxious. "You sure about that knight part? For fuck's sake, I've never met a more covert Casanova."

"Big words for the country boy," remarked Kas with a smirk.

I laughed wetly, appreciating their attempt to break the tension, pleased when I caught the conciliatory look Jake shot Ryder over my shoulder. It wouldn't solve everything, but I hoped it would put an end to the snarky comments. Ryder knew Jake would have his back if something happened, he had to, but he shouldn't have to live with someone who looked at him and saw the ghost of someone else when that couldn't be further from the truth.

Kas nudged my knee when I sat back down beside him, and I sent a small smile his way.

Dinner cooked in no time once the sun finished descending beyond the trees, leaving behind a glittering indigo tapestry. I laid back in the grass, resting my hands over my full stomach and staring up at the many stars. The fire had faded to a dull glow, sending sparks and embers into the sky to dance with the stars above me, and the odd piece of ash hit my legs now and then.

"Stunning, huh?" Liam asked from where he lay a couple feet below me.

"Ben told me that the stars never used to be this bright before the outbreak because of all the light pollution," I replied.

The grass rustled as Jake got comfier, bringing his arms up to rest behind his head. "My uncle told me the same."

A twinkle caught my eye, and I turned just in time to see the flash of light moving across the night sky. Immediately, I squeezed my eyes shut and made a wish, just as Jamie taught me the first time we'd star-gazed. My brain ran in so many directions it was hard to land on just one. I wished that Casey was happy wherever he was. I wished we'd get to the farm safe and sound and that Liam would recover well and we'd see him again back at camp. I wished that the men beside me—

"A shooting star," Ryder murmured, his large hand stroking Mila's fur where she was curled up at his side.

If the moment had me overly sentimental and I reached out to clasp Jake's hand in mine, no one said a word. He squeezed it back tightly, tracing patterns over the skin on the back of my hand as we watched the stars, content to be still for once.

CHAPTER 13

S omeone was outside our room.

I jackknifed up in bed, unsure if I was grateful or nervous that Kas hadn't heard the floor creak. He needed his rest, but fuck, my heart was racing. Ryder was in the living room, keeping watch. Maybe it was him going to bed?

It took me a second to realize that Kas's heavy arm was slung across my waist, locking me into place. It had been hard to fall asleep with him just inches away, sharing the same blankets and breathing the same air. We'd drifted off facing separate directions, but it seemed that his reservations had faded away in sleep, evidenced by the calloused hand cupping my hip, heavy across my lap.

The floor creaked once more, and I carefully pushed his arm from me inch by inch, as silently as possible, then slid to my feet.

A soft knocking reverberated against the wood of the door adjacent to ours and I stopped moving, body frozen at the end of the bed and heart beating so loudly that it almost–but not quite–covered the low *snick* of the door opening and the quiet exchange of voices. I relaxed and, certain it was Ryder, decided to go out to see him, if only just to laugh about the scare I'd gotten.

Only when I cracked the door open and cautiously stepped out, it wasn't Ryder standing before me, but Morgan, wearing a dark nightgown that clung to her curves. It wasn't like she'd run into him on her way to bed; her room was on the whole other fucking side of the compound.

Shock held me immobile, so it made sense that it took me several beats to notice her hand clutching Jake's sleeve, her body angled towards his. He looked past her to stare at me, eyes hooded with sleep. He was shirtless–I could see every defined angle of his golden abdomen from the moonlight around the corner–and loose pants sat low on his hips.

Had he been about to invite her in? Was her seduction working? It had to be, because he was just *standing* there. They'd gone off alone the other day, hadn't they? Maybe they'd forged some sort of connection. What if he'd asked her to come to his room to take advantage of Ryder's absence?

I folded my arms across my stomach, blinking as a miniscule smirk formed across her lips. *Fuck.* I staggered back down the long hall, overlooking the open door to our room.

Someone whispered my name loudly, but I ignored it. My sleep pants dragged across the floor as I walked, bare feet padding softly. Clean hair infused with the scent of smoke brushed my bare shoulders and caught on the straps of my camisole. I entered the living room, sparing a glance for Ryder, who watched me curiously from the couch before exiting the house altogether.

The night air was balmy, and the sky was clear. Moonlight illuminated the front of the home, making the figure standing by the tree in the distance easy to see.

I wasn't so distracted as to walk right towards a possible threat, but when the figure turned upon hearing the front door shut, and I saw the long length of their cane beside their leg, I realized it was fine. I headed in Liam's direction, wiggling my toes with each step in the tall, crunchy grass and hoping I didn't step on a bug or a rock.

He sat when I reached him, patting the ground next to him. Neither of us spoke, instead content to rest our backs against the wide base of the tree and admire the sound of the wind rustling the leaves above us and the bright surface of the moon as it periodically dipped behind clouds.

"What has you out here this late?" he finally asked, minutes or hours later. The silvery light turned his brown hair a cool shade.

My head scraped against the rough bark of the tree as I tilted it back, taking a deep breath in. "There's a girl back at our camp that has four lovers, y'know."

"Four?"

"Yeah. Four."

"I've never heard of such a thing."

"Neither had I... but I've seen them. Affectionate and playful and supportive. No jealousy." On second thought... "At least between them," I added, amending my statement.

He snorted. "You propositioning me?"

"No!" I exclaimed, lowering my voice some. "No, I was just thinking. Anyway, it doesn't matter. Just another example of things I can't have with the people I can't have them with."

Liam smirked. "I'll try not to take offense."

"You ass." I swatted his arm, laughing at his grunt. "I think... Jake is interested in Morgan."

He stared at me, and I had a hunch my lopsided smile wasn't very convincing.

"If you truly think that, I have to wonder how you've survived this long. Clearly, your powers of observation could use some work."

"Ha. Yeah right, I saw it with my own two eyes. Besides–"

"Besides," he said softly. "New territory is scary. The unknown is terrifying, and you've been dropped right at the goddamn center of the maze. I have no doubt you'll untangle everything in that mind of yours and when you do, you'll go great lengths to make it a reality. Until then, I'll be here supporting you along the way."

Tears pricked my eyes at his genuine kindness. I dropped my hand onto his knee, struggling to find the words to thank him, when a frustrated voice rang out behind us.

"What the hell, Sera?"

I swung my head around, scanning the shadows until they landed on Jake's hulking form several feet away as he stalked forward. "Go away," I grumbled, turning back and removing my hand from Liam.

That only served to draw his attention to it, if his bitter huff was any indication. Eyes like burning coals snapped down to the hand now resting at my side, and narrowed. "It's too fucking late for you to be out here, let alone with a stranger."

"Liam isn't a stranger," I argued.

"The hell he's not," he snapped, crossing his arms over his broad chest as he glowered.

Anger flickered to life in the pit of my stomach, a dizzying swirl of frustration and hurt. "Fuck you."

"You need to be inside," he ground out.

"What, with you and Morgan?"

His mouth tightened, and I could hear his teeth grinding from where I sat.

"Whatever," I muttered, standing up to brush off my sleep pants.

I offered a hand to Liam, who shook his head. "I'll be fine out here a bit longer."

Whatever Jake muttered under his breath sounded a lot like it ended in zombies, but I wasn't going to start another argument over it.

He followed behind me, matching my every step, and when I stumbled after stepping on a large rock hidden in the shin-length grass, he commented something about bare feet before swinging me up into his arms without a sound.

I was not as composed. A squeak left my throat, and I struggled until a low growl left his throat and his hand landed on the small of my back where my shirt had ridden up. I was suddenly painfully aware of the scent of juniper on his clothes, hair, and skin, of every single flex and ripple of his arms where they supported me. I gave another half-hearted wiggle to test his hold and wasn't surprised when his grip tightened even further. His gaze snared mine, unflinching in the face of my frustration.

Step by step we closed the distance to the front door, and once we were at the threshold, I was sure he'd let me down, but he continued to carry me inside despite my protests. Ryder watched us vigilantly, but whatever expression Jake made over my shoulder had him staying still, gaze following us with a dark curiosity.

Already at the end of the hall next to the doors to our rooms, I wriggled again with renewed purpose. "I won't," I warned him, voice a low whisper. "Don't you fucking dare put me in there with her."

A noise of disgust was all that met my ears, and then we were entering the small room on the right. As my eyes adjusted to the darkness, aided by the moonlight broken up by the bars streaming in from the small window high up above the bed, I realized it was completely empty aside from the swirling dust motes disturbed from our entrance.

He set me down gently, almost reverently, and I took a big step back once my feet were safely on the ground.

"Sure you don't need me to give you some space?"

"What the hell are you talking about?"

"You know what I mean," I spat. "Morgan. Won't I just be in the way if I stay here?"

His laugh was wicked, and a little cruel. He advanced on me with slow, deliberate steps. An aura of danger ghosted across my skin, sparking hypersensitive nerve endings. It almost seemed as if his eyes were glowing, lit within by some possessed need.

Not once did I fear for my safety.

I had no earthly reason to be so upset. We both knew it, just like we both knew he'd turned her away. She wasn't here, that much was obvious. And yet just recalling her delicate hand on his arm had me seeing red. Fresh jealousy swamped me once more. "Fuck you."

I tried to brush past him in my attempt to exit the room, and got nowhere as far as I wanted to before his grip on my shoulder stopped me.

"You're mistaken," he informed me. "Nothing happened. She knocked on the door, started to spout some shit, and then you walked out. And even if you hadn't, I still would've sent her on her way." That was accompanied by a pointed look. "If you'd've just waited..."

"I waited plenty long enough," I scoffed, the profound relief flooding my system as foreign to me as the burning envy from before.

"Yeah, well, what about Liam? Gonna take him up on his offer?"

"What fucking offer?"

We were panting now. One of his hands slipped from my shoulder to my upper arm and something dark flickered in his gaze as he dropped his eyes to my mouth, scraping his teeth against his bottom lip. "I know what I saw."

"As if," I hissed, yanking my arm away. "You saw nothing. A moment of gratitude for a friend."

"Is that so?"

I wasn't sure when we'd gotten so close, but it took seconds to realize that my chest brushed against his with every incensed breath. I rocked forward as if in a trance, and he groaned, meeting me halfway and sealing his mouth over mine. An arm immediately came up to encircle my back, grasping the bare skin of my hip and tugging me into him, and my mouth parted on a gasp.

It was the culmination of months of longing.

His moan was filthy, and it pushed my desire to new heights. Desperate, I clutched at his bare shoulders and gratefully ground down against the leg he pushed between mine. The pressure was divine, and the soft whimper I let out had him doubling down, stroking his tongue into my mouth to tangle with mine.

Grabbing his hair in my fists, I moved my hips back and forth, breaking away from our kiss to pant. I didn't get very far before his hand landed on the back of my neck, pressing our foreheads together. A good thing too, because without him anchoring me, the sensations would've sent me to the floor. The rough fabric of his pants should have felt abrasive, but it was just textured enough to provide the friction I needed.

Only, once my thoughts intruded, I found myself slowing.

"Why don't I take a guess as to why you're suddenly so quiet, hm?" Jake asked darkly, leaning back just enough to watch my face as he waited for confirmation. I suddenly felt small and nervous; angry butterflies darting around in my stomach.

"None of that," he muttered, reaching forward to grasp my hand in his. It was bewildering to be perceived, to have him actually pick up on my anxiousness and attempt to address it.

Time would tell if he actually knew what I was thinking.

It was hard, but I anchored myself in his gaze, not shying away from his knowing glint.

"You kissed Ryder last night," he said matter-of-factly, oblivious to the fact that I thought my face was going to catch fire. At my incredulous look, he expounded. "The walls are paper thin, darlin'."

Holy hell, was that why they'd been acting so differently today? The reason for all the awkward silences and indecipherable looks? It was hard for me to believe that was the case, but I couldn't think of anything else that had changed overnight.

"Are you mad?" I asked in a small voice. We were nothing, and yet...

"No. I'm not mad. You're a grown woman, with the freedom to make your own choices, whatever those may be. Was that the first time?"

I nodded, gathering the courage to meet his eyes, and found none of the judgment I was expecting. I couldn't believe we were talking about this–*like* this–so openly. Hadn't thought him capable of it. It seemed his gruff exterior held a wealth of hidden vulnerability.

"I'm not mad," he repeated, "but that is not the deterrent you seem to think it is."

With that, he leaned down, giving me ample time to move away, and recaptured my lips. When I didn't pull away, instead making a surprised noise and grasping onto his arm, he deepened it. I wasn't foolish enough to believe he wanted me more than just this brief moment, but it was amazing all the same.

Jake kissed like the rest of the world ceased to exist, lips moving over mine with a singularly focused passion, devouring my mouth and returning my affections hungrily. It was everything I'd ever dreamed it would be in the dark hours of the morning when I was free to explore all the things I tried to avoid during the waking hours.

I pulled away, leaning my forehead against his as I tried to catch my breath, and he dove back in almost immediately, his motions abrupt and if I didn't know him better, furious.

Taking advantage of our position, I used this new familiarity with him to run my hands down the wide breadth of his shoulders, moving onto his biceps with wonder when I realized my hands couldn't fully wrap around them, and letting them drift to his strong, broad chest to caress the muscles there, teasing a nipple into a fine point and moaning when he grunted.

Then the door cracked open, and time froze.

CHAPTER 14

The door had just started to swing shut when Jake spoke, his voice an authoritative rasp. "No. Come in."

Ryder and I both looked at him with a healthy dose of skepticism.

"See, I think," he drawled, "that she wants us both."

Apprehension shot through me so fast it sent my head spinning. Would Ryder walk out? Did the concept of sharing disgust him? Maybe it should've disgusted *me*, but all I felt was an unexpected thrill at having something I wanted so badly within reach.

It was just like Jake to take control of the situation and throw us into a new dynamic. He was braver than I could ever be.

Ryder's head tilted, a predatory glint flashing in his gaze. He took measured steps into the room, closing the door behind him.

His eyes were glittery in the moonlight, jaw sharp enough to carve through stone. It was obvious what he'd walked in on. If he hadn't heard us through the door, or noticed my disheveled shirt or flushed cheeks, it was clear by our compromising position what we were doing. And yet he didn't leave. Instead, he waited for Jake's cue, stalking forward at the permissive nod of his head.

My heart raced, adrenaline making my blood pound.

"Is that true, Seraphim?" Ryder's low voice raised the hairs on the back of my neck, and Jake's lips twisted into a smug, satisfied smirk.

I parted my lips, but only a heavy breath escaped.

"So eager to repeat the other night?"

I'd never seen Ryder look so singularly focused on anything, let alone *me*.

Both sets of eyes glimmered with a greedy hunger in the dimly lit room, reminiscent of a wolf's gaze. And I was their prey. Ryder advanced, closing the distance between us until he was right beside me. Jake had eased me off of him so that I was free to turn if I wanted. So I did. My gulp was audible in the anticipatory silence and elicited wicked grins from both men.

It occurred to me that everything so far had happened *to* me. I'd insisted on accompanying them on the trip, that was true, but I ate when told to, slept where instructed to, walked where directed... wasn't it time for me to *take*?

On the heels of that revelation, I leaned forward, noting the surprise in Ryder's eyes with a perverted glee, and gently brushed my lips against his.

The sound that left his throat emboldened me to reach out and place a hand on his chest, deepening the kiss. He quickly took it over, displaying his same mastery as he had the other night. Ryder swallowed my moan, moving his hand to clasp the side of my neck, thumb brushing against my jaw and I raised up onto my tiptoes so that he didn't need to bend so far, moving my hands onto his shoulders to anchor myself.

Only the sharp exhale from Jake could have pulled me out of my daze. Ryder inclined his head, and Jake's heavy footsteps reverberated off the wooden floors as he approached. And then he was at my back, hand landing on my hips to grip me firmly. I rocked back into his embrace, eyes fluttering shut as he held me against him. They cracked open at the feel of Ryder's lips against my throat, tongue darting out to stroke and teeth nibbling at all my sensitive spots. Jake lifted a hand to grasp my chin, tilting my head back and to the side against his chest, then lowering his head to resume our earlier kiss.

Meanwhile, Ryder's hands traveled the lengths of my sides, stopping further up where he could brush his thumbs along the undersides of my breasts, inciting a fresh flood of desire and a loud moan.

"Quiet," Jake whispered against my lips. "Wouldn't want to wake the others up, now would you?"

I shuddered, my short, stilted breaths filling the room.

He eased himself back, using just his hands on my waist to move me backwards towards the bed. Ryder must've been amenable to this new plan because he dutifully followed.

Jake shifted out from behind me, and Ryder gave me a gentle push. The backs of my knees hit the edge of the bed and buckled, sending me sprawling on the bouncy surface. Jake wasted no time, following me down and hiking my shirt up to leave soft kisses all over my stomach, hips, and then the inside of my thighs. *Shit, is this really happening?*

I bit my knuckle to keep from crying out when he trailed his hand over my leg, drifting towards my center, and used his thumb to rub me over my leggings. My hips squirmed as I begged. "Enough already. I need *more.*"

He tugged my pants down to my thighs and went back to stroking me over my thin panties. I panted, anxious for him to touch me, *really* touch me, when I glanced down to find him watching me with a cruel smirk. The bastard was toying with me!

The hand on my breast startled me, and I jerked my head to the side to find Ryder lying beside me, eyes heavy from sleep and lust. I'd been so wrapped up in pleasure I hadn't even seen him move.

He lowered a kiss onto my lips, swallowing my whine, then wordlessly rucked my shirt up the final distance over my breasts, pulling the whisper-thin cups of my bra down inch by agonizing inch. My now exposed nipples hardened in the cool night air, and I trembled with want, urging them on with a litany of begging under my breath.

Ryder's eyes when he looked at me were black with hunger, and while holding my gaze, he leaned down to pull my peaked nipple into his hot mouth just as Jake pulled my panties to the side and brushed his thumb down my soaking wet pussy. I couldn't have stifled my moan if I'd tried.

More intoxicating than I could've ever anticipated, their combined attention filled me with a wanton, desperate need.

The sudden stroke of something warm and wet against me had my eyes shooting open. The strokes of Jake's tongue started out slow, dragging through my center with an agonizing precision. I whimpered at each pass, stunned to discover that it could feel like this and I'd never known. His mouth felt like ecstasy against me, and with each stroke of his tongue, my mind grew foggier, surrendering to the blatant possession of his grasp on my thighs and the pointed attention he lavished on my clit.

I gave one last ditch effort to try to make sure this was what they wanted, terrified that this was a spur-of-the-moment opportunity they'd grasped hold of. "Y-you," I managed to get out before biting out a choked groan, shaking my head and trying again. "Are you sure? I don't..."

A hand grasped my chin softly and turned my flushed face. "I want this more than you can imagine," Ryder told me quietly. "Allow us to give this to you. No strings, no awkwardness, no fighting. Just working together to please you, like you deserve."

My voice was just a whisper of sound. "Yes."

Jake resumed with a renewed fervor, and I instinctively ran my hand through his hair, holding his head close with a light touch.

"You love it, don't you. His tongue in your tight little hole, dragging through all that slick cream."

"F-*fuck*." When the hell had Ryder gotten such a dirty mouth? I wasn't sure I'd ever be able to look him in the eye again, certainly not if I played that sentence on repeat until the end of time.

"That's it," he murmured, hair falling into his face as he leant down to bite my nipple gently, drawing it back with his teeth and then releasing it. Again and again and again. Ryders's free hand stretched across my body to toy with my other breast, drawing circles around my areola.

"Please," I whispered, hips bucking restlessly into Jake's mouth. He'd begun massaging my entrance, small circles of his thumb that sent shockwaves through me. A low chuckle from the end of the bed hit my ears just as something firm brushed my clit. Ryder clapped his hand over my mouth just before I squealed, muffling the sound.

"Can't have that, darling," he muttered, capturing my lips once more. I groaned into his mouth, as further down my body, Jake licked and sucked in a rhythmic fashion, and when he focused his attention on the two spots that had gotten the greatest response, I bucked upwards. He wasn't delicate, or shy, instead spreading me open with his fingers and working as much of my damp flesh as he could reach, yet never quite entering me.

They worked in tandem to keep me disoriented, the pleasure overwhelming. It felt as if every part of me was being stroked or licked, and I was drowning in it. My orgasm struck without warning, body trembling as my pussy clenched down on nothing.

My nails dug into Ryder's shoulders where he was bent over me, and Jake didn't let up for one second, working me all the way through it. I eagerly latched onto the roughly uttered praise from both men, and after a short while, the aftershocks slowed.

My head tilted back to find Jake wiping his mouth, looking mighty proud of himself, while Ryder pressed one last hard kiss to my lips before pulling my shirt back into place.

I stared at him in awe. Who the hell *was* that? Ryder was so stoic. Aloof and withdrawn, but with an occasional focused intensity that stole my breath. *This* was a whole new side of him that I'd never met before.

How can I come back from this? From wanting them so badly I ache with it now that I've had a taste?

Jake used a towel from the linen closet to clean me up before tugging my pants back into place, and Ryder pushed off the bed to a standing position. It hit me that he was getting ready to leave, so I rolled sideways, hooking his knee to stop him and running my hand up his thigh towards the defined length outlined in his pants.

His light hold on my wrist stopped my progress, and I looked at him in confusion. Didn't he want me to return the favor? Clearly, he needed it. He was solid as steel, just inches away from me.

"No," he rasped. "Tonight? That was about you. Only you."

I looked back at Jake–in a similar state–who nodded. "Everything doesn't have to be a trade," he said softly. "You don't owe us a thing. Now go to sleep. We've got an early morning."

I lowered myself back onto the blanket, sighing when my head hit the thin pillow and hoping beyond hope they would stay. The weight landing on the right side of the bed solved that mystery, Jake settling in like he belonged there.

Ryder hovered, his earlier hesitance returning. I could see it in his eyes; he planned to walk out that door. I doubted he'd sleep with Kas all night, so he'd probably subject himself to the couch instead.

"Come here." I patted the spot on my other side. It was slim, and so I scooted back as much as possible, holding back a gasp when I slid right into Jake's welcoming embrace, his arms winding their way around my stomach so that I was secured against his larger body. "Please."

Ryder moved slowly, like he was giving me a chance to change my mind. Then lowered himself gently into the empty space so that he was facing me. He met my gaze steadily, a strand of hair lying across his face, angling over his sharp jaw, and brushing against his light stubble. A warmth lit my chest as we watched one another, and unable to resist, I wiggled my hand out from under Jake's arm and slid it into the miniscule space between us, watching avidly as he brought his up to meet it, sliding them together. My other settled atop Jake's where it rested on my stomach.

Hands intertwined, my chest rising and falling with his, I matched Ryder's paced breaths until my eyes fell shut without my permission and I drifted off to sleep surrounded by two snug bodies.

I didn't have a single nightmare.

CHAPTER 15

When I was younger, every birthday was spent reminiscing. We had a routine, and Ben never once forgot it. We'd start the day with breakfast—he'd make his special annual strawberry pie—and then we would flip through my baby book while he told stories about my parents. I was forever grateful he'd thought to grab it when rescuing me that day. He wasn't a very sentimental man, but he had been when it counted, and that was good enough for me.

Ben had doted on my parents—leaving his isolated home several times a year to check in on them after they'd met at the farmer's market before I was born—and always made sure to bring us treats from his garden or news from further north each visit.

He never complained about my desire to hear about them. He'd sit beside the fire, rocking in the antique wooden chair that had been passed down through generations, and tell me about the soft yellow paint on my walls that my mother had taken weeks to choose, or the threadbare blanket I liked to sleep that he wasn't able to find when we left, and the animal paintings my father had collected to hang all around the bathroom that branched off of my room. There were only so many he could repeat before I knew them all by heart, but I loved hearing them anyway: soaking in tales of their generosity, their shared humor and kindness.

Above all else, he was the one who was *there*. The one who spent long hours trying to find food I might like when I went through a phase where I refused to eat meat, and who whittled little wooden sculptures to gift to me on special occasions, and taught me everything I knew.

It was a pity that knowledge hadn't helped on the day I lost the house.

The drone of a bee grew louder as I tied off my braid where I sat in front of the wildflowers Morgan had grown, feeling every day of my twenty-six years. I might not have even realized what day it was if not for the uniquely patterned butterfly I'd seen an hour prior that reminded me of the one Ben had carved as a gift for my tenth birthday. It was probably still sitting on my shelf at home, if it hadn't been tossed into a drawer—or worse, thrown away yet.

I still felt Ben's loss keenly. It was on days like today that I lamented the fact that I had a photo of my parents, but that the technology just wasn't available anymore to take a picture of Ben as I'd known him. With no kids or family, and his wife long gone, his last photo had been taken when he was in his thirties, and while I treasured it, it wasn't the same without his deeply lined face and shock of white hair.

A squirrel darted through the grass and up one of the lone trees at the edge of the property, lost to the tangle of branches and new leaves. Good thing Mila was inside, or she'd be halfway across the field by now. Voices rang from the open door to the house at my back and I silently thanked the universe that Ryder and Jake were up and out before I'd even woken up. The sunlight had a sobering effect, and without the hidden cover of darkness, my brain was on full alert, trying to process what had happened. My limbs remained loose and pliant, though tension was slowly returning at the thought of having to go back inside and face them.

We'd run into each other briefly when I'd first walked outside, but aside from Jake's knowing smirk, there'd been no reaction, which only served to confuse me more. The only person to make their stance clear was Morgan, who had upped her attitude to biting comments from my split ends to the circles under my eyes. I supposed she wouldn't have any, given she had nothing to lose sleep over.

The sun's rays were soothing across my bare skin, not yet strong enough to be scorching. It felt strange that I was surrounded by so much open space and not fearing for my life, but I trusted the fencing and their various defenses to keep us safe. For now.

"Sera," Liam called. "Hungry?"

My stomach, previously content to be empty, rumbled loudly. I walked back into the house, inhaling the scent of syrup that filled the kitchen while registering everyone's places. Jake sat beside Morgan at the table, her father across from her, while Kasimir and Jake finished prepping breakfast at the island. I took the folding chair beside Anthony.

Liam limped over to the head of the table at my left, putting almost his entire weight on his injured leg, and I frowned upon realizing he wasn't using the stick or any equivalent.

"What the hell, Liam? You're gonna make your ankle worse." I pushed my chair back to stand, but he stayed me with a hand to my shoulder.

"It's alright. Jake looked at this morning. He said it's healing up nicely, so I'm just testing it out a bit."

"Nothing too strenuous, though. We won't be here forever, and I wouldn't feel right leaving if you were to make it worse."

His lips thinned, either at the warning or the reminder that we would be leaving soon. "It's fine, Sera. All that worry is gonna give you wrinkles."

"That's the least of my problems," I muttered. "And I'd be grateful to even grow old enough to get them. Does it still hurt as much as it did the first few days?"

That prompted a grimace. "Eh. I'm not so sure about running or jumping, but as you've seen, I can use it."

"Don't feel bad for him," Kasimir added from behind us. "I saw him hauling wood yesterday without even trying to ask for help."

"Come on, I didn't *really* need help."

His father gave him a stern look, and I was surprised to find he'd been following our conversation at all. "If they told you to be careful, you should be listening. You don't always know best."

Liam huffed and looked away. I got it, I truly did. If someone who was supposed to love, care, and provide for me picked when to let me risk life and limb based on convenience, I wouldn't be too keen to hear them out.

"Well," Morgan interjected. "He's always been awful at listening. Remember when that doctor at the facility told him to rest after drawing all that blood and he insisted on going to find his friend anyway? He ended up passing out in some random hallway."

She laughed, but she was the only one. Liam's mouth tightened, and I bumped my knee against his in solidarity.

Kasimir finally sauntered over, carrying the large bowl of oatmeal in his hands, and Ryder followed with an armful of various spices and seasonings, setting them down as we all began dishing up.

"Oh, Jake, that's not enough to fill you up. You'll be too hungry to function later. All that muscle needs nourishment."

Refusing to lift my head, I pinched my lips together, so that I didn't laugh or say something bitter. Jake ignored her, going for the brown sugar instead and shaking it over his bowl.

The sudden brush of Ryder's skin against mine as he moved his hand sent my thoughts swirling in another direction. Morgan's dismissive huff melted into the background, and I realized that she, too, had noticed his subtle gesture.

I stole a furtive glance at Ryder from the corner of my eye, admiring his soft expression as he focused on the cat at his feet, digging her nails into his calf as she stretched and begged for food. That he didn't even flinch was ridiculously attractive for some reason.

Trying to juggle my growing attraction to the three of them was taking all my energy, and I had the sudden urge to see Nadira, Jamie, and Heidi, who were already well aware of the crush I'd been doing so well at pretending didn't exist, as well as my inconvenient feelings for Jake. I was certain this latest development would blow their minds.

Our meal went by quickly, and one by one, people left to attend to their own matters. Ryder and Kas stepped out to pump water while Anthony retreated to his bedroom, leaving just Morgan, Liam, Jake, and I. Luckily Morgan was too busy flipping through a torn and wrinkled magazine from four decades ago to bother her brother while he spoke to me at a low volume.

"You've really kept track of every place that you've gone?" I asked Liam.

He nodded, pointing to his head. "Have to. Imagine the one time I try a place I've already cleaned out and there's something waiting for me there, not to mention no supplies. It would be a waste of time, energy, and possibly my life if I slip up."

That should have occurred to me. Maybe it was just more confirmation that if everyone I'd met this past year died tomorrow, I still wouldn't have the skills, knowledge, or strength to survive on my own as they had done. It was a good reminder of the entire purpose of my presence here.

"And you never go into the city?"

His mouth flattened. "I try not to. Too many things better at hiding than I am sneaking. I've had the best luck with some of the more rural buildings. There's a higher chance they won't have been picked clean yet."

Jake chimed in from where he was sitting on the couch, using a small sewing kit to mend a new hole in one of his shirts. "I've found the same to be true. It's why we only head to the city as needed and in groups."

I frowned, remembering their last trip just over a month ago and how I'd briefly considered trying to convince them to let me go but had ultimately chickened out. It was good that I hadn't let myself think too deeply before volunteering for this one, though I often wondered if I'd made a mistake coming along. Every day I grew more attached to them, and every day it would hurt ten times worse if something were to happen. To care about others was dangerous, but especially while tempting fate like we were when we had a perfectly safe camp back home.

Behind me, someone drew me out of my thoughts by winding my braid around their fist. A gentle tug had my head tilting back to find Jake standing behind me, eyes flicking to my lips before letting my braid slip through his fingers. He stepped back to gesture at my furrowed brows. "I've never met anyone who gets more lost in thought than you, darlin'." His gaze was warm on my face, and the slow grin that crept over his lips made a riotous flutter start in my stomach.

The snort from somewhere behind me proved that Morgan was now paying us a small amount of attention and apparently took offense.

Liam grinned, slinging his arm over the back of his chair to face her. "What about you, Morg? Where've you found the most success?"

Her fair complexion gradually mirrored the hue of her hair as she pretended her brother hadn't just spoken, probably because she had no earthly idea on how to respond. When she did speak, she completely ignored her brother. "So, Jake, maybe we can head down to the creek we found last time? I could use some help with identifying edible plants."

"Yeah, but really wasn't that crash course the other day..." Jake's deep voice faded as I studied the cracking paint on the wall behind him, a nice beige color. It was none of my business if Jake chose to go with her or not. It wasn't like I had a claim on all of them.

"Not sure what you've got going on up there, but you should hope the others are less observant than I am, because it's fairly obvious," Liam said, eyeing me skeptically.

I quickly hushed him. "Not a word."

He laughed, but the return of a hand smoothing over my scalp had us both shutting up and turning. I almost missed the look on Jake's face as he stared at Liam before he moved his focus onto me. "I'm going to see if I can catch any fish today. Morgan's going to come along because she wants to look for more mushrooms."

Why was he telling me if I hadn't been invited? Maybe that was a good thing, and the awkward tension that had been riding me all morning would let up.

Honestly, that she most likely only wanted to go to get him alone wasn't giving me much confidence for when we left. None of this was. She still seemed reluctant to help wherever she was needed, and Anthony still retreated daily, leaving Liam to shoulder the brunt of organizing their efforts for after we were gone.

Any response I could have scrounged up disappeared at the casual kiss he dropped on my lips before stretching to his full height and walking off with a smirk, leaving behind a room full of people stunned to silence. Liam seemed giddy, but Morgan's scarlet cheeks matched mine. For different reasons, I was sure. She made a noise then stomped off, leaving just Liam and I.

"Holy shit," he said with a laugh.

"Nope."

"But–"

"Not a word."

I brought my fingers up to touch my lips.

Shit.

Walking over to the small collection of peppermint candies I'd amassed, I noticed that there seemed to be a few missing. Maybe one of the guys had taken a few? I knew they liked them too. I popped one into my mouth, using my tongue to explore the cratered surface as it dissolved, and threw myself into one of the kitchen chairs. Liam had joined the others out back dressing the fish Jake had caught earlier while tending to the fire, so I finally had a moment alone.

Restlessness had crept up on me, which I thought was impossible. Safety never got boring. But I missed the open spaces of camp, the scents of freshly cooked food and the constant bustle of movement. I *could mend that sock with a rip over the big toe*, I mused, grabbing the supplies I needed. Though once I started, it didn't banish the feeling completely, and the sun was setting quicker than I'd anticipated, so I had to work quickly if I wanted to finish without needing to light a candle.

"Oh hello," Morgan said, sounding genuinely surprised when she entered the room and found me sitting alone.

"Hey." I turned back to the fabric I was threading the needle through. Maybe if I didn't give her any attention, she would leave and I could finish in peace.

I should've known my luck wasn't that good.

She settled into the chair across from me, resting her folded arms on the table, and observed me while I worked. "Who taught you to sew?" she asked.

"My... mentor."

Morgan nodded, like this was an acceptable response. "I tried to learn once. One of the girls in the facility had taken an interest in it and thought we could learn together. My favorite shirt at the time was developing a hole in the side, so I figured the timing was perfect. "

"It didn't take?"

"Nah." She smirked, tracing one of the many gouges on the table with her long finger. "Never did get the hang of it."

She was acting almost... nice. Maybe she wasn't so bad in small doses. "It's not too late to learn," I replied, inclining my head towards the needle in my hands. A shout from outside had my stomach twisting, but when laughter followed it, I relaxed. I wondered if the easy camaraderie would bring Anthony out of his shell before we left. He'd already spent some time gathering firewood earlier with Liam, and had instead asked him for guidance on where he could find the best kindling, so that was progress.

Her sickly sweet smile spread and she tilted her head. "I never did get that shirt fixed. But a lovely gentleman who worked in the facility gave me a nicer one several weeks later, and all was well." Morgan leaned back in her chair, expression turning decidedly less friendly as her eyes narrowed. "So you see, it's all about knowing the right people and what they can do for you."

I regretted thinking for even a second that she might be genuine. My initial take was obviously well-deserved.

"Fuck!" I placed my thumb into my mouth where I'd pricked it with my needle.

She pushed her chair back and when she stood, a small clear wrapper fell from the tiny pocket of the jeans she wore. I recognized the shape immediately.

"Is that..."

Morgan smirked, toe brushing up against the wrapper. "Oh that? I hope you don't mind that I had a couple. It's just that you have so many, and I had a feeling they might come in handy." She punctuated her words with a sly wink, and I felt her implied meaning like a punch to the gut.

My body tensed, ready for an overdue confrontation, but she strolled away before I could muster up a response, depriving me of even that. It took me a long minute to swallow my anger before I leaned down and plucked the wrapper from the floor, crumpling it in my fist.

"Hey, you okay?"

"Yeah. Mind grabbing me a band aid?" My finger was still bleeding despite the pressure, and it stung fiercely. I was partly glad Kas hadn't heard what happened, certain that he'd confront her.

Kas immediately grabbed one of the mini first aid kits we all carried in addition to the more comprehensive one that I'd brought. It was probably Jake's. He had a bad habit of setting things down in random places and forgetting where.

Holding the bandage up triumphantly, he approached. The weight of his presence seemed to fill the room, his silent footsteps echoing. He lowered himself to a knee, and I dragged back the hand that I'd extended to take it from him, watching as he took hold of my injured hand, cradling it delicately.

"Here," he murmured, dabbing the drops of blood that rose to the surface with a napkin before his large fingers carefully unwrapped the sterile bandage, exposing its aged, tan surface. The soft touch of the adhesive against my skin made me shudder, both from the slight sting and the soothing warmth of his touch. Time seemed to stand still as he meticulously applied the bandage, his movements precise and unhurried.

His proximity and the feeling it stirred up in my chest quickly over-shadowed the throb of the pressure in my thumb. "You should be more careful," he continued. "Infection is everywhere."

Didn't I know it? It never strayed far from my mind that society had progressed so far backwards. A simple infection could spell death. The virus wasn't the only threat, even if it was the biggest. A simple mistake could cause complications that lead to losing a limb, or worse, your life.

Our eyes met before his dropped to my lips, and all too soon, he was pushing to a stand and gathering up the little pieces of trash.

"Thanks," I said quietly.

His lips curved. "Anything for you, Seraphim."

The atmosphere lightened considerably after he left, like a weight off my chest, leaving me with a lingering mixture of gratitude, curiosity, and an inexplicable longing for more.

Putting away my needle and tucking the mended sock back with my things, I followed the scent of roasting meat to the backyard and took my usual place beside the fire. The evening air was cool, but not freezing, and fireflies danced in the distance so infrequently that I wondered if I was imagining them.

Jake had already prepared a plate for me, and offered it to me once I was settled before he was drawn back into a discussion with Liam.

I balanced it on my lap, listening to the conversations happening all around me and feeling oddly removed. I hoped no one would pick up on my silence.

Though I should've known that hope was futile.

"Everything okay?" Ryder asked, lowering his voice.

"I'm fine."

"How does it feel to be twenty-six?"

My head snapped up. "How..."

He tilted his head, dark hair sliding down to brush his temple. "Come on, Seraphim. I know you like the back of my hand." When I didn't reply, he continued. "I keep track of the date. I remember what you told me back when we were with Gunner."

"You're allowed to just sit here with me?" I asked the man who'd been towering above me as he lowered himself to the dirty floor. All I received in return was a shrug. Across the room, there was a raucous combination of laughter, shouting, and the odd moan.

"You're quiet today," he said suddenly, startling me. His voice had such a deep, soothing timbre, I wished I could hear it more often.

"I think I'm always fairly quiet."

Ryder granted me a tiny smile. "Nah. A troublemaker, that's what you are. I hear you talking all the time."

A quick glance around revealed everyone's attention to be focused on other things. I supposed the only person who would say anything in the first place would be his father, but he'd been out all day meeting with someone. It was rare for Ryder to engage with anyone. He did most of his communicating in grunts and stares, although if I had grown up with this lot, I'd likely be the same.

Thinking about my childhood, my mood soured once more. "It's nothing. Just... my birthday today," I said, the words spilling out of my mouth. "Makes me think about the past is all." I peeked at him out of the corner of my eye, unsure of why I was even talking about this. I always tried to keep things light and happy—no doom and gloom. It was hard enough landing here after admitting I had no clue how to survive by myself, but dwelling on things made them worse. Only, today I wasn't so sure I had it in me to pretend that everything was okay.

"Tell me about them," he commanded, interrupting my thoughts. "Your past birthdays."

"I–Okay." Like he'd unlocked some hidden part of me, I began talking, the words tumbling out. I told him about the desserts I'd looked forward to every year, the stories and pictures, the little wooden figurines. And the entire time I spoke, Ryder sat silently, just listening. When I finally stopped, he made a low noise deep in his throat, sending a tiny shiver down my spine.

"It sounds like you were loved dearly."

"Yeah," I whispered, examining our surroundings since I'd been lost in my memories for what felt like hours. The sun had begun to set, and the noise was dying down as his father's men scarfed down their meals for the night. I squirmed uncomfortably, wondering how long we'd been sitting on the hard floor and contemplating why he hadn't interrupted me so that he could go anywhere else but here, listening to me drone on and on.

"Come on," he said abruptly, climbing to his feet and holding a hand out for me to grasp.

With only a moment's hesitation, I slipped mine into it, marveling at the strength of his grip. He tugged me to my feet, leading me past the random clusters of people and into the small room that he'd claimed as his own near the back of the old school, ignoring the few jeers that rang out.

We hadn't been here long, and yet he'd already made it his own. A collection of weapons rested on the table near the door, and his few belongings lined the cot in the corner, half-hidden under his blanket. He'd chosen a room with the windows semi-boarded over, and though they showed their age, they still held strong. If not for the light streaming through the cracks, it would be pitch dark.

He walked over to his worn navy backpack and dug through it while I focused on trying not to sneeze from the overwhelming scent of the stale, musty air.

"Here." He sounded almost... shy? "I was saving it for a special occasion, but I don't think it gets more special than this."

I looked down at the misshapen chocolate bar in his hand, admiring the bright red wrapper.

He misunderstood my hesitance, rushing to reassure me. "I know it's old... probably been melted and remelted countless times. You don't have to–"

His voice cut off as I threw my arms around his neck, sending him stumbling back a few steps before he regained his footing. Slowly, tentatively, he returned my embrace, setting his hands on my back and sighing when his chin came down to rest against the top of my head.

"Seraphim?"

I blinked rapidly, focusing on his handful of... strawberries? *Strawberries. On my birthday.*

Uncertainty flashed across his face before disappearing. It was so reminiscent of my last birthday, and the chocolate bar that I'd forced him to split with me when he tried to make me eat it all by myself.

"They're nothing special. Obviously. I mean, they're still greenish, but definitely riper than the ones we had the other day. It's just that after I checked the date, I realized I didn't have anything and so I did some foraging and these were the best I could find. Kasimir helped, although I don't think he planned on telling you." His rambling was oddly endearing.

"Oh, Ryder," I sighed, running my hand around the back of his neck and easing him forward so I could press a kiss to his jaw.

His sharp intake of breath was telling, as was the hand that came up to anchor himself using my waist.

The wood in the pit sparked and sent embers flying, and I eventually forced myself to draw back. Plucking a strawberry from his collection, I popped it into my mouth. The tart taste exploded on my tongue, offset by the sweet juice spilling down my throat.

"Thank you," I mumbled once I swallowed my bite, but his gaze was locked on my mouth. "Do I have something?"

Ryder used his thumb to swipe across my bottom lip, eyes flaring at the action. "Just a drop," he said hoarsely.

The sensation of being watched had my focus shifting across the fire pit, where Kasimir sat unabashedly staring at us. The look in his eyes... greedy hunger and the reflection of the flames.

Voices filtered through the night air, and I looked past him to where Liam was drawing Morgan into conversation when she'd been trying—unsuccessfully, it seemed—to get Kas to look at her. Meanwhile, Jake was speaking to Anthony, using his hands to emphasize whatever he was saying. My chest warming, I turned back to Ryder.

"Share with me?" I asked.

There was no way I would fall asleep anytime soon. I'd already tossed and turned for hours, thoughts flicking from the man sleeping beside me to all of my past birthdays, remembering the traditions I'd made with Ben over the years, which inevitably lead to thoughts of the day he'd passed, and losing the house not long after. Not only that, but worries about the journey ahead kept me anxious.

Just like the night before—although for different reasons—I crept out of the plush bed. This time I took a moment to pull on one of the hoodies Jake had lent me, as well as the worn jeans I'd stripped out of hours earlier, and paused to make sure the noise hadn't woken Kas.

I pocketed the utility knife Ben had given me on my thirteenth birthday and the chunk of pine wood I'd grabbed while in the forest the previous day and headed outside. It didn't even occur to me how much I was looking forward to seeing Jake sitting on that couch, taking his turn to keep watch for the night, until he wasn't there.

Ignoring the sick feeling in my stomach, I opened the front door as carefully as possible, telling myself that it was for the best. The minute you started to anticipate someone's presence was the minute you were fucked. I was already in over my head with them. If it were just lust, maybe it would be easier to ignore, but instead it was their unwavering honesty, resilience, and generosity that appealed to me so strongly.

The air outside was brisk and worked wonders on clearing my busy mind. I could smell wildflowers in the breeze as I made my way towards the tree in the distance, grateful that it was empty tonight and that the moon was shining brightly, so I'd be able to see what I was doing.

The bark was rough against my back, and the grass brittle against my legs, but the fresh air stole away most of my discomfort. Using the light of the moon, I pulled out the chunk of wood and started carving along the grain. Steady, shallow strokes that calmed me better than any of the mental techniques I'd tried back inside. There was nothing to mark a design with, so I just went with the flow, stopping every so often to brush the stray wood shavings from my legs.

Working in silence, nothing penetrated my concentration but the occasional hoot of an owl or the scurrying of something small in the brush. When my back started to ache, I shifted to a comfortable slouch, bringing my knees up so that I could rest my wrist.

There was no way to tell how much time had passed before the first muffled shout.

My head snapped up as I was ripped from the deep, trancelike state I'd fallen into while I worked. Morgan was already just a couple feet away, her features twisted with panic and fear.

"Sera, you have to come quick! Jake's been hurt," she cried.

I jumped to my feet, flipping the knife closed in one smooth motion and tucking it into my front pocket along with the carving I'd been working on. "What? What the hell are you talking about? I've been out here for at *least* an hour or two, and he's been inside the entire time."

She shook her head, hair flying. "No, no, we left hours ago to go by the lake for some privacy. You have to come, there's no time! There was a zombie." She uttered her words between huge, gasping breaths, doubling over with her hands on her knees. "We never saw it coming, and neither of us had a weapon. He sent me away to keep me safe, but I couldn't just leave without bringing someone back."

Of course he hadn't been on the couch like I'd expected; he'd already been gone. With Morgan.

Painful knots formed in my chest and bile crept up the back of my throat as my fear for him overshadowed the betrayal.

"*Shit*, hold on, let me get the others."

Morgan grabbed my arm, nails digging into my skin, and pulled. "There's no time. He could be dead right now! It took too long for me to even get here. No way they'll be able to get up fast enough to come."

The palpitations in my heart made it difficult to think. I just knew that we had to *move*.

Had to get to him before something awful happened.

Couldn't waste a second.

Head spinning and stomach churning, I stumbled after her, the word 'dead' ringing in my ears.

CHAPTER 16

T he tall grass near the fence threatened to tangle around my feet while I sprinted, but I made it through unscathed. That Morgan hadn't left the gate unlocked so we could leave quicker was maddening, and I was seconds away from yanking the keys from her when it finally swung open after minutes of fiddling.

It was even harder to run through the crowded forest. The dense canopy of leaves overhead frequently hid the moon and made it harder to navigate. Branches scraped my body, tearing small holes in my clothes, but the overwhelming adrenaline racing through my system drowned out any burn from the scratches.

Morgan kept pace with me, her words whipped away by the wind as we moved. "He... wanted to... show me the... water... at night." A long pause. "We got... busy. Complacent. Didn't even see it coming."

Heartbreak and dread clawed at my throat, making it impossible to speak. So I didn't even try.

Shadows danced in every direction, bony clawing hands reaching out to grab me from the darkness, and yet I still ran, determined to reach him before the unthinkable happened.

Memories of the night I fled from Ben's home tried to intrude and were quickly cast aside in favor of determination.

"How much fucking longer?" I gasped several excruciatingly long minutes later, my lungs aching. Hell, I'd tried to stay limber for this very reason, jogging every morning back at camp, along with some intense stretching afterwards, but clearly, I'd have to make some improvements to my regimen once I got back home.

"Not long. I recognize that tree."

Nothing stood out to me where she pointed. "I don't understand why you didn't bring any weapons," I muttered, more to myself than her. "It's bad enough you left the compound in the middle of the night, but to not bring anything?"

It was so unlike Jake. *He must have been so desperate to be alone with her that he hadn't considered the logistics*, I thought bitterly.

My side developed a cramp, and I knew I wouldn't be able to sustain this pace for much longer. It had to have been at least half an hour or more that we'd been running.

Flashes of Jake's mutilated body hit me every time I slowed; those expressive eyes gone dull and that charming grin frozen forever.

Finally, we reached a spot where the trees thinned out. One moment, I was slowing, and the next everything was a blur of motion. In the span of a single second, I hurtled through the air, landing face down in the dirt several feet away.

The fall knocked the breath from my lungs, leaving my diaphragm spasming as I spat out the soil that had entered my mouth. The laugh behind me froze the blood in my veins, and before I could shake the shock off and move, something wrenched my arms back.

Not something, *someone.*

Morgan finished tying up my wrists with what had to be the longest, most robust zip tie I'd ever encountered in my life. Using my temporary paralysis to her advantage, she wound twine several layers thick around my ankles, binding them together.

The plastic dug into my skin painfully, and the way my hands were bound made it all the more difficult to flip onto my back and face her once I could draw a full breath.

"That was much easier than I'd expected," she wheezed.

"There–" I panted, trying to make up for the previous lack of air. "There was no midnight rendezvous, huh?"

"God, you're so annoying."

What a bitch.

"Jake's okay? Back at the house?" Testing the strength of the zip ties, I grunted when they didn't budge. The grass was damp under my body, soaking through my clothes and adding to the chill in the air. Shivers wracked my body.

"Yes," she spat. "Your precious man never left. I gave him some tea laced with valerian root that knocked him right out."

"Considering he's the one who probably taught you to identify it, the irony is killing me," I replied, my voice flat and hiding the nerves that danced under the surface.

Was she going to kill me? Leave me here?

If she left, I was fucked, but alive. If she stayed... maybe I could antagonize her into getting closer, then kick her or something. Or die. Yeah, that seemed more likely at this point. But damn it, I was going to try.

A foul stench wafted into the clearing, causing me to gag, and even Morgan didn't seem immune. "Like it?" she asked, voice muffled by her hand pinching her nose. "All thanks to the traps Jake taught me to set. In a nice little path leading right to you." Her sing-song tone filled my stomach with lead.

"What's your plan here?"

Maybe if I kept engaging with her calmly, holding back the fear that threatened to choke me, she wouldn't flip out and I could get out of this alive.

The whites of Morgan's eyes shone in the moonlight as she rolled them. "You're so dense, I can't wait until you're out of the way. Then maybe they'll just... move on."

My brain short-circuited at the glint of silver from the knife blade as it left her bag, now clutched securely in her palm at her side. I instinctively curled my legs close to my body as best I could.

"I don't know what you mean. You're the one who keeps leaving camp with them. Why the hell are you upset?"

"He spent the entire time talking about you!" she shrieked, the hand that held the blade shaking.

"I can't control that."

"It doesn't fucking matter. All I need to do is remove you from the equation. You're not even taking advantage of what's right in front of you. Those disgusting looks they give you when you're not looking, jumping to attend to your every need. I know you're the reason Jake turned me down last night."

Shit. Well, if she knew what else we'd done, maybe I'd have already been stabbed, so that was one point for not kissing and telling. "You can't come back from this, Morgan. What will Liam think? Or your father?"

"I'm tired of *starving.* My dad doesn't do anything. Liam is always gone, and whenever he comes back, it's always with less food than the time before. You know how to take care of yourself, but I *need* them. The consistent meals, devotion, protection... You take it all for granted!"

"They're real people with feelings, Morgan. And your brother tries his hardest to provide for you all." It hurt that we were so much more alike than I could've ever guessed. I was shocked to find that she believed me so capable when that was my biggest insecurity.

"Shut the fuck up about my brother already! Honestly, everything was fine before you showed up and started changing everything, making him act like a totally different person."

Did she mean opening his eyes to the fact that destroying himself by trying to do it all alone was pointless? Clearly, nothing I could say was going to change her mind. She wasn't even listening to me anymore, instead just rambling about every perceived injustice she'd experienced since we arrived.

I used her distraction to try to ease the ache of my shoulders, wiggling my hands together to see if there was any give in the plastic tie. All I had to do was make it back and sort this out with the others, because I didn't want to spend one more second with her alone out here.

"You think I don't notice you trying to leave?" Her eyes narrowed. "This is all your fault. I'm sure they'll be so sad when I tell them how I noticed you sneaking out and so I heroically followed you just to see you get bitten. There was nothing I could do. It all happened so quickly. But don't worry, I'll comfort them through it. If they even care, that is."

"You bitch!"

I jerked, still unsure of what I was going to do next but positive it involved my foot on her person somehow, when she used the knife to slash me across the leg. It was shallow, but the sight of blood welling across my dirty jeans shocked me. I couldn't believe she'd actually fucking cut me! And didn't she know how rare undamaged jeans were to find in the right size?

She cackled, and if I'd ever heard her make that sound before, I *definitely* wouldn't have gone anywhere alone with her, emergency or not. *Yes, you would,* the little voice in my head said. *For Jake. For them.*

Morgan backed away, turning to face a tree.

"Are you..."

"Rubbing your blood off on the bark? Duh. How else do you think we'll get a zombie over here?"

White-hot panic threatened to consume me as her words sunk in. She'd mentioned me being bitten, but I was sure it was just talk. A cover story for the fact that she was going to slit my throat and leave me for dead. But bait? That was so much worse.

The scoff when she caught me eyeing the knife was loud. Almost like she'd read my mind, her next words were blunt. "I could just kill you right here, you know. You're not strong enough to break through the plastic and stop me. But I want it to be slow. Painful. Punishment for being greedy and selfish."

Nothing I could say would get her to stop. I was better off directing my energy towards finding a way out of this. My best hope would be waiting for her to leave before I tried to climb to my feet and free myself. Though time was ticking. The scent of the animals she'd caught in her traps, combined with the blood she'd just drawn, could coax out any number of predators.

"I'd better get going now. Don't worry, I'll toast to you in my new life, far away from here. All the food I can eat and all the men I could need... once I lure them in."

"Fuck you," I seethed.

She just smirked, red hair glowing in the moonlight as she exited the clearing. Seconds passed before she disappeared from sight, the sounds of her crunching footsteps swallowed by the forest, and I knew I was truly alone. At least I hoped I was.

The sounds of nature were loud around me: crickets singing and leaves rustling, but even greater was the buzz of the blood rushing to my head. It was impossible to think logically, the fear of the unknown so much greater than I'd ever anticipated when running through worst-case scenarios in the late hours. No more walls or weapons or protectors. Just me and the gaping maw of darkness that threatened to devour me whole.

My wrists ached, along with my entire body, and I really wished I was doing this on more than thirty minutes of sleep. I tried to turn onto my side and cringed at the sharp object in my pocket, digging into my thigh.

Holy shit. A thrill ran through me as I realized what it was. I wiggled onto my side, moving my hips in circles as I tried to dislodge the pocketknife from where I'd shoved it earlier. If only my arms were tied in front of me, I'd be able to grab it easily.

Something creaked in the distance, and I doubled down, my body bucking wildly as I attempted to work the small knife free. The trees pressed in on me, and the scent of my blood filled the air. A sudden influx of panic redirected my struggles to my bound hands, but they proved useless when the plastic binding my wrists remained unbroken. My frustrated cries and grunts bounced off my surroundings, creating an eerie echo that made me flinch.

Focus on the fucking knife.

I used my knees to lift my torso off the ground, doing a strange shimmy in the air and closing my eyes against tears of relief at the dull thud the knife made as it hit the ground. I froze when a branch cracked, the eerie sound confirming that I wasn't alone in these woods.

The flood of static and the frantic beat of my heart made it difficult to hear anything, and I cocked my head sideways like it would help.

A pain-filled moan reached my ears, and I trembled upon realizing that the sounds of my distress combined with the scents of the blood and death around me had lured something from my nightmares. Everyone knew they had heightened senses. It was half the reason we were so damn careful all the time about making any noise, and I'd gone and rang the damn dinner bell. Shit shit *shit.*

Every late-night, irrational, paranoid fear came rushing back at the sight of the undead body ambling in the distance. I caught glimpses of it between the trees–flashes of bright fabric and exposed bone. My stomach threatened to revolt, and I slowed my breathing so I wouldn't pass out by the time it reached me. Instead, I flung myself onto my back, using my bound ankles to push myself across the scrubby ground as my hands scrambled through the dirt for the knife, silently cursing Morgan the entire time.

Another grunt filled the forest, and I whimpered, stretching my shoulders and arms as far as they would go to search the area at my back.

There!

Cool metal brushed my skin, and I flipped my palm to clutch it in my grasp. The flashes of color in the distance grew nearer. Working as quickly as possible, I maneuvered my hands to flip the blade out, wincing as it nicked my finger. My heart thundered so loud I was sure the zombie could hear it.

My hand felt like it might cramp as I twisted it at an unnatural angle to brush the blade against the zip tie, trying to increase the pressure to get it to snap. It wasn't as sharp as it could have been, but it functioned just fine for small tasks. My machete was the important and well-maintained weapon, but I hadn't fucking *brought* it.

The tie snapped open as it broke, and I almost sobbed with relief as I shook out my arms. I was no longer trying to be quiet, instead it was a race to try to free my ankles before the zombie got any closer. It was only a matter of time. I knew that. It was up to me whether I rushed to get free and was able to defend myself once it arrived, or stayed silent and wasted time trying to be discreet so I was less of a target.

Another growl rang out, and I doubled over, stomach cramping, sawing desperately at the twine. The material frayed, but not before the zombie made it to the tree containing my smeared blood, head cocking at an unnatural angle as its milky eyes found me.

It was here.

As it left the shadows and entered the light, I saw it in all its ghastly glory. Its spectral appearance sent chills down my spine. Skin sallow and discolored, the putrid scent of decay added to the general unpleasant aroma Morgan had manufactured.

Exposed bone protruded through patches of battered flesh, a macabre patchwork. Ripped shreds of bright clothing clung to its emaciated frame, hanging in tatters. Its eyes were vacant and hollow, devoid of any trace of humanity and holding an unsettling, glassy quality that pierced through the darkness, reflecting an insatiable hunger.

We stared at each other, frozen in place, for far too long before I snapped into action, frantically chopping at the twine around my ankles.

In my peripheral vision, I watched as the creature moved with a slow, shuffling gait, limbs stiff and jerky, as if controlled by unseen strings. I knew how quick they could be when motivated. Was it just toying with me? Delighted by the fact that its prey was already incapacitated and practically offered up on a platter?

Momentum sent my hand flying back as the rope snapped, and I sprang to my feet, catching my balance as I shakily found my footing. Being face to face with the zombie had my legs threatening to give out, but I had to be strong. Every fear I'd ever had was bundled into this very moment. I was weak, practically defenseless, and soon-to-be dead. But I had to try. I owed it to everyone who'd ever cared about me.

I brought the small knife up, arm trembling as I pointed it towards the creature. Its movements lacked grace or coordination, but there was a relentless determination in its pursuit, driven solely by an instinctual craving for flesh. This could so easily have been me after I'd fled, if I hadn't stumbled on Gunner's camp.

An ear-piercing screech sent me lurching forward, driving the knife toward any part of it I could reach. Running would do me no good, and turning my back wasn't an option.

Nobody was coming to save me.

Morgan was probably just getting back, and for all I knew, she would wait until morning and pretend she'd seen me leaving minutes prior, not hours, so any potential attempts to look for me would be too late.

I was on my own.

The zombie lunged, and I shrieked.

CHAPTER 17

The knife glanced off its body, the small blade taking off a chunk of rotting skin that was of no consequence to the thing before me.

I glanced around, eyes frantic, doing the one thing I swore I wouldn't and bolting for the tree line several feet away. The knife was useless against it. The only thing that might make an actual weapon would be one of the heavier branches nearby.

Shoving aside low-hanging branches as I ran, I heard the telltale noises of it following me as it crashed through the trees.

Too close. It sounded much too close.

There. Spotting a stick nestled among some fallen leaves nearby, I sprinted towards it and swung it just in time to catch the zombie across the face, the force snapping its head backwards. It wasn't enough, evidenced by the way it continued to advance.

This was it. I drew the branch back again, pieces of wood flaking off and hitting my clothes, and a small bud on the side cutting into my hand. The zombie lunged just as I swung, the momentum sending me back a step and out of the range of its bite.

This time it hit the ground with a low keening noise. I clamped my eyes shut against the sight, bringing the branch down again and again until it no longer stirred. Only then did I drop the crude weapon, breaths sawing in and out of my lungs as I swayed back and forth unsteadily, the reality of what I'd just faced rushing in.

Holy shit.

The body on the forest floor was unmoving. Finally at rest, it seemed. Sympathy filled me as I stared at its still form. Could have been me. Could have been someone I loved. The world was so damn cruel.

A far-off noise sounded, and while it could have been an animal, I wasn't holding my breath. Moving quickly, I backtracked to the clearing and took the path that Morgan had first led me down, navigating my way back to the house as best I could. My legs burned with effort while my wrists ached from being restrained so tightly, and the sting on my leg was growing more and more persistent.

For a long period of time, I was convinced I'd gotten lost. My surroundings were unrecognizable, growing dark and twisted whenever the moon ducked behind the clouds, and no matter how far I walked, the forest just went on and on and *on*.

It was a miracle when the trees thinned, and I saw the fence in the distance. It took significant effort not to collapse where I stood. *Not safe yet.*

I scoffed when I reached the fence. She hadn't even bothered to lock it behind her on her way in. How fucking careless.

There was no way to tell what was going on inside as I crossed the field. I was too far to glimpse any candlelight through the windows, or hear any voices. For all I knew they were still sleeping.

My heart cinched as I approached the large structure and heard yelling. I broke out into a run, ignoring the strain in my muscles and thigh until I finally reached the front door, throwing it open as I burst inside.

The room was in chaos.

It took me a split second to process everything. Liam sat on a chair pulled into the living room from the kitchen, and his father perched at the edge of the couch, expressionless. Morgan sobbed into her hands and Kas was yelling, his face redder than I'd ever seen it. Jake crouched behind him, running his shaking hands through his long hair, while Ryder slouched against the wall, features slack with shock.

I heaved in a massive breath, and a stubborn piece of wood that had been tangled in my shirt fell to the ground. A nervous laugh escaped, and I threw my hands over my mouth when it turned into a sob.

"Angel," Jake breathed. I got only a quick glimpse of his reddened eyes before he charged across the room and drew me into his crushing embrace. Over his shoulder, Morgan's face drained of color as if she'd seen a ghost.

He pulled back just far enough to kiss me hard and deep, resting his forehead against mine and sucking in tremulous breaths until I tucked my face back into his hard chest, absorbing his violent shudder. "You're here," he said hoarsely. "What the hell happened? Why'd you try to leave?"

Ryder approached, standing beside us and staring at me like he thought he'd never see me again. "Morgan said..." His voice faltered.

"Ryder," I whispered, letting go of Jake and throwing myself into his arms. It took him a moment to respond, but once he did, he squeezed me with an iron grip.

"Explain," Kas ordered Morgan, voice harsh and laced with a frosty edge. The sheer violence of it had me leaning back to look at him.

"I swear I saw her get bitten. She could be infected right this second! You have to take care of her before it's too late for us all," she cried desperately.

My laugh was bitter. "You bitch." I pulled away from Ryder to confront her, but his hand remained anchored on my arm like he just couldn't let me go yet.

Kasimir looked me over, making sure I was in one piece, before rounding on her with a flat stare. "You said she *left*. That she had a small bag she'd stolen from you and the clothes on her back."

I snorted. *Stole, huh? That was new.*

"You *magnanimously* followed her after she woke you up by closing the door too loudly, and when she told you to fuck off, that she was splitting away from us without all the drama, that you watched as a zombie came out of nowhere and tackled her."

"You have to kill her!" she shrieked, eyes brimming with a frantic, desperate plea. "She's *probably wearing a bite right this very second.*"

"Fuck you," I spat. "I was already outside when you told me Jake was injured."

Jake's head snapped to me so fast there was no way he wouldn't be feeling it in the morning. "What," he growled.

"She said you and her had snuck out to have a private moment together when you were attacked. She 'ran back to come and grab someone' and told me I had to come quickly." I watched as deceitful tears tracked down her flushed cheeks. "So what the fuck did you really do, huh? Wait for me or something?

Every second I showed no symptoms of changing, her frantic urge to make them believe her faded. It was becoming increasingly clear what she had done.

"Don't flatter yourself." She sneered. "I heard you leave and knew it was a gift. I'd planned to draw you out somehow, wake you up without disturbing the others, but this way I could just use my window and pretend like I came from the woods."

Liam's jaw dropped, while Kasimir's expression, if even possible, grew even harder.

"Conniving bitch," I muttered. "Planned the whole thing, along with the creepy animal carcasses and blood sacrifice."

"Don't be so damn dramatic. It was a tiny cut."

Ryder's tone was lethal. "Excuse me?"

"Don't worry, love. I'm alright," I assured him, waving at the minor tear in my jeans.

His double blink made me aware of the word that had slipped out, but our focus had already shifted back to Morgan as she advanced. "You ruined *everything*. I had it all back at the facility! All of my needs taken care of. Then they didn't need *him* anymore, which means we were thrown out into this *wasteland*. The least he could do was get us food, but he *couldn't even do that right!*" She was screaming now, skin a mottled red.

Liam's face drained of color. "Morgan," he croaked, looking at her like he'd never seen her before.

"You're weak," she spat in his direction. "You too," she added with a nod to her father, who didn't react at all. "And *you*. Coming in and changing everything, making everyone feel bad for Liam. I deserve to be taken care of, not you and not him!"

"That's enough," Jake ordered quietly, but firmly.

Amazingly, she closed her mouth. Her chest was still heaving from the vitriol she'd just spewed, and no one had escaped unscathed.

"Wait," Liam interrupted, finding his voice. "She cut you, drew you somewhere on purpose... What was really waiting for you there? You could've just come right back."

I frowned, darting a wary glance at the guys. They were going to lose their shit. "She... tied my wrists and ankles. Adding the fresh blood to the mix must've been irresistible to the undead nearby, because one found me not too long after she left."

Everyone exploded, yelling over one another while Morgan screamed back. Liam was frozen in horror, staring at me like his entire world had just upended itself. I suppose it had, somewhat.

"A fucking zombie?" Ryder shouted, jostling me when his hands landed on my biceps as he frantically scanned my body. "How–You..."

"I killed it," I informed him flatly.

"Enough!" Kasimir roared. The entire room grew silent. "We're done. This was a mistake."

Jake reached down to grasp my arm, lifting my wrist up, so that it was illuminated by the moonlight, and sucked in a sharp breath at the raw marks from the tie. His lips pressed together so tightly they appeared bloodless. "We're leaving. Now."

Kasimir nodded in agreement. "You're lucky I don't kill you where you stand," he told Morgan icily. "It's only for your father and brother that you're coming out of this still drawing breath."

Holy shit. He looked serious about it too. Morgan must've believed him because she shrank back, losing the fire that had kept her yelling. I briefly considered arguing against it, but decided it wasn't worth it. I wanted to be gone just as desperately; never to see this stuffy, suffocating house again.

"Liam," Jake said, waiting until he had his focus before continuing. "You're welcome back at our camp." I made a soft sound, and when Jake glanced back at me, I gave him an encouraging nod. "You'd flourish there. It's up to your discretion whether your family accompanies you or not. Just know that if *she* joins you, it will be unpleasant for her."

If Liam's eyes widened any further, they'd pop right out of his skull. Kas grunted, apparently happy with this outcome. Then he strode into the kitchen, and we all listened to him jostle our supplies around as he collected them.

"Well," Ryder said. "This was a nice detour."

I followed them to the bedrooms we'd occupied, but not without one last glance at Liam's family. They sat silently, Anthony staring at nothing and Morgan fuming. Liam looked dazed, completely unmoored.

It took no time at all to gather our things. Even after settling in, we'd never let them grow unorganized. Every day ended with our belongings in the bags they came in, in case we had to leave quickly. When we reconvened in the living room, the windows revealed the sun to be just peeking over the horizon.

Thankfully, Morgan had retreated to her room, probably not wanting to test their words any more than she already had, but her father and brother remained where they'd been twenty minutes prior. While Ryder and I checked to make sure we had everything, Jake sat with Liam, giving him instructions on how to find the camp.

When we were finished, Kas opened the front door to let the dawn in, and left without another word. Jake and Ryder followed, but I paused in the doorway. Turning back, I approached Liam, noting his defeated posture. "Here," I whispered, pressing the crude heart I'd carved from the wood earlier that morning into his hand and folding his fingers around it. "You're going to be okay. Find the camp, you'll love it there. And take it easy on your ankle. I... left you some food."

Liam's hazel eyes were dull, and his voice bleak. "I found some catnip growing at the edge of the property yesterday afternoon. For Mila. Kasimir has it."

My heart threatened to crack in two. It was impossible not to feel like we were abandoning him with people who would do nothing to make his life easier, who didn't care if he lived or died as long as their needs were met. If we could've brought him, we would've, but I knew he felt responsible for his family. No matter how awful they were, he wouldn't leave them behind.

"You stay safe, and I'll see you at camp. We'll have a feast."

He nodded, face blank.

My mouth twisted. "You'll be okay," I repeated, a statement of fact rather than wishful thinking.

We walked mostly in silence, deep in thought and on high alert, until Jake paused. "We need to stop soon. Sera needs rest."

"I'm right here, you know. I'm fine to keep going."

The burble of a nearby creek filled the crisp, still air and made my mouth water. I considered heading over to it when Jake scoffed.

"You need to rest your leg. I doubt you slept much before everything either. It's okay if we need to take a day."

"Just let it go! I don't need any more special treatment."

"It's not special fucking treatment to want to take care of you!"

I came to a sudden stop, pinning him with a glower.

"Shit," he sighed.

"What's this really about, Jake?"

He flinched, hesitating for only a moment before the words spilled out, like he'd been holding them in for the past several hours. "How could you think so little of me as to believe her?" he asked, swallowing hard. "What were you thinking? Especially after the other night? And to not even grab a weapon or wake one of us up or second guess her at all..."

"I had a pocketknife," I offered, much to his disapproval. "And I found a branch."

Ryder arched a skeptical brow from where he'd come to stand beside me. Always guarding me, even when it wasn't a conscious choice.

"It was a very good branch," I argued defensively. "Got the job done."

Jake advanced, and I instinctively stepped back. The hurt that flashed in his eyes, made even more visible from the soft golden glow of the early morning sun, made me want to erase the distance. "What's going on with you? It's like you've been avoiding us on purpose. Even before what happened this morning."

Kas and Ryder watched me with an equally expectant air, waiting to hear my response.

"Nothing," I mumbled.

My cowboy's laugh was devoid of humor. "Was it the other day?" he demanded. "You didn't like what we did? You regret it?"

Blood rushed to my face at the reminder. It was *way* too early to think about that.

A mortified glance towards Kas had Jake's voice deepening. "Don't look at him. Keep those eyes on me."

The unbidden desire that stirred in response to the harsh edge of his voice spoken with that low rasp took me by surprise. I hadn't thought myself capable of such a reaction with as tired and frustrated as I was.

He must have sensed it, because his eyes grew hooded, and he took another determined step forward. I knew if he reached me, the words would come spilling out, and it wasn't the time for that.

"Okay!" I exclaimed, raising a hand to stave him off. "Yes, I enjoyed it. I don't regret it. I just... I..."

Kasimir's head cocked to the side in an inquisitive tilt, and Ryder gave an aborted jerk, as though he'd just barely stopped himself from reaching out.

Jake continued like he hadn't just shocked the others with his blunt line of questioning. "I liked it. I *loved* it. I want to do it again as soon as humanly possible. But you need to have faith in us instead of running away."

Us.

Frustrated tears flooded my eyes and turned him into one large blur.

"Oh angel, I didn't mean to–"

"No." I sniffled. "I'm not sad. Only tired. I was so scared that something awful had happened to you that it was just so easy to believe her. I didn't want to risk it."

I rubbed my eyes clear in time to see his harsh expression soften. Mila meowed where she sat by my ankles, like she could sense my distress. "And"—I took a shuddery breath in, and released it in one large gust, my next words tumbling out— "I don't understand what this is. You're all..."

"You feel disloyal. Guilty," Ryder said. His voice may have been quiet, but his gaze was pointed and calculating. "Even after we both had you at once. Maybe that's our fault, and all the arguing gave you the impression that you had a choice to make. That we don't know how to coexist."

"What?" I squeaked. "But you–I–You hate each other. Don't you?"

"When are you going to understand that there's nothing we wouldn't do for you, Sera? It's no hardship. Besides, I like Jake just fine."

Kas made a contemplative sound, those pale eyes sharpening as he watched me. Jake's resulting grin was wicked, and he slung his arm around Ryder's shoulders, pulling him into his side and rubbing his hair. "Aw, pretty boy. I'm flattered."

What in the hell?

"He's right," Jake added, letting Ryder slip away. "I'm sorry it took me so long to get my act together. Besides, have you *seen* River and them? I promise you, this is not an unfamiliar concept. Every day I'm subjected to their never-ending flirting." His gaze touched on Kasimir for a split second before darting towards Ryder, dark brows furrowed. "We want you. *Just* you. And it seems useless to fight over it when we could just share; when you respond to us both. No choices necessary. No guilt either. And if you change your mind, that's okay, too."

Why did it have to be now, when things were so dangerous? I couldn't handle losing one more person, though deep down I knew whether things progressed or not, it was already too late. If we parted ways this very minute, I would be just as devastated were something to happen as I would be if I fell even further.

And if I let myself, would I come to rely on them for everything only to be fucked when–*if*–I lost it all and had to start over? I noted the dark promise in Ryder's gaze, the expectant twist to his lips that replaced the aloof mask he so often wore. Somehow, I didn't think I'd have all the time in the world to think it over.

"Okay, then I... Okay." Jake's wry grin was full of sympathy. If my emotions were as transparent as they felt, then everyone knew I had passed overwhelmed minutes ago. "I need to refill my water," I declared. "So I'm just gonna..." I waved in the direction of the rushing water.

I stopped a good twenty feet away into the twisted labyrinth of trees when I heard the footsteps behind me. He wasn't even trying to be subtle. "Seriously?" I whimpered. "I can't have a moment alone?"

Kas raised a dark brow. "I'm surprised you'd want one so soon after what happened this morning."

My jaw dropped, and he let out a string of curses. "I'm sorry, that was... I didn't mean it like that."

It was more shock than offense that had me laughing. "You're such a bastard," I said lightly. "Just hurry up and quit hovering behind me."

His pace picked up, though it took him no time at all with those long legs.

"I suppose you're right," I said conversationally once he was next to me. "It would be foolish to go off alone, especially so soon after that reminder."

A shadow fell across his face. "I can't believe she would do something so dangerous. She deserved worse than a slap on the wrist."

"I think just being her is punishment enough," I said with a shrug.

He grunted. "You were very brave. To take down a zombie alone, especially tied up like you were."

"Not sure it counts as bravery when I didn't have much a choice."

I guessed we weren't going to talk about the awkward conversation with Jake and Ryder. Didn't he have questions? Opinions? Maybe he didn't care. He was still planning to leave, after all.

"Did I say something?" His voice had a husky timbre to it, and I noticed that I'd drifted several feet away from him over the last minute.

"Of course n–"

Ahead of us, through the trees, something flashed.

"Fuck!" Kasimir's hand shot out as he tugged me back into his body, and I felt his sigh in every straining muscle when the color revealed itself to be from a lone shirt hanging from a branch.

"Wow. Reflexes," I said, my head scraping against his shirt as I craned my neck to look up at him. The vanilla scent that seemed to be embedded in his skin at that point surrounded me, suffused with something spicy.

He barked out a laugh. "Lots of practice."

I reluctantly straightened when he still hadn't let his arms fall, moving out of his secure hold. "Is that so?"

Light eyes landed on the abandoned shirt once more as he made a low sound in the back of his throat. "I loved my mom dearly, but she was away at work a lot while my father cared for us, and he wasn't very good at paying attention. I was left doing a lot of the work, which meant developing quick reflexes."

"Us?"

"My younger brother."

Holy shit... Kas had a brother?

"Where is he?" Kasimir's expression shut down, and I knew I'd inadvertently prodded at something painful. "Forget it, sorry."

There was a distance between us that hadn't been there before as he shook his head. I assumed that was it and kept walking until I reached the creek, filling up my water bottle and silently thanking Caelan for the filters he'd given us. I'd still prefer to boil it if I had the luxury, but this was better than nothing since we had no plans on making a fire until the evening, and that was if conditions allowed it. If I let myself dwell on the potential bacteria, I'd never drink at all.

When I screwed the cap back on and readied myself to stand, Kas's voice sliced through the quiet. "He died. Years after the outbreak. It was a good lesson on how harmful attachments and holding onto your old life can be."

My gut twisted. He couldn't have been any clearer.

We lapsed back into silence, this one even more uncomfortable than the one before. Worse, I had a renewed awareness of him now; the way his shirt stretched across his torso with every breath, the soft-looking strands of hair that brushed against his neck, and that little movement he made with his jaw whenever he was lost in thought.

I had to force myself to look away.

We were halfway back to the others when it registered that I hadn't heard his footsteps in a bit. When I stopped to look for him, I noticed he was a couple feet behind me, crouching down and examining an isolated patch of yellow flowers that I must've walked right past without even noticing.

The trees were sparser here at the forest edge, allowing the morning sun to spill down between the gaps in the leaves and bathe his face in gold. I sucked in a breath as his irises became almost translucent from the glow, obscured by the now gilded lengths of his lowered lashes.

Kas stood in one smooth movement, once more towering above me. Resting delicately in his large, scarred palm was one of the small flowers. Each petal possessed a subtle, graceful curve, and its heart held a cluster of stamens and pistils. It was a symphony of pale yellows and creams with an almost buttery quality.

"Here," he murmured, handing it to me.

"Thank you," I whispered, our fingers brushing as I took it from him. "It's so pretty." It was easy to forget about all the good in the world when you stopped looking for it. Flowers weren't something I'd ever stopped to let myself enjoy, always too busy and focused on more pressing things.

"Evening primrose," Kas said, reaching out to rub his thumb along the stem. "My mother used to purchase the oil from these to help with her arthritis. The conditions for it to be blooming right now... it's incredible. Another hour and the blooms would have all disappeared."

"Really?" I tilted my head back to get a better look at his face, my ponytail brushing against my upper back with the motion.

His lips parted as his gaze explored mine. "Yes."

I smiled to myself, twirling it in my fingers. "Lucky for us then."

CHAPTER 18

The sun reached scorching levels overhead. My skin was itchy and hot underneath my loose shirt, and I cursed the onset of summer. I'd always been happier in cooler weather, and dreaded the warmer months.

Everyone paused at the clang nearby, listening intently for whatever had caused it. Several minutes passed where I scoured the barren landscaping for any motion, adrenaline pumping through my veins. Crumbling buildings, discarded trash and belongings, the empty husks of abandoned–and not–cars, but not a single movement. We were on the outskirts of one of the larger cities, but it was a city, nonetheless. Eventually, Kasimir stirred and walked ahead. We filed in behind him, more cautious than before, with Casey fresh in our minds.

Several days had passed since we'd left Liam, and Kas would be splitting off to find his friend soon. He'd insisted on sticking with us through the city, even after being told that we'd be alright without him. Mila sure appreciated his presence, anticipating the catnip he doled out from Liam throughout the day. Right now, she was tucked away in Ryder's bag, having allowed him to pick her up. I thought she'd hate it, but after growing bored with sticking her head out to look around, she curled up happily atop his clothes, probably lulled by his steady pace.

A good half hour passed, spent picking over debris warmed by the sun and sticking close to the shadows. I was getting tired, but this was no place to stop for a break. Cities were some of the deadliest areas due to their crowded populations in the past. As far as I could tell, zombies were a lot like roaches, in that they could endure inordinate lengths of time on barely anything. In fact, I wasn't even sure if they needed flesh to keep moving or they just liked it. Either way, they could survive in almost any conditions, which is why it was so dangerous to be somewhere with a lot of corners and crevices.

A large flock of birds passed overhead, their wings casting shadows against the concrete.

"Stop," Ryder said suddenly.

Like our strings were severed in a single sweeping motion, we all jerked to a stop in unison. My nose wrinkled at the scent carried on the breeze; a putrid odor that threatened to make me gag.

"Hear that?" he asked, turning to us.

Jake cocked his head, his response slow. His dark hair was tied back in a messy knot using one of my ties, though a few shorter pieces had escaped at some point. "Sounds like–"

"Shuffling," Kas interrupted.

I fiddled with the hem of my loose long-sleeved shirt, listening closely. It wasn't quite shuffling, it was too loud for that. A distant groan punctuated the stillness and our gazes locked. A growl followed, and the harder I listened, the more sounds made themselves clear, echoing off the surrounding buildings.

"*Fuck*," I hissed, back going straight as a board.

"Come on," Jake said grimly. "We have to go."

Without another word, we jogged in the direction the birds had flown, all while keeping an ear out for any changes. We were moving up an incline, which slowed our pace some. Kas twisted his head around, and whatever he saw had him biting out a harsh curse.

"Now," he ordered sharply.

I knew it was bad news if he wasn't even moderating his volume.

"I thought hordes were myths?" I panted, trying to match Ryder's pace.

"Definitely not myths," Jake answered. How the hell was his tone so measured when mine was falling to pieces with each step? Damn it. "Just rare. There must've been something here that drew 'em. Whatever it was, it's gone now."

The noises grew louder behind us, and I knew that if I looked, I would see them, so I kept my focus facing forward. I realized the panic was getting to me when all I could think about was how Mila was doing in Ryder's bag, getting jostled every which way. On second thought, I was just glad she was in there. One less thing to worry about.

"There!" Jake shouted, gesturing at one of the more intact buildings with its own lot down the road, standing apart from the others.

It sat three floors tall, shorter than those nearby. The sign very faintly read 'hotel', although the 'o' and 'l' had fallen at some point, leaving behind the lingering residue of adhesive and bleached paint where they'd sat. What used to be a vibrant blue exterior, if the pockmarks and shielded areas were any indication, was now a washed-out denim color.

Terror rushed through me, in sync with my racing pulse. It felt like I was moving through quicksand, but the staccato beat of my feet off the asphalt proved that false. "Are you sure?"

Ryder grabbed my arm when I started to slow, pulling me alongside him. "It's not safe to try to outrun them. Jake is right, taking shelter is our best bet, and that's the only building that isn't falling apart."

Kasimir slowed until I was in front—only overshot by Jake, who sprint-ed towards the front doors—then maneuvered my backpack off, easily matching our pace while carrying it.

"What the hell?!"

"I'm not taking any chances."

I could begrudgingly admit that it was easier to keep up with them without it. Curses rang out when I stumbled and nearly went flying, only held up by Ryder's iron grip. We reached the front of the building just as Jake found a way through the front doors, and went barreling in after him, nearly knocking over the weather-damaged grand opening sign sitting in the lobby.

Whatever Jake had done to get the doors open, it hadn't involved compromising the wood they were constructed from, because they stood intact behind us.

The guys immediately burst into action, grabbing the retractable belt from the stanchions that were blocking the dining area and using it to tie the door handles together. I was just grateful this seemed to be more of a boutique hotel instead of a chain, and therefore didn't have the sliding glass doors that I'd seen from the hotels in more populated areas.

Ryder pushed at the long, solid wood console table sitting up against the wall and shoved it, making sure it wasn't bolted to the ground. Then he swept the acrylic holders scattered atop it and the dusty, yellowed brochures they contained to the floor. Jake rushed over to help him move it, arranging it so that it was against the main doors. I cringed at the screeching noise as the legs scraped against the ceramic flooring once it left the dingy carpet, knowing that if I tried to help I'd just get in the way.

The table was just long enough to hit both ends of the door frame, coming up to about my hips. I could see the beginning of the horde from the sidelights, somewhat distorted from the cracks spiderwebbing throughout the glass.

Someone other than us must have found a way in that didn't involve breaking something because the four floor to ceiling windows–that were still intact–on either side of the doors had been haphazardly boarded over from the inside. Hopefully, whoever had done it was long gone.

"I'm going to look for any other entry points on this floor," Jake called as disappeared from view. He must have had the same realization. We had to be cautious of any possible stragglers.

I frantically scanned the room for something that could sit on top of it, anything that would make it harder for someone to topple over by pushing. Outside, the escalating groans and snarls formed an ear-piercing cacophony.

A coffee table that was sitting in front of two cushy armchairs over in the waiting area off to the side caught my eye. It looked heavy enough to add some weight to the stack and wide enough to block most of the doors. It was damn heavy, and I grunted while lifting one of the corners.

"Let me," Kas ordered, jogging over to pick up the other side.

Ryder groaned as he pushed one of the narrow bookcases behind the receptionist's desk in front of one of the sidelights. I gasped when the wood started to slip, but quickly regained my end and kept walking forward at a manageable pace.

Ryder finished with the bookcase and took over, helping Kas lift the coffee table up and onto the first table, and then we split up to carry anything not bolted down and plop it in front of the towering monstrosity we'd created. The plush, royal blue chairs, the smaller wooden side tables, and the mini circular dining tables from the room the hotel had probably intended to use for buffet-style breakfasts given the breakfast bar that had been installed along the wall. Ben had loved those the few times he'd actually stayed in a hotel before the virus was released, mostly when he'd traveled up north to visit his brother before he passed, and he took great delight in reminiscing about all the food options they'd had.

My gaze flicked to the grand opening sign again, just another reminder of how the world had paused and never resumed. The furnishings had clearly been damaged by the years and not from use. The only signs of people were from the trash scattered across the floor, and the burn marks on the carpet. A suspiciously dark looking spot in the corner had me firming my lips and turning away.

Unlike many of the exposed ground floors of the other buildings in this area, there were no undead inside the building–that we'd seen, at least.

Jake rounded the corner. Much like us, his face was drenched in sweat. "There were two metal doors leading outside. The handle was busted on one, which is probably how the people that did this got in," he said, sweeping a hand towards the chip wrappers, cigarette cartons, and napkins. "I used a few of the doorstops that I found in the rooms on the first floor, then propped a chair against the one with the working handle. This place doesn't have a pool, and the exercise room and business center don't have any exterior walls."

I liked knowing that he'd accounted for every possibility. Obviously, zombies couldn't use doorknobs, but there was no telling who else might come creeping by while we were here, and brute force could accomplish a lot.

"What are the chances of them getting in through the windows in the first-floor rooms?" I asked, my anxiety returning at the prospect. My stomach churned so hard it was physically painful, and I tossed a peppermint into my mouth to try to calm my nerves.

Jake shook his head firmly. "I checked the rooms on this floor and the glass was only shattered in one, so I made sure its door was secure. The glass is old and clearly strained, but very thick. I think we'll be fine."

My shoulders dropped with my deep sigh. Outside, the howls and noises grew to a thunderous level.

"Come on," Kas said. "Let's check the other floors and make sure they're empty, then we can rest on the top floor."

"Assuming the roof hasn't caved in," I muttered. Someone's hand brushed along my shoulder in a fleeting movement.

We made our way up the stairs and checked all the rooms on the second floor. Most contained evidence that they'd been occupied at some point: tossed linens, more trash, and the odd personal belonging. On the third floor, though, at least half the rooms had been preserved.

Nervousness gnawed at me as I stared down the hall, worried that the floor might cave in if we walked on it; however, the building had been brand new over twenty years ago—if the sign in the foyer was any indication—so it made sense that it hadn't deteriorated as greatly as some of its neighbors. The floor had warped in some areas, but aside from a small hole near the stairs, seemed to be stable; and the roof leaked in a few spots but was still standing strong, so I took that as a positive sign.

In a dream world, we'd be taking refuge in a triple-fenced underground bunker, but this would have to do. Actually, in a dream world I wouldn't even fucking be here, so that was a useless idiom.

"You should take this one," Kasimir told me, gesturing at the door to one of the untouched rooms. I walked inside without another word, exhausted down to my very bones, and absently noted as the discordant shrieks grew louder. The horde had to be right below us now.

I stripped back the dusty outer coverings on the bed and collapsed on top of the musty sheets, loving their softness against my skin despite their unappealing scent. After the period in my life spent with ripped, stained, and threadbare sleeping bags and a rolled-up towel or sweatshirt as a pillow, I was much more appreciative of any that remotely resembled a bed or had any cushion. Just one of the many things I hadn't needed to think about before losing my home.

Hours had passed, and the noise from the horde persisted. I firmly believed that the louder they were, the more undead they drew to their group, and therefore, the larger they got. There were periods when the noise lessened, but it went back up to piercing decibels not long after. Right now, it was at a lull, though who knew how long that would last.

The temperature of the room increased as the day progressed. The dim light that shone through the caked-on dirt covering the window gave the room a murky, dreamy quality that made my eyelids grow heavy. It was impossible to keep them open when the serenade of sleep was so irresistible, even with the cloying scents of dust and age filling my nose. Yet I laid there for what felt like hours, and sleep never came.

Moments would pass when I would relax some, and I could see rest in my near future, then a piercing shriek from outside would send my heart galloping once more. There was no way to fully relax, and that fed the memories. Images of running through the woods, branches smacking into my face and legs and leaving behind deep scratches. Shouts and laughter ringing out behind me, the suffocating fear that they would follow. Fear of *everything*. The undead, the unknown.

It had been a hard journey, and it wasn't over yet, but I was in a good place. A better place. Which made the fear of moving backwards so much greater. I knew how easy it was to lose everything that mattered, to be desperate and vulnerable. I never wanted to experience it again, but if I had to, I wanted to be the kind of person who could face it with grit and come out stronger.

Voices sounded down the hall, and I blinked, a subtle twinge pinching beneath my ribs. What was stopping me from going to them? Shyness? Uncertainty? The loneliness digging its claws into my chest far outweighed those.

Before I could talk myself out of it, I cracked the door to my room open and crept out into the hall. My footsteps padded lightly against the carpeted floors, and the sound of voices grew louder the further I went. A sudden creak emanated from beneath my foot, causing their discussion to hush momentarily.

I hesitated once I reached the room I knew they were in, hovering outside and debating whether to knock, but my choice was stolen when the door unexpectedly swung open.

Jake braced himself on the solid frame overhead, cocking his head the longer we stared at one another. I hadn't even heard him get up. I peeked past him further into the room to find Jake and Kas sitting on the overstuffed chairs, watching us. Watching me.

CHAPTER 19

"Seraphim?" Kasimir asked.

My gaze dropped to the floor as a sudden rush of self-consciousness washed over me.

Jake's hand brushed along my upper back in a reassuring motion that instantly dropped the awkward tension from my shoulders as he ushered me into the room. It was a larger suite, with a set of leather chairs by the window on the far wall, and a king-sized bed in the center.

"Do you need something?"

I shook my head.

"You can't sleep," Ryder said, more a statement than a question.

"No." I cleared my throat. "I just..." How could I explain it? The walls were too dark, the rooms too empty, and I needed to see familiar faces.

Kasimir settled deeper into the chair and spread his legs wider, the soft fabric of his dark pants molding to his impressive thighs. "Would you like to rest here?"

My cheeks ignited, and I coughed softly upon seeing the slight smirk tugging at the corner of his lips.

"On the bed," he said, inclining his head towards the massive wooden frame that hosted a plush-looking mattress.

The duvet had been stripped off, and the navy sheets, though discolored, looked inviting. I wanted nothing more than to climb in and curl up with the blankets while they talked around me. But would they feel like they couldn't keep planning with me trying to sleep? The thought of waking up to find myself alone because I'd gotten in the way made me vaguely ill.

Ryder dispelled my doubts with nothing but his quiet reassurance. "Stay, Seraphim. If you want to. Your presence is..." he shook his head, not bothering to finish his thought. The gloomy saffron-tinted light streaming through the window turned his brown eyes amber and gave his dark hair a bronzed sheen, lending him an otherworldly glow.

"Okay," I agreed, and that was it. I climbed onto the bed, rolling into the center, and faced the door, tugging the blankets up under my chin and holding them tightly.

It didn't take long for them to resume their discussion in hushed whispers. Logistics of how Kas would split off to look for his friend when we set out tomorrow, and what the timeline was for when we reached the farm. Although the longer I listened, the more it sounded as though they planned for us to stay with him longer than we'd planned. Extra caution because of the horde. Hordes were rare, at least on the east coast, and usually left multiple stragglers in their wake. Over time, they would disperse as the elements and new lures drew them apart, but it was still safer to stick together. Not like I was opposed, anyway. Having him separate from us now felt wrong.

Their murmured voices and the cozy blankets lulled me into closing my eyes, my breaths growing increasingly heavier. Sleep sang a soft lullaby that only I could hear, drawing me deeper and deeper until I could almost taste it.

A loud shriek from outside pierced the air, and I flinched, body tensing.

The room fell silent, but I could feel the weight of their unspoken communication in the air.

A brawny figure perched on the side of the bed and sent my body rolling into the newly formed depression. I clutched the blankets tighter to my chest and glanced up, surprised but also not to see Kasimir looking down at me. Strands of dark hair fell into his face to obscure his vision as he tilted his head and brushed them back with a casual sweep of his fingers.

"Rest now, Sera. You're not alone. Nothing can get to you here." His rumbling voice had a soothing, honeyed quality that made my stomach do a little flip. Despite the palpable tension between us, he didn't move a muscle; content to keep his distance and watch me with a strangely intimate intensity. That he cared enough to sit with me and reassure me... it was better than any aphrodisiac.

I parted my lips in a silent plea, unable to ask for what I desired, but wanting him to know me so well that I didn't need to.

Moving slowly, Kas reached out and gently brushed the backs of his scarred fingers over my flushed cheek, leaving a trail of heat everywhere they touched. Liquid warmth curled in my stomach, delighted he was so close.

When he went to withdraw his hand, mine shot out from under the blankets to clasp it before it got too far.

His eyes shot to mine, drifting towards Ryder and Jake, before coming back to land on me. I followed the path his gaze had traveled–pleased at the smirk Jake was wearing and Ryder's indifferent yet subtly amused expression–then gave his hand a tug.

He came easily, moving the rest of the distance himself and placing a firm kiss on my forehead. I sighed, keeping my grasp on his hand and brimming with *something* when he awkwardly settled his large bulk onto the empty space at my side. I scooted over to make room for him, drawing the blankets with me. Having him near me made everything make sense.

Jake and Ryder resumed their conversation–now one man short–tacit approval, if I'd ever seen it. Kas made no further moves, holding himself carefully on his side of the bed and watching me with rapt focus. His hair remained smoothed back aside from the piece hugging his square jaw, and I could see the scar running through the right corner of his brow clearer now that we were so close. Same with the dark flecks that swam in his gray eyes. At my obvious perusal, his perpetual frown reemerged, and I couldn't stop my tiny smile.

His gaze lingered on my lips, his own parting the longer he looked, and my smile spread. Only then did his eyes dart back up to mine. "Sleep now," he said gruffly. "I'm here." That he'd phrased it almost like an order was so true to his personality that it only endeared me to him further.

I leaned forward and hesitantly brushed his lips with mine. He had no such hesitance. After a quick moment to process, he was already deepening the kiss with a low groan, his hand traveling to land on the dip in my waist like it belonged there. It was invigorating. Tentative and exploratory and fueled by a desperate, greedy hunger.

"Yes," I whispered as I pulled away, my breath coming out in rapid pants. "You're here."

K as crushed the skull of the zombie that had appeared from around the corner, and I gagged at the sound, clutching Mila closer.

"Grotesque," I cooed to her, nuzzling the soft fur on the top of her head. She meowed, and a rumbling purr soon vibrated against my chest. Good, I liked knowing she wouldn't hate me forever for picking her up. It wasn't something we attempted unless it was an emergency.

She'd–based on fair assumptions–been wild all her life, so it seemed unfair to cart her around when she'd made her own continued choice to stick with us, but I wasn't taking any chances this morning. Though she seemed to like resting in Ryder's backpack on top of his clothes, so that was something. The horde had passed sometime during the night, but we were on the lookout for stragglers. No way would I risk something happening to Mila when we'd come so far. To any of us, for that matter.

For the first time in days, I felt well-rested. I must've gotten over twelve hours of sleep, and my body seemed to have caught up. I vaguely remembered Ryder or Jake sliding into the bed at some point, and I couldn't say if Kas had stayed the entire time, but there had been a constant rotating presence so that I'd never felt alone.

"Here," Kas said suddenly, crossing his arms and staring at the wall before us. He'd been eagle-eyed all morning, adamant that this was the general area his friend was living in. Ethan was like Kas in that he moved from place to place often. Kas would never admit it, but I knew he was worried. He casually let it slip the other night that this was longer than they'd ever gone without checking in on one another, and I knew the horde had ratcheted up his nerves.

I examined the wall, frowning when I didn't find whatever Kas had stopped us for.

"That symbol?" Jake asked, squinting.

As I looked harder, I realized he was right. I hadn't noticed at first, but blending into the pitted dark gray wall were large black letters, crumbling in some areas but still distinct. They must have been painted with an ash or charcoal mixture.

"Yeah," he confirmed. "It's how he tags an area he's staying in. He prefers courthouses and, weirdly, donut shops."

I looked up and realized we were standing in front of the court-house. "Huh."

"We agreed to meet for a check-in two months back, but he never showed. Last we spoke, he said he was coming back here instead of moving on because he'd found a nice setup and he wasn't ready to leave it yet. Should be somewhere around here, so I plan to keep looking."

I took that as the dismissal he meant it to be. "Absolutely not."

My firm tone garnered a few surprised glances. His eyebrows furrowed, and he pressed his lips together so tightly in disapproval that they turned white. Opening his mouth to respond, I cut him off before he could tell us to go. "We're not leaving you to wander around the city that a horde just passed through looking for a needle in a haystack!"

"She's right," Ryder said, so resigned that he almost seemed amused. He gave me a wry smile and addressed the others. "It's better if we stick together. I know we discussed letting you do this on your own and splitting ways, but with the horde so recent and the amount of searching you'll need to do, it would be faster together."

"Yeah, what he said," I added.

Kasimir stared at us, a blank mask in place, before shifting to look just at me. Was he pissed? Did he think we thought he wasn't capable of looking after himself?

"Let us help. You don't have to do it alone." I bit my lip as I waited for his response, unsure of what I would do if he dismissed the idea.

His eyes softened incrementally, and he reached out to pull me against him, leaning down to bury his face in my hair. I gave a startled laugh, hands latching onto his sleeves.

"Sweet Seraphim," he whispered against my ear. "Always looking out for everyone else."

I took a deep breath. "Not everyone."

He held me tighter, and the conflict that had crept over his features whenever he looked at me for the past few days slipped away when he pulled back. Cool, rough fingers reached out to hold my chin in place, and in one smooth movement, he bent down to slant his lips over mine.

My eyes flew open, and I just stared, realizing as he straightened that maybe I should've closed them.

Jake smirked at my frozen state, starting up a conversation with Kas about how we would start the search. Although no one looked mad, I still felt a weird pit form in my stomach, telling me that this wasn't real. Good things didn't happen to me, and if they did, they were snatched away.

Almost as if Ryder could read my mind, he leaned forwards, brown hair falling across his brow, and captured my lips with a kiss. Unlike Kas, he lingered, making sure I knew good and well how he felt, not letting me disappear into my doubts. My mind went blank when his tongue snuck out to swipe my bottom lip, and only a throat clearing had me dazedly stepping back. I felt Kasimir's gaze intimately, his stare hot and intent.

We would be fine. We had to.

Maybe it was time for me to rethink some things.

Walking over to look at the map Jake was currently pointing at, I tried to focus. I admired his practicality, that he'd even thought to grab the map earlier from the corner store nearby. He was so capable, so self-assured. They all were. I'd hoped the more time I spent around them, the more those qualities would leech into me, but maybe they didn't have to. Maybe I'd be just fine as I was.

CHAPTER 20

"**T**his has to be it," Kas said, squinting up at the stately home before us. The afternoon sun cast a radiant glow on his black hair and beat down on my already overheated skin. Jake's golden tone just soaked up the rays, and Ryder had an uncanny ability to keep to the shadows, so I seemed to be the only one who was a sweating, panting mess.

This was only the second location we'd visited, having tried the manor over the hill only to find it completely abandoned, trashed, and covered in dust aside from the three zombies that were wandering the first floor as if stuck in a maze. Kas knew his friend and the type of places he was inclined to choose. It seemed Ethan had a strange passion for moving into obscure mansions and exploring the rooms, unlike the days before the outbreak where he was barely making ends meet.

We were in a small town, just on the outskirts of the city we'd left that morning, and there were only so many places that met Ethan's criteria.

Luckily for us, this mansion had been featured on one of the brochures in the hotel lobby, one of the many Kas had taken to aid his own search once he split from us. It looked promising from the outside. Time and a lack of upkeep left its mark on the once pristine facade featured in the yellowed images we'd seen, and ivy and other climbing plants had woven their way around the aged stones, adding a touch of natural charm to its appearance.

Kas went first, striding down the long driveway and crossing the overgrown lawn to approach the front door with caution. He'd argued that if Ethan was there, he didn't want to startle him by sending us in first. The sun cast long shadows across the weathered walls, keeping him somewhat hidden when he stepped behind a column.

A gentle breeze rustled the leaves of the surrounding trees as Kas pushed at the door, making it harder to hear his reaction, though from where Jake and I stood, we could see the surprise in his tall form. Ryder crossed the distance to join him, and I ignored Jake's plea for caution as I followed. We stopped in the entryway–no Kas in sight–examining our surroundings before going any further. The only sounds were from the acorns plinking onto the roof from the towering trees above us and their branches rustling as they danced in the wind.

The interior was a vision of opulence. High ceilings boasted multiple crystal chandeliers that sent slivers of sunlight across dirtied marble floors and mini rainbows reflecting off of the gilded picture frames that adorned the walls. I wondered what they must've looked like when the electricity still worked.

Plush velvet drapes framed large windows–the lower halves boarded over–inviting the harsh sunlight to dance across the ornate furniture and the intricate patterns of the discolored rugs. Every corner whispered of extravagance, from the remaining unshattered crystal glassware lining the display cabinets to the regal, high-backed chairs that stood like sentinels around the grand dining table. Because of the impressive art collection that the mansion had once showcased, long barriers–that had since been knocked over–and faded signs were set up throughout for the tours it once held.

Jake ventured further into the building, and I followed. Elegant side tables and bookcases that had fingerprints pressed into the wood, and even the grandfather clock had a large swipe across its face.

Someone sucked in a sharp breath from the other room, and I rushed to catch up, jerking to a stop when I processed what we were looking at.

A large pool of blood coated the flagstone floor in the kitchen. It had gathered in the areas between the irregularly sized slabs, turning black in spots and absorbing into the crevices and pores of the stone. Kas cursed as he left the room, his steps no longer measured. Noises echoed throughout the mansion as he worked his way through the remaining rooms, all while we stood there staring at the pile of congealed liquid. A thin trail of ants led to the furthest corner, and I had to look away.

Kas came storming back in, black hair disheveled like he'd been running his hands through it. Something was clenched tightly in his fist, and when I squinted to try to see it better, he uncurled his fingers. A tarnished silver locket with floral engravings sat in the center of his palm, the chain wrapped twice around his fingers.

"This was his sister's," he said, like the confirmation that his friend had, in fact, been here was a death sentence.

"You didn't see any bodies... right?" I asked. After losing that much blood, how could someone have walked out of this room? If they did, they would have ended up nearby, which meant we'd have an instant answer.

Kas shook his head. "Ethan was here, but he would never have left this behind on purpose. So he's either missing or... something happened."

Jake laid a hand on Kas's shoulder, firming his hold. "How about we all take a second look around, just for your peace of mind? Might be better to have more eyes on it."

Without waiting for him to agree, Ryder and I jumped into action, checking behind any and all doors, adjoining rooms, and cubbies. It wasn't long before a shout summoned us to the same spot we'd been in before.

The open back door revealed Kas and Jake to be standing on the grounds, looking down at a person-shaped lump. My stomach dropped, and I hurried to join them.

As I drew closer, the features of the man at their feet became clearer. He was older, maybe in his sixties, with a long stringy beard and dark hair. For a minute, when I looked at him, I saw a different man lying prone and quickly slammed the door on those memories.

I didn't think this was Ethan, but still... I looked at Kas and he shook his head. "Never seen him before in my life."

The sticky, matted hair at the base of his skull made it obvious who the blood in the kitchen belonged to. How had he managed to get out here without leaving a trail?

A heavy sigh left me. After spending time in the stuffy building, the breeze felt cool against my skin, and I leaned into it as I finally asked Kasimir the question that had been on my mind since he first told me about his friend.

"Why do you not just stay together? Why split up each time?"

Kasimir tensed, his expression becoming guarded. "It's for the best," he said stiffly, sounding more like he was trying to convince himself than me. "It's foolish to form connections. Once we'd shared everything we knew, it was safest for him to go. Periodically arranging to meet to trade news and resources makes sense from a practical standpoint."

My chest tightened. He wouldn't meet my eyes, and I knew there was more to it. "I thought he was your friend?" I asked quietly.

"You might call him that. Doesn't mean I'll be broken up if something happened. People die, people go missing, it's just what they do. My parents, my br–" he cut himself off with a muttered curse, his face hidden as he crouched on his heels to run his hands through his hair.

He was so controlled all of the time, a paragon of strength and determination. It was surreal to see him so obviously affected by Ethan's disappearance and still trying to pretend like it meant nothing. That he set out on this journey to look for Ethan at all after he didn't show spoke volumes over what he was telling me now. Everyone found it hard to survive, and good people died every day from things out of their control. It sounded like Kas had tried his best to close himself off from any more loss; although judging by this reaction, he hadn't been too successful.

"Just because you say it, doesn't make it true," I said softly, resting my hand on his brow–just long enough for his eyes to slide closed–pained rapture crossing his face before I walked over to join the others and give him a moment

I flinched when a knock sounded at the door. The others had wandered around the house earlier after dinner, but I assumed they'd retreated just like I had when the noises quieted. While the entirety of the art collection highlighted in the brochure was missing from the gallery, leaving behind empty, faded places on the walls where they'd once sat, and several of the rooms were trashed, the bedrooms were in better shape. I'd found one on the second floor that was largely untouched.

On the large four-poster bed I was lying on, composed of dark polished wood, sat a firm mattress with an emerald duvet draped over it. The wallpaper was ornate, bearing faded swirling patterns, and the windows to my left held drapes of a dull, once rich fabric that were currently pulled to each side to let in the moonlight. The candle I had sitting on the side table cast a gentle glow of light throughout the room that I'd been using to flip through the book I'd found in the study before dinner.

I tucked the peppermint I'd opened not too long ago under my tongue so that it wouldn't get in the way when I spoke and scooted up to lean against the bed so I could watch the door. "Come in."

Ryder took a single step, almost hesitantly, bringing a draft with him. When he didn't speak, I raised an eyebrow, observing him. His features were so dark with just the candlelight, eyes a bottomless brown and his hair almost black. He towered in the doorway like a wraith, face cast in shadow.

"You don't think we'll see anyone." It was a statement, not a question, and there was no need for him to clarify.

"No," I replied tonelessly, plucking one of the pillows from beside me and settling it on my lap to hug it. I wished Mila was here, but she must've been with Kas.

It had been thoughtful of Jake to suggest staying here for the night. Almost half a day that could've been used on travel was spent waiting in the mansion in case there were any signs of Ethan–or others who might know of him. We'd leave in the morning, but I hoped it gave Kas some peace of mind that he hadn't just missed him. Maybe Ethan had been staying here and left for the day to grab supplies or scavenge, or whoever had ended up on the lawn outside knew someone who would come looking for him that we could interrogate. Either way, we'd seen and heard nothing.

"He's worried."

"I would be too."

We sat in silence, and I cocked my head. Surely, he hadn't just come to tell me that. I patted the empty spot in front of me. "Do you want to sit?"

He sat wordlessly. His face was a study in contrasts, longing and apprehension warring for dominance.

"What are you really here for?" I whispered.

Ryder breathed out slowly. "I... didn't want to be alone. Can't stop thinking about Gunner."

I perked up at that. It was the first time he'd brought it up unprompted since it happened.

"I can still hear the sound he made as the blade entered his chest. He looked at me like... like he'd never even seen me before. Like I was the evil one."

"And when you followed me back, everyone kept their distance from you," I whispered. My spirit sank when he flinched. "Even though River, the new darling of their camp, kept telling everyone who would listen that you'd helped save the day."

A tightness constricted my throat as he scoffed, leaning back and sending a rush of jasmine towards me. I fought to keep my head straight and focused on what he was saying, not the long column of his throat while he spoke.

"I'm ashamed that you were there for so long. I should've found someplace for you, set you up somewhere safe."

I held up a hand. "Ryder, your father was a terrible person, but he wasn't responsible for keeping me there. You know that."

Ryder stiffened, and when he went to speak, I cut him off. "I told you before, it was *my* choice to be there. My choice to stay. I had food, water, and my friends. A place to sleep and protection. You could've found me the nicest, safest house around and I wouldn't have left them. Left *you*. And you are not your father. I'm sorry you lost your mother so young, I know–"

"No," he said with a sharp shake of his head. "She didn't die."

My jaw dropped. "What? But you said..."

"What did you want me to say?" His laugh was all sharp edges. "That I was a horrible son? How humiliating. Gunner just liked to tell everyone she died because it was better than the truth, and I followed in his footsteps. Like father, like son."

"Then what happened?"

"She left," he said flatly. His tone was empty, and his controlled temper had fled. He was all raw honesty, and I wished the pillow on my lap wasn't between us. "She didn't die. She left one fucking note in that script of hers I could barely read telling me that she couldn't do it anymore." His voice cracked on the last word.

Fuck the pillow. I pushed it aside and took a chance, climbing into his lap and draping my arms around his neck, resting my head against his neck. My eyes fluttered shut at his sigh, and I snuggled closer once he'd wrapped his arms around my back to clutch at my thin sweater. His body radiated heat, and his muscular frame was much more comfortable than it had any right to be.

He continued, his words coming easier now that we were no longer staring at each other. Well, he was probably still staring at the floor; I was the one no longer looking. "She said that I was a great kid, but that she'd heard some talk amongst survivors that there was a new compound being built, and she'd try her luck there. That anywhere had to be better than with *him*."

"She never came back?" I asked, words partly muffled by his skin.

"No. She never came back."

"You know it wasn't anything to do with you, right? I mean, she said you were a good kid."

His shoulders slumped, like he was carrying the weight of the world, and I held him tighter. "Think about it, Seraphim. If I was such a good kid, why didn't she take me with her? Why leave me behind?"

I had to clear my throat, because I knew my voice would be too thick for me to speak. While I empathized with his mother, my primary concern was the man in front of me who'd been abandoned to her awful husband by her leaving. "People make selfish decisions every day. It doesn't mean that she didn't love you, just that she put herself first." I hoped it didn't sound like I was defending her. Honestly that was the nicest thing I could scrape together in lieu of how I really felt.

Ryder shook beneath me, small trembles at first that grew bigger by the moment, and I started to panic. Was he crying? Upset?

Though when low chuckles reached my ears, I relaxed and swatted the wide expanse of his back. "Damn it, I thought you were crying," I muttered.

His laughter grew. "I love that you're so supportive, but you're much less discreet than you think you are. Anyway, it was a long time ago, and I've made my peace with it."

"What?" I said innocently.

A pinch to my ass made me lurch, and a squeal escaped me before I clamped my mouth shut.

"You know exactly what I meant. Thank you for trying to redeem her in some way for me even if it's obvious that you can't stand her on principle."

"I–You–" I sputtered, blinking rapidly as he used his arms to leverage me backwards so that he was staring down at me where I was reclined in his lap, still lazily straddling him.

His grin was wicked, all teeth and a little intimidating. I'd never noticed before, but his canines came to a point, making him appear almost wolflike. He was devastatingly attractive when he smiled. I wanted him to do it all the time.

I sighed as I watched him, admiring the sharp planes of his face and the way the flickering candlelight played off his hair. His grin softened into something less predatory, and he slid one hand out from behind me to rest it on my cheek.

"My softhearted Seraphim," he murmured.

I couldn't have been the only one whose blood was heating from the contact. I was drowning in it, butterflies swarming in my stomach. Every place his fingers brushed ignited a shower of sparks.

Large hands settled onto my hips as he brought his lips down against mine, all heat and need and urgency. His name left my mouth on a moan, and he shuddered upon hearing it, hands sliding down to my thighs and reeling me in so that we were chest to chest. I gasped at the contact, wiggling when I realized he was hard beneath me.

"Sera," he groaned, hips making miniscule thrusts upward and seeking contact.

I ground down onto his lap, the friction so good it addled my brain.

A hand came up to thread itself in my hair and I paused, a wave of self-consciousness sweeping over me. We all tried our best to keep up on our hygiene using whatever water we could periodically find to rinse off and brush our teeth, but still, I hadn't had a real bath in at least a day. As I felt his fingers catch on a knot in my curls, I realized I hadn't actually brushed them either. I'd gotten so used to taking care of my hair regularly with whatever supplies the camp provided that I hated the reminder of *before*, when I would yank a brush through it, to hell with the frizz, and would put it in a heavy braid after. Out of sight, out of mind.

Ryder lifted his hand, and I bit my lip, focusing on the dark stubble coating his jaw, the hidden dimples I knew to be on either side of his mouth, and avoided the eyes that were scrutinizing me so intensely. "Hey," he whispered, brushing his thumb against my jaw. "What's up?"

"Don't you think... I mean–" I bit out, gesturing at my hair, and then my general body, as though it were fairly obvious. Maybe I just expected him to read my mind, so I didn't have to say it.

I wouldn't have put it past him. He'd done it before.

"Did you know you smell like lavender from that oil you always apply on your temples to sleep better? Drives me wild, always catching it on your skin in the mornings. And it's even stronger when you use that lavender and thyme soap that Halli made. If your hair or your body or anything else is bothering you, we can stop and sort it out, but don't think it makes you any less appetizing." He rested his forehead against mine, breathing the same air for several moments before I surged forward and captured his lips in a kiss twice as urgent as the one before, inadvertently swallowing the peppermint that had been tucked in my cheek.

He was perfect.

Ryder growled out a curse, fiddling with my top to shove down the already oversized front and bare my breasts, taking my nipple into his mouth.

"Fuck," I whimpered, palming the back of his head and running the dark strands through my fingers. It was incredible to me how sensitive my nipples were, how receptive to his long pulls and teasing nips, and I'd never known. Teasing shocks traveled downwards, and I breathed a stuttered sigh when his hand followed, sliding into my leggings and exploring. He bit harder upon discovering the wetness that had gathered, and I clutched him closer, working my hips in a slow rocking motion to make him go faster. He took a break for only seconds to take my shirt off and shove my pants down my thighs.

"Yesss," he hissed, a sibilant curse. A finger teased at my clit, rubbing in small, tight circles before slipping lower and teasing at my entrance. I gasped when he slid it in, shivering at his deep moan.

"I can't wait," I muttered, shoving him back and swinging my leg over so that my left inner thigh was draped over his hips. He worked with me to shove his shirt up and off, and then I settled back down to explore his torso, mapping each curve and dip with my lips and tongue.

Each groan drove another whimper from me. His skin was salty and hot, mixed with the faint taste of the lotion he used and the lingering scent of jasmine. I worked my way downwards, needing his help once again to get his pants over his hips, before he was completely exposed.

Beautiful.

He was barely lit and yet still so clear to me; acres of pale skin and furrowed muscles leading down to a thatch of dark curls and a large cock that twitched hungrily. I pressed a kiss to the tip of him, lips curving into a smug grin at his loud groan. Eagerly, I gripped him at the base and drew him into my mouth, satisfied when his cock jerked.

"Sera," he groaned, hand caressing my arm where it rested across his bumpy stomach. "Please."

I was only there for what felt like seconds before he grabbed my upper arms and yanked me upwards, eyes wide as he panted. "I'm... not yet. Don't want to yet. Inside you."

Watching him lie there, chest rising and falling rapidly with each quick breath, torso glistening with sweat and cock heavy against his abdomen, I wanted him desperately.

Maneuvering onto my back, I pulled him over me, sucking in a breath when he nestled perfectly in the cradle of my hips. His eyes widened, hair falling messily across his brow as he stared down at me. "Condom," he rasped.

I froze, almost ready to cry as I realized we'd have to stop.

He was already shaking his head. "No, I know you don't have one. I..."

Holy shit, were his cheeks going *red*?

"You what?"

"I grabbed some," he whispered. "After we left Liam's, when we stopped at that little store to get the map. But I didn't come here expecting anything..."

I grinned. "You genius, you."

His cheeks only grew redder, and he scrambled off the bed to throw his clothes on. "Just, one moment. Okay? Promise." The door creaked as it shut behind him and in the time it took me to reposition my hair so that it wasn't all bunched up under my head, he had already returned, the foil packet in his hand glinting silver in the dim light.

When he didn't immediately come back to me, I frowned.

"It's obviously expired," he explained, looking uncharacteristically nervous. "Maybe it's not–"

"Ryder, do you want this?" I asked sweetly.

He nodded.

"Then come here."

Every step was quicker than the last, like the closer he got, the more he needed to be back in the same position as before, clothes stripped off again without a thought. The light exposed a long-healed scar on his upper thigh, and it only served to remind me of how much danger he'd been in when we were still with his father and he was treated like a tool and not someone that meant something to me.

"I trust you," I whispered. "And you can pull out to be safe just as an extra precaution. Besides, it was smart of you to grab these. Better than nothing."

The bed shook as he made his way up my body, hands planted on either side of my head as he lowered his head to kiss me.

"I've never done this before," I muttered between kisses. "So it might be awful, and I don't–"

Ryder cut me off with a hard kiss, his next words plain. "Neither have I."

CHAPTER 21

"What?"

"I've never..."

Understanding dawned as I stared at him. "I got that, but I just... I thought... What about Maria?"

"What about Maria?"

"Didn't you two... I thought you had sex with her?"

He settled back onto his heels, shocked, and I used my elbows to prop myself up some. "Never," he replied adamantly.

My jaw dropped. "What do you mean, you didn't fuck her? I saw you two go off together again and again... and when she was bitten, you looked devastated."

"We would talk. She wanted to tell someone so badly about her family. She was trying to work up the courage to take a trip up north to find her brother, so I'd sneak away supplies that she could add to her collection since Gunner was too greedy to just let her have them. When she was bitten, I just... it was crushing to know she'd never get to see him, that he would never know what happened to her."

Shock radiated through me. All those nights, that low burning jealousy in my gut. Heidi had *told* me I'd had the wrong idea and still I was sure I knew best. I'd resigned myself to thinking she had something that I didn't.

"I was rooting for her," he said. "That's all. It was always you. *Always.* The day you showed up, I could hardly take my eyes off you and that never stopped."

Remembering it made my smile grow. He'd been so surly, staring daggers at any of Gunner's men who gave me shit, always making sure I had enough to eat when I let the girls take my portions because I was too 'full,' when really, I felt guilty about being an extra mouth to feed. The little trinkets he'd leave in my bag whenever he came back from scavenging. They warmed my heart to him so quickly I was dizzy with it. He was the first person I'd looked for when I entered a room, and yet I passed it off as a silly crush and nothing more. As something that wasn't reciprocated and could never happen.

"Really? So never once?"

He shook his head.

I'd had no idea. After all, Gunner often provided *entertainment* for his men. I'd just assumed... I sat up a little, lifting my hand to cup his cheek. "How?" I asked softly.

Ryder shook his head, wearing a small frown. "Just never wanted to. Didn't understand what the big deal was."

"Is that still true?" I whispered. "Because there's no... no need for this. I care for you regardless, whether things go further or not. It wouldn't change a thing." I needed him to know that there was no pressure, no expectations. That he wasn't losing me by saying no.

The smile tugging at his lips surprised me. It was small but infused his face with a lightness it had previously been lacking. His hand came up to cover mine, his calluses rough against the skin of the back of my hand. I couldn't stop staring at his soft lips and that enigmatic smile. I leaned forward, almost in a trance, until our foreheads met.

He breathed in as I breathed out, again and again, just existing together. "No," he finally answered, careful to keep his voice low. "I want everything with you. I feel..."

I stayed quiet, letting him think.

"*Alive*," he said on an exhale. "I didn't even know this was possible, that other people hadn't fabricated it out of boredom or necessity. I want you more than I've ever wanted anything, in all the ways I could possibly have you."

Another thought flashed across my mind and made me hesitate, worrying my bottom lip. "Wait. You were first. So how can you not care about... about Jake?" I took a deep breath, mumbling the words I'd been reluctant to admit, even to myself. "Or Kasimir?"

Ryder's smile turned lopsided and knowing. He leaned back, all confidence and self-assuredness now that we were back in familiar territory. Muscles rippled beneath his skin, and his legs, sturdy and long, stretched out miles beneath him. "How could I tell you not to feel something? Command you not to do something like you belong to me and only me? You've not made a poor decision yet, my love, though even if you did, I would be the first in line to support your wrongs. You haven't used the words, but I know there's no competition I'm in danger of losing."

Heat prickled at the backs of my eyes. "Ryder..."

"You have the biggest heart of anyone I've ever met," he continued, "and I have no doubts that there's room for all of us in it. So no, I'm not worried. Or offended or upset or any other negative emotion your brain can conjure up. I love you just the same."

Time seemed to stand still as his confession hung in the air and as the weight of his words sank in, I blinked.

"You do?" I asked, voice barely above a whisper.

He smirked. "You doubt me?"

"No, I... No." I laughed softly, the sound breathless and tinged with disbelief. "You know, I don't think I could stop loving you even if I tried."

His grin morphed into something joyous and free. I'd never seen him wear such an expression before, and I wondered how I could've lived so long without it.

I sat up to press a teasing kiss to his neck, pulling him back down with me as I reclined. My breath quickened as he lowered his head to capture my lips, hips moving as he readjusted his position. His eyes bore into mine with a heated intensity, their brown turning a simmering dark shade.

"There," I gasped, hands gripping his shoulders, his waist, sliding to his hips. Anything to get him closer to me. "I want you."

I pressed my hands to his lower stomach, making small circles with my nails and preening internally when his eyes grew heavy-lidded.

He nipped my jaw, working his way down to my neck and kissing it softly before mapping a vein with his tongue. "Then what are you waiting for?" His hands traced a blazing hot trail down my front with his fingers, driving a whimper from me, rubbing and teasing until he was dipping a finger inside ever so slowly.

"Fuck," he rasped, bringing his hand up to his mouth and drawing his finger down his tongue, eyes rolling back as he tasted me. "Fucking sweet, just like I thought. That Jake got to taste you while I watched... it's all I can think about. How wet you'd be, dripping just for me, spread open on my tongue."

I shuddered at the image, wanting it so badly and yet... "Well, you can't do it now!" I exclaimed. Didn't he see me lying here, shaking in desperation? I needed him *now*. Inside me. Nothing else. "Take me," I whispered, resorting to begging him with each breath as he rolled the condom on with shaking hands. "Take me, take me, take me."

"Sera," he groaned, looking down at where I was spread for him, soaking from the prolonged edging. "So soft. Perfection."

Ryder notched himself at my entrance, staring avidly as he slid in the first inch. I gasped, clutching his arm so tightly my nails dug into his skin. It was bigger than anything I'd ever tried myself, definitely bigger than his fingers the other night. Almost an uncomfortable fullness. I felt myself stretch as he pushed further, and looked up to find his teeth gritted, jaw clenched tightly. His muscles stood out in stark relief, defined and chiseled beneath his taut skin, shaking with the effort it took him to stay still while I adjusted.

His eyes flew up to meet mine, heat and possession dominating the dark color. "Yes," he hissed, throwing his head back. "Yes. Just like that. So good. So fucking good."

Every word he spoke, voice so deep and raspy, made me impossibly wetter, and every breath was almost painful, like I was in stasis as I waited for him to slide all the way in.

Reaching out to clasp his hips, I tugged him close, closing the distance myself. We moaned in unison as his cock filled me completely, hitting spots I hadn't known existed. I shut my eyes before they rolled back, gasping at every twitch of him.

"Open your eyes, Seraphim."

I followed his command, fighting to keep them open even as pleasure dictated they stay shut. He moved, slowly at first, and then gaining speed once he was certain it was ecstasy that kept me speechless and not pain. Over and over, he thrust inside, hips meeting my thighs with a satisfying smack. My hands scrabbled at his back, pulling him impossibly closer so that our fronts were almost flush. The added sensation of my nipples rubbing against his firm chest with every stroke drove me over the edge, and I wound my hands in his hair as I cried out, my release hitting me in violent waves.

I vaguely registered as he pulled back, hand rapidly stroking his cock as he came with a groan into the condom, gasping hard and body twitching identical to mine. He disposed of it while I caught my breath, rolling us over to our sides and laying a steadying hand over my heart on my bare skin.

"Thank you," he whispered into my shoulder, pressing a soft kiss into my skin and sweeping my hair out of my face.

"We're doing that again," I muttered between gasps, elated at his quiet chuckle.

T he sound of a floorboard creaking brought me out of a deep sleep as I blinked blearily at the doorway, memories flooding me of the last time I'd woken like this. Seemed I'd never catch a fucking break. It was too dim for me to see, and beside me, Ryder slept on.

A faint curse came from the hall as someone banged something, and I instantly relaxed upon recognizing Kasimir's hushed whisper. What was he doing up?

I slid from the bed, gently so I didn't wake Ryder, and slipped through the cracked door. More barely audible sounds rang out around the corner at the top of the stairs, and then the creak of the steps as someone descended them. I pulled my long sleeves down over my fists, grateful for my sweatpants, and rounded the corner.

Kas was already on the first floor. I quickly tiptoed down the steps and entered the grand room, instantly spotting him where he stood examining one of the trinkets on a side table, moonlight shining down from leaf-ridden skylights to illuminate him. His frame was powerful and broad, with shoulders that could bear the weight of the world, and a presence that demanded attention.

"Kas?" I asked.

The trinket dropped with a clatter as he flinched, but didn't turn.

"Is everything okay?"

He was silent for so long, I thought he wasn't going to answer, then his shoulders dropped, and he sighed. "You made a noise in your sleep, and I wanted to make sure everything was okay. Decided to walk the perimeter while I was up. You should go back to bed now. You need your rest."

I was so fucking sick of everyone telling me that.

"Face me."

"We'll talk in the morning, Sera. Go back to bed."

"Turn around and face me," I ordered him quietly.

Maybe he really was just concerned for me. Wanted to make sure I was okay. Because he *cared* about me. And I'd wake up tomorrow and everything would be okay. We'd set out for the farm together, as a team.

But then why the hell was his bag sitting by his feet?

It was noticeably emptier, and I knew without even checking to confirm that he'd taken out everything of value to us, every item we'd brought to trade or to eat, so that he was leaving with only the things he'd come to us with and the clothes on his back.

"You're leaving?" I asked sharply, my voice ringing throughout the mansion and echoing off the walls, only serving to emphasize the crack in my words as I spoke.

He turned then, his face carefully blank. Black hair cascaded down to his shoulders, framing a strong jawline that was currently clenched. The scar that started at his temple was almost erased by the silvery light that bathed him in a dim glow, softening his rough features, but it could do nothing to lessen the iciness in his gaze. Those heavy-lidded eyes, a stormy gray, met mine with a challenge.

When he didn't answer, staring at me with that flat, enigmatic look, like I was a *stranger*, I repeated myself. "You're leaving."

"You always knew I w–"

"No," I interrupted. "Don't even try to pull that and turn it around on me. You were never going to leave in the *middle of the night* with your tail between your legs in case... what? One of us woke up and forced you to say goodbye? Asked you to rethink?"

His eyes narrowed, but I scored a miniscule flinch. "Of course not. It's just easier. Surely, you can see that. I would have spared you this if I could."

"Think carefully, Kas. What would you be sparing me? What am I feeling? And why?" To my horror, my voice broke on my next words. "I can't even... To wake up and have you be missing? Gone forever?"

That prompted a reaction. Vulnerability mingled with the resolve in his eyes as he moved jerkily forward before forcing himself to a stop. "It's safer," he bit out.

"For who?"

"Don't make this hard, baby."

"Did you even just fucking hear yourself?"

A frown tugged at his mouth. "I wasn't... I didn't mean-"

"You didn't *mean*," I sneered, hands balling into fists. "I know your friend-yes, *friend*-is missing, and that worries you. It scares you. So you're shoring up that wall, and cutting us out in the process."

"I'm not scared," he argued.

"Oh? And what are you doing right now? Fleeing in the middle of the night because you just love the moonlight so much?" I advanced until I was right before him, drilling a finger into his broad chest and ignoring the way his eyes flashed. "You think I don't know loss?" I hissed. "You think I don't make a conscious choice to set those fears aside for the people I love? I never thought you'd give in to cowardice."

His composure cracked and anguish spilled through before shuttering once more. "Don't you want to spare yourself the pain? Let me do this, before we get even closer. You'll never have to think of me again, never have to worry about how I'm doing or... or lose me. Isn't that what you wanted? Not to rely on anyone and to figure things out for yourself?"

Every single reason he'd just directed my way was straight from the well of his own fears. I knew that. But he was right, I realized. I had wanted that. I'd wanted it so badly that I'd made the reckless decision of forcing my way onto a trip that was so far out of my skill set that I didn't know how I was even standing before him right then.

I was so afraid of having my life ripped away from me again that I'd stopped myself from building it. But I hadn't collapsed and given up after

I'd lost Ben's—our—home. I got up, kept moving, and found a solution, even if it wasn't pretty. And when River came in and shook that up, I followed her based on nothing but promises and a vague sense of trust.

It didn't matter if I relied on someone every day for the rest of my life; that didn't mean I would lose the tempered core of me that kept me moving. And it would hurt if it was ripped away again, it would be devastating, but I would be *okay*. And if I wasn't... that was okay too.

I straightened, meeting his tortured gaze. No way was I letting him slip through my fingers like so many other opportunities I'd been too afraid to reach out and grab hold of. "I'll tell you now, so you'd better fucking hear me. I *care* about you. You could leave the country tomorrow, and I would *still* care for you. Leaving won't change a thing but distance."

"Don't say that," he begged. The mask of detachment fled, exposing the raw emotions that he struggled to keep hidden. "Don't care about me."

"I'm not afraid, Kas. I'm not scared anymore. You're worth it to me. Jake is worth it. Ryder is worth it. I won't throw something so special away just out of fear. So don't you either."

"Seraphim," he whispered, pronouncing my name like he was savoring each letter. My eyes fluttered shut as he traced my cheek with his index finger, hand eventually cupping the side of my face. I leaned my head into the cradle of his hand, opening my eyes to find his already locked on mine.

"There is no world where I would forget about you if I left. But my brother... He was the only thing I had left in my life. I can't..."

"You won't lose me. But I guess you have to ask yourself if it's worth the pain if you did."

"Always," he muttered, thumb brushing against my bottom lip. "I don't know if I could've actually made myself leave. I never thought myself capable of sharing, but I can't picture you without Jake or Ryder, even if I tried."

I waggled my brows. "They're growing on you, huh?"

His chuckle was husky. "I like having them around. It's been a long time since I've had people watching my back, especially whose company I enjoy. But above all, I like knowing you have so many people who... care for you."

"Care," I repeated softly. "Yes. That. It really doesn't bother you that I could feel the same for more than one of you?" A deep breath left me as I worked up the courage to say it plainly. "I know Jake and Ryder said they didn't, but you... you're the anomaly. You could walk out of here tomorrow, like you just tried to do, and settle down with someone else. Someone with a quieter life."

Understanding crept across his features as he processed what I said—and what I didn't. "I don't know if you saw, but I was at your camp for a good week," he said with a lopsided smirk. "I saw River and her guys. I'm no stranger to this. I'd be happy to be a part of your life. Not because I have no other option or because you only come as a package deal, but because I *like* this arrangement. I like having them around, and I like you even better. Even despite the fear."

"So we'll take it day by day."

His gaze traced the contours of my face, a fierce intensity in their depths. "Don't say that on my behalf, Seraphim. I don't need to take anything day by day. I know exactly what I want."

"Is that right?" I said with a light laugh, heart skipping a beat. "No more running away. You're staying."

"Yes," he murmured. "That's right. No more running away."

His mouth, hot and carnal, took mine. Desire mingled with elation to form a potent cocktail, sending a flood of heat surging through me, but I didn't want it to be about me just then.

I wanted to get my hands on him. To show him how grateful I was that he was mine.

How desperate he made me.

In one smooth movement, I dropped to my knees, core clenching at the sound of his hitched breath.

"That's it," he rumbled, reaching down to smooth his thumb over my lower lip, dipping inside my mouth. I glanced up at him through my eyelashes, drawing his thumb in deeper while sucking it and watching as his eyes flared with need.

I adjusted myself on my knees and pulled back so that his hand dropped to his side, then leaned forwards to rest my forehead against his hip–gripping his thighs and taking a deep breath, trembling from holding myself back. I wanted this to be memorable, enjoyable. Not some quick, dirty suck that he'd forget about the next day. I wanted to write myself in his memory. I wanted to be the one he thought about next time he took himself in hand and satisfied his desire when he was alone.

Another shaky breath in and I hooked my fingers under his jeans, sliding them down down down and caressing his hip bones along the way.

He was magnificent. Carved muscles formed a deep v that I wanted to trace with my tongue, leading down to a throbbing, erect cock that was so hard it looked almost painful. Kas grunted pitifully when I leaned in closer just to breathe softly against his skin, alternating hot and cold. His hand found the back of my head, and I liked the weight of it.

I tentatively licked a stripe up the length of his cock, moaning as his hand wove its way into my hair. He let me take things at my own pace, but his impatient grunts and groans made his feelings clear on the matter, as did his tight grip on my scalp. I ran my tongue along him once more, finally taking pity and drawing the tip of him into my mouth, letting it rest on my tongue; the salty, tangy taste of his desire strong. I tightened my lips to form a taut seal and sucked harder, using my tongue to trace along the head.

He moaned loudly, head thrown backward in pleasure, throat bobbing as he swallowed. Thick corded ropes stood out on his neck with each deep sound that left his lips and I had to hold back a proud smirk as I decided to quit with the teasing.

"That's it, sweetheart. So eager to please."

I pulled off his cock with a popping sound to lave attention on his balls, then rolled them in my hand while directing my other to the whatever I couldn't fit and holding it tightly as I took him back into my mouth, deeper this time. An obscene noise left my throat and his hips bucked forcefully, the hand in my hair briefly tensing before loosening once more. "Sorry," he mumbled contritely, voice sounding wrecked when it should have been mine.

"Mmngh," I muttered, working his length harder until it hit the back of my throat then choking slightly. I gripped his hip with my hand when he tried to pull back, doubling down and trying again. I couldn't take much more of him in, but that was okay. He seemed plenty satisfied as it was and there would always be time to try more.

Sloppy, wet sounds echoed around the room as my movements grew messier. Kas was muttering above me, broken sentences and unfinished words about how good it felt, how good I was, how he'd never wanted anything more. My eyes watered and tears graced my cheeks as I took him deeper.

His thigh tensed under my hand while his pull on my hair grew tighter, and I knew he was close. He just needed a little push.

I backed off, preening at his needy groan.

"Use me and come down my throat," I rasped, tilting my head back and opening my mouth for him to use. His eyes clouded over with a dark, possessive need in seconds as he used both hands on the back of my head to slide his cock back past my swollen lips, moving his hips in short, shallow thrusts.

I left my mouth open, occasionally using my tongue. It was sexier than it had any right to be, the way he was fucking my mouth. I dug my nails lightly into his thighs, shivering in response to his shudder, and moaned loudly as my pussy contracted down on nothing.

"Coming," he growled, thrusting faster and harder but being careful to keep them shallow enough that I didn't choke again. He wasn't quite deep enough that I couldn't taste the saltiness of his release, and it lingered on my tongue. I kept there as he panted heavily above me, resting my forehead on his thigh while he softened in my mouth and absently massaged the back of my head.

After a few long moments had passed and our sweat started to cool, I pulled back, licking him along the way and grinning at his quiet, overstimulated grunt.

I sprawled straight back onto the cool floorboards, looking up at him with what I was sure was a smug, satisfied smile while he watched me with hooded eyes and a rapturous expression. "I want to return the favor," he said gruffly, eyes raking over my puffy, spit-slicked lips and flushed face.

"Later," I replied hoarsely. "I don't need anything else. Just wanted... you."

He did what I didn't expect and joined me on the floor, leaning over me to capture my lips in a passionate kiss. If I'd thought he would care where my mouth had just been, it was clear he didn't. He licked into my mouth, surely tasting remnants of himself and the thought made me shiver, though the desire that had filled me moments before had cooled almost like I'd come when he did.

"Insatiable woman," he murmured, resting his forehead against mine. "What am I going to do with you?"

"Keep me," I whispered. "Just keep me."

CHAPTER 22

My bag weighed heavily across my shoulders, making me intimately aware of how much we'd brought to trade. We were fortunate that Casey's things had been easy to split amongst us without adding too much extra weight to our already heavy backpacks. Though items like his clothes, towel, and blanket, we'd hidden for safe keeping at the lodge.

Mila gave a raspy meow, brushing up against Kas's ankle like she could tell something was off. He absently clucked to her, quieter than usual. The zombies we'd encountered earlier had cast a pall on the group as we considered what exactly could have happened to Ethan. I know that Kasimir looked a little closer at the ones we'd run into right outside the city limits.

I made a note to tell Jake we should stop by the mansion on our way back, just in case there was any new evidence of someone staying there or passing through.

"Are you cold?" Jake asked me under his breath. The journey was getting to him too, dull circles emerging under his eyes and a new lethargy to his stride. We were all running low on energy, ready to be somewhere safe.

"No," I murmured back, pulling my long sleeves down over my fists.

It was chilly today. The sky was overcast, and the breeze had a bite to it. To be truthful, I was a bit cold, but it was nothing I couldn't handle.

Ryder shot me a grin from where he was hanging back, making sure Mila didn't fall too far behind when she paused to sniff an interesting-looking plant that hugged the base of a nearby tree.

At least one of us was in better spirits this morning. It wasn't that I was *unhappy*, it was just so draining to be so guarded all of the time. Jake said we were only a couple of miles away from the farm, so maybe we'd get the chance to rest after we arrived rather than being put straight to work.

Jake rolled his sleeves up, exposing tanned forearms. "Wish I didn't run so damn hot."

I looked over to find him wiping sweat from his brow and stifled a smile, placing my chilled hand on his arm.

"Cold." He shivered. "Feels good. Maybe it'll spread through osmosis."

"That's not what osmosis is."

"How the hell am I supposed to know about it? I've never had a biology class in my life unless you count my uncle teaching me about how Molotov cocktails work."

Kas snorted.

Mila stopped and lifted her head, sniffing the air, and I stopped. The scent was faint, but it smelled like...

"Food," Ryder announced. "You smell that?"

We moved quicker towards the source of all the goodness weaving its way through the air. The trees thinned out, and in the distance, I saw wall. It wasn't what I'd expected from a farm. In the agriculture books I'd flipped through, they were all open pastures and gates and tons of land, but the farm we were looking at resembled a fortress, and the fence was practically solid. Fence posts emerged from the ground and supported sturdy planks that were topped with vicious looking metal wound with barbed wire. It was tall too, and all I could see over it were the tops of buildings. The closer we got, the more silver I saw glinting in the dirt in front of the fence, and it didn't take me long to realize they were half-buried sharpened spikes.

Jake whistled. "Looking good as ever."

"And you trust these people?" Kasimir asked. I knew him well enough now to parse that it wasn't anger riding his tone, but wariness.

"Like anyone else back at camp," Jake replied seriously, all teasing vanished. "They've helped us out in the past through some hard times, times when we didn't have much to spare in return. The journey is rough, and they made it anyway, just to lend a hand. So yes."

Kas's eyes were crystalline in the gloomy light provided by the darkening clouds, riddled with hesitance and concern, such a stark contrast from his pitch-black hair. He looked tired.

I reached out to grasp his arm. "It'll be okay, Kas. I trust Jake, and Nix had only good things to say about them. But even if something goes wrong, we're a team. We have each other's backs."

He hesitated, eyebrows drawing together, before sighing heavily and nodding. When I went to remove my hand, he caught it before it could fall, giving it a tight, reassuring squeeze.

Jake grinned, all boyish charm and none of the tension from before. I loved how easily he could switch modes. "Kas and Sera sitting in a–"

I slapped my hand over his mouth, a smile rising unbidden at Kasimir's deep chuckle.

Jake's eyes danced above my hand, and when I removed it, he leaned down to press a quick, reassuring kiss to my lips.

We'd be okay. We had to.

The heavy gate was open when we approached, revealing a small group of people that were waiting to welcome us. It was amazing how much land was hiding behind the tall fencing.

A large house sat in the center just before us. Its exterior was adorned with weathered wooden panels, complete with a welcoming front porch that held a tiny crowd watching us approach. Looking at the large windows–in good condition and framed by white-trimmed shutters instead of being boarded over–made me think of camp and how lucky we were to live somewhere that didn't require us to triple reinforce every door and window.

Every building on the property held a certain rustic charm, especially the colossal barn behind the house, showcasing the passage of time through its aged exterior. The patches that stood out against the rusted metal of the roof told me they took upkeep seriously.

Lush fields of wild grasses stretched into the distance, and I could see moving figures interspersed with what looked like grazing livestock. Just around the corner I saw a glimpse of color, and realized that it looked awfully similar to the garden we had back at camp, just on a larger scale. More outbuildings dotted the land, but they were too far for me to really see what they were. Maybe cabins?

Jake was greeted with a kind reception, jokes and kisses on the cheek, while the rest of us received handshakes and firm nods. A bald man almost engulfed by the coat he was wearing immediately pulled him aside to give him details on the harvest and how their supplies were doing, while a tall woman came to stand before us.

She was only a head shorter than Kas, and though lean, her crossed arms were subtly defined with wiry muscle. The shorter woman at her side wore a welcoming smile; the flowy red dress that peeked out from under her coat, matching her crimson hair and the rosy tint on her pale cheeks.

"Gabrielle," the taller woman said, her stare assessing as she extended a hand to shake mine. Her grip was firm and steady, long fingers chilled by the cold. She wore a light coat as well, and I envied them both as I shivered at the biting chill brought by a powerful gust of wind.

Just by the way the others looked to her for cues, I knew she was in charge. She had the same wary, jaded look in her dark brown eyes that Merikh had acquired after years of running the camp in his father's shadow along with his brothers.

The guys and I introduced ourselves one by one, and when the silence stretched afterward, the smiling woman at her side spoke up. "I'm Haley. It's rare that we get fresh faces around here."

My smile dropped. "Casey joined us," I said stiffly. "But…"

"Oh! Oh, I'm so sorry. I hadn't even…" she trailed off, looking flustered and upset.

Gabrielle spoke, her voice marginally softer. "Most of the people here don't leave. We have some who venture out to scavenge, but it's been a good amount of time since the rest have felt the acute fear of the undead up close."

It wasn't quite a condolence, but I took it as the acknowledgement it was. Somehow, I knew that she didn't fall into that category. She seemed the type of leader to take on the dangerous tasks herself.

An older woman walked up behind them, tall, dignified, and almost an exact replica of Gabrielle, just with silvery locs instead of a short pixie cut. "Well, come on. Don't let the poor things freeze. And perfect timing because your bread is done baking." The last part was addressed to Haley, whose grin resurfaced at the news.

For the first time since we'd started speaking, Gabrielle's straight-face demeanor cracked, and she heaved an exasperated sigh. "We're coming, grandmother."

Haley turned to joke with the older woman as they started walking towards the large house, and my eyes widened upon spotting the deep mark traversing up from Gabrielle's back and onto her neck once she followed. Half-hidden by her coat, a long line of twisted scar tissue stood out against her dark skin, a stark reminder of the harsh cruelty our world was capable of.

Jake caught up with us, the man he'd been speaking to hurrying off in the other direction, and kept pace with me. His hand tangled with mine, thumb moving in soothing circles, and I squeezed it once, a pleasant feeling settling in my stomach.

I wanted to breathe a sigh of relief. We were *here*. We made it. But the journey back loomed in my thoughts, bringing a sinking dread that I couldn't shake.

The house was marginally warmer, the fire in the hearth doing a good job of heating the entryway. Those who had been hovering on the porch offered us curious nods as they filtered out, leaving just us seven.

"Here," her grandmother said, sweeping her arm towards the over-stuffed velvet couch in front of the fire. An identical couch sat to our left and to our right were two emerald green wingback armchairs. "We've got freshly baked food here that you can eat, then you can rest."

She grumbled at Gabrielle as she retreated to the kitchen; something about keeping us standing in the chill after a long trip. Haley followed her in, and the sounds of clinking dishes and low conversation ensued.

When I stood to help, Gabrielle raised a hand. "Best you just sit. It might not have been an order, but you should treat it like one."

That had me sliding back into the soft couch. On either side of me, Kas and Jake's thighs pressed against mine, the pressure soothing. Combined with the heat from the flames and the heavenly scent coming from the kitchen, I was close to falling asleep.

I drifted in and out as Jake talked logistics, little snippets reaching my ears as he told them about the journey here and asked about the horde. When thin napkins were brought in, each holding a slice of dense bread drizzled with honey, I sat up straight, mouth watering at the sight.

Ryder laughed softly at me from where he sat on Jake's other side as I dove in, moaning at the sweet taste on my tongue. Kas went stiff beside me, and before I could see what was wrong, his large hand settled on my thigh.

A look around revealed everyone to be tucking into their own slices, and so I glanced at him discreetly, surprised at the way his gaze raked over me, full of heat.

To hold his attention when he had freshly baked food in front of him? That's how you knew it was love.

Fuck.

It was my turn to freeze, thoughts tripping over themselves as I tried to backtrack. *I didn't mean that. I mean, he doesn't love me. Just like I don't love him. Or those light eyes, always so easy to read even when the rest of him is reserved, and that cute way he greets Mila when he thinks no one is looking, and...* Ah, fuck. I didn't see that ending well.

Misunderstanding my sudden shift in mood, he withdrew his hand to return to his snack, and I already missed its absence. How the hell could this have happened? When I really examined what I felt for Jake and Ryder, that warmth behind my chest was the same as what I felt for Kas. Admiration, lust, and appreciation intertwined to form something I hadn't thought I'd ever find. They were all so different, but I needed each of them. Did they know that? *Could they know how terrifying the prospect of losing myself to them is?* I stood by what I told Kas last night, but that didn't make it any less intimidating.

A voice cut into my thoughts, making me realize I'd just been staring at the last bite of my bread. "We were hoping you could stay at least a few days," Haley said from where she was curled up on the armchair to our left, bare feet tucked under her legs. "Maybe a week."

"My wife is generous," Gabrielle added dryly, taking the hand clasped in hers and bringing it to her lips for a quick kiss, prompting a broad smile from Haley. "We know you're probably needed at home, but we don't get much news from the outside and with the increase in pregnancies lately, we have fewer hands than usual."

My thoughts flew to Heidi. I hoped she was doing alright. I missed her dearly, Jamie and Nadira too. We hadn't been apart for longer than a day or two in the entire past year, and I knew they'd be in disbelief about how things had changed in the short while I'd been gone.

Maybe not so much about Ryder, since they'd always suspected *something* was there, but more the fact that there was more than one of them. Though I supposed after spending time with River, it didn't seem quite so foreign a concept. And the more I thought about it, they probably wouldn't be all too surprised about Jake either. Damn, was I really so predictable?

Jake set his napkin down on the scratched wooden coffee table and leaned back against the couch, legs widening just enough to press mine tighter. "We took longer than anticipated to get here, but we can stay as needed. They'll be worried when we don't come home around the time we expected, but won't launch any kind of search party until at least a month passes."

Gabrielle nodded, resting her arms on either side of the plush chair. "Great, here's what we need..."

J ake flopped onto the king-sized bed, landing with a bounce and letting out a soft sigh. "Fuck, I missed this."

The cabin was just as cozy as the farmhouse. Located near the edge of the property, it was structured much like the new ones back at camp, with a large room that consisted of a fireplace, dining area, and kitchen, then a bedroom at the back. The plan had initially been to sleep in the communal area closer to the barn, but since one of the pregnant women had recently moved into the farmhouse for her last trimester, we had it all to ourselves. Gabrielle had been a paramedic before the outbreak, and liked to keep anyone close who might need care.

One of the first things they'd traded when establishing a relationship had been the knowledge and expertise that allowed our camp to get water running through the pipes. Haley told me that the water wouldn't get warm here like it did back home, but I'd been expecting to bathe in a pond or something equally uncomfortable, so any alternative was welcome news. The bathroom across from the bedroom was small but tidy, and I was eager to shower off the whole damn journey.

"You go," Kas said, gesturing towards the shower. "We'll wait."

I didn't have it in me to argue, even though I felt like I should. Instead, I pulled a clean set of clothes from my bag and set them on the bed, then took my dwindling bar of soap and headed to the bathroom.

The rectangular window on the far shower wall provided the room with just enough cloudy light that I was able to navigate perfectly without lighting a candle, and when I pulled back the curtain, I was surprised to find several bottles already on the shelf. We'd been told to use whatever was left behind, but still...

Flipping the top of the cap on the bottle marked with an 's,' I inhaled deeply, recognizing the scent of gardenia. I set my things aside and flicked the water on, only flinching a little when the water noisily worked its way through the pipes for a minute before shooting out in bursts. Shivers racked my body at the temperature, but it was still so much better than a lake.

The cool tiles under my feet were grounding, as were the muted colors of the walls and the soft play of light as the clouds shifted outside the window.

I faintly heard what might have been a knock at the front door, but ignored it, knowing the guys would handle anything that came up. I used my soap to scrub vigorously at my skin and all the little marks and bruises that had cropped up over the past couple of weeks. The skin of someone who worked hard, and persevered. Ben would be proud of me, I just knew it. Peeking at myself in the mirror across from me, I looked like an entirely different person. The anxiety I wore like a cloak had receded somewhat, leaving behind clear gray eyes and a more youthful looking face, while sun exposure had brought out more of my freckles, sprinkling them liberally across my cheeks and nose.

The small room smelled of flowers mixed with the minty aroma of my toothpaste, and it reminded me of home so strongly that I had to close my eyes.

A short knock sounded at the door.

"You okay, Sera?"

I nodded before realizing that Jake couldn't see. "Yeah, all good." I'd shut the water off some time ago and had just been standing, shivering, lost in memories.

"Okay. Kas and Ryder went next door to use their shower. A courtesy so that we didn't have to spend any longer dirty than necessary."

That was kind of them to offer.

I wrapped the soft and stained towel draped over the rack against the wall over myself after soaking up some of the water from my hair and tucked the corner in, then opened the door, not expecting to stumble into Jake.

"Woah there." He steadied me by grasping my upper arms, going stiff when he realized I was only wearing the towel. "I–Your clothes. On the bed."

A laugh escaped me, and I patted his bearded cheek as I extricated myself. "Kind of you to notice."

"That's me. Kind."

I hummed, entering the bedroom and looking back at him where he stood in the doorway, eyes fixed on my face with a deep concentration. He held himself with a rigid tension, almost vibrating in place as we watched one another.

"You're so..." he breathed, gaze drifting down before shooting back up.

"Bruised? Soggy?"

He shook his head slowly, and it was then I noticed the simmering heat in his stare. Hands grasping the door frame, and an expression like he wanted to eat me whole; he was spellbound.

At some point, he'd lost his shirt, probably so he could wash it, but it meant that his entire golden torso was exposed—revealing muscles carved with precision that led down to a defined V-shape, made more visible by the pants slung low across his hips.

A rush of answering heat engulfed me and made me bold.

The towel slipped inch by inch, the drag roughly satisfying against my skin as it exposed my damp upper body. His sharply indrawn breath was audible in the near silent room, and I was grateful that the bedroom window was angled towards the fence so that no one would walk by and get an eyeful.

Jake watched my newly unveiled skin with a rapturous focus, and I allowed the towel to drop even further. My breasts were bared to him, then my belly. We both knew it was intentional, this tease, though by his quickened breaths I didn't think he minded.

"I heard you and Ryder last night, angel."

My cheeks flooded with heat, but I thrust my chin up anyway, like that wasn't a little embarrassing. "And?"

He stalked closer, a smirk playing at the edge of his mouth. "And I'm thinking unless you're too sore, I'd like to hear those sounds up close." His dirty, crooked grin was slow to spread, and wickedly attractive.

"Oh," I uttered, the towel dropping completely at my surprise.

"You were good for him, hm?"

"Y-yes."

"Gonna be good for me, too?"

I shrugged, backing up with each step he took until my legs hit the edge of the bed and threatened to buckle.

"That's not an answer, Seraphim."

As always, hearing my full name in that deep, rasping voice sent a shiver throughout my body.

"I think you like it when I'm a little bit bad," I whispered, letting myself fall backwards onto the bed.

His eyes flared, almost all of their rich brown swallowed up by the dark abyss of his pupils, impatiently demanding a response.

"No. I'm not too sore."

He joined me on the bed, hovering over me to look his fill and capturing my lips in a demanding kiss before pulling away much too soon.

I started to protest, but stopped when I realized he was sliding down my body, leaving kisses against my clean skin. My stomach, the insides of my thighs, my ankles, everywhere he could reach. It was a tortuous, exquisite pleasure.

Hungry eyes met mine when he reached the apex of my thighs, pressing a singular kiss to my pelvic bone.

"C'mon," I groaned, tossing my head back and waiting for him to take away the ache his teasing had created.

"Beg for it real needy like and I might consider it," he growled, head tilted.

Sucking another choked breath in, I spread my legs further so that I was totally on display for him.

"Please, cowboy. I need you."

Another kiss, this one lower and punctuated by the sweep of his tongue. His groan as he parted me was filthy, and I arched at the sudden sensation. "*Yes.* That's it."

Lips and tongue made quick work of me, working in unison to explore every inch to see what brought me the most pleasure. When he added his fingers to the equation, I bit down hard and narrowly missed my tongue. *Fuck*, why was he so good at that?

"That's it," he murmured, voice muffled and sending vibrations through me. "Such pretty noises, all for me. Missed this pussy."

I whimpered louder, sliding my hands in his tousled hair and scoring my nails over his scalp, pleased when he groaned and targeted my clit, giving it a quick nip. No longer teasing, he used targeted movements to make me moan so loud I almost shoved my fist into my mouth to muffle them, spreading me open to expose me further and sucking my pussy so hard I could see the hollows of his cheeks stark under his beard. The noises were obscene.

"Right there," I gasped, rocking my hips when he used one hand to tug me closer so that I was practically riding his face. The fingers stroking me in the exact spot I liked, coupled with the firm suction on my clit, ensured I was done for. I came with a cry, holding him in place with a frozen grip while my orgasm crashed over me.

I registered him wiping his face off onto his discarded shirt when my vision finally cleared, pushing to his feet with a smirk.

How was it that I was thoroughly debauched and naked while he was still clothed, cock throbbing fiercely behind the worn layer of his jeans? I gaped in awe of the picture before me. Roped muscle on top of muscle, every inch of him cut and defined. Golden tanned skin and dusky hair covered every inch of him. I sucked in a sharp breath, momentarily frozen by the enormity of my desire.

The front door squeaked as it opened, and I looked at Jake, only to find him smirking. "Your call, darlin'. Wanna cover all that creamy skin up? Or you wanna get even dirtier?" The deep growl in his words had my tired body responding with a fervent *yes*.

I reclined more fully onto the bed, my nakedness on total display, watching Jake as the footsteps grew closer. A smoldering intensity burned in his gaze, stoking the fire deep within me.

Kasimir turned the corner, already wearing a secretive smile. "Could hear you all the way from the front door, baby. That was one hell of an orgasm." Ryder followed him in, dark eyes snapping to my prone form as he scanned me up and down.

Feeling mischievous, I adjusted my hips so that my legs fell a little further apart, exposing more of me to the room. Then I stretched my arms overhead, creating a natural arch to my back that lifted my breasts upward. Being on display sent a dizzy, toe-curling rush to my head.

"Fuck, sweetheart," Kas growled, prowling towards the bed with a predatory grace. His dark, damp hair hung loose around his face, framing that strong jaw and full lips, and the white shirt he'd pulled on after his shower was sticking to his skin in random spots. He stripped it off halfway to me, so that I could feast my eyes on the entire length of his pale, scarred torso.

Chiseled and defined, his muscled abdomen formed a landscape of rippling contours. I reached out to touch it, when he plucked my hand out of the air and set it on his chest, sliding it down slowly over every single bump and curve.

I inhaled a shakily, eyes darting up to watch him.

"I want to taste you," he declared.

Jake laughed, settling into the chair at the right of the bed with a casual sprawl. "You're going to have to make her come again if you want any of that delicious fucking cream, because I already took everything she had to give."

"Ah, I don't think that'll be so hard. Hm, Seraphim? How about you? I bet you're wet right now." He traced a finger around one pebbled nipple, winking when I gasped. "Dripping for me already."

That finger trailed down my chest, to my belly button, then even further. "You'll come for me, won't you? You're so eager to please, how could you not?"

"Kas," I groaned.

That cruel mouth curved into a knowing smirk. "Just this once," he whispered. "I'll take pity on you." I grinned, and it earned me a hard kiss.

My pulse quickened as he settled his bulk at the end of the bed, wasting no time before licking me boldly.

"Shit!" I writhed at the sudden pressure, eyes darting over to where Ryder still stood by the door. His hard length throbbed where it lay trapped by his jeans, and damp hair curled onto his forehead as he watched me with heavy-lidded eyes. I beckoned him over with a hand, shivering when Kasimir inserted a finger and sharpened his tongue to a point before flattening it once more.

I glanced down at Ryder's thighs in front of me, and in seconds, he'd stripped off his clothes so that I had full access to him.

"You want this, Ryder? My hand on you?"

Black eyes flared as he snarled. "You know I do. Enough teasing."

"You're tellin' me," I murmured, crying out when Kas flicked my clit.

"Now that wasn't very nice, was it, Seraphim?" he asked casually.

Jake laughed when I gritted my teeth together. Wrapping a hand around the burning, hot skin of Ryder's cock, I moved in slow increments, watching raptly as pleasure crossed his face.

In turn, he toyed with my nipple, observing which motions received the best reaction as it hardened to a point under his finger. Leaning down, he drew it into his mouth, sucking with a steady pressure.

"Love these tits," he muttered. "So fucking full and soft; pretty and pink and craving my tongue."

I threw my head back on a moan that became exasperated when Kas stopped entirely. My head shot up in frustration to find him immersed in focus and ignoring my increasingly desperate pleas as he spread my pussy open and watched as it clenched down around nothing. Jake snickered from behind us, honey-brown eyes half-lidded and hand on his own cock.

"Your pussy's wide open for me, did you know that? Gaping. Begging for my tongue in your hole."

"Fuck. Kas, your *mouth*..." His breath as he laughed against me was warm. "Please," I begged. "Keeping going."

Ryder sucked harder, drawing a moan from me.

"Say my name," Kas ordered, brushing his lips against my clit.

I trembled, hands flying to his shoulders as I sucked in a harsh breath. "Kas," I gasped. "Kasimir, please."

His lips curved into a wicked grin where he was using his tongue on the crease of my thigh. "Fuck, I love my name in your mouth. The only thing better would be my cock."

A full-body shiver consumed me at that. When Jake cursed, I beckoned him closer, gripping his hip and twisting my upper half somewhat onto my side so that I could feed his cock past my lips.

His low groan spurred me to take him in further, choking for only a split-second. Ryder used his teeth to tug at my nipple, sending a shot of pleasured pain straight to my pussy, where Kas had just inserted another finger.

"I said I'd take pity on you, and I will," Kas informed me darkly. And with that, he finally delivered the sensations I'd been chasing. Licking, stabbing, and sucking; using his entire mouth to drive me to the edge.

I whimpered around his length, my full mouth sending vibrations through Jake, whose eyes snapped down to mine, glittering with need. "That's it," he murmured. Tiny thrusts of his hips sent him deeper until he was as far as he could go. I relaxed my throat muscles, using my tongue and hand to drive his fevered moans up in intensity.

My other hand stroked Ryder's cock still, but I'd added a twisting motion, tightening my grip each time I reached the head. "You don't mind waiting your turn," I said with a laugh. "Always did like to save your dessert for last."

He gave me an unrepentant grin. "Can you blame me?"

Jake's hips stuttered, and he paused. "Oh fuck, I can't..."

"That's it, cowboy." I increased the suction until he flooded my mouth with his come, sharp pants and growls escaping his lips as he pulled out inch by inch, using his thumb to wipe at my lip where a drop had had escaped.

Before I could even speak, Kas curled his fingers, powering in and out of my cunt with a singular goal in mind. My body snapped up in response. "Yes!" He kept up the rhythmic motion as I tightened around his fingers, adding a hard suck to my clit until my orgasm struck without warning, sending shockwaves through me that obscured my vision.

Kas didn't waste a second before rolling the condom on and pounding into my still contracting pussy as my orgasm stretched on, prolonged by the new angle he was hitting. He slammed into me with a fevered intensity, giving me the pace that I craved.

"Please, *yes*, there," I rambled on a sob, absently wondering when Ryder had even given it to him. A glance at Ryder revealed him to be watching me tremble with a dark stare. My eyes dropped to where his cock had been abandoned during my orgasm and I let my lips part, tongue extending.

His breath hitched. Instead of feeding it right to me, he tapped it on my tongue, then stroked the head of his cock over my nipple, leaving behind a clear, sticky trail. I was lucky I had larger breasts because I was able to bring it up to my mouth and lick it off, holding his gaze the entire time. Kas must've been watching, because he groaned, snapping his hips a little harder. Even Jake gave a raspy moan where he lay beside me.

"*Fuck*," Ryder snarled, biting out curse after curse. His patience snapped, and he pushed into my mouth with a pained groan. "Our dirty angel."

Ryder's hand fisted my hair as he fucked my mouth, staring into my eyes with an intensity that made me clench down hard around Kas. All too soon, he was coming down my throat, a hiss escaping his clenched teeth as he threw his head back. Instead of collapsing beside me once he finished, he bent down and kissed me to his satisfaction.

An over-sensitized whimper escaped me after he pulled back. "Kas, I d—don't know if I have another in me."

"You do," he snarled. In one quick move, he flipped me over so I was on my hands and knees. The new position sent a renewed jolt through me, and I shook as, almost immediately, my pleasure crested once more. This time aided by Kas who as he slapped my ass so hard he probably left a handprint as he chased his own release. The thought of seeing his mark on me in the mirror the next day made me cry out. I felt him fill the condom inside me, a liquid heat that I knew I wanted to feel bare one day, and bit back a scream as my sore muscles contracted around him. I collapsed in place, half on top of Ryder, who pressed a hot hand to my back.

My ragged gasps took ages to slow. "Oh my god," I groaned. "We're doing that again. After a decent, and perfectly respectable recovery period."

That startled a laugh from Kas, who had just come back from washing his hands as he handed a damp rag to Jake, who started cleaning me off.

Even my laugh sounded tired as I took way longer than I should've to pull on the oversized shirt Kas tossed at me once I was wiped down, hardly able to move. "Maybe I'll let you three share the bed and I'll take the couch."

Jake snorted, hooking me around the waist and rolling me over with a playful growl, not stopping until I was plastered against his chest where he lay in the middle.

"This works," I said, my voice muffled by his chest. I could feel the deep rumble from his laugh under my cheek and gave an involuntary smile in response.

"Y'know," Jake said sleepily, giving me one last tug so that I fell perfectly within the cradle of his body. At my right, Ryder laid a large hand across my inner thigh, finding me with unerring precision, considering his eyes were still closed. "I think I just might build us our own place when we get back. Why not, right? We're constructing them, anyway. Not like we can fit four people into either of our current places."

Kas snorted to our left. "Oh? Am I included in this headcount or is there another man you have your eye set on? So sure I want to move in with you?"

"You know there's not," I groused. "What, are you scandalized? Don't worry, Kas. I'd never ask you to ruin your stellar reputation." Shifting a bit, I snuggled further into Jake, jerking with a squeal when Kasimir pinched my ass lightly.

"You know damn well I want to," he said with a rumbly laugh.

Jake's voice was nothing more than a faint mumble now, fading in and out as I slowly but surely drifted off. "Good. We're in agreement. We'll wake up early to watch the sunrise, angel. I know how you love those. And we'll have a big bed, big enough to fit everyone, with an even bigger kitchen..."

CHAPTER 23

I covered my mouth at the sight of the largest goat climbing atop the dirtied plastic playset. Another pair charging at one another caught my eye and reminded me of two Ben used to own–Daisy and Mildred. Mildred was a crotchety old thing, but she loved Daisy fiercely, always entertaining her antics and making sure she was looked after even when her high energy was too much. She couldn't stand the rest of them, but those two had been thick as thieves.

The scents of livestock and soil were comforting, reminding me of all the positive times I'd had when Ben was still alive. It was so easy to only remember the end.

The fence shook as one of them banged into it and made me vibrate. My weight was currently supported by the crude wooden structure, as I wasn't sure I could stand on my own yet. I thought weeding and planting hadn't sounded too hard, but it was back-breaking, taking up most of the day and leaving me with sore muscles and aching knees. My clothes were coated in a fine layer of dirt since the worst of the clumps had been brushed off earlier, and the sweat had since cooled on my body, so I was no longer the color of an overripe tomato from the exertion.

After several days of lighter work to give my sore muscles a slight rest so I wasn't too worn out for the journey back, I thought I would have more energy. That failed, because I totally felt like I'd been trampled by a horse.

Even worse, I hadn't seen the guys all day as they'd been put to work elsewhere. Jake had dropped by to let me know they were given an errand for a nearby homestead, and I'd tried not to think too hard about that, so I could do even a crumb of work without checking the entrance every second. The incessant churning in my gut hadn't left all day, but that didn't stop my aching stomach from protesting loudly that it had been too long since my last meal.

"Hard day, huh?"

One of the girls I'd met that morning approached–Adriana, I thought her name was. Her dark hair was tied back like mine, but several pieces escaped to frame her elfin face, and her tan skin was currently flushed with a deep pink.

"Yeah, exhausting." Succinct, but I never was good at making conversation with strangers. I braced my hands on my lower back and bent until it cracked, letting out a relieved sigh. It was a good kind of tired, not borne of fear or necessity but hard work and contribution. Made me feel useful.

Adriana smiled affectionately as one of the goats bleated. "I just came over to tell you that dinner is ready. We have a buffet-style line set up in the barn. You'll love it, lots of creamy dishes and fresh food. One of the best parts of living here, aside from the safety, is the delicious meals every night. Being able to actually fill our stomachs is a blessing."

My stomach growled at the mere mention of the meal I could already scent on the breeze. "Thanks for letting me know. I'm starving."

The short walk was spent stretching my arms every which way and trying to relieve some of the stiffness from my muscles. *Maybe I can talk one of the guys into a massage...*

The sounds of a commotion rang out as I approached, and I immediately went on alert. There was a stark difference between casual, everyday noise, and alarm. Why the hell had I thought a weapon would just get in the way while I was working? I should've known better than to trust we'd be safe here. It was my worst nightmare come true. I'd freeze and lose everything, too cowardly to act and too frightened to run.

Shouting filled the air, and I took off at a run, Adriana hot on my heels. We rounded the corner of the barn to find a circle of people near the entrance, half of them pacing and waving their arms and the other half watching in silent horror.

I slowed to a jog when I spotted Jake and Ryder, not stopping until I'd reached them.

"What the hell is going on?" I gasped, doubling over while I examined the scene and realized someone was missing. My heart dropped into my stomach and nausea made my stomach flip. "Where's Kas?"

Jake tipped his head, looking grim. I straightened and noticed what had been hidden behind the wall of people before. A man laid squirming on the ground, foaming at the mouth.

Kasimir stood above him.

He looked like an avenging angel, skin deathly pale despite the golden light from the dying sun but contrasted by his raven-black hair. His face wore a twisted grimace, and when I instinctively stepped forwards, he jerked his hand up. Like despite his singular focus on the rabid man, he was still aware of my every move.

"Get her out of here," he growled.

When the set of hands settled on my shoulders, I shook them off, taking a step away. No way in hell would they get me to leave. What the fuck was happening?

"Is he infected?" I whispered, knowing the question was pointless. It was obvious the man had been bitten.

Gabrielle, who had been silently standing at the back of the group–shoved her way through. Her face was a blank mask, and in her hand was a large blade. "All of you go," she commanded.

The group dispersed, but not without rushed whispers and a few grumbles. I refused to move, gaze fixed on Kasimir, and so Ryder and Jake stayed behind too, as well as a man I'd never seen before at Gabrielle's right.

"This is why we have a protocol," she said, softer this time. "Because every life is so important now, and a single mistake can risk everything. I'm sorry for your loss, Otto."

I swung my attention to the men behind me, realizing that it just as easily could have been them. The groaning body at my feet had been walking, talking, and living, just minutes prior. How quickly he deteriorated. It was heartbreaking.

Jake laid a reassuring hand on my upper arm, his grip permeating the chill that had enveloped me.

Otto spoke bitterly, but his devastation was clear to see. "We could have gotten the fucking supplies some other time, but Ian just had to go for it. You're lucky the rest of you weren't bitten."

Taking a second look, I realized that my guys were speckled with dirt, blood, and sweat. It seemed that something had gone wrong on their short supply run and instead of turning back, the bitten man had forged ahead against better judgment.

Everyone paused when the man twitched. His skin was rapidly paling, now a sickly gray color, and his veins were darkening. The bite on his arm was gruesome, reddening as the infection spread. He was still conscious, still biting back words, but his eyes were rolling wildly.

Kasimir stood taller, pain and something more troubling flashing across his face as he took the blade from Otto. "Go. No one should have to kill their own brother."

I sucked in a sharp breath. His brother... No wonder he looked so hollowed out. To survive for so long with your family at your side only to lose them like this... I hoped he had a good support system, because he was going to need it.

Otto looked as though he might argue, but one glance at the resolution Kas radiated had him rubbing his face and walking back to the house where more onlookers gathered. Gabrielle offered Kas a short, grateful nod and followed, but not before adding one last request. "Just... wait until after Ian turns, okay? Once he's completely gone. He deserves that dignity."

It made sense, but it was still so damn risky. Every fiber in me urged me to eliminate the threat while it was still incapacitated on the ground. Watching Ian shake as he turned into something else was horrifying and painful to watch. I swore never to do it again. I understood her reasoning, but was it kinder to spare him the process of turning while he was still aware or kinder to end it when he was no longer present?

We waited, tuning out the murmurs in the distance and watching diligently when Ian gave a strong lurch.

A disturbingly mournful moan left his throat when he moved to his feet in quick, jerky motions, twisting his body to whoever stood closest.

There was another pained gurgle, and it was clear what was left of Ian had disappeared. The zombie lurched toward Kas, and Jake grabbed it by its discolored arm, holding it in place to make this as painless as possible.

Only everything went to shit the second the zombie tore free, using a strength beyond any newly turned I'd ever seen. Ian was a large man in life, and that had persisted in death. With his muscles and physique still intact so soon after turning, his size was used to his–its–advantage.

Lunging at Kas with a speed none of us had anticipated, I realized immediately what would happen. Kas would be bitten before he could even position his arms to defend himself. Jake was still regaining his balance and Ryder was even further behind us, but I was closest. I could *help*.

Without giving it a second thought, I threw myself forwards and tackled the zombie from behind.

We landed with a thud that knocked the breath from my body, and in seconds Kas was ripping it off me and plunging the blade through its skull. Glimpses of losing Casey filled my mind, reminding me of a different fall and a different tragedy.

The minute I caught my breath, I scrambled back and to my feet, almost running into Ryder as I fought to keep my balance. He reached out to steady me and I firmly told myself that it would be bad if I just sunk into his grip, even though I wanted nothing more than to collapse into his arms.

It didn't save me from the pure fury on Kasimir's face as he strode up to us.

"What the *fuck* was that?"

Ryder's steady presence at my back helped me temper my response. Why the hell was he angry? I'd just saved his fucking life! "Excuse me?" I shot back.

Kasimir shook his head, fists curling and uncurling in rapid movements. A spray of blood stained his shirt, but fortunately hadn't reached his face. "What were you thinking? I had it handled. You should've just stayed back. Don't *ever* do something so reckless again."

"I'll do it as many times as you need it. You almost got fucking bitten!"

"No, *you* almost got yourself killed for *nothing*. I had it under control!" he roared. He shook his head, his next words were spoken with a frigid finality. "You shouldn't even be here. You're a liability. A distraction."

Each word sent me reeling. It would've hurt less if he'd hit me. "You don't mean that," I whispered, searching his gaze for any hint of remorse.

Kasimir scowled. "I've never meant anything more. You're going to get someone killed."

I forced myself to keep standing straight, even as his words echoed on repeat in my mind, constricting my lungs and making it hard to breathe.

"*Fuck you*," I gasped through the tightness in my throat. How could he be so angry over me just trying to keep him safe, especially after we'd both ended up alright?

I didn't feel Ryder's hands leave my arms, just like I didn't register that I was retreating until they'd faded from my sight.

Kasimir was so strong, so self-assured. The kind of person who'd do anything for those he cared about. I just never thought I would be on the other side of that. Every insecurity I'd ever had came roaring back, drowning out the sound of whoever was calling my name behind me. My fear of everything falling apart, of losing everyone I loved because I was too fucking weak and cowardly to *fight* for what I wanted: like my home, my belongings, everything I'd called my own. It only took one evening for me to lose it all.

Maybe Kas was right. I never should've come.

CHAPTER 24

"Sera?"

My head hazy, I blinked groggily as the trees came into focus. Dusk had settled in, the sky painted in soft hues of orange and pink, and the air carried a touch of chill. My stomach ached, as did my chest, and only when the memories came rushing back to me did I realize why.

The owner of the voice knelt down beside me and let out a deep breath. "Thank fuck. We were worried sick. What the hell were you thinking going off on your own like that?"

I rolled over and groaned as the blood rushed to my head. "I was thinking that I was safely behind their walls and deserved some time alone to think." Deserved some time to process how we'd gotten to this point and how I could begin to separate myself from them without letting Kasimir know just how much his words had struck me. I hadn't meant to fall asleep, but I wasn't surprised my body took advantage of my stillness after the day I'd had.

Jake rested his arms on his knees and watched me with solemn eyes. "To brood, you mean."

"I'm not brooding! Besides, even if I was, I think I earned the right. Wouldn't you?"

He shook his head slowly. "C'mon Sera. That's not you."

"Maybe you don't know me then."

"You can't scare me off, darlin'. I'm all in."

"Shouldn't be," I grumbled. "Didn't you hear him? I'm a liability."

"Ah, you know he didn't mean that, Sera."

"Didn't he? Why else would he say it?"

Jake settled into a more comfortable position and rested his arms atop his bent knees, giving me a knowing look. "Why do you think?"

"I don't know. That's why I'm asking you!"

That earned a small laugh. Jake tilted his head up to the sky. "What do you know about Kasimir's brother?"

I frowned. "His brother? He–" I paused to think, trying to recall our conversations. "He died, he said."

"Did he tell you how?" Jake pushed.

"No, but... what does this have to do with what happened?"

"You need to talk to him."

"Cowboy..."

"Come on, angel." He jumped to his feet with an agility no one should have after a day on their feet and extended a hand to me. I hesitated to take it, worried that I was making a mistake. What if I saw Kasimir, and he repeated it all, but this time added more? I wished Jake would have just let me languish there tucked under the trees.

I sighed, trudging alongside him. All around us were the sounds of the farm winding down, voices ringing out from various corners and echoing across the fields. Chickens clucked in the distance and somewhere close by a fox yipped, reminding me that the world was so much larger than it currently felt.

Once we were on the familiar trail that led toward the east side of the farm, passing one of the smaller greenhouses I wanted to visit, I realized he was taking me to the cabin we were staying in.

Maybe Kasimir isn't there, I thought to myself. *He might be halfway across the farm helping with something or... dealing with the aftermath of what happened to Ian.*

Just recalling it sent a shock of pain through me.

You're a liability. A distraction.

Turning down the path shaped by countless footsteps before us, we soon broke off to make our way towards the solitary cabin by the wall. Evening had descended gradually during our long walk here from where I'd fallen asleep, and light from the hearth glowed from within, sending shapes through the windows to dance over the grass outside.

Jake stayed unnaturally quiet, as though he sensed that any conversation would lead to questions he couldn't–or wouldn't–answer. That he was even advocating for me to speak to Kas after hearing the things he'd said... it stung, seeming a little like a betrayal. Although logically, I knew he would never push for anything that might hurt me in some way. That alone told me I shouldn't expect to hear more of the same sentiments from Kasimir.

I didn't even get up to the front door before it was flying open and Kasimir was snatching me off my feet. He pulled me to him in a shuddering embrace, holding me like I'd been gone for weeks and not hours.

"I looked for you," he rasped, clutching me tighter. "I thought... I don't know what I thought. That you left, maybe. Ryder had to force me to stay behind to let you come to me."

Sure enough, Ryder stood behind him in the doorway, a sympathetic curl to his lips as he watched us. He winked when he noticed me peeking up at him from where I was tucked against Kasimir's chest.

Kasimir vibrated with tension as he moved his hands to my upper arms and leaned back to scan me up and down, turning his attention to Jake.

"Sleeping in the crop of trees to the south," Jake said with a smirk.

Satisfied that I was okay, he let out a relieved breath. "Don't ever disappear like that again. Please." His dark brows furrowed as he tried to parse through his emotions to put them to words, and I had to wonder if this was the first time aside from Ethan that he'd truly worried over another living being in the past decade. *I really scared him, huh?*

I frowned, stepping away. "You hurt me. I needed time."

"I'll give you all the time you need, but only where you're *safe*. To come so close to losing you, then have you disappear like that? It nearly killed me."

"Kas, I–"

"Promise me," he insisted, pain flickering in his eyes and turning them cloudy. To see him so twisted up over *me*, dark hair disheveled from his hands and lines bracketing his mouth...

"Fine," I acquiesced. I could give him that, because I would want the same. It wasn't different just because he was larger than me, or stronger. Everyone was fallible. And if he ever tried to test me on it, citing something about strength or capability, I'd clear the misconception up fast. That went for the others, too.

Jake reached down to slip his hand into mine, leading me inside. I followed easily, plopping onto the couch before the fire and snuggling into the blanket that laid across the back. Kas followed, looking unsure. He was so large, always so confident. The kind of person who could handle any situation, any challenge. But right then, all that commanding energy had morphed into anguish as he watched me. The scar through his eyebrow seemed deeper in the firelight, as did the grooves lining his forehead. He closed his eyes and let out a deep breath, his first easy one in hours, it seemed. "You scared me."

"You don't think I was scared? Of course I was. I was terrified."

"Seraphim, it's–"

"No," I insisted, cutting him off. It felt so freeing to be able to speak the words that had been festering inside me for so long. "I lost my home because of cowardice. What else will I lose? One of you? Never."

Jake swept my cheek with his thumb, such a casual, gentle touch that meant everything to me. "We've all been afraid, Sera. I've never felt fear like I did when you were lying next to Casey, and I didn't know how badly you were injured."

"You don't understand," I rasped. "I didn't even fight for it. Ben's home was all I had. It was where he taught me to keep going after he passed, and I just let them take it. You were right, Kasimir. I am a liability. It was so... so senseless. Such a waste. How could I not save *you* if I had the means to do so? To do things right this time?"

I called it Ben's because it was easier that way. Less painful. If I had no claim to it, then it wasn't like it had been taken from me. Ripped from my grasp. Deep in my heart when I had to acknowledge it, I knew it was as much mine as his. I was raised in that home. Loved in that home. But the more time that passed, the more I realized a home was just a house without the people who made it so.

"What happened?" Ryder asked. He laid a comforting hand on my knee.

My voice was flat. "It was around my birthday, my first without Ben, and I was lonely. Almost a year by myself and I was feeling nostalgic, so I thought I'd pick some strawberries, like he used in the pies he baked every year. Except there were none growing close to the compound. So I ventured a little further out than usual. I did everything he taught me to: moved silently, kept a watchful eye on my surroundings, listened closely. Never even found any goddamn strawberries, just heard a noise and bolted. But whoever it was had followed me back. I could hear them moving through the forest behind me once I reached the house. I locked everything up and shut myself inside, too scared to leave for weeks after that and assuming they'd gotten turned around before they realized the house was tucked away further down. Honestly, it was probably my fault for even running. Maybe they would've just asked me a couple questions and let me go if I'd stayed."

Jake pulled me close, tucking my head under his chin.

"It took one trip out for them to make their move," I muttered. "There was an issue with the well, and I left to check it out. Imagine their surprise when they realized it was just me in that huge building, and not the many faceless people they thought they'd need to kill to take it over."

"You were forced out, and they moved in," Kasimir surmised.

I nodded. "It was awful. Being shut away like I was, I had no idea they were camped out just down the road, formulating a plan. Of-fucking-course it would've been easy for them to keep looking until they found it. Which they did. People don't just disappear."

"I'm angry on your behalf," Jake rumbled, "but grateful beyond belief that nothing more sinister happened."

I shuddered, recalling the many horror stories I'd heard growing up when Ben was trying to teach me about the realities of the world. "I know. Me too." I hesitated. Sharing that was one thing, but this felt so much more vulnerable. "I admire you, you know." They were silent, waiting, and I wet my lips. "I feel–*felt*–like I could never possibly measure up."

Ryder was already shaking his head, ready to protest, and Jake's face was twisted in denial.

"Yes," I said sharply. "Kas, you lost your family, and you kept pushing forwards. You didn't let it turn you bitter." Kasimir frowned, about to object, but I continued. "Jake, your uncle died and instead of giving up or making some reckless decision, you found the triplets. You made a new home for yourself." His lips parted, and I faced Ryder. "And you. You had the courage to kill your own father when, horrible person or not, he was the man who raised you. Then to move to a new place and start all over, knowing how much they disliked you for it? All because you never lost your moral compass."

Jake shot him an apologetic look at that, to which he received a wry eye roll and a miniscule grin.

"I wanted better for you," Ryder mumbled. "You couldn't stay with us forever. It was the better deal, and I got to wipe out some of his corruption in the process, which I'd been planning for a while."

"I joined the first group I saw when everything fell apart, and while I could never regret meeting the girls, or you, or ending up where I am today... What if I'm not strong enough the next time I lose everything? River kept going after her dad died. She stayed true to herself, and even when she ended up back there, she didn't just sit down and take it. Me, however..."

Kas bent over to clasp my hands in his, bringing them into his lap. His thumb brushing soft circles over my fingers helped me relax some. A hand reached out to rest under my chin, tipping my head up from where I'd been staring at our tangled grip. Jake's expression was so soft, so honest. Tears pricked the back of my eyes and I blinked rapidly to clear them. "You're the strongest person I've ever met, Sera. Not just because of what you can do, or how you survive, but because of your heart. You're the best person I know, and I'm honored to have met you. You throw yourself into everything you do, but helping others is something you excel at. You think it wasn't pure chance and faith that had me going with them that day?"

Ryder interjected, his voice deep and sure. "I fell in love with you the moment I saw you. Having you end up there with me... of all places? I thank fate often. To be yours is an honor."

No amount of blinking would hold back the tears from falling, in fact now it only sped them up.

Kas let go of my hands to swipe his thumbs over my cheeks, clearing away the salty trails. "You're never going to be alone again. Not with us here. But even if you were, I know you have the determination to keep moving forward. You're not dependent on us, or a burden. I never should have said that."

"I know that now," I said with a watery laugh. "I wouldn't have it any other way."

Kasimir exhaled deeply as he watched our hands, pulling his free after several moments. "I still owe you an apology."

Ryder gave me a quick but passionate kiss before making a move to leave. Jake looked from him to me before turning to follow, when Kas held up a staying hand. His voice when he spoke was infused with gravel. "You're in this, right? Committed. For Sera."

"Ours," Jake said with a smirk, brown eyes dancing, while Ryder tilted his head in agreement and offered me a discreet curve of his lips.

"Then stay. You'll want to hear this too. If you hurt her like I did, I'd want to weigh your apology in my place."

I let out a slow, steady breath as they joined me on the couch. Jake scooped me up into his lap, positioning me so that I was resting against his chest, and Ryder pulled my feet into his lap, thumbs working over the tired muscles with a gentle pressure. To have them all together like this... I felt lighter somehow, like something had lifted, but I didn't know what. Maybe it was just the relief of knowing that Kasimir hadn't meant what he'd said. That saying it had hurt him as deeply as it did me to hear it. Or maybe it was that they all fit together so well, that they were so invested in me and my well-being. Watching them interact made butterflies dance deep in my stomach.

Kas lowered himself onto the table in front of the couch, resting his forearms on his knees as he watched me. "I owe you an apology," he began solemnly. "I shouldn't have said what I did. I was..."

"Scared," Jake supplied helpfully, a sly grin tugging at the corners of his lips. "You were scared."

If I'd thought Kas might be irritated, or try to correct him, I would've been wrong. He just sighed, smoothing the area between his brows as if rubbing away any tension. "Yes," he agreed. "I was scared."

"But why?" I blurted out, adjusting my position so that I could face him a little more fully. "I was fine. You stopped it before it could turn on me. Yeah, I was scared too, but I had faith that you would keep me safe."

"Seeing you–" he broke off with a rough growl, trying again. "That you would ever put yourself in danger for me is unacceptable. I've only just found you. If I lost you because you would ever dare put me above yourself? I couldn't..."

I was sympathetic to his cause, but there was no way I'd ever not act in a situation where he was in danger and I could help. Jake took one look at me and tightened his arm around my waist. "What he said, angel. Don't even try it."

I shrugged. "We'll have to agree to disagree."

Ryder shook his head, thumb working the high area of my arch. "I'll follow you from this life into the next if it comes to it, so I'd rethink that strategy if I were you."

"What the hell?" I threw my arms up before crossing them over my chest. "That's not the deal! Why is it so hard to accept that I'm not just going to stand by and watch something happen to you if I have the power to stop it?"

"Love doesn't work that way," Kas informed me unapologetically, his silver gaze holding an electric charge as he watched me. His mouth formed a rueful smile at my shock. "Oh, come on, Seraphim. Really? You can't tell me you didn't know."

My back flew straight. "Oh what, between the *'you're a liability'* talk and the attempt to run out last week?" The hurt that flashed across his face made me wish I could take back the words.

"You're right. I shouldn't have said that. I didn't mean it and I'm sorry it hurt you. You're incredibly capable, I know this. And I'm sorry I almost left. I just..." he sighed.

"Scared again?" Ryder commented, hiding his amusement behind his typical mask.

Kas grinned again, but it was anything but happy. "How'd you guess?" He adjusted his position and tilted his head back so that he was looking at the ceiling when he spoke, throat bobbing with each word. "My entire family is dead, as you know. My parents died when the virus mutated. They were out picking up our rations for the week. I was seven."

I flinched, and Ryder's hand moved from my foot to span the length of my ankle, his tight grip comforting.

"You said you had a brother. How old was he when they died?" I asked.

"He was only four."

Jake grunted, his other hand coming up to land on my stomach when I made a quiet noise.

"He died when he was fourteen, and I was the one who killed him."

CHAPTER 25

M y sharp intake of breath was harsh in the silent room. The flames crackling in the hearth weren't enough to lessen the oppressive silence that had settled over us after Kas dropped that statement. There had to be some way that he'd twisted it, because I knew Kasimir, and the man sitting before me had not murdered his brother in cold blood like he seemed to be suggesting.

"What are you talking about?" I asked. "What do you mean, you killed him?"

"I've never told anyone this," he said tonelessly, gaze darting from Jake to Ryder to land back on me. "He couldn't speak, but I knew he was scared. He had to be. Maybe I was seeing things that weren't there, but I can remember it so clearly. He... His eyes..."

"Kasimir." I couldn't stand seeing him so upset, eyes glazed over as he relived the memories.

"It was my fault."

"How?" Ryder asked. His head was tilted to the side as he watched Kas, maybe recognizing something in that tortured tone.

"He was hungry." Kasimir's voice broke on the last word, and I couldn't take it anymore. I disentangled myself from Jake and Ryder, got my feet under me, and stood. Taking Kas's hand, I pulled him along with me over to the chair at the right of the couch and pushed him into it, climbing into his lap after so that I was completely swallowed up by his hulking body.

Immediately, his hands came up to circle me, as if I were a stuffed animal or a safety blanket. Like she sensed the tension in the room, Mila cracked an eye open from where she was napping on the rug in front of the hearth. The room must've passed her approval because she closed it once more, drifting back to sleep.

"Okay," I whispered, laying my hand over of his and lacing our fingers together. On the couch, Jake spread his legs to take up the spot I'd vacated, and Ryder rested an arm on the pillow beside him. Both their gazes were steady as they waited for Kasimir to find the words.

Kas pressed a soft kiss to the top of my head before continuing. "He was all I had left. We'd done pretty well for ourselves: staying hidden, staying safe, finding edible food here and there. Those first few years were..." Lines of anguish etched themselves across his forehead. "Torture. I was much too young to keep both him and myself alive, but we managed somehow. It was a miracle. Things got easier as we grew older, and I learned through trial and error. I did all the scavenging and exploring, only bringing him along once I knew it was safe, otherwise he was holed up in an old treehouse we'd found deep in the woods in some suburbs. But, of all things, I caught a fucking cold."

"Shit," Jake said softly.

Kas nodded. "Best I can guess, he was tired of waiting for me to get better and worried about the dwindling food supply, and decided to venture out on his own while I was sleeping. I knew we were getting low, but I figured it'd be better to go hungry than for me to look for more while I was sick. If I died, he'd have no one to look after him, and I couldn't risk it."

I brushed my thumb along the back of his hand in sweeping back-and-forth motions, silently prompting him to continue. This would be the worst part.

"I was half-delirious with the cold and interrupted sleep when he came back. To this day... I don't know why or how."

My heart twisted violently in my chest, sending a cold shock throughout my body. *Please tell me he doesn't mean what I think he does. Not Kas...* Thinking of him at seventeen, losing the only family he had left in the world and assigning himself the blame all these years made a hot pressure build behind my eyes. I sniffled discreetly, trying not to draw attention to myself.

"Sera–"

"Go on," I interrupted him in a stuffy voice. He needed to get it all out already so I could start telling him it wasn't his fault, using logic and facts rather than pure conviction, which I knew he would dismiss. I felt his deep sigh with every cell in my body.

"He had a bite mark on his arm. I didn't notice it at first–but I definitely noticed how his eyes were struck through with red. The foam building in his mouth. He was turning so quickly that he must have used the last bits of *himself* to find his way back to me. Some days I'm not sure if I'm more grateful he came back so I would know what happened to him or less so that I wasn't forced to... neutralize him."

Ryder flinched at the word "neutralize." It sounded so impersonal, but it held a wealth of meaning when Kas said it. He'd tried to keep it impersonal, but the very word implied that he had to take down the zombie of his own brother, the little boy he'd practically raised all on his own.

Jake frowned. "I'm not seeing how this is your fault."

"It's obvious, isn't it? If I'd just been more careful not to get sick or brought home more food so we wouldn't have run out as quickly, then maybe he wouldn't have gone off on his own. Wouldn't have come back with that hollow look in his eyes. The worst part is that to this day, I'm not sure if he came back because his brain was already changing and he knew where to find a guaranteed meal, or because he didn't want me to bear the weight of his disappearance, forever searching for him and coming up empty. Maybe he wanted a merciless end, and he didn't care about the mark it would leave on me. Whatever the reason, I took care of it. Like I always did."

Aaaand the floodgates are opening. I tucked my face into my knees where they were curled up near my chest to try to muffle the sound of my wet sniffles and discreetly wipe the tears away.

"Key word being 'maybe,'" Ryder pointed out fruitlessly.

Kas made soft unintelligible shushing noises as he gathered me up even closer, unfurling me so that my teary face was exposed to the room. "Oh, don't be sad for me, love. It's been a very long time."

A few more tears slipped out, and I quickly knuckled them away. "I don't think it ever hurts less. Besides, it kills me that you think it's your fault, even after all these years. You were just," I hiccoughed, "a kid doing the best he could."

Jake got to his feet and retreated into the kitchen. The sounds of running water and opening cabinets reached my ears until he reappeared into view with a damp washcloth. Kas took it from him with a murmured thank you, using it to brush the tears away with the gentlest touch, so incongruent with his large, scarred hands.

"She's right," Ryder added, looking down at his feet. "I know a thing or two about being young and making hard choices. It was tragic what happened, but that doesn't mean it was your fault. Hell, there were a million other things that could've gone wrong. Sometimes things happen simply because they do."

Kas bent to press a kiss to my cheek, his stubble rough against my skin and his hair tickling me as it brushed my neck. I caught his cheek with my palm before he could pull back and pressed a firm kiss to his lips. It was wet and tasted of salt.

"You don't want the same thing to happen to me," I said after he pulled back, my voice nasally.

Ryder stood to go into the kitchen but paused on his way, running a hand through my hair, and letting the curls slide through his fingers to drape across Kasimir's broad shoulder.

"I couldn't bear it. I'd give my life a thousand times over before I let anything happen to you."

"On that, we're in agreement," Jake added from the other room, where he was rinsing the washcloth.

Ryder gave my hair a little tug where his hand was still buried against my scalp, and when my eyes flew up to meet his, he gave me an unapologetic shrug. It seemed he, too, was of the same mind.

I rolled my eyes. They would never have to know just how deeply I felt the same.

I would do anything to keep them safe, even if they liked to pretend I wouldn't.

CHAPTER 26

"You have everything you need?" Gabrielle asked while visually inspecting everyone like she might find some sort of glaring issue that would delay us. Haley had already sent us off with her blessing, and a few well-bundled treats.

"We're all set," Jake informed her.

The crisp morning air carried an aura of anticipation that made me jittery. All around us buckles were snapped into place and boots were triple laced as we got ready to set out, each small sound ratcheting up the expectant tension.

Our bags were heavy with fresh supplies. We'd been able to trade for all the essentials—cuttings from a multitude of their thriving plants, dried and well-preserved seeds, excess tools and materials we could use in the ongoing construction, and plenty of wool fabric made using the sheep they kept in the south pasture.

Beside Gabrielle stood a shorter man with tanned brown skin, whose narrowed, hooded eyes scanned the group just as watchfully as Gabrielle, looking for anything out of place. His hair was shorn close, and he wore a machete strapped to his hip like I did, where he could easily reach for it. Kas helped me sharpen mine last night so that any of the events on the way here wouldn't affect its performance on the journey back.

I liked knowing we had people looking out for us and making sure we had everything we needed. It gave me a false sense of confidence that everything might just go right this time. We were so close to being home, and once we got there, I wasn't sure I'd ever leave again. My short-lived adventurous streak had all but disappeared. It had taken me this whole time to realize there'd never been any 'test' required for me to give myself permission to feel safe. That debilitating fear of the unknown that kept me up night after night, terrified some faceless monster would snatch the entire life I was building out from under me, had quieted to a whisper. Fear would still haunt my every move, but I had a tighter hold on it now. I was ready to start *living*, and I finally didn't feel ashamed or weak for wanting to do that safely back behind the fortified walls of the camp.

A tug on my backpack sent me reeling into Ryder, who chuckled and steadied me. I looked behind me to find Jake tugging on the straps, making sure it was secure.

"A little warning," I quipped, raising an eyebrow.

He pressed a kiss to my hair to hide his smile, and Ryder spun me to check the straps across my front. Mila meowed from the new special section at the front of his backpack, where she had the whole space to herself.

Jake tsked when I squirmed, pulling on the straps again. I threw my arms up as I exclaimed, "Seriously?"

"You wanna check me, sweetheart?" Kas asked with a chuckle. Like the first time I'd met him, his clothes clung to him with a tantalizing snugness: a form-fitting black shirt, dark cargo pants, and hefty combat boots.

"I'd be surprised if you haven't already checked *yourself* at least four times."

He shrugged. "So I'm big on preparedness."

My heart–lighter than it had been when we'd first walked through those doors–thumped steadily as they pulled open the gate at the entrance.

Kas came up on my left and slid his hand into mine, giving it a comforting squeeze. "We're going to be okay, Sera."

I pulled my ponytail tighter and took a deep breath. "Yeah."

On my other side, Jake rested a hand on my shoulder and leaned in to press another kiss to the top of my head. "Kas is right. We've got this."

Calming my agitated nerves by tapping the fingers of my free hand against one another, I looked back and waved to Gabrielle where she'd moved to the porch, then walked through the gate to the outside.

Our night at the mansion was uneventful. The traps we'd placed at the unbarricaded doors hadn't been disturbed, nor had any of the ground-floor windows, so it was safe to assume no one had returned in the time we'd been gone.

I didn't think Kas had expected otherwise, but he was still noticeably quieter that day. We'd all shared the bed in the room closest to the top of the stairs, and I'd spent the night running my fingers through his hair to get him to finally sleep. The others picked up on it and joked more easily, drawing him into conversation often so that he didn't disappear in his thoughts. It seemed almost like Kas hadn't realized what an important role Ethan played in his life, and now that he was forced to confront the fact that he *was* indeed a friend and not just a convenient resource, he was left vulnerable to the worry we all experienced for those we cared about.

For breakfast, we ate some of the fresh provisions Haley had sent with us. It wouldn't be long before we ran out and were left eating granola and jerky again. If only canned food wasn't too heavy and didn't take up so much space, then we'd have some more variety.

With no plans to spend any of the day in one place like we'd had to on the way up, there would be no fishing or foraging to break up the monotony. I tried not to think of all the variety and flavor in the meals they'd served back at the farm. They'd had *goat butter*, for fuck's sake. I hadn't had butter in years.

As the forest path stretched ahead, our tired footsteps fell in sync. Running water was audible in the distance and I looked longingly towards where the trees parted. The day's journey had been a long one, leaving me yearning for a brief respite. The promise of fresh water was almost irresistible.

"Just think," Ryder said, noticing my despair. "You'll be able to shower in no time as soon as we get back."

I looked down at my stained shirt and sullied jeans with a frown. "I miss being clean."

Jake made a thoughtful sound and passed me a peppermint, flashing me a sly grin when I gaped at him. "You have more? I thought they all ran out!"

"I couldn't let you have them all at once. Then what would I pull out whenever you need cheering up?"

I was too excited to be annoyed; he was right. It was small, but had totally turned my mood around. Popping it into my mouth, I groaned happily as the minty taste hit my tongue.

"We should get you some other flavors," he mused. "Maybe your new favorite is just out there waiting for you to discover it."

"Curiosity killed the cat," I muttered around the one already in my mouth. "I'd rather we just never left camp again."

Jake's eyes dropped to where my lips pursed as I tucked the candy in my cheek, so I shot him a wink.

"But satisfaction brought it back," he crooned, leaning in closer and lowering his voice. He batted his lashes innocently as he asked, "Are you going to satisfy me, Sera?"

A rough shiver racked my body at the heat in his eyes and the way his voice deepened, taking me out of our current surroundings and transporting me somewhere much more intimate. Then I remembered my tangled hair and growling stomach and snapped out of it.

I straightened, clearing my throat and raising an imperious brow. "No. Now, if you'll go on about your day, I have things to do."

Kasimir burst out laughing, elbowing Jake as he teased him, and I watched them both with a hidden, pleased smile.

We made such good time that we neared Liam's home in just a little under a week. Part of that was due to the fact that we'd encountered relatively little zombies compared to the journey up, but also that we didn't make any unnecessary stops and instead powered through each day from sunup to sundown at a grueling pace.

I wished we could have stayed at the lodge for a night, but because it was out of our way and we already knew where we were going, we didn't bother to stray from our current path. Though I missed the luxurious grand room and the convenience of the wood-fire oven, the thought of returning home even quicker than anticipated was satisfying enough to make up for it. We'd slept on the ground before; it was no hardship. Especially when, this time, I'd been surrounded by warm bodies, nestled from the cold.

The longer we walked, the more familiar the landmarks grew. Like that peculiar tree in the distance that Jake said resembled a statue last time, or the bed of primrose, where the flowers all lay dead on their stalks under the intense brightness of the midday sun. We passed the general area where I'd been lured by Morgan, souring my mood. I tried not to scan the forest floor morbidly for anything out of place, any pop of color, but it was impossible not to. When I didn't find anything, I wondered if that was better or worse. I rubbed my arms as the sun dipped behind a cluster of clouds and a chill settled in the air.

"We're close," Ryder said, kicking aside a dead branch that was in our way.

He was right; it wasn't very long at all before the long length of their fence came into view.

A strange set of nerves filled my belly. I felt like I'd abandoned Liam, even after we gave him instructions to get to the camp. I hoped he'd decided to go. That he was halfway there by now, or better yet, safely behind their walls and not spending one more day suffocating in this place where he was supposed to be free.

We hadn't spent a lot of time debating what to do about the locks on the gate, thinking we'd just call out to grab their attention. Raising our voices seemed preferable to cutting all the locks open and compromising part of their security measures.

Only, the closer we got to their land, the more it felt off. The gate was... cracked. The locks weren't broken, just undone, lying uselessly around the wires.

"Jake," I whispered, pointing at the streak of reddish brown painting the metal of the fence. My heart leapt into my throat as I tried to think of plausible reasons for the blood but came up empty.

He cursed under his breath, taking Kas to look around the immediate area and leaving Ryder with me. No one had suggested we try to check out the house yet. Why? I wasn't sure. What if they needed us?

My eyes flew wide at the sound of rustling behind us. When Ryder's gaze darted toward where Jake and Kas were further back along the fence, I knew he'd heard it too. If everyone with our group was in view, then who—or what—had made the noise? I braced myself for a ghastly surprise, bleached bone or torn skin, but the face that suddenly appeared had none of those things.

"Liam?" I gasped. I lunged forward when Ryder stopped me with a firm arm across my front. "What the hell, Ryder?"

He let his arm fall and inclined his head toward Liam. I took a closer look, realizing why he was so hesitant to approach him. Blood soaked his front, and his eyes appeared vacant. His shirt was ripped down the center, leaving the side of his torso exposed, and there were... bites. Scattered across his skin. "Oh, fuck," I whispered. My heart plummeted as I looked at my friend.

Had he turned? Was he *turning*? Just what the hell had happened here?

"Hold still," Ryder commanded, then strode forward. He grabbed hold of Liam's shirt and used it to wipe away some of the blood obscuring the bites. I bit my tongue, half worried he was in mortal danger and the other half wanting him to help Liam faster.

A closer look at the now cleaned bites revealed them to be healed, old enough for scar tissue to form, partially concealing the marks. Some were fresher than others, but they were still clearly from the past. There were only about six in total, which was six too many.

Ryder nodded to himself. "He's not infected. Just in shock."

I tried to grab Liam's attention, but it was like he was staring right through me. His gaze had a haunted quality, and he looked more like when we'd first found him than ever.

"It's going to be okay, Liam," I uttered gently as I plucked a spare cloth from my bag and wet it with some water from my bottle. Taking over for Ryder, I pressed the balled-up fabric to the blood that covered his face. Ryder must have deemed it safe to leave me with him because when Kas and Jake came back, he stepped a few feet away to explain in low tones what had happened so far.

After several long minutes of cleaning the gore from him, and the repeated rinsing of the cloth, his eyes snapped to mine. His face was clear of blood now, and all that remained was a set of fresh, deep scrapes over his left cheek and a new scar that ran from just above the left side of his jaw down to his neck. Weary hazel eyes landed on me with an unwavering focus as Liam came back to himself with a deep sigh that sounded faintly of a sob.

I opened my arms, and he collapsed into my hold, burying his face in my shoulder as his own shook. Dread filled my gut as I wondered what could've gone so wrong. Jake wandered over wearing a frown, resting his hand on one of Liam's shaking shoulders. I could only shrug when he looked at me with a question on his face.

"It'll be okay, whatever it is," I whispered. "We're here now."

CHAPTER 27

T he fire crackled in the pit as Ryder stoked it and sent quick periodic looks Liam's way. Instead of hunkering down somewhere else, we'd stopped for the day at Liam's house since it was closest, and I really didn't want him traveling while he was so out of it. He hadn't spoken all afternoon, instead letting us take him to the creek to bathe, then spending the rest of the time lying on his back near the fire and staring at the sky.

"Here," Kas murmured, handing me a plate of rice and beans and tipping his head towards Liam.

"Thank you," I whispered, bringing it with me as I plopped down in the grass beside him. He didn't register my presence, but when I nudged him with my elbow, his eyes flicked to the plate I held.

I handed it to him, waiting until he had a solid grasp to pull away. "You should try to eat. You need the nutrients."

Jake and I exchanged a look over his head from where he was sitting cross-legged in front of us, hair pulled back into a loose bun.

Liam sighed, setting the plate down with a solid thump. "Might as well just tell you."

I kept my voice was gentle as I tried to reassure him he wasn't under any obligations to tell us anything. The last thing I wanted was for him to hurt any worse. "Liam, you don't have–"

"No, you should know who you're eating with. It was all my fault."

"Okay." I exhaled slowly. "What happened to Morgan? And your dad?"

His swallow was loud. "I convinced them to come with me to your camp. I knew Morgan wasn't going to be welcome, but I couldn't just... leave them. Even after everything, it felt wrong." He hesitated, like he was waiting for us to jump in and argue, but we stayed quiet. It was easy to see how he'd felt that way. Leaving anyone behind in a world like this was tough, especially family, even if it was the healthy thing to do.

"So... we got maybe a few hours away, when my dad needed to rest. It was so hot out, and he was exhausted. I told Morgan to go ahead and check the nearby houses for one that wasn't destroyed too badly and was empty. They were just across the street, so I could keep an eye on her if anything went wrong. I was going to do it but there'd been a noise behind us, and I didn't trust her to protect our dad if I left her with him and went instead."

I pursed my lips in silent agreement. She'd sooner leave him to the zombies than break a nail trying to help him.

Liam paused to gulp down some of the water we'd given him before continuing. "There was this red one at the end of the street that she said was perfect. I had my dad stand up, and I brought him to it. She did an okay job. The door was broken, but the inside wasn't trashed, and it seemed completely empty. My dad went upstairs to rest in one of the bedrooms while I was unloading our stuff on the first floor when he screamed."

"You don't have to say anymore," Jake interjected with an uncharacteristic softness. Kas nodded in agreement. Of anyone here, he probably understood best how Liam was feeling.

"Nah," he muttered, the rest of the story coming out in a spill of words. "It is what it is. I went up, and he was already... gone. It was feasting on him. Must've been hiding in the closet or something because I noticed it was cracked. I yelled down at Morgan for not actually checking like she'd promised–which I never should've done–because she ran up the stairs to just fucking stand there and stare. I hadn't even killed it yet; didn't know how to go over there and just... pull it off him. The one time she ran to danger instead of from, and she just starting fucking *screeching*. It filled the whole house. Drew the zombie's attention immediately. I'd run up to help so fast that I didn't think to grab my bat, so when it lunged at her, I threw myself in front of it. Took us both down. When she finally snapped out of it and got up to run away, it used my face to claw itself up and grabbed her ankle to bite into it. It was too late so... I did what I had to, then came back here."

I cursed under my breath, squeezing my eyes shut. His family hadn't been perfect, but he still cared for them. To lose them like that, over something so preventable... it had to be equally infuriating and devastating. Morgan had damned the entire family with her recklessness, and Liam still felt like he hadn't done enough just because he dared to give her a little responsibility instead of doing everything himself, like always. I could be furious with her, but he had guilt twisted up into it that distorted things. Everyone knew that diligence was essential to survival. It was the reason we'd checked the entire hotel like we did even though we were only using a few rooms on the top floor. Zombies could survive *anywhere* and would come out when least expected. I knew the guys had no love lost for Morgan either, so it was commendable that they didn't immediately speak aloud where my thoughts were going.

Jake moved over to sit behind Liam, patting his shoulder gently. "I'm sorry. It's not your fault; I hope you know that."

He scoffed. "I knew better than to give her a task like that. It would have been so easy to do a second check on the house."

"Even at the end, you threw yourself in front of her," I added. "You did everything you could; it's just that sometimes even that's not enough. That doesn't mean you failed, just that the circumstances were beyond your control."

He didn't respond, just stared down at the grass, and I knew we'd lost him. He'd have to think through it himself to reach that conclusion eventually, if he ever did.

"And the bites?" I asked.

"The bites," he repeated, sticking his tongue in his cheek as he thought. "Didn't you ever wonder why they sent me out to do all the work? It wasn't just because I was the most capable or the most willing."

Fresh horror filled me anew as I processed his meaning with what I knew about his time at the facility. "Are you saying..."

"They felt I owed it to them. After all, why should they be expected to scavenge when I was the one who could be bitten and live? When the facility no longer needed me and it was my fault we had to leave?"

"That doesn't mean you'd stay living!" I sputtered. How ignorant could they have been? "You might be immune, but that doesn't mean you can't catch other things from them. And a bite is one thing. You could've had your throat ripped out! I mean, I just can't..." I shook my head in disbelief, unable to find the words. I'd never hated a person as strongly as I did right then.

He laughed bitterly, pulling his knees up to his chest.

"Did they know?" I demanded. It mattered to me. If their son–their brother–had come home with supplies for them bearing fresh bites across his chest... and they'd kept sending him out even after that like some kind of sacrificial lamb...

His slow nod confirmed it, and I bit my tongue until it bled to keep from responding.

Ryder crossed his arms as he looked down at him, eyes hard in a way I usually only saw him regard strangers, reminiscent of the man he'd been when he doled orders out to his father's group. "I'm assuming you were all packed up for good when you first set out?" When Liam indicated that yes, he had been, Ryder continued. "Good. Make sure they're all by the front door tonight and be ready to leave in the morning to head back with us. In the meantime, you should get some rest."

Liam went to stand, his face blank.

"Here," I said, hopping to my feet and holding out the plate for him to take. He reluctantly grabbed it and brought it with him inside, but I just hoped he actually ate it. Though, knowing Liam, he would've never taken it if he wasn't planning to. He was the least wasteful person I knew.

Once he was out of earshot, I turned on Ryder. "What the hell was that?"

"He doesn't need coddling, Sera. He needs to feel useful." Ryder gave me a wistful smile, tucking a loose curl behind my ear. "I seem to remember you trying that very same technique on someone else. Besides, your anger isn't going to help right now. You need to process it separately."

I rolled my eyes. "I can't help it."

"I know, love."

CHAPTER 28

I stopped fixing my ponytail when a high-pitched shriek rent the air. We knew the cities were more populated since the horde passed through–so many areas for them to split off and get lost in–but the entire morning had been one after another after another.

We were all exhausted and running on fumes, and with the way things were going, it was possible we would need to stop just outside the city limits for the night instead of traveling the rest of the distance home. Already the sun hung lower in the sky, casting the various structures in long creeping shadows with even longer skeletal fingers, and sending a chill through the streets.

That another zombie was already so close didn't bode well for us.

"Ryder," I hissed, pulling my machete free. He stashed away the bottle he'd been drinking from and palmed his knife. Behind us, Liam stumbled and let out a low curse from where he'd tumbled face-first on the asphalt. Of all of us, he was the most tired. Jake swore while he helped him up, ushering him over to the shade of a half-destroyed bus stop so he'd be out of the way for this next confrontation. Kas broke off to help, rushing over with a near-silent jog when he realized Liam was moving too slowly.

The screech cut off abruptly, leaving reverberations bouncing in my ears.

"That's fine, right?" I whispered nervously. "A good sign."

Silence echoed, the tension in the air palpable, and our group held its breath, every sense alert to the impending danger.

Movement exploded.

In a flurry of motion, a sudden surge of undead figures–not just a singular zombie, as I'd expected–emerged from behind the car wash, their ghastly forms contrasting starkly against the dimming light.

There had to be at least six of them, like that first prolonged wail had been a battle cry, or a siren call. My heart constricted painfully, muscles tensing as they went weak from fear then remembered to do their jobs. We'd faced countless of these situations in just the past day alone, but this time felt different. The exhaustion that clung to us like a second skin made it difficult to think, so I moved on impulse, acutely aware that a single misstep could cost us dearly.

They swarmed us in seconds, leaving our group without even a moment to form a plan before we had to defend ourselves.

My machete slashed through the air, meeting flesh and bone with an eerie cadence. What had been so unfamiliar to me the night Morgan led me out into the woods was now approaching a habitual ease that twisted my stomach. We should've never taken this path back home, steering clear of it no matter how many days that would add to our journey.

The zombie closest to me, wearing bright pink rags and a gold necklace that winked in the light, stumbled back when my blade hit its skull with a bone-chilling sound. My arms ached from the effort, and if I could move at all in the morning, it would be a miracle. I tried not to look too closely at its features after it fell, worried I would see something too similar for comfort.

Adrenaline surged, sharpening my focus as I met another threat head-on. There was no room for error, and my entire field of vision cut down to exactly what was in front of me. Ryder and I moved as a synchronized unit, our movements fluid and almost rehearsed from spending so much time with one another. It didn't matter that we hadn't spent it fighting, we were still intimately aware of the other's nonverbal cues and signals.

My blade lodged in bone more than once, bringing me back to a place I didn't want to remember on a day similar to this one.

Kas and Jake held their ground beside us, their weariness momentarily forgotten as survival instincts took over. They were poetry in motion, muscles bunching and flexing as they moved. Each hit found its mark with precision borne from years of experience.

Minutes that felt like an eternity passed, each second marked by the distinct sounds of violence and the scents of sweat mixing with the metallic tang of blood. I stumbled when I aimed my machete too low and it cut through weakened flesh like butter, the momentum carrying me towards the creature, and was quickly snatched back against a hard chest to avoid a deadly collision.

Tired bodies dodged debris and waste as we darted from place to place, filling in where another couldn't while avoiding the gnash of frenzied teeth. No one asked me to sit it out or hide, but they couldn't have even if they'd wanted to, given our exhaustion was reaching dangerous levels and we were outnumbered. Just because the beings before us were dead, didn't make them less of an opponent. Mindless hunger was an insidious thing, compensating for strategy with pure energy.

The occasional pained grunt or sharp curse rang out as, one by one, the first group of zombies and any latecomers drawn by the noise were incapacitated.

And then, just as quickly as it had begun, it was over. The last zombie fell, its lifeless form joining the growing pile as Liam took his bat straight to its skull.

A strange mixture of exhilaration and lethargy swamped me as I surveyed the scene, my breath ragged and body aching as it struggled to realize the threat was now gone. "Thank fuck for that," I sighed, flicking the blood from my blade. "I could go for some fish." My hair had stayed in its ponytail but could do with a good wash. My clothes, however, were a lost cause and would likely have to be burned.

Kas snorted, reaching over to pluck something from my hair. I considered myself lucky to miss whatever it was. "Aim higher." A droplet of sweat rolled from his hairline onto his temple, following the curve of his scar.

"What, like candy?" Ryder remarked, bringing his water back out to resume his drink. His dark, stiff clothing made wet once more was a gruesome patchwork of the day's encounters.

Liam made a pained sound, drawing our collective attention like a magnet.

"Liam?" I asked, voice sharp.

I followed his gaze over to Jake, whose eyes locked with mine before he looked down.

In the end, it only took a split-second for my heart to shatter into pieces as I followed his line of sight to the unmistakable shape marring his arm amidst the torn, bloody fabric of his once white shirt.

The bite revealed itself like an arrow had magically appeared and pointed straight at it, just to turn around and stab me in the chest after.

My world shifted in an instant, a surge of devastation threatening to overwhelm me completely. I fought off the rising panic and despair, clenching my fists so tightly that my fingernails left deep, raw indents on my palms.

"No," I uttered, my voice cracking. "Not again."

His gaze lifted to meet mine once more, and I could see the mixture of fear, guilt, and resignation swirling within it.

But the inevitability is what killed me.

His voice broke as tilted his head, his words a desperate plea to spare me. "You have to go, darlin'. You don't wanna see this."

The thought of abandoning him tore at my heart. Wasn't he scared? Why was he still thinking of me and not himself? I fought hard to prevent the hot pressure of tears from escalating into something worse as I stepped closer to him, my hand reaching out to rest on his chest. "We're not leaving you," I said, proud when my voice only wavered a little despite the anguish threatening to overwhelm me.

Jake's honey-brown eyes softened as Ryder joined me as a reassuring presence at my side, his large hand an anchor on my shoulder.

I knew he wouldn't force me to go, even if Jake commanded it.

"Listen," Jake said firmly. "You need to kill me after. Like Ian. I don't want the chance to hurt anyone and I... I can't exist like that."

A solitary tear escaped to trace its way down my cheek as I stared up at him, refusing to look away even for a second.

Kas nodded, face set like he'd never received a more important task. Regret and resignation weighed heavily on his features. "It's nothing I haven't done before."

"No," Liam said. "I can do it. What's the worst that'll happen? He'll bite me?"

For Liam to give that to us, to make it so Kas didn't have to bear the weight of another person he cared about, was everything to me. Especially since he didn't know the circumstances of what had happened to his brother. We tried so hard to be strong, to persevere, to push through the memories and the fear and the uncertainty to survive, but some things didn't leave us no matter how hard we wished they would.

I would never take him up on it.

Some things needed to be seen through until the end, and this was one of them. I would gladly carry this memory–the worst I'd ever had, and would most likely ever have–to my grave, grateful just to know I'd used every single second I had left with him, and then some. Liam moved to Jake's side, their silent exchange speaking volumes.

My movements clumsy, I made myself walk forward on unsteady feet to meet him, eyes closing in agonizing relief when he didn't push me away, instead bending to press a hard kiss to my mouth.

How he could be so soft and warm and *alive* with the virus inside of him?

I loved a dead man walking.

His eyes fell shut in a tortured expression and his lips parted on an exhale. Tears painted our lips with salt, and I wasn't entirely sure they were all mine. He kissed me back like it would be the last thing he ever did. Which I supposed it would. I ran my fingers along his jaw, sweeping my hand down over his neck to hold the back of his head close.

He pulled back enough to cup my face, and I took advantage of his stillness to catalog his features inch by inch, committing his every detail to memory.

"You'll be okay, angel. You've got Ryder and Kas to take care of you. And you'll take care of them too. You're good at that."

I shook my head in denial, the growing numbness making it hard to focus. The rapid cycle through what this *meant* took up too much space for anything else.

"Yes. Have I told you I loved you? It feels so strange now that I haven't. I've thought it every day since I met you, but I never gave you the words."

"You didn't need to," I murmured, laughing wetly and cutting it off before it turned into a sob. "You're good at showing it. Besides, I love you too and I've never told you. But you knew that, didn't you?"

"Yeah," he whispered, brushing his thumb over my cheekbone and catching a stray tear. "I knew."

Beside us, Liam took hold of Kasimir's arm and drew him to the side, muttering in low tones as they discussed logistics.

"You don't feel anything?" I asked, afraid to hear the answer.

"Just tired. Like I have a cold."

I had no time frame for when things would worsen. Casey had died more from his injuries than the virus, and Ian was already long infected before I'd stumbled onto the scene.

"Sera, you really need t–"

"Stop. I'm not leaving."

"Seraphim?" I looked at Kas where he stood beside Liam. He wore an odd expression as he beckoned me over.

"I'm not leaving," I said stubbornly, feet planted in place. "Whatever it is, he can hear it."

Jake brushed his thumb across my cheek again at that, and Kasimir grunted. "Fine. I just didn't want to... make things worse."

I frowned. "How could you do that?"

He grimaced, pointing at Liam, who stepped forward. "Jake, you mentioned that when your grandparents died, that neither you nor your uncle contracted the virus, right?"

Jake nodded slowly.

Liam darted a hesitant glance at me. "That's near impossible. It had a 94% mortality rate. Those odds... they're usually indicative of some type of immunity. To not even suffer symptoms at all after direct contact..." he trailed off, brown hair gleaming in the setting sun as he faced Jake. "That's typically the first thing they look for in the facilities, is your experiences with viral contact in the early days."

A fragile hope filled my chest, so delicate and visceral that it ached beneath my breastbone like it was trying to claw its way out.

Ryder made a considering sound. "You're saying... he might be like you. Immune."

"So, we wait?" I whispered.

A slow grin spread across Liam's face. "By my estimate, it's been around three minutes. A bite can take anywhere up to five minutes to take effect. For him to even be standing there like he is, almost completely unaffected... Yeah, I'd say with pretty good odds that we won't need to wait."

My muscles lost their rigidity, as if someone had severed my strings. Kas caught me before my knees could buckle and pulled me into his embrace, never once turning me so that my eyes had to leave Jake for even a moment. I dissolved into choked sobs then, the culmination of every single emotion I'd held back for his sake. Ryder clapped Jake on the back, leaning in to sweep a warm, calming hand over my back.

Strong arms surrounded me as Jake pulled me into his chest. Kas pressed a firm kiss to my head before relinquishing me into his grip, and I wound my arms and legs around him, vowing never to let go.

"Hear that, darlin'?" he murmured into my hair. "I'm not going anywhere. You're stuck with me for life."

My body shook as a thread of laughter filtered into my cries. "I love you, cowboy. In this life and the next."

EPILOGUE

Ryder pressed a hard kiss to my lips just as Nadira walked up, hand linked with Thomas's. She grinned as he whispered something in her ear, pausing to respond before crossing the space to us.

"Sera!" she enthused, looking down at the dress I was wearing. "You look stunning. I haven't seen you wear a dress in months."

She wore a similar one in a bright orange color that complemented her dark skin. Jake's hand brushed against the small of my back as he partially listened while holding a conversation with Grey about the new cabin he was planning. I tucked my peppermint candy into my cheek so that I could respond. "I didn't feel like it for a long time. I wanted to wear things that would be easy to run in."

Letting go of the chokehold I had on my fear had helped more than just my state of mind. Every aspect of my life had improved. When we ate meals, I no longer spent the entire time worried that it would be my last one. I would always feel safer having a separate stash in case of an emergency, but the constant low-level anxiety that would haunt me had lessened. It would never fully disappear, but it was more manageable now. I woke in the mornings and my first thought was for the men beside me, and not what I had lost or what I was worried about losing.

Though since we'd been back, Jake never strayed far, sensing that I would need that extra reassurance for some time to come. It would be a long while before the devastating memory of that day faded to something less painful.

She smiled softly, leaning into Thomas. "Good."

A loud yell pierced the air, and we snapped our heads around to seek the source, both recognizing the voice instantly. Kas frowned from where he was speaking to Ethan across from us, watching as Jamie marched over to Ethan and slammed something into his chest.

As fate would have it, he was the very man I had encountered at the start of our journey. I'd been shocked when he approached Kas as if he knew him after we got back. Not a day went by that I didn't tease the guys about how, if I were as untrusting as them, he might never have reunited with Kas. Apparently, River had immediately been suspicious upon hearing his story once he'd arrived and asked him about Kas to confirm. He'd decided to stay and wait for him to return and hadn't left since.

"Keep your fucking present!" she shouted, grinding her foot into the dirt.

Ethan smirked, hand flying up to hold it to him. "What, you didn't like my gift?"

"You know damn well that wasn't what I meant the other day," she hissed.

I exchanged a look with Ryder, who shrugged. Jamie growled under her breath, giving Ethan a glare that could cut glass. To his credit, he didn't even react, instead matching her stare with a hard, unflinching resolve. It would infuriate her that he was so calm.

Sure enough, her eyes flashed, and she spun on her heel to march off, red curls bouncing with each frustrated step. At the last second, she shouted, "Maybe I should've just given it to Liam!"

Ethan's eyes flared as her words hit him, and the second she was gone, his body let go of its tension as he responded to Kas. It was like getting her all worked up had invigorated and bothered him at the same time. He didn't like her distress, that much was obvious, but he didn't mind poking at her while he tried to figure her out; like a puzzle that needed solving.

"What's up with them?" Nadira asked me, frowning as she watched Jamie turn the corner.

"I'm not sure," I answered. "Maybe Heidi might know?"

We hadn't seen much of Heidi in the weeks since we got back–Jamie probably saw her the most since they lived together–but we'd all come out today for the shower River organized for her. It had been more of a party, a camp-wide event that everyone was welcome to attend to celebrate the birth. I wished Liam were with us, but he wasn't much for socializing lately. I'd see if someone could bring him some cake later.

Those of us closer to Heidi had spent the first half of the day at her cabin, catching up and presenting her with our gifts as we revisited old memories and new dreams. Jamie had seemed alright then, but it was hard to tell with her. Although she seemed like she wore her heart on her sleeve, she actually kept things a lot closer to her chest than anyone realized.

A child ran by with a slice of cake in her hand, screaming as a little boy bolted after her, hollering about sharing, and Nix laughed as he strolled up behind them.

The sound of my name being called had me searching the crowded space until I saw River waving wildly from the side of the building. I nudged Ryder, tugging him after me as I went to see what she needed.

"It's time," she gushed, eyes sparkling. "Khira said it started maybe half an hour ago."

A rush of excitement surged through me. "Kas!" I yelled. "Jake, c'mon." They withdrew from their conversations and jogged over, worry written across their faces.

Ryder wore a small, secretive smile as he informed them, "It's time."

I jumped in place. "Let's go already! We're missing it."

Kas laughed at my enthusiasm, slipping his hand into my free one. "Alright, baby, we're coming."

River split away at some point on our way back to the cabin so that it was just us. My eyes remained glued to the empty spot where our future home was going to sit as we passed it—the one Jake had promised and had already gotten to work on delivering. He captured my lips in a quick kiss when he noticed my attention lingering.

In no time, we were back at my little cabin that we'd all been staying in since we got back. It was a tight fit, but we made it work. I jogged up the steps and pulled the door open gently so I didn't startle anyone.

"Thank you so much for keeping an eye on her," I told Khira where she was sprawled out on the floor next to the faded yellow blanket in the kitchen, brown curls splayed around her. She just giggled, cooing nonsensical words at Mila before sprinting past us and calling for her dad to tell him the good news.

Walking over to the black cat in the center of the blanket, I gasped when I noticed the squirming babies nestled up to her stomach.

"Oh shit," I whispered loudly. "She was right! Babies!"

We'd taken Mila to a person here who used to be a vet when she'd started acting strangely. I'd been sick with worry that something was seriously wrong, but they confirmed that she was just pregnant. There was no exact time frame for when we could expect the babies to arrive, so we just kept an eye on her. Once she grew even larger, we made sure someone was around to supervise when we were out, just in case.

She seemed to be behaving fine, licking her newborn kittens happily. Each one of the little black and orange balls of fur received an equal amount of attention from her, squirming in one big pile as she nuzzled them. Everything we were warned to watch out for didn't seem to be happening. Instead, she seemed safe, happy, and content to stay where she was while she loved on them.

"Wow," I uttered, as one of them squeaked. "Oh my god, we're cat parents!"

Ryder burst out laughing, tugging me into the main room when Mila shot him a judgmental look, and Kas sent me an indulgent smile as he followed. "Cat parents, huh?"

"It would seem so," Jake said, dropping a quick kiss on my lips.

"Good that we're using protection, because that's as close to babies as we're getting in a long long time. I can't imagine what you three would be like with a little human. I feel like you'd dig up a notebook or something just to set more rules and actually have a hope of remembering them." I snorted.

Kasimir's eyes flashed. "What's so wrong with rules? You love them, even if you like to say you don't."

A rush of warmth washed over me, my stomach flipping. He was right. Just thinking of that deep voice feeding me commands while I was at his mercy...

"Oh, she likes that," Ryder rasped, moving to my side to spread a hand across my stomach, sliding it to my side to brush my waist.

I swallowed thickly when Jake fixed me with a dark stare. "I'll see you without it one day. Completely exposed to me, skin to skin and raw, so I can fill you up with my come."

"What?" I gaped at him.

"What?" Jake watched me with a sly grin, eyes lowering as he took me in. The sheer sexual energy rolling off him in waves hit me hard. "Of all the things I've said to you, you think the fact that I want to fill you up until you're dripping with me is far-fetched?"

A high-pitched sound left me and Kasimir laughed. "I think she likes the idea."

My heartbeat thrashed in anticipation as Jake advanced. In one quick movement, he spun me around so that my back was pressed up against his front. Wrapping his arm underneath my breasts, he pulled me to him tighter and used his other hand to maneuver my chin to press a hard kiss to my mouth.

I hummed, grinding my hips back to rub against him and stilling when Kas clamped his hands down on them from the front, stilling me. Ryder took over the kiss, leaning in to capture my mouth while palming my breasts and teasing each of my nipples to fine points.

Kas groaned when he pushed his hips forward to grind his cock into my stomach. I could feel it pulsing through his jeans, hard and desperate for me. My eyes flickered shut as behind me, Jake did the same.

Ryder switched with Jake, escalating my increasingly frantic need to be *touched* as his body rubbed against mine and his hand snaked around to my stomach while Jake slanted his head to sink his tongue deeper into the kiss. I moaned helplessly as Ryder brushed a hand against my pussy, a fleeting movement that left me aching for more.

Leaning my head back on Ryder's shoulder, I watched as Kas flipped my dress up. A snort escaped me when his eyes grew wide. "Naughty girl."

Someone nipped at my neck. "Take advantage of it," I snickered, rocking my hips.

"I have another job tonight. You'll have to beg someone else."

I turned pleading eyes onto the men beside me, cheering internally when Jake winked and made his way around to my front. Dipping a finger inside me, he pulled it out to watch it glisten and stuck it into his mouth with a rapturous expression. "Any other night I'd be licking every inch of you," he informed me. "But I can't wait right now."

He stripped down, watching me with an unwavering intensity, and rolled on a condom in seconds. The view made my stomach flip. Packed ridges of muscle on his abdomen glistened with sweat, and his cock stood proudly against them. Lining up with me while I was still standing, he thrust home with one hard push of his hips.

Ryder swallowed my squeal with a kiss that was all carnal, tongue dipping into my mouth to stroke along mine. I ran my hands up Jake's flexing front, nails scratching across a nipple, satisfaction filling me when his hips stuttered. Eyes that were previously heavy with desire, flew open at a tentative pressure behind me. Kasimir shushed me, leaning down to kiss my neck and nip my ear as he whispered, "You didn't think we'd leave this hole out, did you? I'm going to stretch you nice and good, Seraphim. And one day, you'll take both of us like the eager to please angel I know you are."

I shuddered violently both at his words and the brush of his lips against the shell of my ear, not as intimidated as I'd expected to be at the thought of them taking me at the same time. Just the mere idea was burning me up inside.

A tremulous moan left me, the loud sound cut off by whoever grabbed my chin and pressed their lips to mine urgently. "She can't wait," Jake observed, not a question. My body's response to the roughly spoken words was clear.

I jerked my head up and down in agreement, gasping when the finger at my ass returned, this time slick with lubricant. Kas's finger circled my hole, brushing up against Jake's cock that was hammering into me mercilessly. The momentary stretch and burn as he confidently stretched me had me clenching my eyes shut, although the quick brush of pressure against my clit from Ryder drowned out most of my discomfort. I murmured my thanks, rocking back and forth in small motions to ease the pressure.

"She's so hot," Jake moaned, tweaking my nipple. He'd paused some in his movements, allowing me time to adjust to the new intrusion. Hands smoothed down my hips and sides, around my stomach and down my arms, both soothing and heat-provoking; Ryder's encouraging whispers only serving to relax me further.

The finger currently occupying my ass moved deeper, and when I gasped at the slight sting, even more distractions were employed across my body. Soon Kas was able to saw back and forth comfortably.

"You're good?" Ryder asked from my side, catching my cheek so that he could meet my eyes to judge for himself.

I nodded, head lolling back and eyes already shuttering once more at the onslaught of pleasure, but he tightened his grip just a little, clicking his tongue in consternation. "Give me the words, love."

"Yes. So good," I whimpered.

He smirked, going back to my neck and sucking my skin into his mouth with deep pulls to leave a lasting bruise I would admire later, while his hand snaked its way down my front to reach my clit. My breath hitched at the extra pleasure added just from that small, consistent touch.

Jake groaned long and low, when I clenched down impossibly tighter around him. I'd never heard such desperate moans from a man before. Even among the men being serviced back at Gunner's, they were stoic and stubbornly silent. Jake was vocal in his pleasure, grunts and moans falling from his lips, head tilted back in rapture. I gasped in response, hips working tirelessly back and forth to chase my own pleasure when he slowed.

He fisted a hand in my hair to pull me close and fuck my mouth with his tongue, matching each slow, hard thrust. With Ryder's hand at my clit and Kasimir fingering my ass, his free hand gripping my hip with bruising force, I reached a new high, biting down on my hand so that I didn't shriek as I trembled with the force of my orgasm, relying on the men around me to keep me on my feet.

"That's it, darlin', I'm coming–" Jake moaned brokenly as his dick swelled inside me, and Ryder applied more pressure to my clit, moving to take Jake's place when he pulled out. I was still coming when he pounded into me hungrily, his pace grueling.

Ryder's deep groan echoed off the walls as my cunt pulsed around him, eyes drifting down to watch my breasts bounce with each hard thrust. The finger from my ass withdrew, and I turned my head to slant my lips over Kasimir's as he rose to his full height. He grabbed my chin to hold me in place so that he could give me his tongue and his dark stubble was rough against my chin. "Love those pretty gray eyes, Seraphim," he muttered against my lips.

My eyes dropped when I felt something brush against me and I realized that his throbbing cock had bumped into my hip. I reached out to grasp it, keeping my lips locked with his as I stroked it to the rhythm of Ryder's hips.

Movement had me opening my eyes–not realizing they'd even closed–as Ryder shifted to thrust into me from behind while Kasimir slid to my front. I took advantage of the new position, running my hands up and down his carved abdomen and pressing small kisses to any part of him I could reach. When he growled impatiently, I grinned and returned my hand to his cock, hooking the other arm back around Ryder's neck so that my entire body was stretched out for them to use. Jake murmured approvingly from where he watched.

Kas palmed my chest with one hand, the other reaching down to rub my clit in tight circles. Already, I could feel the tension winding tight once more. Ryder whispered into my ear, telling me how good I was doing, how tightly I fit around him, and how perfect I was.

I tightened my hold on Kas, and he snarled as he snapped his hips to fuck my hand harder, coming with a tortured groan and slicking his own passage through my fist. Sharp pants escaped him as he pulled away from my grip, muscles twitching all over his body as he came down from it, his rough, scarred hand reaching out to rub his come into my skin with a possessive growl.

With no one in front of me to stop him, Ryder wound a hand around my curls and bent me over. I grabbed onto the coffee table, a small whimper escaping with each powerful snap of his hips.

"Make yourself come," he ordered, hand smoothing down my back to leave a trail fiery heat and rhythm stuttering as he filled the condom. A low moan left him as he bit down on my shoulder to muffle any further sounds. I followed his direction, reaching down to roll my clit between my fingers and crying out loudly when the pleasure grew to unbearable heights, only intensified by the bite. My entire body quaked with the force of my release, rendering every muscle in my body useless except for my pussy where it contracted around him.

Knowing damn well that my legs would be jelly after a session like that, Ryder scooped me up and deposited me in the center of the bed, muscles still trembling. I moaned as the plush surface cradled my back, cuddling into the soft blankets Kas had found around camp by trading various things because he knew how much I loved their light purple color.

Someone wiped me down with a damp rag before retreating again, and the quiet drone of conversation made my eyes grow heavier.

"Love you, Seraphim," Kas said when he returned, pressing a kiss first to my lips and then to my forehead. I giggled when his stubble tickled my skin, squirming as much as I was able.

Ryder echoed the statement when he brought a pair of sweats over and helped me shimmy into them while I was still horizontal, giving my hand a quick squeeze.

"Always love you," Jake whispered as he passed me a water bottle and waited until I was done drinking to take it from me and set it on the nightstand.

I made a deep, satisfied noise. "Love you too," I mumbled. Kas slid in behind me, molding his long form to my back, and lifted the covers for Ryder, who got in on the other side. I curled my legs slightly to twine them with his, reaching over his waist to clasp Jake's hand where he joined last at the other edge, grinning when he pressed a noisy kiss to my hand.

"All of you," I rasped, struggling to keep my eyes open.

Ryder laughed, palming the back of my head to kiss my hair. "What, love all of us?"

"Mhm, always. Forever."

I couldn't remember ever being happier than I was then, tangled up with limbs on all sides as we desperately tried to cram into a bed that hadn't been made with us in mind, soft snores coming from the kitchen as Mila slept, and the afternoon sun casting its golden rays over the blankets.

I couldn't wait to live the rest of this life with them, growing old in the cabin Jake had envisioned for us in a place where we were finally safe, with a new litter of kittens underfoot to care for.

AUTHOR'S NOTE

To each and every one of my readers, I don't know where I'd be without

you. I'm eternally grateful to everyone who's picked up a copy and joined

me on this journey. While it was an enlightening experience to write River

and her strong personality, Sera was much more familiar to me in all of her

fears and anxieties. To everyone who can relate, you're not alone.

Reviews are appreciated and help my books get seen if you have the time :)

Milton Keynes UK
Ingram Content Group UK Ltd.
UKHW040800131123
432470UK00008B/518